THE PARADISE GARDEN

TALES OF CASTLE RORY
BOOK 5

R. MARSDEN

Hurogol Press

Published by Hurogol Press 2024.

ISBN: 978-1-917063-09-8 (Paperback Edition)

ISBN: 978-1-917063-10-4 (Ebook Edition)

Hurogol Press

www.talesofcastlerory.co.uk

To Debbie, Pat, Simon and Stephanie, who have provided constant and heartwarming encouragement.

Without their positivity, I might still have written this Tale, but you wouldn't be reading it.

CONTENTS

JOIN THE HOUSEHOLD!

Join **The Castle Rory Household — an exclusive and free club for my newsletter subscribers!**

Members of **The Household** will receive *Mansurah: Jonny's Tale*, an ebook *only* available to **The Household.**

You'll also get my newsletters, full of exciting medieval facts, quizzes, stories and background information.

All you need to do is subscribe to my newsletter and that's it, you're in!

To subscribe, and to know more about Lord Rory's adventures, please go to: www.talesofcastlerory.co.uk

ALSO BY R. MARSDEN

Tales of Castle Rory

Book 1: The Box of Death

Book 2: The Soldier of Fortune

Book 3: The Man in the Moon

Book 4: The King's Ransom

Book 5: The Paradise Garden

Book 6: The Foucois Legacy

Book 7: The Minstrel's Daughter

Book 8: The End of Time

Exclusively available to members of

The Household:

Mansurah: Jonny's Tale

(your free e-book when you join **The Household!**)

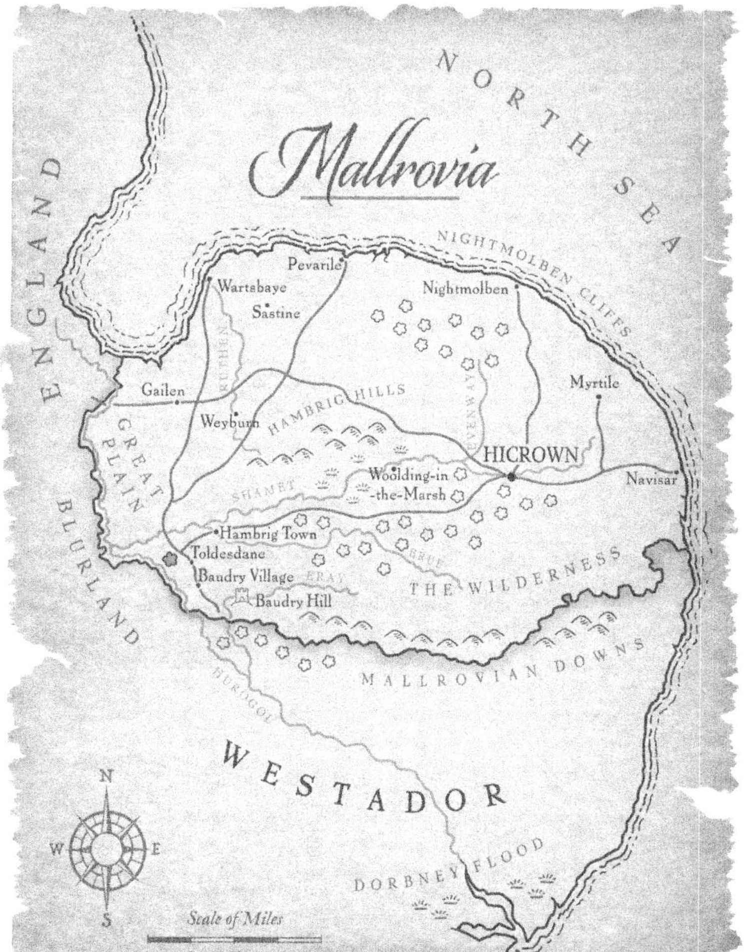
Mallrovia
NORTH SEA
ENGLAND
NIGHTMOLBEN CLIFFS
Pevarile
Wartsbaye
Sastine
Nightmolben
RUTHEN
Myrtile
Gailen
Weyburn
HAMBRIG HILLS
GREAT PLAIN
HICROWN
Woolding-in
-the-Marsh
Navisar
SHAMET
Hambrig Town
Toldesdane
Baudry Village
ERAY
BRUF
Baudry Hill
THE WILDERNESS
BLURLAND
MALLROVIAN DOWNS
BUROGOL
WESTADOR
DORBNEY FLOOD
N
W
E
S
Scale of Miles
0 5 10 15 20

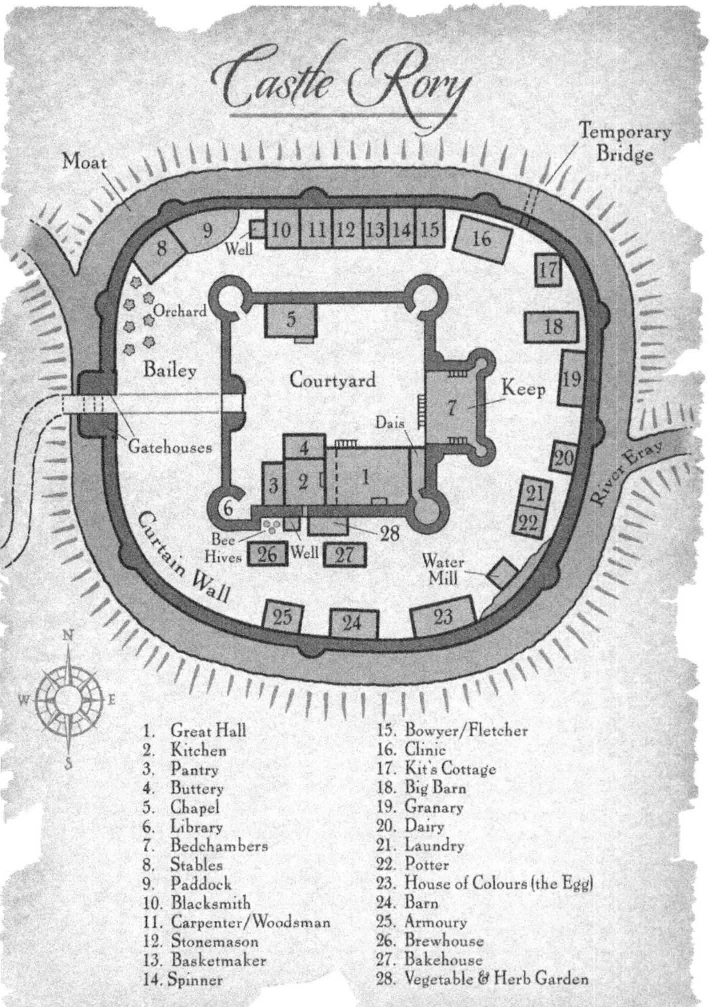
Castle Rory
Temporary Bridge
Moat
8
9
Well
10
11
12
13
14
15
16
17
18
19
Orchard
5
Bailey
Courtyard
Keep
7
Dais
Gatehouses
4
2
3
1
6
28
Bee Hives
Well
26
27
20
21
22
River Eray
Curtain Wall
Water Mill
25
24
23
N
W
E
S
1. Great Hall
2. Kitchen
3. Pantry
4. Buttery
5. Chapel
6. Library
7. Bedchambers
8. Stables
9. Paddock
10. Blacksmith
11. Carpenter/Woodsman
12. Stonemason
13. Basketmaker
14. Spinner
15. Bowyer/Fletcher
16. Clinic
17. Kit's Cottage
18. Big Barn
19. Granary
20. Dairy
21. Laundry
22. Potter
23. House of Colours (the Egg)
24. Barn
25. Armoury
26. Brewhouse
27. Bakehouse
28. Vegetable & Herb Garden

PROLOGUE

May-August, AD 1244

The chickens are being difficult, as usual. As soon as he grabs one and pulls it out of the way, another takes its place, flapping and squawking and pecking furiously at him, and then, because he is absolutely as clumsy as Shakira always tells him he is, he'll drop at least one of the eggs he's been at such pains to collect. The mess will spread all over the straw-covered stones, and his feet, somehow drawn to trample in it, will slip and slither and slide. Then, of course, he'll let go of the chicken he's holding, and it'll flap even more, working itself and the other birds up until the whole place is in uproar.

He is almost crying with frustration. Why does this always happen to him? His sisters can be sent to the hen coop for the morning eggs without any of these problems. Even the younger one always returns with a basket of fresh brown eggs, and no sign of broken yolks or chicken shit on her at all. Why has his mother sent him, when he's so useless?

The eggs, most of them broken now, are not worth bothering with. His basket is up-ended on the floor, and, in a temper, he kicks it to the far corner of the coop. The chickens squawk, and one flies deliberately into his face, its beak pecking viciously at him. Instinctively, he takes a step backwards and slips in the muck. He lands hard and painfully on his backside. Scrambling to his feet, he runs out of the coop, forgetting to shut the door. He doesn't care. He hates the chickens *and* their eggs.

Elmira is a serene woman. When her thirteen-year-old son barges in, his face streaked with tears, his entire body covered in chicken mess, bits of eggshell and other muck, she barely raises an eyebrow.

'Go and wash yourself,' she tells him quietly.

He curses. He could have thought of that for himself, surely. He bangs furiously out again and goes to pump some water.

It takes most of the morning to wash his clothes and himself. His sisters titter at him as they pass. Shakira is two years older, Amira two years younger; both are cleverer and find greater favour with his parents. He sits on the stone wall in the sunshine. If anyone asks him why he's not working, he will say he has to wait for his clothes to dry. And if they rebuke him for getting them dirty so early in the day, he will simply stick his tongue out. But though he sits on the wall until the sun rises high in the sky, no one challenges him and his tongue stays in his mouth.

But thirteen-year-old boys soon get hungry. He doesn't relish pleading for food, since that'll simply give his family the chance to ask him pointedly where this morning's eggs are. Perhaps he should find something else for the family to eat. But what can he get? He has no money. Inspiration strikes. Berries! He can collect a huge pile of berries, and his mother will make a pie or a pudding and she'll be pleased with him and his sisters won't laugh. Also, the berries will be in the hedgerow, and he can creep along there unseen. Hardly anyone comes along the dirt track that leads to the farm.

The boy slides down from the wall. He goes back to the hen coop and retrieves the egg basket, averting his gaze from the inhabitants, who open their beaks and stare malevolently at him. This time he closes the door. Still naked, and clutching his basket, he runs out of the yard and comes to the edge of the woods. Here the hedges grow wild, their vivid green foliage usually bright with red and purple berries. He stares, perplexed. No berries. Where are they? Did someone else get to them first?

A peasant woman comes strolling along the track from Mula. Her basket is full of food. She stops dead when she sees the boy, and he realises he's left it too late to hide.

'What's happened to you?' she caws. 'Did you forget to get dressed this morning? I'm an old woman. I shouldn't be seeing what you're showing me!'

He flushes, and instantly covers his penis with his hands. 'Where are the berries, old woman?'

'Berries? At this time of year? Are you mad?'

Oh. This isn't the time of year for berries. He feels the old woman's eyes on his nakedness, his shame, his failure to provide. In a fury, he flings himself on her. She crumples to the ground under his onslaught. Her eyelids flutter; she isn't dead.

'Someone will come by,' he mutters, standing, though he's pretty sure they won't. 'Someone will help you, old woman.'

He picks up her basket of good, fresh produce and hurries home.

As he hoped, Elmira is pleased with him. He's pulled his *djellaba* on again before entering the house, and his sisters, smirking, haven't told on him for once. He plonks the basket down on the table and watches as his mother exclaims in delight at the food.

'This will last several days, my son,' she says with a smile. 'How could you afford to buy so much for us?'

'I messed up with the eggs,' he admits. 'I wanted to make up for it. I hurried to the market in Mula. Most of this was on offer at a good price.'

His mother smiles, arranging bread, fruit, olives, cheese, pickles and cured fish on the shelves. He feels on top of the world; his mother is pleased with him and his sisters look disgruntled. They never like it when he finds favour with their parents – a rare enough event, after all.

Over dinner, Elmira shows the children a letter. 'It's from that young man who was here a while ago. Do you remember him? He stayed with us for about a year, and your father really liked him.'

'He was from Persia,' the elder daughter says dreamily.

'And you were in love with him.' The boy's tone is mocking. Shakira flushes, but remembers vividly how she adored the young man, and how nice he was to her, though she was only seven at the time. He danced with her! That's the part she remembers most, his dancing, and his beautiful voice with its delicious Persian accent.

'How old was he when he came here?' the younger girl asks. She barely remembers him at all.

'Only fifteen,' their mother says, looking up from the letter. 'Do you want to read what he says?'

'Read it out to us,' the boy says quickly. He knows he'll find it hard to decipher the strange handwriting.

Elmira reads out the letter, which tells, as all such letters do, of heroic achievements by the writer. The children hear that the young man is now settled in a far-off country called Mallrovia. He has made a wonderful friend with whom he lives and works. He is discovering new and exciting things every day, and he is about to embark on his greatest and most ambitious project to date, the creation of life!

As one, the children gasp. 'The creation of life!' breathes Shakira, her eyes huge.

'Apparently so,' her mother says drily. She doesn't read the whole of the letter out to them. The young Persian is not only ambitious, he's boastful as well, and she is not sure he's reading his Qur'an every day, as a good Muslim should. The younger girl, Amira, folds her hands in her lap. She is glad she doesn't remember this visitor; he sounds dangerous. But the boy's eyes are glowing. Without realising it, he crushes the clay cup he's holding, and the stem breaks off. His mother looks sharply at him, but he's thinking of a young Persian boy, far away in the north, mixing precious, exotic substances and chanting powerful spells to make a living, breathing creature like himself.

Elmira folds the letter up. 'Your father will want to read this,' she says, tucking it away inside a clay pot that stands on the table. 'Remind me to tell him of it when he comes.'

The children are looking forward to their father's return from Mula, the nearby town. But Elmira isn't expecting him back today. 'Tomorrow,' she tells them. 'Tomorrow he will be here. He has been doing business with many men in the town, and it all takes time.'

The girls are chivvied off to their chores on the farm. The family is not well off and they have no servants. But in any case, Elmira believes that young women should learn how to cook, sew, wash and clean. Their brother, left to his own devices, decides to go and see if anyone has rescued the old woman he robbed this morning.

The boy trots briskly along the track. The old woman is no longer where he left her. Presumably, she suffered no ill-effects, got up and has walked home. Minus her basket of food, of course. The boy stops. He's heard something. Shouting. And the sound of many horses. An army! Where is it? He spins round, listening. The pandemonium he can hear is near Mula. He picks up his pace, lopes half a mile and then breaks into a run. He runs hard, his sandals flapping on the stony track, and, finally, he sees it, right outside the town. There are many horses, and men are putting up tents; everyone is shouting and running around. The boy feels dread creeping through his body. It starts in the soles of his feet, and it moves up his legs, through his groin, into his stomach and into his chest, and he stops breathing for a short while. Then the dread moves on, lodging in his throat like a scuffed-up dust cloud. Finally, it gets to his eyes, which blur and dim in fright.

The boy turns. He runs like he's never run before, back home, back to his mother and sisters.

'They're here!' he gasps. 'The Christians! They're in Mula! What are we going to do about Father?'

Elmira clutches the table in shock. Fiercely, she interrogates her son, finding to her horror that he's not making it up, he did indeed see the men with their cross-emblazoned surcoats, the fine, head-tossing stallions, the boldly striped tents of the rulers of Castile, León and Aragon, and the array of deadly lances, swords and battleaxes. Most frightening and telling of all, Elmira hears of the trebuchets, ballistas and siege towers, massed at the gate and walls of the little town, ready to batter it into submission if it refuses to surrender to the Cross of Christ.

'Children!' Elmira cries, calling the girls from their chores. 'We must pray for our home and our land, and most of all for your father. Come, wash your hands, and pray with me.'

Dutifully, the three children wash their hands in a bowl of almond-scented water, bow their heads and recite their *salat*. Elmira follows with the *dua*, and then more prayers to Allah, until the sun sets behind the apricot groves and there are no more prayers to be said.

The boy hardly sleeps that night. In the first light of dawn, he gets up, pulls on his clothes and steals out into the yard. It's a three mile walk to Mula. He doesn't know what he'll find, but he knows he must go there. He is careful not to wake his mother as he passes; her face, though, is streaked with tears, and that disturbs him. His father doesn't need tears, he needs help.

The boy sets himself a pace he can sustain for three miles, a good Arab lope that makes the yards flash past. And there, at the side of the track, is the old woman. How did he miss her body yesterday? He could have sworn she wasn't there. He allows his pace to falter for a few moments as he gazes at her. Did he kill her? He kicks at her corpse, rolling it over slightly, revealing the knife wounds in her back. He recoils. Someone else has been this way. The boy resumes his run, but slows down long before he reaches the Christians' camp. They're already up, and the campfires are burning. Food is cooking, smelling good, making the boy's mouth water. He creeps into the outskirts of the camp.

Somehow, he must enter the town and find his father. It's not going to be easy.

As the day wears on it becomes clearer and clearer just how difficult the task is. At first, the boy thought the whole of the town was under attack, but people are coming and going through the gate. He creeps nearer to the strong, majestic entrance, observing carefully. All the traffic in and out is Christian. No Moors enter or leave the town. Shields and lances flash in the sunlight. Huge, tall men with crosses on their surcoats stride importantly around the camp, or ride their big horses into the town with a sense of purpose.

The boy creeps closer, until he's too close; someone grabs him by the scruff of his neck, hauling him to his feet. He's challenged by a bearded conquistador, whose expression is searching but not angry.

'I'm checking things out,' the boy improvises. He glances down at his Arab dress, his sandalled feet. 'I'm in disguise. I've been sent to mingle with the Moors. Find out what their plans are. Then I have to report back.' He is surprised at how confident he sounds.

'You think they'll accept you?' the man sneers. 'Tell you their plans? You're only a child! Who sent you, boy?'

'He did,' the boy says, nodding towards the grandest of the tents. 'He knows I can do it.'

'Prince Alfonso sent you? Then you'd better get on with the job. He doesn't like being kept waiting.'

The man lets him go. The boy, astonished, hurries through the gate, thinking fast. The first thing the man will do, of course, is check with Prince Alfonso, whoever he may be. And this Prince Alfonso will deny having dispatched an Arab urchin inside the enemy's walls, and then someone will come after him and probably kill him. But a plan is already forming in the boy's mind. He'd said he was in disguise. So why not?

It turns out to be easy. In the town square there are many people. Indeed, it looks like all of Mula has gathered here, and someone on horseback, one of the Christians, is addressing them. They will starve to death, he tells them, if they don't surrender the town. Once they've surrendered, they'll be well treated. They have nothing to lose by agreeing, and everything to lose by holding out. But a Moor calls out something rude to the knight on his fine horse.

'It is your own fault,' the Christian replies scathingly. 'You should have respected the Pact of Alcáraz. The rest of Murcia agreed to it, but this town did not. This is what happens when you break an agreement.'

'We never made an agreement,' come the shouts of protest, but the knight lashes out at the speakers, who fall to the ground.

'Respect the treaty,' shouts the knight. 'Come to your senses. Don't let your women and children starve to death!' With a flourish, he canters out through the gate.

The boy wonders why the Christians don't just take the town by force. A siege seems unnecessary. But there, on the ground, is both his reason and his salvation. The bodies of several Christians and their squires lie in the dirt, trampled on by the Moors who've lived in this town for centuries and see no reason to let foreigners from Castile take it over. And perhaps they also command the Castle of Alcalá, so the Christians dare not move against the town.

The boy waits until people have drifted away, before running over to one of the younger looking corpses. Swiftly, he strips the clothes off the dead squire, and hurries back to the shadows by the wall. But it's not enough to don different clothes; he must make his face change as well. Parts of the town wall have been hollowed into alcoves and watch towers; the boy knows them well. He secretes himself into one of the alcoves. He changes his clothes, and rips up his *djellaba*. With a small, spit-dampened piece of it, he smears chalky residue from the wall over his face, ties his hair back with another strip of cloth and adjusts his mobile features, experimenting with different expressions.

He exits the alcove and stands on the edge of the square. Some townspeople throw stones at him and he makes a rude gesture back. He hasn't yet seen his father, but for now he must play the part of a Christian squire so convincingly that even if his father popped up next to him, he wouldn't recognise his own son. The boy feels full of excitement and self-belief. He straightens his shoulders and marches out of the gate, back into the Christian encampment.

Days pass. The boy changes his disguise frequently. Sometimes the Christian squire walks purposefully around the camp, as if on some mission for his master, though he's vague as to the identity of the knight he serves; other times he helps the cooks, appearing in a greasy apron and Castilian headgear, serving bowls of mutton and spiced fruit to the invading army.

Then again, the horses and ponies need a lot of looking after, and another stablehand is always useful for cleaning the tack, shovelling muck or filling nosebags. The young Arab, who always hated labouring on the farm, finds himself working day and night in one capacity or another, but, to his astonishment, he enjoys it. He improves on his disguises, learning how to change his skin tone, hairstyle, teeth and clothing to suit each role. He picks up phrases in Castilian, perfecting his accent by listening acutely. Nobody challenges him. No one realises that the lowly stableboy slouching around today was yesterday's nobly born squire. Different roles suggest themselves to him all the time, and his mind works busily on how to submerge himself into the new look, the new job, the new character.

Early on, he worked out there was, after all, no point in trying to rescue his father by himself. Far better to wait until the townspeople surrender to the Christians. They will, of course. Once they've eaten the animals, the grain and the produce, once they've eyed each other up with hungry eyes and rumbling stomachs, someone will have the sense to give in. And then, he reasons, he can simply walk in and find his father. Assuming he's one of the survivors.

Days become weeks. The boy discovers his disguises are reusable. The squire, the stablehand, the cook's assistant and the blacksmith's apprentice can all resurface every few days. People nod to him now. Sometimes they send him on genuine errands. He's even met the great Prince Alfonso of Castile, and it's Alfonso who recognises something in the boy and teaches him to play the flute. The young Arab realises that the great *reconquistador* has taken a liking to him. Which is dangerous. So far, he's avoided answering questions, staying too long in any one role, or getting close to anyone. But it's hard to say no to Alfonso, who's young, exuberant, and full of music and fun. So the flute lessons begin, followed by singing, and the music-making goes on late into the night. The boy gets fidgety. He's accustomed to using the nights to change his persona, and now they're taken up with Alfonso and his music. It's difficult, and becoming more so every day, so it's with great relief that, finally, one cool, damp morning, the boy hears a shout go up from inside the town. Trumpets sound and there's a huge commotion. Mula has surrendered.

The young Moor is ready. He has prepared for this day and he knows exactly what to do. He dons his Templar surcoat, picks up his sword and shield and saunters over to collect 'a horse for my knight, if you please, sir.' A horse is duly presented to him, and the boy walks the animal back through the camp as if taking him to one of the knights who are readying themselves for a triumphant entry into the city. The boy joins a few other squires, who, one by one, greet their masters and help them prepare for the procession. Eventually, only the boy himself is left. Bounding up into the saddle, he jams a helmet on his head and joins the tail-end of the line.

Inside the city the conquerors are rounding up the surviving townsmen, women and children. And there, on the edge of them all, stands the boy's father, emaciated and gaunt, but still just about alive. The boy watches. Everything depends on what happens now, and he has not been able to make a plan for this part. The townspeople are moved in a single phalanx, herded like cattle out of the town. Women are wailing, children are crying and clutching their parents' hands. There are many dead bodies, and a great stink arises from them, together with swarms of bloated flies. The boy's father, head bowed, shambles off with the rest of the captured Moors. Just outside the gate, the boy dismounts.

He steps forward and pulls his father away from the walking dead.

A knight stops him roughly. 'What are you doing, boy? Where's your master?'

'Don't stop me, sir.' His tone is assertive. 'The prince wants to see this one.' He gestures towards Prince Alfonso who's sitting on his horse, sternly watching as the prisoners file past. 'A special wish. My knight is with him now.' Which could easily be true, since the prince is surrounded by Templars and others.

The knight draws back. As the boy has long since discovered, a self-assured tone makes one unassailable. He pushes his father roughly towards the prince. But as soon as the knight who challenged him has turned away, the boy uses his Templar shield to hit his father on the back of his head. As the man collapses, the boy calls for help, and another squire comes running. Together, they get the unconscious prisoner onto the boy's horse, the man's body sprawled over the horse's neck. The boy gives the squire casual thanks in the Castilian vernacular, waving him back to his duties. He leaps into the saddle and quickly spurs his horse away. It's the most dangerous moment of all. Will he be noticed? Called back? Chased after? Shot at? None of these things happen.

As he rides homeward, he rests his hand on his father's back, hoping he hasn't actually killed him. It takes very little time for the warhorse to travel the three miles. The boy can soon see the familiar shape of the farm, and he drives his horse faster along the dirt track, willing his father to survive and be all right. The yard is deserted, but the boy is glad of that. He doesn't want his mother or his sisters to see the Templar cross on his surcoat and shield, the bright sword in his hand. And he wants to revive his father before they surprise the family with their reappearance. His mother must surely think both he and his father are dead by now.

He pulls off his Christian garb, then hurries to the pump to fill a bucket. The water, he throws into his father's face. He laughs as his father comes to, shakes his head in surprise and looks at his son in astonishment.

'I rescued you, Papi!' The boy's delighted grin says it all. 'I did it! I got you out of Mula and away from the invaders. And now we're home!'

'Home? Where is your mother?'

'She'll be in the house, of course. Come, let's surprise her!'

But how do you surprise the dead? The boy's father, in spite of only just regaining consciousness, grasps the situation much more quickly than his son does. He drags the boy outside, away from the death and the decay. The bodies must have been lying on the kitchen floor for weeks. The boy hears his father's words, but he can't deal with them.

Robbery. Rape. Murder. Bastards. *Fucking, fucking bastards.*

1

THE MOST BEAUTIFUL AND WONDERFUL WOMAN IN THE WORLD

June, AD 1267

The cockleshell was my prize. It shouldn't have been, of course. The true prize must always be the sheer, awesome knowledge that you have made it to the shrine of Saint James the Apostle.

And I had. I had gazed in awe at the tomb, along with so many other pilgrims. I'd said my prayers, though they'd been more dutiful than heartfelt, but I'd knelt and bowed my head in genuine humility. Saint James the Apostle did not acknowledge my prayers or my presence in any discernible way, but the bad-tempered sacristan eagerly took my money when I entered the cathedral, and grudgingly handed over my cockleshell as I shuffled out with everybody else through the ornate and stunningly beautiful *Gloria Portico*.

I had worked hard for that little shell. I had walked a thousand miles from Castle Rory in Mallrovia to Santiago das Cunchas in the country of Smander, which lies in the north-west corner of the Iberian Peninsula. A long and arduous journey, which had taken me more than four months. I'd brought little with me. No horse, for I travelled on foot. No weapons, save a small dagger in case of trouble on the road.

I did bring my gittern, a beautiful stringed instrument. It had been made in Corsica, but was found on a market stall in Peterborough in England. It so took the eye of Master Kit that he bought it with his own money. And gave it to me. I'm not very good, but I do love playing it. My gittern, in its soft leather case, was slung around my neck during the entire long walk to Santiago. And Santiago, strangely, is in Kit's country, or at least, the country where he grew up.

Around a year ago Kit returned to his fortress on the top of a mountain here in Smander. Many people left Castle Rory at about that time, most of them people I'd thought would always be there, people I counted as family. But I learnt, the hard way, that they didn't share my view. They were family to me; I was not so to them. And my home seemed empty and dead without them.

It wasn't just that, though. I'd lost my honour as a knight. For several months I tried to live with it. But I couldn't sleep and I barely ate anything, so I took to having all my meals in my library, where no one knew if I threw the food to the castle's dogs, or if, having choked some of it down me, I brought it all back up again behind the courtyard wall. I was attempting to be Lord of Hambrig, the same man everybody knew, while slowly coming to acknowledge that I was unable to do my job.

Baruch, a rabbi in Hambrig Town, helped me a lot to start with, and on his suggestion I threw myself into several building projects, all of which were successful and, ultimately, profitable. The most ambitious and profitable of all was the new shipping dock, known as Hambrig Wharf. It's already in use as a *kontor* by the northern European countries trading as the new Hanseatic League. And I took Jonathan, that fatherless boy, under my wing and promised him a good education. I looked after Tessa, my long-lost cousin, as well, and I made the two of them into another 'building project', organising their education, finding them suitable work and companions, taking an interest in all their activities. I had more energy than I'd ever had before, yet I was empty inside. I had forfeited my honour and could see no way to retrieve it, no matter how many good deeds I found to do.

No one suggested this pilgrimage to me, but five months ago, towards the end of an unseasonably warm February, I threw my gittern strap over one shoulder and a satchel with a few possessions in it over the other, told Ben, who's in charge of the garrison, and Rachel, who's in charge of everything else, that I was going on a journey and had no idea when I would return. I walked out through the gatehouse and pounded down Baudry Hill to the Wartsbaye Road. I headed south, and I didn't look back.

And now the pilgrimage is done. I've punched a small hole in the corner of my cockleshell and strung it on the lanyard that holds my keys and always hangs around my neck. I've spent a further three weeks in the palace of King Xisco of Smander, who is as courteous and hospitable as ever, even though his daughter, Begoña, who was my bride, died in my bed eighteen months ago. But he has another daughter. Aldara is unmarried and still at the palace, an unattractive woman, probably in her thirties. At first I paid her little attention, but she turned out to be interesting to talk to and good company.

I, however, am not good company. The pilgrimage has

not achieved the result I'd hoped for. I was under no illusions that my honour could be restored by abasing myself before a shrine, but I'd hoped the long, solitary journey would reveal my true self and shine a light into the darkness of my soul. For a while I thought that had happened. The Way of Saint James was so hard, the terrain so difficult, the whole journey so punishing, it absorbed my every effort, and I came out of my deep despair as I negotiated forests, rivers, mountains and the ocean itself. But as I finally knelt before the effigy of the apostle, I felt all the inadequacy, the humiliation and the torment flood back through me, like a great tidal wave of sorrow and regret. And afterwards, in the sunshine outside the *Gloria Portico,* I clutched my little cockleshell and wondered what it was all for. Many pilgrims stood there. Hundreds. They must all have had their own reasons for doing this. My reasons were no better or worse than theirs, and I was neither a better nor a worse person than any of them. They surrounded me, and some spoke to me, and many I recognised from the journey we'd all just made; but in spite of all that, I felt utterly alone.

King Xisco knows I'm leaving tomorrow. He says he has a surprise for me. He has promised to reveal his surprise at supper this evening, so I shall put away my journal and go to his splendid and sumptuous great hall for what is bound to be a wonderful feast. I will touch little of it, but I'm looking forward to a new discussion with Aldara, who's interested in many things, and in spite of my scepticism, the 'surprise' intrigues me.

The surprise turned out to be Kit. He arrived in Xisco's palace in Santiago on 13th July, his twenty-sixth birthday.

Years ago, King Xisco bestowed a territory on this young man, albeit far from the capital and in inhospitable country. High up in the Red Mountains is the fortress of the Duke of Casuel, which is Kit's proper title, though he never uses it. He's an enigma, a man who puzzles, infuriates and fascinates me in roughly equal measure. And I was thrilled to see him.

'You know each other of course.' Aldara always comes straight to the point. 'His Grace used to be a frequent visitor to Santiago. Then he stopped coming. It is kind of him to return now; we appreciate the honour, don't we, Father?'

King Xisco merely smiled. But Kit had loved Begoña, not Aldara, and it was Begoña, the king's youngest daughter, who had travelled the same thousand miles in the other direction, from Santiago to Castle Rory, to be married to me. She had died on a sunless afternoon in December, just three days after our wedding.

However, under the king's practised hand, the conversation settled down, and Aldara did not pursue her barbed comments against Kit.

Kit was mercurial as ever, with brief, flashing smiles, dark, mysterious eyes and curly black hair that flicked up from his forehead. 'I heard about your pilgrimage, Rory. The news of it got here before you did. Whom did you leave to run your estate?'

I shrugged. 'Everyone. They all know what they're doing.' I didn't want to talk about it. 'I'm leaving tomorrow. Should be home by the start of Advent.'

'You will take Aldara with you?' Xisco's question sounded almost by-the-way, as if the answer were already decided. But it was the first he'd mentioned it, and Aldara gazed at her bread on the table in an attitude of calm resignation.

'Whatever for?' scoffed Kit. 'Aldara belongs here. Helping the queen. At least, that's what you've always told me, sire.'

'It was the case once, Kit,' Xisco said. 'It was the case when I had two daughters.'

'All the more reason now—' But Kit should have known not to interrupt a king.

'All the more reason now, Kit, to observe more closely and speak more judiciously. If Lord Rory will take her, Aldara will accompany him to Hambrig.'

'Of course,' I said. 'On a long journey, a pleasant companion is worth their weight in gold.'

It was an hour after supper, and I stood with Aldara in the palace grounds, an area of sloping grass with a low stone wall at the end of it. Beyond the wall I could see the ramshackle cottage where Kit's mother once lived. I'd heard of it, but this was the first time I'd seen it. It's derelict now, but even when smoke had curled from the roof and cooking pots were being scrubbed outside, it could still only have been a hovel. I bit my lip. I don't think Kit has ever been inside, nor would he want to.

I had asked Aldara what was behind her father's request.

'Lord, I'm thirty-one years old,' she said obliquely. 'I'm unmarried. My father is hopeful—'

'That you will find a husband on the road north?'

'That I have already found him, and that he will take me home.'

I drew in my breath sharply. Why would Xisco take such a risk?

'We don't blame you for my sister's death,' Aldara said earnestly. 'We knew how ill she was. My father was wrong to bring her to you. It was too difficult a journey, and her health was too poor. He wants to make it up to you, lord. He is offering you a healthy wife!'

I said nothing. She's too old. I like her, but I don't want to marry her. 'You can come to Mallrovia if you'd like to, Aldara. But...'

'You won't marry me?'

'I won't marry you.'

There were no tears and no harsh words. She's unlikely ever to marry, and that's hard for a woman in her position. Xisco should have married her off years ago, but perhaps the queen wouldn't let him.

Later, I spoke with Xisco, a man I like enormously. I was honest with him.

'She can have children,' he assured me earnestly. 'I'm certain of it.' When I said nothing, he continued. 'Yes, she's thirty-one. But she's young at heart! And I know she will bear you children, Lord Rory.'

'How can you know?' I asked. I didn't want to upset the man, or insult his daughter, but it's an unconditional requirement that the woman I marry should give me an heir. Or what's the point?

Xisco looked resolutely into the distance, where the sun was slowly setting, which gave me my answer. He didn't know for sure. *Couldn't* know. Some women are barren, and all women become infertile at some point.

'Have you asked her?' My tone wasn't hostile. I just needed to know.

Xisco turned to look at me. 'I have asked her. She says she is able to bear children. I have to trust her, don't I?'

Perhaps he does. But I don't.

I wandered through the great hall, now cleared of its food trenchers, tables and benches, and I went to my room. Sitting on my bed, I pulled out a rolled-up parchment from inside my jersey. It is the latest instalment of this long-running journal. I had a piece of charcoal too, and I scribbled down two questions. And then their answers. *Do I want to marry Aldara? Categorically, no. Should I marry Aldara? Almost certainly, yes.*

Prosperity, peace, security, stability. These things Aldara brings to a marriage, a union between her father's Iberian nation and my estate of Hambrig in the tiny, and sometimes struggling, country of Mallrovia. What would my father think? *For God's sake, boy, get yourself a wife! You don't have to love the woman and she doesn't have to be pretty. Just get a wife and get a child. Preferably in that order. Oh yes, and have enough children to ensure that at least one of them survives.*

Spookily, my father is now sitting next to me, leaning his back against the wall where the window looks out into a pretty courtyard filled with long rays of golden evening sunshine.

I look at him sidelong. My skin prickles, as it always does when this happens. My father's ghost. No one but me believes in it, but then, no one but me has seen it. Or heard it. He looks the same as he always looked in life: stern, even forbidding; upright and without any deceit or dishonour. His voice, as always, registers disappointment. I've let him down again. I am not the Lord of Hambrig he hoped I would be. I am not the eldest son he wanted. But I'm what he got, and so he makes the best of it. My younger brother, Nicholas, currently in England, would not have made the grade either. As for my sister and my youngest brother, Thomas – well, they're both dead. So Father has no choice. But his pained tone tells me how far short I fall.

You've messed up with this marriage thing enough times. So what if Aldara isn't your dream bride? You're too old to be choosy. I married your mother, the most beautiful and wonderful woman in the world. It's a pity you couldn't have found someone like her when you had the chance.

All right, I think, locking my fingers together behind my head and stretching out on the bed. I'm deliberately avoiding looking at him, though I can feel his penetrating gaze on me. *All right, I'll marry her. You're right, Father. I can't pick and choose anymore. It doesn't matter who she is or what she looks like.*

As I think these thoughts, I recall Aldara: her plain Iberian face, black hair pulled tightly back and tied in a knot behind her head; her arms hanging by the sides of her short-statured, square-shouldered form, clothed in a long black *cyclas*. None of these things mean she won't make a good wife.

You don't know her at all, says Father in an annoyed tone. *She may well be up to the job. And if you refuse her, who else is there? Who else is going to offer you his daughter's hand?*

And with that, he gets up and stalks off, disappearing out of the door, vanishing into the air. Until next time. His words make sense, but I'm resentful. Aldara is not the wife I want, and Father should have known that. She is no replacement for *the most beautiful and wonderful woman in the world.*

2

THE DREADED PASO DAS ROCHAS

Small, wiry ponies were waiting in the courtyard the next morning; they were hung with capacious bags and saddled ready for the road. I saw three, and the reason for the third was made clear when Kit sauntered out of the palace portico, dressed for travelling.

We would be a disparate lot. Aldara rides well, Kit is awkward on horseback, and I manage pretty well, in spite of the pain I still occasionally get. I call it the firepain, since it was caused by a fireball slamming into my body as I tried to escape from a burning building.

Our ponies were used to the rough country; they needed little help and they seemed to know their way. The fastest and most direct route led through Kit's territory of Casuel and over the famous Red Mountains.

'Everyone calls them that,' Kit explained. 'But their real name is the Aquilanos Mountains. They *are* red though!'

They certainly were, and, in the distance, I saw how strangely shaped some of them looked, their jagged peaks pointing to the sky, scrubby grass nestling around the bases, but little other vegetation anywhere. I'd never seen mountains like them.

In the foothills we came to the village of Narij. I knew of this village, and the sharinga trees that grow on the slopes of this one mountain, at the top of which is Kit's home, the Fortress of Casuel.

I looked up, shading my eyes. The fortress loomed large above us. 'Is your mother still there?' I asked Kit.

'Of course. Iago is with her, and Iago's wife, Enes, as well.'

'And Xurxo?'

Iago and Enes work for Kit on his Casuel estate. Xurxo is their son.

'He said something about coming with us. We'll probably meet him further on.'

I frowned. I'd expected to go home on my own, just as I'd travelled solo on the outward journey. Now I was to be riding with Kit and Aldara, and perhaps with Xurxo as well. It's not that I don't like them. But they will not help me in my quest, for they don't even know of it. Since I failed to feel any more honourable for having made the pilgrimage, I was hoping to recover my soul on the way home; but you need solitude for such things. I know this from my time in Palestine. Solitude is sometimes the only way to reconcile who you are with what you've done.

But there are good things about having companions, and soon I was glad I had my friends with me. The most treacherous part of the passage through the mountains was *O Paso das Rochas,* the Pass of Rocks. I'd not had to navigate this pass on the *Camino Frances,* which takes you north of the Red Mountains to a place called Villafranca. Now, the Pass of Rocks lay some five miles ahead. Kit told me Xurxo definitely wanted to join us.

'Join us? For the day? For a quick "hello"? Or for the whole journey to Hambrig?'

Kit made a face. 'You didn't expect to be travelling with all of us, I know. Xurxo likes Hambrig. He wants to live there.'

That evening a sturdy mule picked its way over the craggy red landscape. The rider looked comfortable, familiar with the rough terrain, one hand loosely on the reins, the other waving enthusiastically. Xurxo.

'You belong *here,'* I told him bluntly. 'You're Kit's man. He needs you, surely. And even if he doesn't, your father certainly does. You are Iago's voice.'

We'd stopped to let Xurxo catch up with us, and now Kit and Aldara were making a fire so we could sit round it and eat some supper together.

Xurxo smiled happily. 'No, no. *Sappo* is Iago's voice, Lord Rory! Remember when I told you that?' Xurxo told me long ago that his father, who is dumb, gave his voice to a pet toad, an animal we all call Sappo. 'My father is back in Narij,' Xurxo went on. 'Back with my mother, Enes. And *O Señor* himself suggested I come with you.'

O Señor. It's Kit's title round here.

'This is the right time to tell you,' said *O Señor*, his mouth full of soft Smanderino cheese. 'I'm returning to Hambrig as well. For good.'

Enes had fallen ill again, and Iago, her husband, was hard at work all day, so he couldn't care for her. Joy, Kit's mother, had offered to take Enes in and look after her on the mountain top.

'Anyway, I've been dispatched with a message for Cristina, since it's not certain Enes will live much longer,' Kit said.

Cristina is Xurxo's sister, and she lives in Hambrig Town.

'But why won't you come back to Casuel after that?' I asked.

'I've discussed it with my mother. She wants me to stay with you. She's perfectly capable of running Casuel anyway, and when Enes dies, Iago will take over and Joy can come to Hambrig.'

I felt sorry for Enes.

Xurxo and I awoke just before a chilly dawn, and we stoked up the fire so we could sit by it and talk in low voices. Mostly remembering the events of last year, when the Dorians attacked us, and everyone was pretending to hold King Xisco and his daughter hostage.

'You are troubled,' Xurxo observed.

'It's nothing,' I said. 'An old man's misplaced nostalgia, that's all.'

'You're hardly an old man.'

'That's all you know. I certainly feel like one.'

'Come on then. We should rouse the others and get on our way before you become too ancient to make the journey!'

There were caves. Many caves.

'They are connected by passageways,' Xurxo told me. 'But we should not use them. They're not safe.'

We didn't use the passageways, but we did use the caves, trying to make sure we reached one by nightfall every day. They were dry, and much warmer than huddling together outside in the chill night air. I asked Xurxo who had made the caves and the passageways.

'The people who mined the gold,' he explained, scratching at the rock in the side of the cave we were sitting in at the time. 'Can you see it?'

A thin line of yellow glowed in the red dust.

'It's not a real vein,' Xurxo explained. 'There are many tiny crystals still within the rock. But there was a great deal of gold here once. Smander is a rich country, and this is the reason. But Casuel, the very source of the gold, is its poorest territory. You know why? It's called *ruina montium.*'

My Latin was up to that. 'Wreckage of mountains?'

'They used water, flooding the tunnels they dug to wash out the gold. The water broke the rock and smashed the mountains.'

'Who did it? Who mined the gold and smashed up the mountains, Xurxo?'

'The Romans.'

My God. That was centuries ago!

Xurxo gave a grim smile. 'I can see you think that was too long ago to matter. But to Casuelos, it matters.'

'It's the gold that makes the rocks look red then?' I asked.

'Yes. The rock is *arxila.* That is the Smandego word. I don't know it in English.'

'It's clay,' Aldara told him.

'If you go through the passages,' Xurxo said carefully, 'you can still find the remains of the Roman soldiers who died in the mines they made. Skulls. Bones. Whole hands and feet sometimes.'

I've always known how clever the ancient Romans were. But to cause whole mountains to topple over? To harness the power of water, even the meltwater from snow in the high peaks, and wash the rocky rubble down the slopes into a complex drainage system from which gold nuggets could be extracted – *that* is organisation on a larger and more productive scale than I could contemplate.

I approached the Pass of Rocks feeling more confident now. Aldara had been telling me that bandits and robbers lurk there, but the four of us should surely be able to see them off. At the start, the Pass was an easy climb. Then it grew steep, and finally it became steeper still, winding tortuously. The narrow track had a sheer drop to one side, while a constant stream of loosened stones threatened to knock us out from the other side, where the mountain rose almost vertically above our heads. We led the ponies and the mule, and progress was slow and difficult.

Kit slipped on some loose rubble and fell, banging his knee against a sharp outcrop. His pony skittered in fright, which upset mine. Aldara kept her head and soothed the animals. I helped Kit up, but blood ran down his leg and his face was contorted in pain. We decided he must ride. Aldara bandaged the gash, and we got him onto Xurxo's mule. We trudged on, and I revised my opinion of the Pass. If bandits lurked around the next bend, we wouldn't know until they were upon us. With a wounded man, Xurxo leading the mule, and Aldara inexperienced in combat, I was a lot less certain we could outwit or outfight them.

The Pass of Rocks is well named. After climbing higher and higher, it eventually took a turn into a steep-sided rocky gorge.

'It will bring us out on the other side, and we will no longer be in Smander,' Xurxo explained. 'Then there is the downhill part, which is worse than we've had so far. That is where the robbers will be waiting.'

So I hadn't needed to worry about bandits on this part of the mountain. I looked across at Kit on the mule and made a decision. 'We'll stop here for a bit. We can't make a fire as there's no wood, but we'll rest for an hour, and everyone will drink some water.'

Xurxo looked anxious. 'Is that wise? We should aim to be down the mountain before dark. We have little time to spare. And little water to spare also.'

On my instructions, Aldara had used some of our precious water supply to wash Kit's leg and clean his wound. Kit was still in the saddle, but I wondered if he'd actually fainted. His face was almost white, and he was swaying so much he'd soon fall. We lifted him down and sat with our backs to the mountain. I passed the water skin round and everyone obediently took a swallow. Nobody spoke. Kit lay on the ground, his eyes closed, his breathing shallow.

The gorge was in shadow, and the air was filled with dust. I noticed, after a short time sitting here, that it was harder to breathe. The others were turning red with the dust that landed on us. I could see no birds and no animals, no plants, trees or life of any kind. Were we the only living things here?

We heaved Kit onto the mule, trying to make him comfortable across the saddle. We tied him on so he couldn't fall, even if the mule tripped. Which it wouldn't, Xurxo assured me, because it's a mule bred in this country. I nodded but didn't want to talk; the dust was in my mouth, choking me.

Xurxo had no weapon on him. Aldara had tied her barbette around her forehead; she looked more like a bandit than a royal princess. She'd also tied her gown up to give her an easier ride on the Pass.

'*Son unha muller bandida!*' She laughed. A female bandit, perhaps, but an unarmed and defenceless one. I decided we would all ride again, and Aldara could lead the mule.

But she challenged me fiercely. 'You think Xurxo is a better fighter than I am?'

Xurxo was almost certainly stronger than Aldara, although he was barely any taller. And I'd never seen either of them fight. 'Just lead the mule, Aldara,' I said. 'Someone has to, and, for now, it's you.'

The end of the gorge did not bring us back into the sunshine, because the sun was behind us and the mountains cast huge shadows over the land. Spread out before us, though, whether in sun or in shade, was the *Corona de Castilla,* the Crown of Castile. This massive state, bigger by far than Mallrovia, was created fairly recently, and now the whole gargantuan area is ruled by one man: the King of Castile, León, Toledo, Murcia, Jaén, Córdoba, Seville, and Lord of Biscay and Molina. *Alfonso X.*

We began the descent. It was hard, as Xurxo had said. Even the little Smanderino ponies, born to this landscape, found it tough. I led the way, my blade in my hand, but I saw no bandits. Nobody leapt out at us as we picked our way down the steep and slippery slopes of the Aquilanos Mountains.

We moved eastwards, across the north of the country,

parallel to the coast but never within sight of the sea. Everyone was subdued, and very little was said. Xurxo asked one question: where would we spend the night? I shrugged. We're no longer on the *Camino,* and there will be no pilgrims' hostelries within a day's walk. We must make shift where we can, and try to strike the well-known route as soon as possible.

We made our camp by the side of a vineyard, a good five miles from the Red Mountains. The stream nearby would supply water for cooking and washing. Xurxo began cooking something on a blazing fire, and Kit, once he came to, made a rapid recovery, though he can't put much weight on his right leg yet. The night was warm and dry, and our spirits had recovered in the relief that we'd successfully made it through the dreaded *Paso das Rochas.*

3

SOME QUESTIONS WILL ALWAYS REMAIN UNANSWERED

Xurxo served up a meal of scrambled eggs and pears, which he'd obtained from the vine-grower. There was wine too, and by the time we'd finished, the stars were clear in the night sky, the fire was still going strong and there was a contented silence among us. Everyone was relaxed now the Red Mountains were behind us, and I felt very comfortable by the fire, with a couple of rugs under and around me, a full stomach, and a light heart at the thought of going home. By my calculations we'd be in Santo Domingo de la Calzada in around ten days, and from there we could pick up the *Camino,* the Way of St James.

The days passed quickly, and they all felt similar. Sometimes we lodged in a barn or a farmhouse; sometimes we camped under the stars.

Four days from Santo Domingo everything changed.

Three warriors appeared over the brow of the hill. They wore full-face helms and flowing cloaks in red and gold.

I looked at Xurxo. He shrugged. 'These will be important men. They wear the coat of arms of the *Corona de Castilla.*'

When we were a few yards from the riders, we halted. So did they.

'*No vayas más lejos.*' Their spokesman moved forward slightly, his visor catching the sun. The dazzling reflections blinded us for a few moments.

'He says we must go no further,' Xurxo murmured.

'Tell him we are just passing through. We want to get to Santo Domingo de la Calzada and eventually cross into Aquitaine.'

Xurxo called across the gap. Behind me, I heard Aldara say something to Kit.

The Castilian rider removed his helm and I saw a Mediterranean face, long black hair and a bushy black beard. The man's eyes were cold. He continued, his voice stern. '*Puedes cruzar a Francia. Pero primero vendrás con nosotros.*'

'We must accompany these men,' Xurxo told me. 'They have not said where to.'

I nodded and bowed.

'*Señor Rory, bienvenido a la Corona de Castilla. De nuevo.*'

Startled, I turned to Xurxo. 'How does he know my name?'

But it was the Castilian who answered, his English thickly accented. 'We know who you are. We watched you travel through our country weeks ago. We noted your pilgrimage to Santiago das Cunchas. We waited for you to return with Princess Aldara. We did not expect to see other Smanderinos with you, but they, also, are welcome.'

'Where are you taking us?' I asked.

'First, I will introduce myself. My name is Yehudah ben Moshe. I serve the king.' It seemed we were not to know the names of his two companions, nor see their faces, since they were still helmed.

'Señor Yehudah,' I said formally, 'I present Xurxo and Kit.' I waved vaguely at my dusty, travel-stained group.

Yehudah ben Moshe gazed at us, unsmiling. 'We will now go on our way, perhaps to complete your pilgrimage. We will escort you to Santo Domingo to meet King Alfonso, the Holy Roman Emperor. He has expressed a desire to talk with you.'

I'd been through Santo Domingo de la Calzada once already, as I walked the *Camino Frances*. There'd been no king there then. Alfonso's name is known to everyone, and I've been told he's as clever as he is ruthless. Why he should want to see me, I had no idea. But we'd intended to go there anyway, so I bowed to Yehudah and his companions, who turned their horses round and led the way.

As I said before, every day is much the same at the moment, so I'm not keeping this journal in such detail as usual. We've been travelling around twenty miles every day, in company with Alfonso's men. Aldara has enjoyed the ride, and she is a cheerful and interesting companion. Kit is quieter than usual. He's not a horseman, and his injury still troubles him. Xurxo is our spokesman, talking with Yehudah and his companions, communicating with them on our behalf. We finally learnt their names: Isaac and Joseph. Joseph is short and middle-aged, a bespectacled, reserved man who has said little so far. Isaac is younger, lean and light on his feet.

Isaac smiles at Aldara far too much. He's useful though, good at organising our lodging in the hostels, negotiating prices with the monks and finding us the most comfortable beds. As for Yehudah, he's a strange man. Tall and stern-looking, his mouth seems fixed in a permanent sneer. Xurxo says he's knowledgeable about many things, but he wouldn't be my first choice of travelling companion.

Four days after we'd met the three Castilians, we rode dustily into town. Alfonso moves his court around. He travels a lot, and with him travel scribes and scholars, translators, scientists, and anyone with great knowledge or wisdom. Oh yes, and lawyers.

Yehudah led us up a sun-bleached track towards a magnificently decorated building. I'd have called it a palace, but Yehudah told me it was just someone's home, commandeered by the king for the time being. I sucked in my breath in astonishment; King Philip lives like a pauper by comparison. But then, the Crown of Castile is huge and mighty. You could fit Mallrovia into it a hundred times over.

We were shown to sumptuous apartments, served with savoury and sweet delicacies on gilded trays in our chambers, servants washing our feet and hands, fresh clothes laid out on our beds... It's all quite extraordinary. When I travelled south, crossing the Pyrenees, and following the *Camino,* I met no one who had even heard of Mallrovia, although the monks in the hostels along the way were always politely interested. So it's odd to be awarded such lavish treatment on our arrival at the court of King Alfonso X. And my audience with the great man is, so they tell me, tomorrow morning, which means I have plenty of time to myself this afternoon. I have personal servants, provided by the king's household, and they will meet my every need. As for Aldara, Xurxo and Kit, I have no idea where they went, and the questions died on my lips as my servants simply shushed and soothed, smoothed my bed yet again, pressed more sweetmeats upon me, refilled my flagon of good red wine and glided out of the chamber, leaving me with a little bell with which to summon them, should I require anything at all during the night.

So now I have the time to get my journal up to date. This journal is personal to me and I have shown it to no one, nor will I. It's my dream that one day, maybe a long time from now, someone will read my *Tales of Castle Rory* and understand how and why we did what we did. As for *this* Tale, hopefully by the end of it we will know why the mighty King Alfonso wanted to see me in his sumptuous palace. But maybe not. It's my belief that some questions will always remain unanswered.

4

PYJAMAS?

Mass in Santo Domingo took twice as long as it does in Castle Rory, and the church here is a hundred times more ornate than my austere little chapel. This morning, in the cavernous church of Santo Domingo, where the language and liturgy were familiar, although not exactly the same, Aldara, Kit and Xurxo stood next to me at the front – it seems we are guests of honour – and I got my first glimpse of the King of Castile, León, Toledo, Murcia, Jaén, Córdoba and Seville.

He's tall, with dark, wavy hair and an interested, expressive face. Intelligent brown eyes locked just once with mine. Questioning me? But then he smiled, and those eyes lit up in welcome. I smiled back, as the priest walked through the crowd, swinging his thurible as best he could in the press of worshippers. Afterwards, Yehudah appeared out of nowhere and steered me out of the church and back towards the palace. I know it's *not* a palace, but I can't help calling it one.

'This morning, you meet the king,' Yehudah said sternly.

'Are you going to tell me why?'

'He will tell you.'

I was led into a huge hall. Yehudah presented me to King Alfonso, bowed and left.

'Are you comfortable, Lord Rory?' the king asked. He was seated in a high-backed, beautifully carved chair on the dais. The dais was raised higher than we in Mallrovia normally have them, so he was looking down on me as I stood before him. His English was like Yehudah's: perfectly intelligible, but with a strong Castilian accent, and his voice was pleasant. 'Here, in Santo Domingo? I hope you find your chamber agreeable.'

'It is delightful, your Majesty. On our way here from Smander, we've stayed in many hostels—'

'Yes, they are of great use to the pilgrims on the *Camino.* And the monks make a fortune from such travellers.'

I'd scarcely have thought they made a fortune. They charged little enough, though it's true many pilgrims pass their way. I realised we had to get through these pleasantries, and I wondered when we'd get to the real reason for my invitation to the palace.

'If there's anything you require, you must let the servants know,' Alfonso continued. 'Food, wine, women – you have only to state your preference.' He looked at me searchingly.

I thanked him, and assured him I would not hesitate to list my requirements – should I have any.

But Alfonso seemed to be waiting for more.

'There is nothing at the moment, sire,' I said at last. 'I've eaten well this morning. And the wine is excellent.'

'Good, I am glad to hear it. But you have not mentioned women. What are your tastes?'

'I was married, sire. My wife died and now I am unmarried. I have no "tastes".'

He did not miss the disdain in my last sentence, and I

saw the speculative look on his face. He turned suddenly. There was a servant by the door; there had been no one there before. King Alfonso clicked his fingers and the servant disappeared, reappearing a moment later holding a young boy by the wrist. The boy was brought before the king. He stood with his head bowed, his shoulders dejected. Although he looked so dismal, he was nice looking, and he had been dressed in an expensive gold-embroidered tunic; dainty sandals on his feet.

'This is Diego,' Alfonso said, without a single glance at the boy. 'The son of a friend of mine.'

The king waited. Diego looked at the floor.

'I don't understand,' I said.

'It's of no consequence.' He waved a hand, and the servant oozed into place and, without a word, escorted Diego out of the hall. After a short silence, Alfonso said, 'I think that when I asked your taste in women, you did not understand me fully.'

Oh, but I understood him fully then, and I was suddenly furious. So furious I forgot I was in the presence of the mightiest king in Christendom. 'You were asking if my "taste" is actually for young boys? You thought I might want to fuck Diego. Is that it?'

'Do not rant at me, Lord Rory of Hambrig,' the king said calmly. 'Do you read the ancients? Many had such tastes. I needed to be sure. Your outburst tells me a lot. You do not sleep with other men, and you have a fiery temper. You are also a man with a reputation for courageous leadership and bold decisions. I like such things, but however desirable those qualities may be, I like even more that you chose to walk the *Camino*. Why did you?'

'Many choose to do so. There was nothing special about my pilgrimage.'

'I think there was. You needed to do it. I do not know your reasons, and I know you will not tell me them, but you needed to show humility. And now that you have done so, you are returning on horseback with an assorted retinue and a new agenda for your country. Your king will be delighted to see you, and you will be welcomed home with a triumph.'

I highly doubted that.

'My daughter,' said the king suddenly, and the light bantering tone disappeared completely, 'my *eldest* daughter, would make a good match for you.'

I was thunderstruck. 'A good match, sire?' Did he know what he'd just said? Was I really being offered the daughter of the self-styled Holy Roman Emperor?

'Indeed. Do you doubt it, Lord Rory? A union between Castile and Mallrovia. That would be a truly valuable thing – no, it would be a *priceless* thing. How do you think it would look to King Philip? Would he want you to miss such an opportunity?'

I knew exactly how it would look to the King of Mallrovia. Philip, if he learnt of this offer, would not allow me to refuse it. Mallrovia joined by marriage to the mighty Crown of Castile? Philip would explode with excitement! But why would Alfonso suggest such a thing?

'Tell me what the deal is, sire,' I said, and he laughed. He beckoned to me and I mounted the dais and sat in the high-backed chair that was next to his own, and Alfonso put his cards on the table. Or at least, *some* of them were put there.

Just before dinner I grabbed Xurxo. 'He wants Jabir! Jabir and Joan! He wants them in his court, and he wants them to bring Sappo. In return, I get to marry this daughter and Philip gets to feel even more pompous and important than he already does!'

Xurxo frowned. 'Is it what you want?'

'I don't want Joan to leave Hambrig.'

There, I've said it.

Jabir ought to be important to me too, but it's Joan I really care about.

'Aren't you prepared to let go of Joan for this opportunity?' Xurxo asked.

It wasn't as simple as that. Xurxo understood nothing. 'Look, he wants Jabir to compile some complicated tables of the planets and the sun and the moon. And he wants him to try yet again to create the Elixir of Life, which is why he's asking for Sappo, I suppose. I don't know why he thinks he needs Joan, but he insists she come here as well.'

'Because Jabir won't come without his woman?'

'She's not his woman, damn you.'

'Ah. I'm sorry. I did not understand.'

Aware I'd lost my temper with him, I stalked off to my chamber and looked around it in a foul mood. Too much gold, too many tapestries, too many soft, sumptuous silken bed coverings. I'm used to coarser stuff, whitewashed walls, frayed rugs and worn linen. All this glaring luxury hurt my eyes.

I lay on my back on the bed, my eyes closed, and thought about Alfonso's offer of marriage to his daughter.

Even for Jabir's services, it seemed lavish, a bargain of far more value to Mallrovia than to Castile. Unless, of course, Jabir was worth more than I thought he was. He was the cleverest, most intelligent man I knew, yet he had failed more than once in his quest for the Elixir. I didn't know why Alfonso thought Jabir would succeed in Castile when he'd failed in Hambrig. Joan once said Jabir would do anything for me. But would he do this?

For, while King Alfonso clearly thought he had only to offer me a prize worth having and I would command Jabir and Joan to set off for Castile, the truth was very different.

Jabir wouldn't budge unless he wanted to. And he wouldn't want to if Joan didn't want to. And why would either of them want to? What, I asked myself, was Alfonso offering *them?*

I went to find out.

'*What am I offering them?* I'm offering them the chance to work for me, in this great and wonderful kingdom, in the warmth and sunshine of Castile and León. I'm offering them the opportunity to work alongside the best Christian, Muslim and Jewish scholars in the world! I'm offering art, poetry, music and literature, science and song, astronomy and astrology, conversation and discourse at the highest level. They will find all these at the court of *El Sabio* and nowhere else!'

'Even so, they may not want to come.'

He looked at me in disgust. 'You, Lord Rory, have observed it for yourself. You will go home with these observations, and with your glowing report. In this way, all will benefit. You get my daughter's hand in marriage. Your textile worker and your alchemist get the opportunities I have just spelt out for you. And I get the benefit of their expertise and intellectual ability. Everyone is happy.'

'I'd like to meet your daughter,' I said, at last, God knows why. Last year Philip said he wanted Mallrovia to 'play with the big boys'. Well, they don't come much bigger than King Alfonso X, *'El Sabio',* of Castile. And I still didn't understand why he was so keen to have Jabir in his court. There were many men like Jabir here already. The place was full of men and women from the East. Different languages could be heard throughout the palace, and, over the midday meal, I'd listened in to animated discussions concerning the new celestial 'tables' Alfonso spoke of. I couldn't see why he needed Jabir as well as all these other, equally erudite, Islamic scholars.

'You shall meet her.' The king nodded affably. 'You shall meet her tomorrow. For now, you are simply an honoured guest, Lord Rory, and I hope you will continue to enjoy the best hospitality we can offer.'

And I did. The food was excellent; servants stripped and bathed me in pools of soft water, and then dressed me in a sumptuous crimson tunic. The weather continued to be warm and sunny from dawn to dusk. During the afternoon, I sat in an orange grove, idly picking and eating the ripest fruit, soaking up the hot sunshine, and deliberately not thinking of Alfonso's deal.

And it was there that Aldara found me.

'I have been searching for you,' she said.

She was wearing a new gown. It was made of silk, coloured a beautiful sky-blue which set off her dark complexion. Over it was a gossamer-thin surcoat in a creamy-white colour, its long, wide sleeves reaching to her wrists. The surcoat floated behind her as she walked towards me. Around her head was wound a turban of the same sky-blue material as the gown, fastened in place over her right temple with a large blood-red ruby. On her feet were pretty, jewelled sandals, open at the toes. Aldara will never be a beauty, but the clothes relieved her plain features and disguised her solid shape. I couldn't help it; I gasped at the sight of her.

She laughed. 'I have been washed from head to foot by handmaidens, and these clothes were found for me. Do you like them?'

'They are most beautiful,' I said, sincerely. 'You've been well treated, then?'

'Very. At least half a dozen maids have been allocated to me, and they will hardly leave me alone. They're forever enquiring if I need anything. Sometimes they bring what I need before I even know I need it!'

I smiled. 'And Isaac? Have you seen much of him?'

'Isaac? Of course not. He is not allowed in the women's quarters.'

But Isaac hadn't struck me as a man who'd bother too much about the rules.

'How long will we be staying here?' Aldara asked.

'Not much longer.'

I was anxious to be off. The sunshine was wonderful, the oranges sweet and succulent, the surroundings opulent and luxurious, but I had a yearning to be on the top of Baudry Hill, dressed in my oldest jersey and my worn russet breeches, the wind in my hair, while I bit into one of the sharp little apples that grow on the hardy, gnarled trees in our orchard. That longing was painful and acute.

Aldara, who has never been to Hambrig, knew nothing of my feelings, but she felt my tension. 'Are you all right?'

'I'll be better when we're on the road again. Will you have to return those fine clothes, or are they yours to keep?'

'Mine to keep,' she said, dreamily, fingering the thin fabric of the surcoat.

'They won't be much use to you in Hambrig. Your toes will go blue with the cold in those sandals, and that coat will blow away in the wind.'

Aldara flinched. I stood up, flinging orange peel and pips onto the grassy bank that bordered the grove.

'I'm sorry you're angry,' Aldara said. 'It will be supper time soon, and—'

'No supper for me. I'm going to my chamber. If anyone asks, I don't wish to be disturbed.'

The servants' fussing has got on my nerves, and I sent them scurrying away. I have gone to bed. *We're leaving tomorrow,* I think as I lie there, wide awake. *No more Castilian court, I've had enough of it.*

But you must meet this daughter of Alfonso's, says my father.

Why must I? What if I prefer Aldara?

Don't be ridiculous, boy. This is the sort of opportunity hardly anyone gets. No Mallrovian has ever married into such prestige. Xisco will understand you couldn't marry Aldara. He will find her another husband. She will be all right.

I open my eyes and see my father sitting on my bed, his eyes serious, his forehead creased in a frown of disapproval.

Father, I'm not a child anymore. I can make my own decisions.

If that's truly so, why do you need to say it?

Because you doubt me! You've always doubted me!

Only when you're making mistakes, boy. Serious mistakes. Do I come to you when things are going well? Do I visit you when you're happy?

No, he does not. My father's ghost visits me at times like this. But it doesn't help, so what's the point? Generally, his visits make me feel worse than ever. And now he's keeping me awake when I want to sleep.

You wouldn't be asleep anyway, he says with a short laugh. *Don't be a fool, boy. You're far too worried about this proposal, and also Aldara, King Philip...*

Tell me then, I say angrily. *What should I do about King Philip?*

It should be obvious, he says sharply. *You'll have to live with Philip a lot longer than you have to live with Alfonso or Xisco. Philip would want you to marry into Alfonso's family. In fact, he will be furious if you don't. Now is the time to live up to our family motto, Fac Fiat. Make It Happen.*

But I like Xisco—

Which hardly matters, boy, does it. You don't marry a woman because you like her father. You marry her to gain political advantage, and to get an heir to your estate. May I recommend you get a move on with both these things?

I don't know why my father never uses my name. I'm always 'boy' to him. I was 'boy' when he was alive, too. Is it any wonder he thinks I act like a child? In the soft, fading light, I'll finish writing this strange day's record in my journal.

I strip off all my clothes, and slide under the soft, fluffy sheets, ignoring the silken outfit someone has left out for me. What's the heathen word they use? Pyjamas?

5

CONTINUE YOUR JOURNEY TO HAMBRIG

In the hall the tables were laden with fruits, sweetmeats, cuts of lamb, breads, pastries, honey and flagons of wine. I ignored these and went up to the high table on the dais, where sat King Alfonso X of Castile. And by his side, a young woman. I halted before the dais and looked up at the two of them.

'Greetings, Lord Rory,' Alfonso said in his thick English, and his tone had become sweet again. 'Please come and join us at the high table. And I will introduce to you my daughter.'

On the dais, I bowed to the woman, kissed her hand, and learnt that her name was Rosa. She was beautiful. Her English was far better than her father's, although still with a marked Iberian accent, and the tone of her voice was almost harsh. Her eyes were dark, and, as they gazed into mine, I saw a challenge. I rather liked it. My lips brushed the back of her hand, but she did not smile at me. This was a woman who expected men to listen, and, almost certainly, to obey her. I smiled briefly at her, offering my own challenge.

'You will eat with us?' Alfonso asked.

'Certainly, sire. It will be a pleasure.'

And it really was.

'You will be married here, in this house in Santo Domingo. You will spend two further days here. After that you will journey back to your castle on the hill. You will take with you the three men whom you met on your journey, together with a letter for Jabir of Tusa. This letter will explain his part of our arrangement, and what he and the Lady Joan will gain by joining my court. My men will then escort the alchemist and his lady to Castile, and their instructions will be to meet me in Seville as soon as possible. I will send word of their safe arrival back to you, and from that moment on, they will cease to be your responsibility.'

It was so very final. *They will cease to be my responsibility.* Father, in his chastisement of me last night, hadn't once mentioned the Lady Joan. She was always *his* responsibility, and after his death and my return from Louis's ill-fated Crusade, she became my responsibility; but apparently that is all to be overturned. And, to a large extent, it already has been. Now Jabir looks after her, but they are still tenants of mine, and that counts for something. It seems I'm to lose even that.

'What do you think, Xurxo?' I was back in the orange grove, and I'd hauled Xurxo over there as well. I'd spent a long time explaining everything to him, and I wanted his opinion.

'I think King Xisco will not be happy, Lord Rory.'

'I know he won't be. And you don't have to call me

"lord", not when it's just the two of us. You think I should reject Rosa?'

'You're asking my counsel? If so, it is that you should wait. You have forged a strong bond with my country and with my king. I would urge you not to throw that away. It is interesting that King Alfonso is so determined to have your Islamic alchemist he is prepared to give you such a precious gift. She is a very beautiful woman, and she will not be without suitors. And, meaning no disrespect, Lord Rory, her father could choose a more powerful ruler than you with whom to make his alliance.'

'I know that. Which is why I don't know what to make of it. You counsel me to wait – but what for? And until when?'

'I will find out more tomorrow, before you marry the Castilian.'

I didn't see Aldara all day, but, towards evening, I saw her standing close to the lithe, handsome Isaac. He was speaking; she was listening. They were doing nothing wrong, but it made me uneasy.

I have accepted Alfonso's offer. My father is clear this is the right thing to do. Xurxo's counsel to 'wait' is impractical. Alfonso needed an answer at once, and I want to go home. Rosa is most suitable, and her age, bearing and pedigree are perfect. I've been in love just once in my life, so I know and remember vividly how it feels, and I've sworn never to let it happen again. Nor has it, but there is something about Rosa. She is beautiful and calm, not unlike my Kathryn. My gut twists as I think this, and I've had to put down my quill to breathe deeply. I won't think of Kathryn. Only Rosa.

The morning of my wedding promised another sun-drenched beautiful day. This wedding was to be without fanfares or fuss, it seemed – a quiet ceremony outside the big church. Alfonso had briefed the priest, and the marriage was to take place just after daybreak. Almost no one was there. I had no special outfit to wear, so I appeared in my travelling clothes, though I'd burnished my sword and had the ever-ready servants clean and polish my boots. I stood by the church door, looking around for Rosa and her father. The priest stood a little way off, his hands folded inside the sleeves of his cassock. In the still morning air, I heard a shout, and someone swerved around the corner of the church. It was Xurxo, and behind him pelted two members of Alfonso's guard, their daggers drawn.

'What's happening?' I cried, my hand reaching for a dagger that wasn't there.

'Something you need to know,' Xurxo panted, though he had doubled over and was gasping for breath. The priest raised his hand and the two warriors stopped where they were. 'This isn't what you think it is,' Xurxo gasped. 'The girl Alfonso wants you to marry – she's his daughter, but not by his wife. She has no standing! She was born out of wedlock, *before* he married Queen Violante. He's laid a trap for you!'

'Is this true?' I turned to the priest. 'Is Rosa illegitimate?'

The priest's narrow face gave nothing away. '*Dominus sit in corde tuo, et in labiis tuis, ut digne et competenter annunties Evangelium suum: in nomine Patris, et Filii, et Spiritus Sancti.*'

I ignored him. 'Xurxo, how do you know? Where is Alfonso?'

'I advised you to wait. But you did not. So I had to act in haste. I have our horses ready, your bags are packed, there is no time to waste! We must run!'

'I am not running. I need to speak to Alfonso.'

The priest was still chanting in Latin, his arms spread wide, his face growing darker by the moment. Xurxo was staring at me, and in the distance I saw he was right. The ponies and the mules were ready at the gate, my saddle bags were full, and there, looking towards the church, stood Aldara and Kit. With great efficiency, Xurxo had mobilised our party.

Xurxo is a good man, and I trust him. But I could not simply take him at his word. And yet, suspiciously, Alfonso and Rosa were already late. As the bells chimed for Prime, a line of monks appeared and filed into the church. The priest, standing to the side, bowed his head and would not look at me. There was no sign of my bride, nor of her father.

I went to find them.

I ran him to earth in his solar, though I don't know if they call it that here in Castile. In Mallrovia, as in England and France, the king's solar is a suite of rooms where he sleeps, rests and relaxes. And where also, apparently, he plays music. I heard the music from some way off, and it drew me to the room. The door was wide open, and the king was sitting cross-legged on a stool, strumming a gittern and singing softly.

He looked up. 'Tomorrow. Not today, no, not today. I think you misunderstood.'

'I did not misunderstand, sire. You told me it was to be today, and the priest was expecting it to be today.'

'Oh, that's Luca! He's often confused. No, no. The wedding is *mañana.* Tomorrow. And you, I hear, enjoy music as well?'

'I play the gittern a little,' I said, looking at the instrument he was holding. 'Mine is exactly like yours, sire. *Exactly.*'

He laughed, took the strap from round his neck and held the instrument out to me. I wondered why he was offering it; then I examined it more closely.

'But this *is* my gittern,' I exclaimed. 'Your Majesty, what is happening here?'

'You brought it with you, did you not?' He chuckled. 'The servants who have been attending you reported that you had a musical instrument among your possessions. I must ask your forgiveness, Lord Rory. I had your gittern brought to me this morning. I have been composing a new *cantiga,* and I am very pleased with it.'

I began to wonder if I were dreaming. I absolutely *know* Alfonso said the wedding would be this morning. The priest clearly also thought so, and so did Xurxo. Yet instead, the king stole my gittern and now he was calmly sitting in his chamber writing a song.

'Would you like to hear my *cantiga?*' Alfonso asked, still holding the gittern out to me.

'I'd like to know why you offered me the hand of your illegitimate daughter. Without informing me that she has no standing and leading me to think this was a prestigious match. And I'd like to know why you changed the date of the wedding.'

Alfonso said nothing for a few moments. Then he slowly nodded. He put the gittern's strap around his neck again and rippled a few chords. And then he sang me the song.

Rosa das rosas, e fror das frores,
Dona das donas, sennor das sennores.
Rosa de beldad e de parecer,
E fror d'allegria e de prazer.
Dona en mui piadosa seer,
Sennor en toller coitas et doores.

Alfonso looked up. 'Did you understand the song, Lord Rory?'

I shook my head. Xurxo had mentioned a trap, and I felt like I was well and truly caught in one with no idea how to talk my way out of it.

'*Rosa das rosas e fror das frores, dona das donas, sennor das sennores.* It means, rose of roses and flower of flowers, woman of women, lady of ladies.'

'It's about your daughter, Rosa?'

'No. It is one of my *Cantigas de Santa Maria.* A pious song to the Holy Mother.'

'Then I don't see the connection, sire. It is a beautiful song, but—'

'You don't see the connection? Here I sit, playing your gittern and writing a new *cantiga*, perhaps my best yet. There are more verses, I didn't sing them all to you. They speak of devotion to the lady, of love and forgiveness, and – finally – of the singer's wish to be the lady's own troubadour.'

When I stayed silent, he sighed. 'I will teach you the song, and I will write it down for you. I need you to understand, but I can see it is not easy for you.'

Still I said nothing. He made some utterance in his own

language, rose from his stool, went over to a cupboard against the wall and took from it another gittern.

'You see?' He flourished the instrument at me. 'I did not *need* to use yours! It was symbolic. Symbolic of our union. Our two countries joined in the match between your noble self and my lovely Rosa.'

'But she is of low status, your lovely Rosa,' I said doggedly.

'That is not how it is here. Here in the passionate south, things are very different. We are not austere and aloof as you are in the north; we do not hold ourselves back. And we do not condemn a royal princess of the house of *El Rey!*' He sat down again and ran his fingers along the strings of his gittern. The instrument was more intricately decorated than mine, probably much better in quality. Mine had turned up on a market stall in a small English town, whither it had somehow made its way, probably via the bartering hands of several traders and ship owners.

I had not been invited to sit, and I still wanted to understand. 'Lady Rosa is of equal standing to children born in wedlock?'

'I have already answered that question.' His intelligent, dark eyes met mine for the first time. '*Rosa das rosas e fror das frores, dona das donas, sennor das sennores.*'

'But you said the words are not about her! A song to the Holy Mother, that's what you just told me.'

'And so it is,' he agreed calmly. 'But how strange that my daughter's name comes up in the refrain. Over and over again you hear it. What do you make of that, Lord Rory?'

I decided I could do with Kit by my side at this moment. He would soon unravel this double-talk. I was simply bewildered.

I tried one more time. 'Rosa's mother is not the queen?'

'Rosa's mother was Mayor Guillén de Guzmán, a noblewoman in my father's court. She was a wonderful woman and we had a great love. She gave me two daughters, Rosa and Beatrice. Beatrice married very young. The King of Portugal. They have many children, though none is named after Beatrice's mother. If Rosa gives you a daughter, I would like it very much if you called her "Mayor". You are thinking you will be in good company?' Alfonso asked, idly strumming his strings. 'The King of Portugal is a powerful and intelligent man. I doubt he would have married a woman of "no standing".'

I stood rebuked, but Alfonso was smiling. 'Shall we play together? You would like to learn my *cantiga?*'

I could hardly refuse. We spent the hours between terce and sext playing music. I learnt his new *cantiga*, and several others, all of which tell of miracles performed by the Virgin Mary. And, because he pressed me to, I played him the two songs Kit had taught me, and then he wanted to learn them too. To my surprise, I found I was quite good at instructing him, and he learnt quickly, enjoying *Reis Glorios,* and, particularly, *Gaily the Troubadour.* I could explain *Reis Glorios*, a song composed by a troubadour from Limoges. But the other song, with its strange English words, is an enigma. Years ago, Kit told me the song hasn't been written yet. It's from 'the future'.

Alfonso has not officially met Kit. He eyed me quizzically while I floundered to describe my enigmatic minstrel. It proved impossible, and in the end we both laughed, and agreed there are things that just can't be explained. Nor had he explained the postponement of the wedding. Had that been to confuse me? To prove Alfonso had the upper hand? But he did not need to prove that.

Perhaps he'd simply changed his mind. He's *El Rey*. He can do what the hell he likes.

I married Rosa early in the morning of 2nd August in Santo Domingo de la Calzada. Strangely, the sun, as it rose over the eastern end of the nave, was obscured by grey cloud, and soon after prime was rung, a drizzly rain began to fall. Rosa was unperturbed. She stood on my left, silent and accepting, as Luca, the priest, pronounced us married. I walked away feeling no different. Feeling nothing. Rosa is beautiful, more beautiful than Begoña, my wife of only four days, and infinitely more so than Aldara, Begoña's sister. Yet I know I have let Xisco down. Betrayed him and both his daughters. Xurxo avoided me this morning, and I didn't blame him.

Alfonso offered to provide an escort for Aldara to return to her father in Santiago das Cunchas. Aldara met me in the orange grove, wearing the same beautiful sky-blue gown and jewelled sandals.

'Lord Rory. Congratulations on your marriage to the beautiful Lady Rosa.'

'You cannot mean that, Aldara. I know you and your father had different hopes.'

'Whatever my hopes may have been, I expected this,' she said, surprising me. 'No, that's not quite true. I didn't expect it so soon. I didn't realise Don Alfonso would offer you his daughter. You had to accept. But I did expect that, sooner or later, you would find another woman more attractive and more desirable than I. My father knows it too. He will be disappointed, but not surprised.'

'You are an attractive woman, Aldara.' It was clumsy, and I hated saying it. Surprisingly, though, it was also true. She might be plain-looking, but she was attractive in many other ways. I couldn't put that into words, though. Such things are beyond me.

Aldara smiled, her eyes still holding mine. Eyes filled with emotion. Only two other women have ever looked at me like that: Kathryn and the Lady Joan. Kathryn because she loved me; Joan because she understood me. I caught my breath in dismay.

'You are to return to Santiago,' I told her. 'Alfonso's men will escort you.'

'I would like it, lord, if you would take me to Mallrovia as planned. I do not wish to return to Santiago, and most certainly not with Alfonso's escort.'

'Why? Everything has changed.'

'There are several reasons. First, it would be humiliating for me to return to my father without a husband. Second, I do not trust Don Alfonso. And third, I still wish to marry. There is no one in Santiago of whom my father would approve. I am a Smanderina princess, and as such I have value. I believe King Philip has an unmarried son?'

I was startled. Prince Barney is indeed unmarried, and King Philip has been looking for a suitable match for him for some time. He might well consider a Smanderina princess to be exactly that. 'All right, Aldara. You will continue your journey to Hambrig.'

6

HIS APPARATUS CAN GO TO HELL

I returned to the orange grove after dinner, thinking to find more solitude, or, even better, to speak again with Aldara, should she decide to join me there. But she didn't appear.

Isaac turned up instead. 'Lord Rory, please would you come? His Majesty has requested your presence.'

It sounded important and I went at once. And what did the King of Castile want? More music. We made music together all afternoon, and *Rosa das Rosas* was played and sung over and over again, until it was stuck in my head and in my fingers, and my gittern strings resonated to the melody and the harmonies of Alfonso's *cantiga.*

It kept the king happy, but my mind wasn't on the song. My marriage to Begoña had been swiftly followed by her death, her secret burial and the lies and subterfuge that followed. And my stomach twisted and cramped in its familiar dance as I remembered that Aldara, Begoña's older sister, must never learn of this. But she *would* learn of it! I was suddenly sure of that. And then word would get back to her father. Philip will say it doesn't matter anymore. Not now Mallrovia is allied to the Crown of Castile.

'Your thoughts are not on my *cantiga,*' Alfonso said reprovingly. I realised I had not been paying attention for some time.

'I'm sorry, sire. I love your song, but there is a lot on my mind just now.'

'Indeed. Would you care to share your thoughts with me?' He put his instrument down, crossed his legs on the stool and waited.

'I was thinking of my good fortune in marrying into your family. Having planned for an alliance with Smander, you have given me a greater prize.' Which may or may not turn out to be true.

'You will reap the benefit of both, in fact,' Alfonso said smoothly. 'Smander itself is about to join the Crown of Castile.'

The tone was matter-of-fact, as if the words didn't matter that much, but the implications were huge. And it could only mean one thing. Alfonso had either forced or negotiated an annexation. The Crown of Castile is enlarging, and so is its status and its power.

I made the only response I could think of, though I thought it a lame one. 'King Xisco never mentioned it to me.'

Alfonso smiled thinly. 'I think you'll find he did, Lord Rory. But obliquely, perhaps?'

At first I didn't get it. Then I did. 'Begoña? And – Aldara?'

'He is trying to create other alliances. Friends in high places.'

'But Mallrovia—'

'With respect, Lord Rory. Mallrovia is small fry. Henry now...'

'English Henry?' I asked, startled.

Alfonso inclined his head. 'Many years ago, perhaps more than ten years past, I created an alliance with Henry of England. Against Louis of France. You fought on Crusade with Louis.'

Is there anything this man doesn't know?

'It was all on account of Gascony.' Alfonso sighed. 'I could have had Gascony. Gaston and I had it all worked out. But in the end there was a diplomatic marriage between my daughter, Eleanor, and the English prince, and it was Edward who got Gascony. Still, that's all in the past now. When did you get back from Crusade?'

'In the autumn of '53.' How long ago that sounded.

'And that's exactly when all that Gascony business was going on. So, you see how it is? Henry is a powerful king and a useful ally. Mallrovia is on the English border, and Philip and Henry are the best of friends. They have to be, for otherwise England would swallow up Mallrovia. Do not look so affronted, Lord Rory, you know it's true. It's the same with Smander, a once-powerful nation. But now, an isolated one. And between Smander and the rest of Europe lies the Crown of Castile. And who is in control of Castile? I am. Xisco thought to promote an alliance with England via Mallrovia.'

I was angry. 'And now you're doing the same?'

'I am doing the same.' He smiled again, and I was beginning to dislike that smile of his. 'I am doing the same. And you, Lord Rory, in the middle of the annexations, the negotiations and the ceding of land, have the most to gain. Whether you marry my daughter or Xisco's can make very little difference to *you*. But to your country, and to Smander – it's everything.'

I took up my gittern, bowed stiffly to Alfonso and walked

away. To be a pawn in anyone's game is anathema to me, but to have been used to trick my friend Xisco of Smander made me furious. It was also humiliating, as Alfonso knew very well.

In the doorway, I turned to face him. 'I have not yet consummated my marriage to your daughter, sire. Perhaps I will not do so. Perhaps I will revoke the marriage.'

Unperturbed, he shook his head. 'You will consummate the marriage, Lord Rory. You may well feel mortified by these events, but you will feel even more so if King Philip hears that you have thrown away this opportunity. Philip is a man with a great hunger. He hungers for glory. Your marriage to Rosa, and the heirs she will give you, these things will make a big difference in Mallrovia. But if there's no marriage, or if there should be no children from the union, then, perhaps, King Philip and his little independent coastal state will be forgotten.'

'Forgotten? Or deliberately side-lined?'

'Does it matter?' Alfonso asked carelessly. 'Either way, there will be no more ships at your *kontore*. No more trade with your merchants. No more recognition of your sovereignty, and perhaps Henry of England, or Edward when he succeeds him, will annexe you, and that will be the end—'

'Enough!' I cried. 'This is monstrous! Mallrovia is already part of the Hanseatic League! We have free trade agreements and rights to sail in European waters. Even Castile can't change that!'

But the smile was spreading until it was a wide grin. 'Sadly, Lord Rory' – and Alfonso sounded not the least bit sad – 'sadly, it is all too easy to reverse such agreements. Easy, also, to cancel such rights. Easy, in fact, for the League to expel Mallrovia.'

'But why? Why would the League want to do that? Mallrovia contributes a huge amount; our manufacturing—'

'What do you manufacture?'

'Textiles. Wool, cloth, garments, bags. Glass and flint too, but mainly textiles. There's a massive demand.'

'Of course there is. And there will continue to be. Trade will continue, whether your country is in or out of the League. It will just cost you more... In any case, as I've already said, you, personally, have everything to gain. I have had your chamber made ready. Tonight, Rosa will be brought to you. I have given you a beautiful and valuable bride, Lord Rory. Spurn her not, or it will go badly for you, for Mallrovia, for Hambrig and for King Philip. The repercussions will be severe and long-lasting. Do not do this to your people, the people who depend on you.'

Alfonso's voice followed me down the passage. 'Play my *cantiga* to your wife tonight. Rosa is a music lover!'

Our group now consists of eight people. Aldara and Kit were the first into the sunlit courtyard in front of the palace this morning. Alfonso's three men-at-arms closed up behind them, and Xurxo, Rosa and I were the last to muster there. Alfonso didn't deign to see us off. I've seen him briefly today and wondered if he would talk to me. He did not. Everything he needed to say was said last night. I stowed my gittern in my saddlebag and climbed into the saddle. Yehudah walked his horse over.

'I have the letter from his Majesty King Alfonso of Castile to your alchemist and his wife. It will be safer if I look after it until we arrive. His Majesty has charged me to hand his invitation personally to Jabir of Hambrig and the Lady Joan.'

Jabir of Hambrig! That is not the alchemist's title at all. In fact, he has no title. The man has no status whatsoever. He came to Mallrovia an itinerant beggar, and wandered the streets of Hambrig Town, squatting in the gutter, begging for food, unable to support himself. How or why he came, nobody knows. Eventually he was found and taken in by Sir Bernard of Hambrig, a man who did nothing but good in his lifetime. Bernard gave Jabir a home, and somehow Jabir became a knowledgeable man. Perhaps he'd always had great knowledge. Jabir is clever. A genius, some would say. And hopelessly in love with Joan, a woman ten years his senior.

A servant opened the big gates and the eight of us clattered out onto the dusty white track that leads out of Santo Domingo de la Calzada.

We followed the trail to the huge mountains that separate Navarre from Gascony. Aldara has brought a substantial purse with her, and she insists on paying for every third hostel we stay in.

'I would not be costing you money if you had sent me back to my father,' she explained on the first night she jingled her purse in front of me.

I frowned. 'Don't show people your money, Aldara. You'll be robbed in the night!'

'I don't. It is only to you that I'm explaining.'

'You wouldn't be on your way back to your father if we hadn't spent several days in Alfonso's court,' I pointed out. 'In fact, there would only be four of us, not eight, if I hadn't married Rosa.'

'That is true,' she agreed without rancour. 'And perhaps

that would have been good. But then again, eight is better than four. Safer and stronger.'

'I don't understand you, Aldara. Why aren't you angry with me?'

'Would it help if I were?'

'It would make sense.'

Yehudah also has money, and he and I paid for the other accommodations between us, so our funds are lasting well. Sometimes we even splashed out on the better beds the monks had to offer, rather than simple straw bales in the monastery outbuildings. The ride was, in fact, pleasant and easy-going.

Although the mountains between Navarre and southern Gascony are much larger than Kit's Red Mountains in Smander, the passes are easier to travel through, and we encountered no problems. On the other side of the mountain range we lodged in a small monastery. Our three Castilians are an odd bunch, and all very different. Joseph is clearly a very intelligent man, knowledgeable too. As dusk fell, he stood in the cloisters and gazed into the darkening sky. I joined him, and my lips mouthed the familiar names of the stars I could see.

'You're interested in astronomy?' Joseph turned a searching gaze on me.

'My grandfather used to tell me stories,' I explained. 'Ancient tales of the Greek heroes, mythical beasts and the gods who lived on Mount Olympus.'

Joseph smiled. 'I grew up with those stories too. But the reality is even more fascinating.'

'What reality?'

'The reality of what the stars really are, and why they move as they do in the night sky. Did you not study astronomy in the Quadrivium?'

I had, of course, and enjoyed it, too. But nothing that was said to me then had contradicted Grandfather. And there had been no mention of 'the reality'.

Joseph intoned the names of the stars, giving short snippets of information about them, but I wasn't really listening. He has a dry, monotonous voice, and, though I'm sure he knows a great deal, he didn't inspire me to listen or learn. So I was unaware of the exact moment he stopped talking about the night sky and started quizzing me about Jabir.

'I have heard that your alchemist, Jabir ibn Hayyan, has acquired many interesting books.' Joseph's voice was muted to little more than a whisper.

'He's not ibn Hayyan—' I began.

'*The Book of Knowledge of Ingenious Mechanical Devices* for one,' Joseph continued reverently. 'It was written by the famed mathematician, Ismail al-Jazari, inventor of the Castle Clock and other wonders. I have never been able to lay eyes on a copy of this book, much less own one. But soon, soon that will change. When we reach Hambrig and we meet your great alchemist, Lord Rory—'

'He's *not* ibn Hayyan,' I said again. 'Though he claims to be related...'

'He is from Persia, I believe,' Joseph said, and I confirmed that was so. 'Many wonderful discoveries and inventions began in Persia. Why do you suppose he travelled to your country?'

I admitted not knowing the answer to that.

'It will be so much easier for him to work in Seville,' Joseph mused. 'It may be difficult for him to transport his apparatus, however. Does he have much in the way of apparatus, Lord Rory?'

I shrugged, uninterested in the transport of Jabir's 'apparatus'.

'Because,' Joseph continued earnestly, 'all at Don Alfonso's court will be very interested to see the way such a man works.'

Will they indeed.

Joseph began babbling another absurd question, while I slipped away to find the lay brothers' dormitory, where I chose an empty bed and flung myself upon it. Jabir, and his 'apparatus', can go to hell.

7

I CRASHED DOWN ONTO THE TABLE

These have been hard days, climbing northwards through Gascony and along the shoreline of Aquitaine. We kept to the coast road here, and although we found fewer hospitable monasteries, we were also less likely to become the prey of footpads and robbers.

'Why are you worried?' Aldara asked, riding by my side for once. 'There are eight of us, and six of you are fit, strong warriors! We are not likely to be set upon.'

'Better safe than sorry,' I answered, though in my mind I disagreed with her counting. Alfonso's men, who'd looked such fine warriors when we first encountered them, seem less and less like fighting men the longer we spend with them. Yehudah is tall and imposing, but he doesn't strike me as a fighter. Joseph is a short-sighted, middle-aged academic, more likely to run away than stand his ground. I wouldn't want to be dependent on either of them. I don't yet know about Isaac. With his athletic build, perhaps he would be reliable if it came to it. As for Kit, he's a musician not a warrior, and he's still troubled by his injury. With Xurxo the only man I can really count on, I'm taking as few chances as possible.

The further we got from Smander, the more cheerful Aldara became. Riding along with me now, the morning sun climbing into the sky, she looked relaxed and happy in the saddle. The clear blue sea sparkled on our left, and the wide grassy track meandered ever northwards. Aldara's hair was escaping from her wimple, but she didn't seem to care. She no longer wore the sky-blue gown, but had acquired a simple brown shift from one of the many markets in Gascony, and it suited her.

Turning round, I saw the others strung out behind me. Xurxo and Yehudah were engaged in a discussion where neither seemed prepared to concede a point to the other. It's ongoing, this conversation, some kind of political wrangle involving who is the rightful landowner of the Duchy of Aquitaine. I fervently hope we'll hear no more about it once we leave said duchy and enter Brittany.

Behind Xurxo and Yehudah came Joseph and Kit, and there was no communication between those two at all. I shouldn't imagine Kit would be any more receptive to Joseph's tight little lectures than I was.

Bringing up the rear were Rosa and Isaac. Weeks ago I'd thought Isaac over friendly with Aldara. That stopped as soon as I married Rosa, and since then he's spent more time with my wife than I'm comfortable with. Rosa, I thought, watching them, should be riding with me, here at the front of the column. Instead she's at the back, and her companion is the far too good-looking Isaac, a man at least ten years younger than I, and whose conversation seems to be extremely stimulating.

Aldara broke in on my thoughts. 'You don't like it?'

'No.'

'Then put a stop to it.'

'I will.'

'You're not concerned about her pregnancy?'

'There's no pregnancy, Aldara. We did not make love on our wedding night. I've explained my reasons to Rosa and she understands them. I do not want to undertake this long and difficult journey with a pregnant wife. But nobody else knows.'

'Then – you are not legally married at all?'

'I suppose not.' Slightly disconcerted by Aldara, and wishing I hadn't told her, I changed the subject. 'I thought of asking Yehudah to give me Alfonso's letter this evening.'

'That's a good idea, and something you should have done a long time ago.'

Who does she think she is, this woman? 'The time was not right before, Aldara. We needed to be far enough from Castile.'

'But now you will have no recourse against Alfonso, will you?'

In a flash of anger, I rounded on her. 'Aldara, you speak out of turn.'

She dropped back, leaving me riding alone, and the morning seemed to have lost its glitter.

In spite of that, the day passed serenely. We stopped for a quick dinner and a swim in the sea in some cove or other. Isaac is as proficient as Xurxo with fire and food. Soon there were sizzling cubes of meat on thin, sharpened sticks roasting over flames contained within a circle of large stones on the beach, and in addition there was samphire and some sort of chopped up seaweed, salty and sour. This time the meat was chicken.

We arrived this evening in a large town called Bordeaux, famous for its vineyards and the quality of the wine they produce. I sent Isaac and Joseph ahead to find lodgings for us, and we arrived in time for supper at a fine merchant's house. I asked why we hadn't gone to an inn.

'The man who owns this house overheard me asking about lodgings,' Isaac said, his dark eyes cast down. 'He offered us rooms. And a good price for them, too. His housekeeper will cook our supper, included in the price. I thought it wise to accept the offer.'

'It's only for one night, Isaac.' I wished he'd look up; I was sure he was keeping something back.

But supper was excellent, and I had to concede we wouldn't have eaten nearly so well in the local hostelry.

With our panniers and bags loaded down with flagons of good red wine, we left Bordeaux early the next morning and journeyed north towards the Duchy of Brittany. Four days later we arrived in the town of Saintes, on the banks of the River Charente. The town is surrounded by a high wall, with an ornate gate at its southern end. As we clattered through the gate, the first thing we saw was a large church. It dominates the town. I sent the secretive Isaac in to ask about lodgings, and he dragged us off to a dingy little place near the town wall. I looked at him in consternation. Surely this wasn't the best Saintes had to offer?

'The priest directed us here,' Isaac said sulkily. 'I didn't know it wasn't to your taste—'

'Well you do now. Get out and find somewhere better.'

He flushed. 'With respect, lord, it's late and I'm tired, and I'm not actually *your* servant—'

'Get out!' I roared at him. 'Find us somewhere better than this shithole, or you'll be nobody's servant!'

I was furious. Not only with Isaac, but also with Joseph for his pontificating nonsense, and Yehudah for his unbending, sneering arrogance. All three have got on my nerves today, and I'd give a lot to be rid of them.

'There may not be anywhere else,' Xurxo suggested. We'd gone back down to the square, and we waited a good while, but Isaac did not return. Tired and hungry, I led my group back to the squalid little lodging.

A youngish, bearded man was standing in the doorway. 'My name is Franco, and I am the proprietor of this – ah – shithole.'

We trooped inside and were soon sitting in the hall of his boarding house, drinking wine from tall jugs.

I apologised to Franco. 'I didn't realise you could hear me. I insulted your house; I am sorry.'

'I think all of Saintes heard you! You were very displeased with your servant for bringing you here.'

I explained we were tired, dirty and in need of rest and food. Franco's house seemed somewhat basic. But we were grateful, nonetheless. And the wine was very good.

Franco was concerned he didn't have enough rooms for us all.

'We can share,' I said with a shrug. 'If the women have one room—'

'Ah!' Franco exclaimed. 'The women!'

I looked at him in surprise.

'I will explain,' he said hurriedly. 'Here in Saintes we have special accommodation for ladies. Especially noble ladies such as you have in your party. I will have them escorted immediately to the *Abbaye aux Dames.* It's a Benedictine nunnery with accommodation for visiting ladies.'

Franco arranged for Aldara and Rosa to be escorted to the nunnery, so now there were six of us, but even so it would be cramped in Franco's foetid little hostel.

Isaac has disappeared, and so has his mule.

'He said he would do it if he met the *Justiciers,*' Yehudah said obliquely.

'Do what? What the hell are you talking about?'

'Isaac knew we might find the *Justiciers* here in Aquitaine. The *Justiciers?* They are known in Castile as well as here, and in Brittany too, you'll find. I am surprised you do not know of them. Their mandate is to exterminate the Jews. Isaac, Joseph and I knew we would be targeted, but I told Isaac we should ask you for your protection. Still, he knew you didn't like him. He said he would go home if the *Justiciers* made themselves known here.'

I had not heard of this group. 'They're vigilantes then?'

'They are led by a man whose uncle was the Grand Master of the *Vendicatori.* Maybe you have not heard of the *Vendicatori* either. They operated years ago in Sicily, but they have been shut down now. You are right, the *Vendicatori* were vigilantes. A secret society who worked at night, killing those whom they decided were a danger to others. They did not particularly target Jews, however. The *Justiciers* are their legacy, and their goal is more specific, and more deadly. They are committed to removing the Jews from the face of the earth. Many Jews have been killed in this country, and even in Castile, although King Alfonso offers us protection.'

'You said the *Justiciers* have made themselves known. How did they do that? Have you seen them?'

'Why do you think we've been sent to this hovel? You made Isaac go into the church to ask for accommodation.

He met the priest, who turned out to be the leader of the local *Justiciers.* Isaac panicked. We will not see him again.'

Joseph is also of the opinion that Isaac will be attempting to make his way back to Castile and Alfonso's protection, but both he and Yehudah believe Isaac has little chance of escaping the *Justiciers*. The zealots will pursue him, and they will show him no mercy. I wish the man had spoken to me first.

Xurxo, Kit and the two remaining Castilians retired to the room we were all to squeeze into, but I stayed and shared another tall jug of wine with Franco, and we discussed Isaac's flight.

'You knew he was a Jew?' Franco sloshed more wine into my goblet. 'You *must* have known!'

'His name's a bit of a giveaway, but he doesn't look particularly Jewish, and he doesn't wear the yellow tunic or the badge.'

'But you found out? Did he tell you?'

'No, Franco, he didn't tell me, but we shared rooms and we bathed in rivers and I saw for myself.'

'Then why did you come?'

'We're on our way home! We had to come.'

'You should have avoided Saintes. The *Justiciers* were alerted by the priest; he's their leader. Isaac will be caught. He should have stayed with you.'

'That's why the priest sent us here?'

'Of course. You were right when you said there are better *logements* in Saintes. But none of them will accept Jews. They'd be punished.'

'Do you accept Jews, Franco?'

He smiled wryly into his goblet. 'We need more wine, you and I. It's going to be a long night.'

I hadn't started out with the intention of staying up all night talking with Franco. Nor with the aim of getting drunk. But both those things happened, and I thought Franco was a wise man who understood how people think and behave.

'Why do the *Justiciers* hate the Jews?' I struggled not to slur my words. We were well into our fifth or sixth wineskin by then. I liked Franco; he was good company. So was his wine.

'Everybody hates the Jews. And now I need to introduce someone to you.' He got up from the table and called softly through a doorway. Someone came into the room. My eyes wouldn't focus, and I had to blink and squint to see who was there.

It was a girl. Young, not tall, but with loose limbs, black hair and olive skin, which was free of blemish. She wore a simple white cotton shift and her feet were bare. Franco beckoned to her, and, rather shyly, she approached me, her movements graceful, slim arms held across her body. About fifteen years old, I guessed.

'This is Sara.' Franco drew her forward. 'She will look after you tonight.'

But I kept seeing two of her, my head was fuzzy and I couldn't think properly. What I *did* know was that not only did I not want to sleep with this child, but I'd be no use even if I did. I struggled to explain, while Sara's shape shimmered disconcertingly in front of me. Giving up, I crashed down onto the table.

8

IT WAS TIME TO SEE FOR MYSELF

I was still lying across the table when I woke next day. Franco's young whore was also still there, standing by the door. Someone had cleared away the wine, and there was no sign of Franco. I went to the door and called for the others. They came tumbling into the hall, and I was relieved to see they were all there.

'Who's this?' asked Kit.

'My name is Sara,' said the girl. '*Le patron* would like me to accompany you on your journey home. I can serve your wife and the other fine lady.'

I shook my head. Had I agreed to something I'd no memory of? But Joseph, approving, said, 'That is well. Lady Rosa will be glad of a maidservant.'

I left them all to get to know each other. I'm not interested in Franco's women. I'll tell him to keep the girl. I don't need her. My wife is managing very well without a maid.

Kit and I sat on a low wall in the marketplace in the centre of Saintes. Sara, for some reason, had trailed along with us. I'd sent Xurxo and the two Jews to the *Abbaye aux Dames* to fetch Rosa and Aldara back. I still hadn't paid Franco, but he'd disappeared and I was anxious to get back on the road.

Kit looked over at me. 'You don't want the girl to come with us, are do you?'

'I don't remember Franco mentioning it. It won't happen.' I was watching some small boys trying to feed an apple to our ponies, which were tethered to a nearby tree.

'I think Lady Rosa would like it.'

'Maybe so,' I said, absently, shooing the small boys away. 'I won't be asking her, Kit. We don't need this girl. Franco offered her to me last night. Even if she were to be useful to my wife, we don't need that sort of girl in our group, it'll just make trouble.'

But Sara overheard our conversation. 'Please take me. I won't be any trouble, and you may need my help. I understand this country.'

I shook my head, unwilling to add further complications to the journey.

The three of us waited for Xurxo, Joseph and Yehudah to bring Aldara and Rosa to us. We waited a long time. The sun rose high in the sky, the marketplace now thronged with townspeople, and still there was no sign of the rest of my group.

'I'm going to find out what's happening,' I said to Kit. 'Stay here. And Sara, you stay here as well.' I slid down from the wall and made my way to the church at the side of the square.

The building was dark and cold. I had to wait for my eyes to adjust. Once they had, I saw the priest standing at the far end.

'Mon Père,' I called. 'Do you know Franco, who owns the boarding house at the north end of the town?'

He shuffled down the length of the church, bare feet slap-slapping on the cold flagstones. *'Non, je ne le connais pas.'*

'Then, do you remember my companion, Isaac? He came here to ask you where we might stay the night. You directed him to Franco's boarding house.'

The priest scratched his head. *'Non, monsieur.* It was not I who did so. Perhaps your friend spoke to someone else, maybe one of the acolytes. Or an altar boy. Is there anything else I can help you with?'

It was a dismissal, but I didn't care for it. 'I don't believe you.' I moved closer to him. He was, perhaps, the same age as Laurence, our chaplain at home. But in all other respects he was completely different. Flinty eyes met mine. A mat of grey hair lay flat on his scalp, almost as if it didn't grow there but had been placed carefully upon it and would be removed at night, or in a high wind.

'It is a shame you don't believe me.' The priest's voice was toneless. 'It would be better for you if you did.'

'You're threatening me, *mon Père?*'

'For your own good. Here in this town there are men who would be displeased to know you called me a liar.'

'The *Justiciers*?'

'A secret society of men who have vowed to bring justice to this town.'

'Who is their leader?' I knew the answer, but wondered what he would say.

'I lead the *Justiciers*. My name is Yan.'

'Is Franco dead?'

No answer.

'Where are Xurxo, Joseph and Yehudah?'

Yan stepped right up to me. He peered into my face. His breath stank and the grey mat of hair, up close, looked even more artificial. 'You are asking all the wrong questions.' Spittle jumped from his mouth. 'Here is the question you should be asking: what do the *Justiciers* do in this town?'

I resisted the temptation to step back from him. 'All right. What do the *Justiciers* do in this town?'

He licked the spittle up and nodded approvingly. 'My father's uncle was a member of the *Vendicatori*. My great-uncle was the Grand Master for ten years. He led the *Vendicatori* to do many good things, to right many wrongs, but he was hanged as a criminal. Here, in Saintes, I started the *Justiciers* two years ago, and it, too, is doing good in the world. We have rescued people who were wrongly arrested, and we have killed those who were persecuting the innocent. "Justice For All" is our motto and our goal. We will not allow power-seeking despots or corrupt petty officials to deflect the course of truth, justice and equality. The *Justiciers,* slowly and surely, are showing that peace, opportunity and justice will make a better world than oppression, evil and violence. In this, Saintes will lead the way, and the world will follow!'

I recognised the demented fanaticism in his eyes. I'm more afraid of men who want to force people to be good than those who know they're evil. Men like Yan have blood on their hands, but they think it's in a good cause so it doesn't matter.

I remembered that feeling.

In Egypt and in Cyprus.

Slaughtering the Infidel because his beliefs were different from ours.

Knowing with absolute certainty that God was on *our* side, not theirs.

Knowing that our violent behaviour was sanctioned by the Almighty, who rode with us into battle. The ruined cities we left behind us, the dead warriors on both sides and the wailing women and orphaned children were all part of God's plan to rid His earth of the Unbeliever.

'I'll return to my original question,' I said. 'Where are my companions?'

'The Smanderino? He was sent home. You see? No killing, no wounding, no maiming. Just a peaceful instruction to leave Saintes.'

'What of the Castilians? And what has happened to my wife and to Lady Aldara?'

He sighed. 'I see you do not understand. The Jews have been dealt with. You asked about the Jew named Isaac. Isaac is dead. He was a coward, running home to Castile, but he did not get far. My officers saw to that. The woman you mention, Aldara of Smander – we have no quarrel with her, nor with your lady. We have given them our protection.'

I've seldom heard more chilling words. Xurxo has been asked to leave Saintes, presumably under some sort of threat. Joseph and Yehudah have been 'dealt with', and the women have been given 'our protection'. I put my hands on Yan's shoulders. He did not flinch or try to move away. My thumbs inched towards his throat.

'Tell me where they are, *mon Père.*'

'You are a stupid man, using that threatening tone. You already know I am backed up by the entire society of

Justiciers. And you know we do not respond to threats or violent behaviour. So take your hands off me and step back. Only then shall I tell you what you want to know.'

I took my hands from his shoulders and stepped one pace back from him.

'The Jews, as I said, have been dealt with.' His voice was still toneless, and there was no more spittle. 'They are not dead, but one of them has been beaten, as an example to the others. He made a terrible error, which could not go unpunished. The Smanderina is tending his wounds. You will find them both in the *Abbaye aux Dames.* Go there now and tell the *abbesse* I sent you. Then take your wife and the Smanderina away. You will not be stopped.'

'It's as simple as that?'

The mat of grey hair nodded. But I did not for one moment believe him.

'What do you know about the *Abbaye aux Dames?*' I was staring into Sara's strikingly attractive face. I still knew nothing about her, but I intended to put her to the test. Kit was no longer with her, and she couldn't, or wouldn't, say why; but then, Kit does often take himself off without a word to anyone.

'It's right there.' The girl nodded towards some railings opposite the marketplace. 'That's the *abbaye.*'

'Do you know the *abbesse* there?'

'You cannot trust her! Is your wife in there?'

I looked at her sharply.

'I overheard Franco,' the girl said quickly. 'Franco

mentioned sending the women in your party to the *abbaye*. Your wife and one other?'

'Does Franco use you, girl? You're a whore?' Though it was obvious she was.

She looked down at the ground. I began to ask her about the priest.

'Don't trust the priest either, sir!' Sara interrupted. 'He's one of the *Justiciers!*' The girl took a deep breath and approached me more closely. 'I know you don't know anything about me.' Her voice was high and soft, her eyes limpid. 'I want to prove myself to you. I will show you I am worthy of being in your group and travelling with you. Let me enter the *abbaye*. I will bring your wife out to you. I swear I can do it.'

'How?'

'I have a plan.'

We honed the plan between us. Sara would ask for sanctuary in the convent, pretending the *Justiciers* were after her. I would stay in the marketplace, playing my gittern and singing. I would be facing the *abbaye,* so that the crowd, gathering to enjoy my music, would be facing away from it. As soon as Sara brought Rosa out, the two of them would mount one of the ponies and ride away. After a short while, I would pack away my gittern, collect a few *soux* from the crowd, saunter over to the tree and ride off. The three of us would meet outside the town wall.

'I'll have to go back after that, Sara, and so will you. I need to find the others from my travelling party, and you belong here. With Franco.'

I thought the plan had a reasonable chance of succeeding. If it did, then the *Justiciers* would have been foiled, and we would have to make a very quick escape from Saintes. If Sara's plan failed, I would have to come up with something else. I doubted even the *Justiciers* would lay hands on Rosa, daughter of Alfonso, King of Castile, but Aldara might be a target, and the other two Jews would probably be hunted down and killed.

I arranged myself back on the wall with the gittern's strap around my neck, my right hand grasping the short quill. An ostentatious tuning-up of the instrument's strings. A few chords and discords. '*Sorry about that,*' I muttered. A passer-by helpfully asked if I knew what I was doing, and I was able to gesticulate up the road away from the *abbaye* and tell him in execrable French what I thought of him. Insulted, he called to his friends to come and support him. A tavern nearby proved a source of folk willing to come over and adjudicate the argument. Now I had a crowd around me. The man I'd insulted stomped off in a rage, but by then he was unimportant. I sat on my low wall, twanged the strings experimentally, and eventually someone called out, 'Go on then, *salaud*. Give us a tune.'

I started with one I know well, *Reis Glorios*. At first, the crowd couldn't hear properly. They crept forward, and nearly toppled me off the wall. I stopped in mid-verse and motioned them back.

'Well, sing up then, *salaud!* We can't hear you.'

Salaud. Son of a bitch. It would do. I played and sang raucously, and the crowd did not disperse. Rather, others joined, swelling the ranks, obscuring anyone's view of the *abbaye's* walls, including my own. No matter. I carried on with my recital. I followed *Reis Glorios* with two English songs, and then one in their own language, which they loved. But I was getting desperate. I had no idea if Sara had been successful. Over the press of people, their various hats and bonnets moving around at the back of the crowd, I simply didn't know if the ponies were still tethered to the oak tree, or if Sara and Rosa had ridden off. Or, the possibility making my stomach lurch, if Sara had betrayed me. Was she also working for the *Justiciers?* Had I been reckless to agree to her plan? Perhaps the whole thing had been cooked up by Franco and Yan, and even now Aldara and Rosa lay dead in an alleyway, or in the silent cloisters of the *abbaye.*

So what should I do? Play another song? Make some pretence that necessitated my standing up so I could see over the heads of the crowd? Perhaps play the next song wandering amongst them, edging my way to the back to get a view of the nunnery. The crowd wanted more music. They began to jeer. The *'Salaud'* taunt was taken up and became louder and more insistent.

'N'arrête pas!' the back rows screamed.

'I'll give you another song if you pay me,' I shouted back. 'Drop your *soux* in my hat!' And I flung my woollen hat onto the ground.

'He must be joking,' someone declared loudly. 'With a voice like his, we should pay him to shut up!'

My singing is nothing special, but it's not that bad. It was nowhere near as beautiful, though, as the singing that floated over the crowd from the other side. Everyone stopped hurling abuse at me, and all listened.

Rosa das rosas, e fror das frores,
Dona das donas, sennor das sennores.

A girl's voice. Ethereal and perfect. People gasped. The crowd parted. I saw her step between the two groups of silent listeners, walking as if to meet her lover, her footsteps delicate but unhesitating, her head held high, a flame of passion in her eyes, and that song on her lips. Sara came towards me, and I, almost in a trance, began to play the accompaniment. We performed the song together.

Unbelievably, Sara knew the whole song, all four verses and their refrain, and the crowd hung on every word, absorbing the music into their souls. When we finished, Sara made a simple curtsy, and I bowed flamboyantly. Coins chinked into my hat, many, many coins, and it was passed to me almost reverently.

'Play here again,' they all said. 'Every evening. The two of you. We want to hear your music again!'

We laughed, promised to be back and strolled away. 'Where is she?' I hissed to Sara as soon as I could.

'Change of plan,' she explained in a low voice. 'I got your lady out, but I could see you were in trouble. I told Lady Rosa to ride off. No one saw. Then I came to rescue you. Now all we have to do is catch up with your lady. I told her to wait for us outside the town.'

'You did the right thing. Now go and take my wife to Poitiers. I will find the others and meet you there.'

Could she do it? Could I trust her to do it? She'd been resourceful so far, and sometimes you just have to take a gamble. I watched Sara hoist herself into the saddle of the remaining mule, gather the reins and set off for the town gate. She didn't look back, and I prayed she would not double-cross me. I'd not seen Rosa, and I only had Sara's word for it that my wife had been liberated from the *abbaye*. It was time to see for myself.

9

THE JUSTICIERS ARE EVERYWHERE

'So was it just our bad luck that we stopped in this town where this organisation exists? And just Joseph's bad luck that his faith was noticed and he was beaten for it?' Aldara, in the Paradise Garden, was angry.

I'd had all kinds of trouble getting the abbey gatekeeper to admit me, but the use of Yan's name eventually convinced him. The *abbesse* received me, but said very little. She told me Aldara and Joseph were in the infirmary. Joseph could not be moved, but she would send for Aldara, and if I would be so good as to wait in the Paradise Garden, Aldara would join me there. The Paradise Garden? I hurried to find it.

I'd seldom seen anything so lovely as that garden. Inviting pathways led between bowers of climbing roses, the air heavy with their scent. Shady arbours had been formed in recessed alcoves, while in the centre was an astonishing fountain, the water rising to ten feet in height before falling into a square pond. On each side of the pond was a stone bench, so you could sit and watch the sunlight play on the water and listen to the delightful plashing sound as it fell, bubbled and rose again. Around the fountain, the garden was arranged in four distinct quarters, and between them were beautiful, narrow channels of fresh, still water. The whole garden was as lovely and refreshing as its name had promised.

As I waited for Aldara, I wandered along the paths, discovering new wonders and intriguing little grottos around each corner. I ducked under arches of honeysuckle, strolled between beds of glorious lilies and violets, and eventually came to the furthest quarter of the garden, which consisted of a paved circular courtyard, edged with huge rose-pink pebbles. Against the south-facing wall a beautiful old vine was growing, its fruit gorged with the promise of excellent, full-bodied wine. On the other side stood a painted dovecote, and the soft, cooing sound of the doves was the backdrop for my conversation with Aldara.

She had walked through the garden towards me, and now we sat together on a carved bench.

'I don't think it's bad luck at all,' I told her. 'It's my belief that the *Justiciers* knew about us before we got here. We were sent to Franco's hostel by Yan, the priest, and he runs the group.'

'So Alfonso's behind it? You must have discussed our route home with him?'

'I did discuss it with him. But he couldn't possibly have got word to Yan before our arrival.'

'He wouldn't have needed to. He just had to make sure you stopped in Saintes. Perhaps he recommended it for the wine they make here, or the quality of the inn. I don't know, could have been anything. Can you remember if he mentioned the place?'

'I know we spoke of it, yes. But I don't remember who mentioned it first. And then Joseph—'

'Joseph was the bait. Or Isaac was. Isaac and Joseph must have been chosen by Alfonso because he knew the *Justiciers* would get to them. It was a set-up.'

'How is Joseph?'

'Very badly hurt. Three *Justiciers* set upon him. He was unarmed and he's not strong.'

Middle-aged, bespectacled Joseph, with the dry, sententious voice, anxious to teach me 'the reality' of the stars. He couldn't possibly have defended himself.

'Will he recover?'

'He'll live. But he won't be able to move from here for a while.'

'I'm sure he'll be well cared for by the nuns.'

Aldara's eyes opened wide. 'Oh no. I thought you understood. *I'm* caring for him, and I want to continue to do so.'

I frowned. 'I thought you wanted to travel with me to Mallrovia.'

'I do want to do that. And so does Joseph. And we hope to be married in your tolerant and wonderful country.'

I was taken aback. Joseph is hardly the husband King Xisco would have chosen for his daughter.

'I would have married you if you'd wanted me,' she said.

Too late for that. I closed my eyes, hearing the splish-splash of the fountain, the incessant cooing of the doves and the birdsong in the trees. I caught the heady scent of roses and lavender, feeling the woman close by me. Her gown rustled, and I smelt soft perfume from her body. How would it have worked out if I'd married Aldara while I was still in her country? Would Alfonso have sent his henchmen to get me? Almost certainly not. We would not have encountered the *Justiciers*, and Aldara and I would not now be sitting in the so-called Paradise Garden in this convent. *A simpler life.* That's what I would have had with Aldara. And a simpler journey home, too.

'I did want you,' I said, unsure if that were true. 'But then—'

'You got a better offer.'

'It'll sound trite, but I did it for my King.'

She laughed. 'It sounds very trite! Your king doesn't care whom you marry, Rory. He just wants you to marry and have a child. I know this because my father has told me all about you. *And* all about King Philip of Mallrovia. Joseph needs a wife. And I need a husband.'

'It's a business deal then?'

'You could put it like that. I am thirty-one years old. If I don't marry now, I never will, and that would break my father's heart.'

'You're a Christian and he's a Jew.'

She shrugged. After all, Joseph is from the court of Alfonso X of Castile. I doubted Xisco would have religious objections.

'I need to find Xurxo and the others, Aldara. Unless they, like Isaac, have been murdered by the *Justiciers*.'

We stood up. 'Now listen,' Aldara said quietly. 'But don't let it look like you're listening. Gaze around, admire the garden. Point to things. But while you're engrossed in the flowers, the birds and the trees, I'm going to talk and you must listen without showing it.'

I did as I was told. While I was looking all around, and gesturing at the prettiest flowers and the wondrous landscaping, Aldara spoke softly to me.

'Xurxo and Kit will have been sent away by the *Justiciers*. The *Justiciers* can't risk angering Castile. Castile is too powerful, and it's growing bigger every year. The Crown of Castile has conquered many kingdoms, and Smander is alone in withstanding its reach, but we won't be able to hold out much longer. Little Smander will be swallowed up in the Crown of Castile before long. Ever since Andalucía, all of Castile's neighbouring states have been wary.'

I began to walk around the garden, pretending to sniff the fragrant roses, looking into the waters of the tranquil pool, strolling along the gravel footpaths. Aldara followed, picking daisies as she went. '*You* are safe as well, of course. You have married into the most powerful family in Europe. The *Justiciers* are a small group of fanatics, but they're intelligent enough to know their limits. Here, though, they are safe. The *abbesse* is Yan's sister. Between them they control the town.'

We couldn't pick daisies for ever. I straightened up, my back aching.

'Who's listening or watching, Aldara? Why have we had to pretend not to be talking?'

She answered very softly, her arm around my waist as if we were lovers, her lips close to my ear as I bent to listen. An observer might have thought we were kissing. 'This courtyard is overlooked by a large dovecote. And behind the dovecote there's a hut. And in the hut there's an evil woman who reports everything she sees, under cover of the birds and the noise they make. This is the Paradise Garden. Paradise can be a dangerous place.'

I looked over at the dovecote. It was a large structure, and the birds coming in and out, cooing to each other, did an excellent job of concealing whatever lay behind it.

'Who's the spy behind the dovecote? To whom does she report?'

'It's just one of the nuns. She reports to the *abbesse,* and *she* has daily meetings with the priest.'

'So Yan gets to know everything that happens here. There's got to be a reason for that. What's going on in the *Abbaye aux Dames?*'

'I've told you everything I know. Hopefully the nun behind the dovecote has heard nothing of our conversation and thinks we have been admiring the garden all this time.'

'Whatever the nun thinks, Aldara, nobody will believe I came here simply to look at flowers with you. There's more to it than that.'

The big, gaudy dovecote stood about twenty yards to my left. I ran. I was at the structure in moments and dodged behind it. Aldara was right. Hidden in a carefully cut-away recess in the hedge was a small wooden hut. With the dovecote in front and the hedging to each side, you wouldn't see it from any angle. The door was wide open. As I threw myself into the hut, I heard scrabbling and then a soft thud.

The hut was empty. A low wooden bench occupied most of the interior, but behind the bench was a small door, which was flapping itself shut even as I looked wildly around. I flung the little door open. I'd have to bend double to get through it, but a woman could do it more easily. I folded myself through the doorway. I was in a strange part of the garden. Grassy paths led in all directions. Tall trees and hedges bordered the paths, so I couldn't see where they went. I had no way of knowing which path had been taken; it was a brilliantly constructed escape route. I wouldn't know which way to go, and if I took the wrong path, my guess was I'd soon be hopelessly lost, and would wander round in circles, unable to get out of the maze. So whoever had been spying on me and Aldara was now safe. I squeezed back through the little porthole and sat on the wooden bench.

All right then. I'm spying on people in the Paradise Garden. What can I see? Answer: nothing. Well, that wasn't completely true, I could see the large dovecote directly in front of my hide. It was painted a drab grey on this side, not at all like the vivid, colourful pictures of trees and birds you see from the garden itself. The birds fluttered in and out from both sides of it, and their noise would mask any sounds I might make.

I leant forwards, almost into the doorway itself. Still nothing but the back of the solid-walled dovecote. I frowned, frustrated. What's the point of a spyhole when the spy can't see anything? She can't hear anything either. I must be missing something. I looked around more carefully. There were two pieces of string dangling from the roof. Perhaps they held the door shut when there was nobody in here.

And then I saw it: a ledge built into the front of the hut. On the ledge there was a long hollow tube – made of metal, copper perhaps. I picked it up. At first, I couldn't see how I was supposed to use it. It must be part of the spying apparatus, but how? Again, I scrutinised the interior of the hut, but there was nothing else. I got up and stepped outside. The gap between the doorway and the back of the dovecote was small, less than two foot in width.

But to the side of the hut, fallen over as if abandoned in

a hurry, was a wooden triangular structure. I placed the feet of the triangle on the ground between the hut and the dovecot. On top of the triangle was a grooved piece of timber. It was the right size for the copper tube to lie in, a cradle for the tube, and a support too. It was exactly the right height off the ground for someone sitting on the bench to put their eye to it. I leant forward again, the long copper tube resting on the tripod. But the tube was *too* long. If I leant forward to steady the tube, its near end projected over my shoulder into the hut. I couldn't put my eye to it. There must be something else.

This time I discovered it by accident. It was the final part of the apparatus. I pushed the tube towards the dovecote. It was several inches too long, but then I found it was disappearing inside the dovecote. And then it stopped. I pushed a little harder, and there was a faint click. The tube had engaged with something inside. My heart started to beat faster. The tube was supported, somehow, inside the dovecote, and also on its cradle outside. It was steady, and I no longer needed to hold it.

Sitting on the bench, leaning forward just a little, I found there were soft leather pads on the shelf on either side of the doorway, and these made comfortable supports for my elbows. Now the tube was exactly the right length, and I could put my eye to its end. When I did, I gasped in amazement. I thought I might see a small circle, a tiny part of the Paradise Garden on the other side of the dovecote. But I could see the entire garden, though the view was distorted, the level surfaces curved and the distances shortened. I saw Aldara, standing by herself, making a necklace out of the daisies she'd picked. There was no one else in the garden. I thought – wishing I knew more about such things – there must be some sort of glass lens fixed into the other end of the tube. Not the copper tube I was looking through, but the one that must be set up inside the dovecote, the window onto the garden.

How many people meet here, I wondered? The *abbesse* obviously sends everyone here, and then she dispatches one of the sisters to sit where I was sitting, to watch. But you'd need to be able to hear as well, or you'd learn nothing. I looked around again, conscious that I needed to look for something clever. I caught hold of the two looped pieces of string. They were slippery, and I guess they'd been waxed. I pulled on them. Tumbling down from the rafters came a couple of metal cylinders. I put the cylinders to my ears. And there we were! All the sounds from the garden. The fountain splashed, the birds sang – and Aldara was singing too:

Rosa das rosas, e fror das frores.
Dona das donas, sennor...

I left the hut, its copper spy-tube still in place, the metal cylinders swinging from their waxed strings, and I ran over to Aldara.

'Did you know how it worked?'

'No. But I suppose *you* do now.'

'Why were you singing that song?'

'I like it.'

I sank down on the grass. Who was the spy? What had she seen? Why was my presence here so important?

Aldara sat down next to me. 'At least we can talk openly now. You chased the nun away, I suppose.'

'I never saw her.'

'I should get back to Joseph. He needs constant attention.'

'Take me to him.'

'You won't be allowed into the infirmary.'

'Can he travel?'

'No, he's too badly injured. My advice to you is to take Lady Rosa home now and leave the rest of us to join you when we can. Although perhaps Xurxo and the others are already heading back to Castile.'

'Yan, the priest, told me Xurxo was. He said the Jews have been "dealt with". I don't know where Kit or Yehudah are.'

'That's bad,' Aldara said thoughtfully. 'Anything could have happened to them. Just remember two things: one, the *Justiciers* are everywhere. You can't trust anyone not to inform on you. And two, Joseph and I *will* come to Hambrig. But he can't be moved yet. We will join you later.'

'And the others?'

She shrugged. 'As I said. The *Justiciers* are everywhere.'

10

I'VE ALWAYS BEEN ABLE TO SING LIKE THAT

I rode out of Saintes, heading back towards Bordeaux. To everyone I met, in every village through which I passed, I asked the same question: 'Has anyone been seen travelling along this road? A man on horseback? Average height, dark green beret, rides well. Going to Bordeaux. Have you seen him?'

Nobody had. It's approximately three days' ride from Saintes to Bordeaux, and if no one had seen him on the first day, then Xurxo hadn't come this way. Isaac was dead, and Yehudah had probably run away. What sort of an escort were these men? Jews, all three of them, not good in a fight, unable to defend either themselves or the rest of us, and destined to be persecuted in the very places Alfonso knew were on my route. Alfonso, I had decided, was playing his own game, and one for which I did not know the rules. Which meant my wife, Rosa, was almost certainly part of it.

I turned the mule's head once again and made my way back to Saintes.

I'd arranged to meet Sara somewhere between Saintes and Poitiers, although I hoped the girl would go all the way to Poitiers with Rosa if need be. I was also aware that, for the first time since we set off from Smander, I was on my own and no one knew where I was. I slid down from the saddle and took my gittern from its bag, slinging it around my shoulders. I tied the animal to the same oak tree outside the *abbaye* walls, and spoke to the same gatekeeper, giving him the same fiction. It worked before, and it worked again. He jerked his head towards the Chapter House, where I'd met the *abbesse*, but, foolishly, he didn't trouble to escort me this time. I walked down the gravel path, then, out of sight of the gatehouse, I veered off to the left and entered the Paradise Garden. Again, I was the only person there. Or so it seemed. I peered behind the dovecote and found the little spy-hut empty.

Sitting by the cool fountain, I took my gittern in my hands and played a melody. *Rosa das rosas e fror das frores...*

Someone came into view, one of the sisters. When she saw me, she stopped.

'I heard the music. I didn't realise a stranger was here. Who are you?'

'My name is Nathaniel. I'm a friend of Aldara's.'

'Aldara? We have no one of that name here.'

'She's working in the infirmary.'

'Ah, then I might not know her. She's a lay sister?'

I nodded.

'It doesn't explain your presence in the garden, however.

Who let you in? Have you seen the *abbesse?* We rarely allow men in here.'

'I did speak with the *abbesse*, sister. She asked me to wait here for Aldara.'

'I'm not sure—'

I didn't wait to find out what she wasn't sure about. I decided I'd been speaking with the sister long enough for the spy to have arrived and settled down in the little hut. I sprinted across to the dovecote and heard the sounds of someone frantically trying to escape through the back, but this time I was quicker than she was. Flinging myself into the hut, I hurled the bench to the side, lunged forwards and pulled the nun towards me.

'Please let go of me, sir,' begged a frightened but familiar voice.

Shocked, I tore off her veil and wimple. As the sister I'd been speaking to in the garden cautiously approached the dovecote, calling to me by my fictitious name, I stared into the face of Franco's whore, who was meant to be escorting Rosa through France.

'What are you doing?' I hauled her to her feet. *'Where is my wife?'*

'She is safe, sir, but you must get out before you're arrested. Sister Nona has gone to get help. The *Justiciers* will be here soon.'

'I'm not going anywhere. What the hell's going on here?'

'I'm employed by the *abbaye.* I watch what happens in the Paradise Garden. I report to the *abbesse*, and she tells Yan the priest. Yan is the Grand Master of the *Justiciers*, a vicious, dangerous man. You should keep out of his way, sir.'

'Come with me.'

'I can't come with you. The *abbesse* knows you're here, she knows you've spoken with Sister Nona, and she expects my report. If I don't go now, she will have us both arrested. Sir, if Yan gets to you, you will not live to see tomorrow. Please believe me!'

'You're coming with me, Sara. We're both getting out of here, and we'll both live to see tomorrow. Put your nun's garb on again, look like you normally do here. Then *you* arrest me.'

Staring in astonishment, she arranged her wimple and veil and stood up, dusting herself down.

We stepped out of the hut and Sara grasped my wrist.

Nuns were pouring into the Paradise Garden.

'I found him with Sister Nona in the courtyard,' Sara told the *abbesse.* 'What shall I do with him?'

'You have done well, child. I know this man; he was here before, speaking with one of the lay sisters. I will send for Yan.'

The *abbesse* tied my wrists tightly behind my back. I don't know what she used, but it cut my flesh and it hurt like hell.

'Take him to my office, girl. Yan will meet you there.'

Sara pushed me, and I stumbled forwards. She'd promised to prove herself to me and this was her chance; if she were working for the *Justiciers,* I'd soon know. Even with my hands bound I could knock Sara out and make my escape. The *abbesse* and her brother would not be pleased with their little informer if that happened.

We walked across the lush grass. On a pink gravel path, Sara pushed me to the left, the way to the office. Not my plan, and I half-turned, but Sara pulled on my arm, causing the strong, thin ties to embed themselves in my wrists, and I cried out.

'No, no, don't make a sound,' Sara whispered frantically.

'I am taking you to the infirmary. We are going to rescue your friend.'

We slipped down a passage between two long, low buildings, and there Sara cut the ties around my wrists.

'Where are we?'

'This is the lay sisters' dormitory. And over there's the church. We need to wait here for a short while. You'll hear the bells go for compline and the sisters will go in to pray. That's when we move. The infirmary is right in front of us now. We've passed the doorway already, but we'll double back to it soon.'

'Joseph is too ill to move.' I was thinking aloud. 'That's what Aldara claims.'

'We need to rescue a sick man as well?'

'He was beaten up by the *Justiciers.*'

'Then if we don't move him, he'll die anyway. The *Justiciers* aren't going to let him survive. Now we must be silent. We can't let anyone hear us.'

We pressed ourselves against the wall of the lay sisters' dormitory, and after a short while the bells chimed out from the church. I kept my eyes down, hearing feet on the gravel, the nuns' measured walking, two by two, into the great abbey church. I've seen it enough times in Hambrig Abbey, and I don't expect it's much different anywhere in the world. Two by two, filing in to take their places in the nave and the choir, to give thanks to God for his ministry on earth and theirs too, to chant psalms and the rest of the liturgy, and then file out again and go back to work in the fields, the kitchens, the library or the laundry. Or perhaps, since it's compline and the end of the day, to their dormitories for private prayer before bed. Such is the religious life, no matter where you live.

The crunching of the gravel came to a stop. We waited a

bit longer, in case there were any latecomers. Sara put her hand on my arm and we hurried softly down the narrow passageway until we reached an open doorway. I followed the girl up a flight of wide, stone steps, and emerged in a large, airy room. It had big windows, all of them unglazed, and it was bright with evening sunshine. We walked down the length of the room. As far as I could see, all the beds were empty. When I got to the other end, I found it a much more shadowed part of the infirmary; there were no windows here. In the furthest, darkest part of the room lay the solitary patient.

I didn't look at the man in the bed. 'Now tell me the truth,' I growled at Sara, swinging her roughly round. 'Where is my wife?'

'I got her away, I told you. I did not lie. She will be waiting in the countryside beyond Saintes.'

'You were supposed to go with her. You were told to take her to Poitiers. Yet you turn up here, working for a group that commits murder—'

'No, sir, that isn't how it is. I only ever pretended to work for them. It was – it was necessary. I can't explain now. Lady Rosa is well, and she is where I told you. The other lady will be somewhere in the convent. I will find her, and I will bring her to you. Two women will easily move in and out of the *abbaye*. Please take your injured friend away while you can!'

I looked down at the man lying on the palliasse. He was pale, bandaged, seriously hurt, without his spectacles, and unconscious. I bent down and slid my arms under his body. I lifted him and hurried back through the passage between the beds, down the stone steps, out into the narrow corridor between infirmary and dormitory, back to the gatehouse. What if the gatekeeper had returned? I could neither explain myself nor fight him off. I gritted my teeth and turned the corner, Joseph's head bumping up and down on my shoulder. Out of luck. The gatekeeper was back; but he wasn't looking in my direction, and I stopped moving and slunk back a bit. I laid Joseph down on the grass and approached the gatekeeper, who turned when he heard me.

'Hey! I was told you'd been arrested,' he yelped. 'I'm waiting for the *Justiciers* to come and take you away!'

'Well, maybe they'll take you away instead,' I suggested. Before he could query that strange idea, I rammed him hard in the stomach, and he crashed into the stone wall behind. I sprinted back to Joseph, and in moments, I was out of the convent and had somehow hoisted the injured man onto my mule. I jumped into the saddle and flicked the reins. We began at a walk, picked up the pace, started to trot, which turned into a clumsy canter, and soon we were out of Saintes altogether. I slowed down, my eyes flickering from side to side, hoping to find Rosa waiting, as Sara had promised.

But it was Rosa who found me. Very sensibly, she'd concealed herself in a shady copse of larch and beech by the side of the road. Or perhaps Sara had advised it. As soon as my wife saw me riding towards her, she showed herself.

'Rosa, thank God!' I exclaimed, jumping down and hurrying to her. 'Thank God you are safe.'

'It is entirely thanks to a young girl,' Rosa said primly. 'She is pretending to be a nun in the convent, but she told me she is now one of our group. I thought she would come with you.'

'She's bringing Aldara. They will join us later.' I had no great confidence in the statement; Sara's loyalties could lie anywhere, and if she's being paid by the dubious Franco, or the more obviously evil Yan, then I doubt she's on my side. She'd told the truth about Rosa though.

With no physician it will be hard to care for Joseph. Aldara is well meaning but untrained, and Joseph needs trained medical help. What he *doesn't* need is a long, hot, dusty ride over bumpy terrain, draped over the stiff leather pommel of my mule's saddle. I'm writing my notes as I sit here for a few moments. Rosa is dosing, leaning against me. Her eyes are closed, and her breathing is slow and steady. The red disc of the sun is well over in the west. In an hour or so it will have set, although the sky still has that brittle brightness that's so common this far south.

I moistened Joseph's lips with water; there's no shortage of that, thank goodness, with rivers and streams running everywhere. But his body was burning hot. I put him in the shade of the trees, trying to make him as comfortable as I could. As I watched him, he stirred. Opened his eyes. Reached out to me.

'Can you hear me, Joseph?' I asked, positioning myself so he could see my face.

'Very thirsty,' he croaked.

I fetched a skin of water and held it to his lips. Water dribbled everywhere, but he managed to drink some. Then more and more.

'Go easy. A little at a time.' I've heard Stephen making sure his thirsty, feverish patients don't make themselves sick.

'Help me up.' Half-sitting, Joseph struggled to raise

himself further. I got him leaning back against a tree, and I think he felt a bit cooler. I collected some dead wood and an armful of larch cones, and lit a small fire.

Leaving Joseph resting against his tree, the fire crackling strongly inside a circle of stones, I walked along the track and soon arrived at a largish village. I managed to buy bread, milk, cheese and mackerel from some peasant folk whose patois was unintelligible. In the setting sun, I hurried back to our little roadside camp. Rosa was awake and watching for me, but Joseph had fallen asleep, although only lightly. He woke up when he heard and smelled the mackerel sizzling on the fire. I didn't know if today was a fish day or not; I'd lost track of the calendar, but I didn't think God would mind too much either way. The bread I'd been given was light and spongy-soft. I broke it open, fitted the hot mackerel fillets inside, added a lump of the soft, white cheese they favour round here, and closed Joseph's hand around the whole thing.

'Bite into that,' I said, handing a hunk of bread to Rosa and doing the same with my own bread, cheese and fish. The mackerel tasted of the sea, the bread was soft and mealy, the cheese creamy and fresh. Joseph managed to eat just under half of his, which I thought was good enough. I was about to kick the fire out when I heard the sound of travellers on the road. Not robbers – they'd have been quiet and stealthy. Rosa looked at me, questions in her eyes. In the gathering dark, I peered through the trees.

'Is it them?' breathed my wife by my side. 'Is it Aldara and the nun who saved me from the *Justiciers?*'

It was.

In front of the other two women, Rosa rounded on me. 'When Yehudah took me to the convent, I thought you had abandoned me. I thought you'd decided you did not want me after all. I am a Castilian, and the king's daughter. You should not have humiliated me.'

'I married you.'

'And then you shamed me.'

Sara's eyes darted from me to Rosa and back again. She knew perfectly well what Rosa meant.

'I did not mean to shame you. I explained it all. I don't want you to be expecting a child on this long and difficult journey. Which is proving even longer and more difficult than I'd anticipated.'

'You explained it, yes. But you didn't tell me everyone would know.'

'I didn't know everyone would know.'

She wouldn't look at me. 'In the *abbaye*, they said I could join them. I would rather do that than be treated with disdain.'

'No!'

I couldn't bear it to happen all over again. I'll not lose another woman to a nunnery. I told Rosa nothing of Kathryn and what had happened to her all those years ago, merely stating that Rosa was married to me. There would be no more talk of convents.

'But where is everyone else?' she cried angrily. 'Isaac? Yehudah? Xurxo and Kit? Where are they all?'

'We are going to find out, lady,' I said grimly. 'But for

now, I need to get you to a place of safety. Sara, in the morning you are to take Joseph, Lady Rosa and Lady Aldara on towards Poitiers. You won't get there tomorrow, or even the next day, so you must find somewhere comfortable where you can all spend the night.'

'I will do my best, sir,' Sara said.

I had one more question to ask her. 'That singing in the marketplace. The people loved it. How did you learn to sing like that?'

'I've always been able to sing like that.'

11

LE VICOMTE D'AULNAY

We stayed in our little camp until dawn. The fire glowed, fizzed and crackled all night, and the two women and the girl slept well. Joseph slept too, but I remained awake, thinking about what to do in the morning. My mission now was to locate Xurxo and Kit, the two people I could utterly depend on; the others, I wasn't nearly so sure of. Sara had behaved strangely, and I still didn't know if I could trust her. As for Aldara, she was a woman bordering on no longer being marriageable. Her father, King Xisco, knew that. There had been deception there too.

At first light, I mounted my mule and turned him towards Saintes, hopeful of meeting my two friends and even the unsmiling Yehudah. I met nobody. Into Saintes I trotted once again, hating the place now. Franco's sordid boarding house, the market square, the *Abbaye aux Dames*, the church where the odious Yan presided – all these unpleasant places greeted me in turn. The sun rose higher in the sky. The abbey bells rang for terce.

Yet again I tied the mule to the oak tree outside the

abbey walls, and walked across the square to the church. The gloomy interior showed no pinpricks of candlelight. I searched the building. Yan wasn't there. Back outside I blinked in the sunlight.

'Tu cherches ton ami?' called a voice from outside the tavern. It was the man who'd first called me *salaud*. He was propped against the doorway, holding a flagon of ale. He waved it at me. *'Il te cherche aussi!'* And he broke into guffaws of raucous laughter.

'*Tu sais où il est*?' Maybe he did know where my friends were. Though I thought the man was likely bluffing. Or drunk.

'*Oui, salaud. Sinon, pourquoi je te parlerais?*'

But I had to wait a good long time before he deigned to impart his information, for the flagon of ale had to be consumed first, down to the last drop. Finally, I learnt that Kit had been in the tavern most of the night but had gone out first thing to look for someone. My rude acquaintance spat blobs of slime onto the cobbles when I asked further questions.

By dinnertime I'd searched the whole of Saintes to no avail. I bought bread and cheese in the market and wandered down to the river to eat a frugal dinner before abandoning the search – and that's where they were. All three of them somehow together, in the midst of a discussion as to how to go about finding me. I can't say it was a joyous meeting, but we were all relieved to see each other.

'What's happened to Isaac? Do we know if Isaac was killed? The priest told me he was,' I said, handing out my bread and cheese and wishing I'd bought more.

'He's not dead, but the *Justiciers* have got him,' Xurxo said glumly. 'Joseph had a lucky escape.'

'What about you, Yehudah?' I asked. 'How did you escape the *Justiciers?*'

'He was in hiding,' Xurxo said. 'Luckily, I found him. But we shouldn't waste time looking for Isaac. He'll be dead by now, but even if he isn't, you can't beat the *Justiciers,* there are too many of them.'

Kit looked up. 'You clearly haven't seen Rory in action. What do you think, Rory? Should we hunt for him?'

'It depends,' I said slowly. 'Xurxo thinks he's probably dead already, but we've had more than our fair share of luck so far.'

'That's true,' Kit said. 'I was lucky to find Xurxo—'

'Pah!' Xurxo exclaimed rudely. 'That wasn't luck! *I* found *you.* Word travels faster than people do, and everyone in Saintes knew where you were. I made sure to waylay you before the *Justiciers* did.'

'But they're just a group of people who think they should be in charge of law enforcement.' Kit's voice came thickly through a mouthful of soft French cheese. 'Though they've no authority to do so. They carry out punishments on people who they say have broken the law. The law as *they* see it, that is.'

Which described the *Justiciers* pretty well.

I said, 'Yan told me he'd sent you back to Castile, Xurxo. Yet in reality you were all in hiding. I'm guessing he didn't even know who you were. Yan was bluffing.'

'He is a dangerous man,' Xurxo said seriously.

'I believe he is. And the *abbesse* is involved as well.'

'Of course. The *abbesse* is Yan's sister. They run the *Justiciers* between them. If anything, she is the more dangerous of the two.'

The more dangerous of the two. Sara had worked for the *abbesse.* And I'd sent her on her way with my wife. 'We must catch up with them,' I said. 'It won't be difficult. Sara and Aldara are walking. There are only two mules between the four of them.'

We retrieved our various mules and ponies and got ready for the journey north from Saintes. It hadn't escaped my notice that in all that time Yehudah had said nothing at all.

We rode until an hour or two before sunset. There had been no sign of Joseph and the women by the time we reined in at a place called Aulnay. It was only small, like most of the towns here in Aquitaine, but there was a church and a smallish kind of castle. I led my party up a terraced, vine-covered hill to the dilapidated gatehouse. There was a chance we might find accommodation for the night, and I would make enquiries about the others. They must have been seen from this castle on its hill – if anyone was keeping a lookout.

'*Vous êtes sur le Chemin de Saint-Jacques*?' queried the guard, a scruffy man, unkempt and ill-dressed.

I confirmed our status as pilgrims, now on our way home.

'*Mais pas le Juif?*'

'Ah, well, you see, the Jew is a fellow we have picked up on our way home. Not a pilgrim himself, naturally, but a man on a journey, nonetheless, and there's safety in numbers, as everyone knows. He seems an honest sort of fellow, and we are happy to travel with him...'

'*Et vous-même? Vous êtes seigneur?*'

'Yes, indeed, I am a lord, and so is one of my

companions, the Duke of Casuel in Smander, who, along with one of his countrymen, is a genuine pilgrim like myself, and we would all be so grateful for some hospitality... but you should stop asking us questions and tell me who is the lord here?'

'*C'est le vicomte! Le vicomte lui-même est ici. Je vais vous présenter.*'

He left his post and took us along passages and up staircases and into strange round towers. The castle was like no other castle I've ever seen. Every part of it seemed run down and in poor condition, and it was very easy to get lost in. But the longer it took to get anywhere, the more concerned I became. Perhaps this servant was just leading us round in circles, a grand tour of Aulnay Castle, with the aim of getting us completely disoriented.

'How much more of this?' Kit grumbled from behind me on a narrow, twisting stairway.

'How should I know?'

We emerged from that stairway into a circular chamber at the very top of one of the towers. The chamber was in darkness. Our guide motioned us to stay where we were while he stepped into the room. I could see a shadowy figure further in, but who it was, what it was doing, even whether it was sitting or standing, was impossible to tell.

'*Monsieur le Vicomte. Je vous présente le Seigneur du Castle Rory en Mallrovia et le Duc de Casuel en Smander avec leur entourage. Ce sont des pèlerins.*'

'*Chretiens?*'

'*Trois Chretiens et un Juif, Monsieur le Vicomte.*'

A whispered conversation ensued, our guide stepping further into the room.

Kit glanced across at me. 'All very odd,' he mouthed.

Damn right, I thought.

After some more indistinct whispering, the gatekeeper tiptoed back to us. *'Monsieur le Vicomte vous verra.'*

'Parlez-vous anglais, Monsieur?' I asked the shadows on the other side of the room.

'I will translate if need be,' the scruffy servant said from behind me. 'My English is good, *seigneur.*'

Xurxo swore in Smandego, and at the same time Kit pulled something out of his clothing. I knew without looking that it was one of his firecrackers. And I knew, also without looking, that we were in danger. I turned, stepped forward, and at the same time put out my hand and shoved the gatekeeper backwards. I heard him try to keep his balance, and then Xurxo's voice. But I was approaching the shadowy figure by the wall. It was a man, that much I could see now, a man standing up, but leaning on something. A stick perhaps.

'Who are you?' I called to him, while still several feet away.

'My name is Thuban, and I am the *Vicomte d'Aulnay.'* His voice was halting and reedy, and with an accent I couldn't quite place. Not French.

I felt rather than heard Kit move, turned to him and shook my head. I didn't want him to unleash his firecrackers just yet.

'I know my name is odd,' the viscount continued. 'You will remember it. It is growing dark and you have journeyed far today, I think. We shall talk again tomorrow.' Thuban beckoned to his servant. 'Rastaban! Take these people to their rooms. They're staying in the *chateau* for now.'

Rastaban led us on a much shorter route this time, and we quickly arrived in another tower, where there were several partly furnished bedchambers, all of them shabby to the point of dereliction.

'*Vous pouvez prendre n'importe quelle chambre que vous aimez*. Choose any room you like. You will find the *chateau* a vast improvement on the "shithole" in Saintes!' Rastaban shrugged dismissively while scratching coarsely at his genitals, and then disappeared down the winding stone steps.

'How does he know about Franco's place in Saintes?' Xurxo asked incredulously.

I shook my head. I didn't see how the gatekeeper and his master could have known anything at all about us. I turned to my minstrel. 'Kit, you are to investigate this tower, and any passages that lead off it. Yehudah, you stay here; and Xurxo, you're coming with me. We need to find out what's going on.'

Kit vanished up the steps, and Xurxo and I went back down to ground level. Outside the tower was the courtyard. It was mostly in shadow, although some evening sun lit up the vines that grew against the crumbling walls, shining onto an ancient apple tree leaning its gnarled trunk against the south-eastern corner. But the place was deserted.

'Either the *vicomte* isn't at all wealthy,' I whispered to Xurxo, 'or he's a skinflint. He's spent no money on this place for a long time.'

'Or,' suggested Xurxo seriously, 'he doesn't actually live here.'

'You go south and west. I'll take the north-eastern tower and the outbuildings on this side. Meet me back here in an hour.'

We separated. Kit was already scoping out the north-western tower. From the top, and in daylight, he would get a good view of the countryside all around. It was dusk now though, and the hillside would be rapidly darkening. I hurried over to the tower opposite, but its main door was locked. An axe would have made short work of that, but I only had my light dagger. I saw no other way into the tower from the courtyard, but there might be a door on the other side. An archway had been built into the western wall. I dodged through it and found myself in a vineyard. Over to my left I could see the roughly cobbled track we'd ridden along from the south-west. To my right were some low buildings – barns probably, and my guess was they contained wine presses. The grapes looked fat and juicy, ready for picking and crushing. But it was too late in the evening for anyone to be working in the vineyard. To get to the north-east tower, I'd have to skirt round two sides of the chateau. I pulled the dagger from my belt and began my circuit.

I looked along the length of the north wall of the chateau. Here there were hen coops, and also a well, sunk deep into the ground. As I made my way eastwards, I saw a small door in the wall, and realised I'd not spotted it from inside the courtyard because the ancient vine hid it from view. The chateau as a whole looked as neglected and crumbling as its courtyard. I began to think Xurxo's theory might be correct. Thuban didn't live here, and the likelihood was that *nobody* lived here. I arrived at my goal. And there it was. A wooden doorway into the north-eastern tower. No actual door – that had fallen through long ago.

I stepped inside. Immediately, I was under attack; carrion crows squawked in my ears and flapped around me, pecking at my face. Bats dropped from perches high up, rats scuttled across my feet, and I tried to fend the whole pestilential lot off by flailing my arms around, kicking out strongly and keeping my head down. As far as I could make out there were no steps and no chambers; the tower was just a shell. Slipping on bird shit, keeping my hands up to protect my face from the angry rooks, trying not to gag at the awful stench of the place, I made a hurried escape from the tower.

To meet up again with Kit and Xurxo, I completed my circumnavigation of the chateau, walking down to the south-east tower. The sun at my back was all but gone now. My hands were covered in scratches, grazes and bite marks, but there was nothing I could do about that. I arrived at the gatehouse in the southern wall, where I met Rastaban again. He looked surprised to see me pop up from outside the chateau.

'You did not find *les chambres* to your liking?' sneered the man, looking at my filthy clothes.

'No, I did not. What other rooms do you have?'

'*Aucune*.'

Really – none?

Unhelpful.

'*Où sont mes amis?*'

'*Lesquels?*'

'*Il y en a quatre*.'

Four missing people: Sara, Joseph, Rosa and Aldara. I held out no hope for Isaac. Rastaban shrugged, uninterested. He produced a bottle of wine from somewhere and uncorked it. He allowed himself a long swig, then held it out. It was coarse and harsh on the throat. He laughed at my expression.

'*Fils de pute anglais*,' he observed rudely and inaccurately, and it was my turn to laugh. We shared the bottle, and then another and another, though this time I was careful only to pretend to drink. Rastaban became as coarse as his wine, his insults flowing as freely, his supply of both never-ending. After a while, as full night descended, and the gatehouse grew dark, Rastaban slumped onto the ground. His head fell forward. He snored. Fast asleep, he pissed in his breeches. But, among the rude French epithets, obscene gestures and crude jokes, I'd gleaned information. I'd learnt exactly where the others were. Now I just had to meet up with Yehudah, Kit and Xurxo, and then we could take our leave of the repulsive gatekeeper and his strange master, *le Vicomte d'Aulnay*.

12

MY FATHER UNDERSTOOD ME

Thuban found me before I found my companions. And when he did, I got a shock. Standing in the courtyard, I heard a strange clicking noise behind me. In the dark of the tower room, where I'd first spoken with him, I had not properly noticed the appearance of the *Vicomte d'Aulnay*. Now I saw an elderly, hunched-over man, hobbling on two sticks. He was thin and haggard, clearly in pain, yet with sharp, dark eyes and a firm, square chin. His face was the only part of him that looked normal. He was much older than I'd thought, and in far worse condition.

He stared defiantly back at me. 'This is why I keep to the darkest places, Lord Rory.'

But I'd seen worse. 'What happened to you, Thuban?'

'I do not talk about it. And in any case, it is supper time. You will, of course, join me.'

'Not yet, thank you. I am looking for my companions, Kit and Xurxo. And when we are all together, I will leave you to your darkest places and I will go and find the rest of my group.'

'You know where they are?'

'Your servant, who's drunk and unconscious, has told me everything.'

'Did he tell you about me?'

'No, he didn't, Thuban. But I wish he had.'

'Tut tut. He missed the whole point of the plan, then, *l'imbécile.*'

'You told him to get drunk and answer my questions?'

'Ha ha. You don't have to tell a Frenchman to get drunk; you just make sure he has plenty of *du bon vin rouge*. But yes. He was supposed to talk to you. It sounds as if he did that a bit too willingly, but never mind.'

'I don't understand why you didn't just tell me where they were. And why you made your servant lead us all around the chateau before allowing us to meet you.'

'It is true you don't understand. But you will. As you say, you have to find Xurxo and the duke, and I do not know where they are. You can see I am not much use at chasing around, so you will have to do that yourself. I will sit here and wait for you. You will find a lamp in the gatehouse, with oil and flints and whatever you need.'

I felt my way back to the gatehouse, located the oil lamp and then set off on my rounds. I found both Xurxo and Kit in one of the barns, and there, too, were Sara, Rosa, Aldara and Joseph, just as I knew they would be. Rastaban had locked them in, but it was an easy matter to unbar the door and release them.

'Why?' stormed Kit, who's got a temper on him. 'Why did that idiot lock us up?'

'I have no idea,' I answered, 'and we can't ask him because he's dead drunk. We'll spend the night in the confounded chateau after all, then continue our journey tomorrow. And it's a very good thing we are all together again.'

'But we are not all together.' Joseph's voice was accusing. 'Isaac is not with us.'

'The *Justiciers* have him,' Xurxo explained shortly. 'And that means he's a dead man.'

Aldara had been caring for Joseph and he was recovering well. So long as he leant on someone strong, he could walk, but he was no easier to get along with. We all trooped back around the wall of the chateau and entered the courtyard.

Thuban was still there. 'Good. Now you must find the *chambres* Rastaban showed you, which is where your other Jewish friend is waiting. And tomorrow there will be food.'

'I thought there was going to be food tonight,' I said, angrily. 'Supper time, you told me.'

'That was long ago, Lord Rory. The hour is late. We must all get some sleep. Please. After you.'

I knew why he waited. The south-east tower was the only one with habitable rooms, and my party made their weary way to it. Thuban and I listened to the clump-clump of boots up the stone steps. He levered himself up, refusing my offer of help.

'I have been like this for a long time. I have learnt to manage most things. Some things I cannot do, and I have learnt to accept that. Now, follow your friends. Get some sleep.'

'What about you? You're not going all the way back up to that dingy room, are you?'

In the lamplight I saw him smile. A friendly smile. 'No, Lord Rory, I am not. I have a ground-floor room. Naturally, Rastaban did not show you that one. And do not worry about your wounded friend. It was to be expected, you know. The *Justiciers* don't like the Jews.'

I walked with Thuban as he limped painfully into the

tower and opened the door to his chamber. It was a spartan room, almost bare, the walls crumbling and damp with moss growing up them.

'Do you live here, Thuban? All the time, I mean?'

'No. But this is where I have chosen to be for the time being. Goodnight, Lord Rory of Hambrig.' He hobbled in and shut the door on me.

I climbed wearily up to the top of the steps, where the chamber was at least less damp, less mossy and less rank. There was no bed, but someone had piled rushes into a sort of mattress on the floor. No doubt it would be teeming with insect life, but I didn't care. I tugged off my boots, pulled my shirt over my head, slipped out of breeches and braies and collapsed into the straw. I didn't even have the motivation to write my journal before I crashed into sleep.

A large wooden wagon stood outside the gatehouse, and Rastaban was busy piling bales, boxes and barrels into it.

'Going somewhere?' I called.

He spun round. '*Bonjour, Monsieur le Menteur.*'

I don't take kindly to being called a liar. Reaching him in two strides, I lifted him up by his dirty tunic so his toes danced just off the ground, and I asked him what he meant by it.

'*T'es menteur. C'est tout.*'

Kit came sauntering up, a lump of half-chewed bread in his hand. He bit into it, then stood, watching. Rastaban was still struggling to keep his balance; I had not let go of him.

'Why do you say Lord Rory's a liar?' Kit called out. 'I've known him lie. But I wouldn't call him a liar. They're not the same thing, you know.' It was the patient, instructive tone of one used to talking to idiots.

I dropped the servant. 'It's of no importance. This man's of no importance either, and he's clearly on his way somewhere. And the sooner we get on ours, the better. Do you know how Joseph is this morning?'

Kit shook his head.

I asked him where he'd got the bread.

'I found it. I don't recommend it though. It's weevilly.'

Right, I thought. 'Supper time' never materialised, and it didn't look like 'breakfast time' was a thing here either.

'Get everyone together, Kit,' I said, watching him hurl the rest of the weevilly bread into a bush. 'Horses, mules, packs, the lot. Make sure the women are all right. We leave within the hour.'

He ran lightly back to the tower, and on the still morning air I heard voices. Kit relaying my instructions, hopefully. Female voices sounded, and there was even a song, drifting out of one of the topmost openings in the tower wall.

Rosa das rosas...

I went to check on the animals, and by the time I came back, satisfied they'd eaten their oats and were watered and rested, there were a great many people in the courtyard. I didn't see Thuban, but protracted farewells were not on my agenda.

Counting heads, I decided Kit had done a good job. 'Listen, all of you. We're going to head north-west of here, to Poitiers. Gather your possessions, eat something from out of the saddlebags, load your packs onto your mules, muster at the gatehouse.'

Sara helped pack the bags for the men to lift up and secure onto the mules' saddles. She folded blankets and shawls and rearranged baskets of bread, grapes and rounds of soft French cheese. I was impressed with her energy and good spirits, but I had bad news for her. I called her over to me.

'I'm sending you back to Saintes. You've helped me a lot, and you were good to my wife, so I'm sending you back with a good-sized purse, which I hope will help in whatever—'

I had to stop. The girl had thrown herself onto her knees in front of me. 'Please let me come with you, sir! I can help your wife and I will follow all your orders and not be a nuisance! I'll do anything you ask, but please don't send me away!'

Surprised, I replied, 'You belong in your hometown, girl. And Franco, if he's still alive, will be looking for you.'

'Franco won't care about me. I was working for him, that's all.' I knew that already. Men like Franco will always need girls like Sara.

'Who is your father, Sara?'

But she didn't answer.

'Whoever you are,' I said eventually, 'and whoever your parents are, you belong in Saintes, and that's where I'm sending you. If necessary, I'll have one of my party escort you there. That's an end of it. Now go and make yourself useful, and remember what I said. I'm grateful for what you've done, and I'm giving you a fair amount of money. Your father, whoever he is, will not be disappointed.'

I've hoisted myself onto the wall, my journal and my quill in my hand. Poitiers has been my next destination all along, though I didn't anticipate it taking this long. From Poitiers we'll go to Tours, though it will be a hard journey with an injured man.

I'm mulling over my conversation with Sara – and some things Rosa told me earlier this morning.

The girl, said my wife, was wonderful. Sara found the best watering holes; she kept everyone's spirits up by telling stories and singing songs in her lovely voice. When they arrived at the chateau in Aulnay, it was Sara who spoke nicely to Rastaban, and Rastaban, with no mention of the viscount apparently, allowed them to sleep in the wine-pressing barn. I'm glad the girl impressed Rosa. She's obviously from a wretched family, but at least they will be a lot better off in a few days' time.

Thuban interrupted my thoughts and my jottings. He beckoned to me from a doorway. Understanding his reluctance to be seen by everyone, I jumped down from the wall and went to meet him. He was leaning heavily on his sticks, and his legs were shaky.

'Thank you, Thuban, for your hospitality,' I said, although the chateau wasn't his, so the hospitality wasn't his to give.

'Tell your men to unpack the mules,' Thuban said quietly. 'Put your belongings into the wagon. I can see Rastaban has not explained.'

'Explained what?'

'Two important things. One, we are coming with you. We have a large wagon, which will do until we get to the Vienne. I cannot ride a horse or an ass. You understand.'

But I did not understand. 'Why? Why do you want to come with us? Is this a trap, Thuban?'

If so, it was a very silly one.

'No, Lord Rory, it's no trap. Well, perhaps it was, just a little. I enticed you here, you and your group of pilgrims. It has its uses, this chateau, being on the Way of St James. I wish to go to your country. I have heard of your alchemist from Persia, and I wish to see if he can cure me of my disease. Travelling with you will be safe for me. I have long wanted to make the journey, but Rastaban, though he means well, is not much protection. And I will be useful to you, since I know the lie of the land. You were going to Poitiers, then on to Tours I believe, but the road is difficult, and many footpads lurk in the hills. I have a better route to the coast. We'll travel up the Vienne, first—'

'The Vienne? What's that?'

'It is a river. And it connects to another river, the Loire. And the Loire connects to the Sarthe. Then we go overland for a short distance, before we embark on another river, the Eure, and finally the River Seine, which will take us to the port of Honfleur. From there we take a ship to England, and then it is over to you.'

'What happens to the cart? At the first river – the Vienne, was it? What do we do with the cart?'

'We dismantle it. It comes to pieces, and is easily reassembled for travelling by road again. It is constructed for that very purpose, Lord Rory.'

I raised my eyebrows and he nodded. 'This plan has been years in the making. I have been waiting for this opportunity these last fifteen years. Fifteen years of deteriorating health, utter reliance on Rastaban, though he's never let me down, and the hope of, maybe one day, finding a cure. Although Rastaban is a good servant, I can't call him a friend, and there are things I should like to be able to do for myself. Personal things. The things that give a man dignity.'

'Have you had this cart ready and waiting all this time, Thuban?'

'All this time. The chateau also. It has been here, slowly deteriorating, just like its master, waiting for you to arrive. But we didn't allow the cart to fall into neglect. That has been maintained and kept in good condition, the wheels and axles oiled monthly, just in case you came.'

'Me?'

'You, or someone like you. Someone strong, someone on his way back to Hambrig, following the Way of St James.'

'There must have been many such pilgrims. It's a popular route.'

'Oh yes. There have been many old men, many young ones too, but none who fulfilled my exacting conditions. Not until now.'

'And what are these "exacting conditions"?'

He refused to tell me. I think he was frightened I wouldn't take him. I *would* take him, though, if only because the wagon would allow Joseph to travel more comfortably, and would make the whole journey a lot more pleasant for the pack animals, and, therefore, for all of us. As for going by river, it's actually an excellent idea. I didn't use any waterways when I made my pilgrimage from Hambrig to Santiago das Cunchas, partly because I wanted to follow the waymarked *Camino Frances*, but mostly because I was punishing myself. And that meant not taking any easy routes south. A good many people in Hambrig thought I was running away.

Let them think what they like, my father advised me. *You've looked after them to the very best of your ability for many years. They'll manage without you for a few months, and appreciate you all the more when you return.*

'All right. You and your servant, and your well-maintained cart, will join our party. And what of the second important thing?'

'The second important thing is the child you know as Sara.'

Thuban clicked his fingers, and Sara herself slipped out from behind him. Thuban propped one of his sticks against the wall and put a hand on the girl's shoulder. 'Sara has told me you intend to send her back to Saintes. But this child is not from Saintes, neither is she who she seems. I wish to present this child to you for training as your squire. I have been told you are in need of one. This child is the son of a friend of mine. His name is Guido.'

At first I thought I hadn't heard him right, and then, as he nodded, and Sara ducked her head in embarrassed silence, I decided I didn't believe a word of it. This girl could not be anyone's squire, and as for being 'the son of a friend of mine' – well, that didn't seem possible either. But I knew only too well how deceptive appearances can be. The girl's eyes did not meet mine. Thuban's hand fell to his side, but Sara stayed where she was. Silent. Denying nothing.

'Is this true?' I asked slowly.

No answer, though her hands fluttered a little at her sides.

Thuban, also silent, was watching me. Looking for my reaction, perhaps. What he didn't know was that I've come across this before. When I was on Crusade with my friend Jonny, escaping from Caesarea Philippi, we were helped at one point by a woman who turned out to be a *khanith.* A *khanith* is an Arab male who dresses and acts as a woman. They're scarce, and not always welcome, but they have a recognised place in society. And Jonny and I will be eternally grateful to the *khanith* who risked his own life to help us find our way to the sea.

'Guido is a tormented soul,' Thuban explained softly. 'He has no place in Saintes, not with the *Justiciers* about. No one will accept him to do any work or be part of our society. It was not so bad when he was a young child. But now he is almost grown, yet he will not change his ways. Guido believes he should have the freedom to be himself. Without it, he is no longer alive. But does this actually help him? What will he do? Where will he go? How will he work if no one will take him? The freedom he claims as his right to life can be the denial of someone else's. He did not understand that, not at first, but he understands it now, and he knows it is a problem for all of us, not easily resolved. I made a promise to his father that I would secure Guido's future, and so I am asking, no, *Monseigneur,* I am *begging* you to take this boy as your squire. Take him home with you and train him. He is a quick learner and you won't regret it for a single day.'

'Have you spoken to a priest?' I asked, for surely this poor child must be the church's responsibility. I did not think I wanted a *khanith* as my squire.

'No priest can help us. He would give Guido sanctuary, it is true, but there is no work Guido could do in Saintes.'

'You think the life of a lord's squire is an easy one?'

'I think you are a good lord, and you will make sure Guido changes into the young man he was born to be.'

I took a deep breath, and thought, *what about Jonathan?* But Jonathan might not want to be my squire. He's English. He may want to return to England. I wished I'd had the sense to speak with Jonathan before leaving on my pilgrimage. If he had accepted my offer… well, Guido would have had to stay here and take his chances.

But I hadn't spoken with Jonathan. And right now I had no doubt that Jonathan and others would be amusing themselves in Castle Rory, with no steward to keep an eye on them and no strong garrison commander to maintain discipline among my household. I sighed. My home situation was a mess, and I admitted to myself that that's one reason I took to the Way of Saint James. I needed to leave it all behind for a few months.

'I'll have to think about it,' I said.

Sara – Guido? – looked at me in desperation. I guessed that if I'd agreed in the first place to take her with me, if I hadn't insisted on returning her to Saintes, the revelation that she was a boy would not have taken place. This offer to become my squire – it was a last anguished attempt to get out of Saintes for good.

Thuban was looking, not at me, but at the boy, if that's what Sara actually was. I was still unconvinced. Somebody was lying, and it was not at all clear who. I thought of Rosa and of how Sara had helped her. I thought of Sara's unnamed father, who had, no doubt, been murdered by the *Justiciers,* and of Thuban's promise to give the child a future. And so, boy or girl, I knew what I had to do.

'All right,' I said. 'All right. I do need a squire. I'll take you, Guido. And then, Thuban, when he's a grown man, I'll send him back to you. That's the deal.'

Thuban nodded gravely. In that instant, I decided I rather liked him.

'Why do you dress and look like a girl?' I asked Guido bluntly.

'I am a girl.'

That was disconcerting. And unexpected. The *khanith* that Jonny and I met in Caesarea dressed as a woman, but he didn't think he *was* one.

'What did your father think about that?'

'My father understood me.'

13

IT HARDLY MATTERS

I told my group the new plan for our journey north, and they all grinned in delight. Joseph was helped into the cart and propped himself up against a soft bale of something or other. Bags and packs were bundled in. Last to get on board was Thuban himself, who struggled manfully across the courtyard, unwilling to let anyone think him incapable.

Halfway across, he stumbled. Xurxo sprang forward to help, but Thuban somehow regained his balance. Sweat was pouring down him, saliva ran from his mouth and his spindly legs were shaking. His head shook too, and, far from making an unobtrusive passage across the courtyard, he was now an object of fascination. Realising this, he stopped, raised his eyes and looked about him in horror.

Rastaban noticed what was happening at the same time. He'd been lashing down some barrels in the cart, but, seeing his master's distress, lumbered over to him. He took his arm, but Thuban swung his stick, catching Rastaban on the leg. It hurt. Rastaban cried out and stepped back, and Thuban let out a great torrent of cursing, though not in French. But swinging his stick at Rastaban had unbalanced him, and he lurched forward, tried desperately to save himself from falling – and failed. The servant, nursing his bruised shin, did not move. Like a beetle that had rolled onto its back, Thuban couldn't get up. He struggled, failed again, and lay where he'd fallen. *The things that give a man dignity.*

I walked over to him, reached down and hauled him to his feet. I handed him his two sticks, turned and walked away.

We were ready. Thuban, Joseph and Rosa were riding in the cart, along with all the baggage, and there was a damned lot of that. Thuban and Rastaban had more than doubled the amount of stuff we were carrying with us. But they also had a draught horse, a big beast called Albert, pronounced the French way. Rastaban was to ride Rosa's mule.

There was still, it seemed, the matter of Isaac.

'What about Isaac?' Yehudah confronted me, just before I gave the signal to move off.

'We can't help him now, Yehudah.'

'I cannot believe you would walk away from helping a friend.'

'He's a *friend*? I thought he was part of Alfonso's plan to ensure I don't renege on my agreement with him.'

'That too. But *El Rey* never thought you would go back on your word. You are known to be an honourable man. And it is because you are honourable that I ask you now not to abandon Isaac. He needs your help.'

'If I'm so honourable, why did *El Rey* send you three with me in the first place?'

'It is time to tell him, Yehudah,' Joseph called feebly from inside the wagon.

Yehudah rounded on Joseph, his face dark with anger. 'You be quiet! You have been enough trouble already. It is *not* time, but now you have said that, we shall have to.'

'Indeed you shall,' I murmured.

Thuban was restless. One of the least convenient symptoms of whatever disease has struck him, is the need to urinate frequently, something he needs help with. Rastaban had to slide down from the mule and help his master with this, while Yehudah and I argued outside the chateau. Thuban was anxious to start, and I didn't blame him.

'Whatever it is, you'll have to tell me later,' I said to Yehudah. 'Now get going, or we'll leave you behind as well.'

Furious, he mounted his mule, and our whole party lumbered off along the track to a fork, where we turned right to go almost due east, heading for the River Vienne at Saint-Germain-de-Confolens. It would take two days to get there.

Thuban's problems became more and more apparent, and more and more difficult, the further we travelled. We needed frequent stops. After the third or fourth stop in only two hours, I told Rastaban we couldn't keep drawing to a halt for him to get down, climb into the cart and help his master pee over the side.

'*What* then?' growled Rastaban. 'You want him to disgrace himself?'

I told Xurxo to get in the cart and to help Thuban

whenever he needed it. Rastaban didn't see why I'd asked Xurxo and not him.

'You're leading,' I told him shortly. 'You're the one who knows the bloody way, so you stay where you are. Xurxo, get in the cart.' Thuban didn't seem to mind the new arrangement at all. Perhaps he saw the sense of it. I harnessed Xurxo's mule behind Albert, and we began to make better progress. Thuban needs to drink a lot as well, so we refilled the water flasks, bladders and skins frequently. It wasn't my intention to stop anywhere for the night, and I got Yehudah to make a duty rota so everyone could get some sleep in the cart at some point.

Guido is also a problem, as he refuses to answer to his name. Kit rode alongside me for a stretch. 'You're not put off by his appearance?' he asked.

'No, I'm not. Why should I be?'

'He's – different.'

'I don't know if you're thinking of Felix,' I snapped. 'Guido's nothing like Felix. Felix didn't look or act like a girl. He was an obnoxious child who liked to have sex with other boys. And he was evil.'

'And I warned you about that long before you came to realise it for yourself,' Kit said, serious for once. 'I wasn't thinking of Felix, as it happens. Though now I'm wondering – did you ever find out how he died?'

But I'm not prepared to go into that. Not with Kit, nor anyone else.

'You don't mind that Guido dresses in girls' clothes?'

I was annoyed at the stupid hints and loaded questions. 'Look, all of that is going to change. If Guido is a boy, he will be my squire. He won't be wearing girls' garments much longer, so there will be no problem.'

But Aldara also wanted to have her say, and at one place

where we stopped for a rest and a drink, she brought up the subject. And, being Aldara, she came straight to the point.

'Sara is a girl, lord.'

Now how could that be true, when Thuban had told me, in front of Guido, that he was a boy? Nor had Guido denied it. Though, when I remembered how Franco had offered the girl to me for my pleasure, it was hard to know whom to believe.

'I know what you're thinking.' The dratted woman thought she could read my mind. 'But Sara is a girl. And Guido is a girl in his head.'

None of that made any sense to me, and I decided to ignore it.

At mid-morning on 27th August we arrived in Saint-Germain-de-Confolens, having seen its hilltop castle from some miles away. As soon as we'd come to a stop and seen to the animals, people began unloading the packs and looking after Joseph and Thuban. With Aldara's words in my head, I decided to confront my squire-to-be. In my heart, I didn't believe the child was a boy. The more I saw of Sara, the more I knew she was female. In which case – who was Guido? This business had to be sorted out; it was as plain and simple as that.

I made sure we were completely alone. 'Take your clothes off, Sara.'

Some people are shy, and some are not. That's fine. But Sara was hysterical.

'Please don't make me do that, sir, please don't!' she begged, practically throwing herself on the ground in front of me. Her sobbing and pleading made so much noise that in the end everyone gathered around, thinking something catastrophic had happened. Even the invalids came to find out what was happening.

'What is the matter with Sara?' Rosa asked, watching the child writhing on the ground.

'I told her to strip.'

'But why?' asked Joseph at once, his dry, clipped voice grating on my nerves.

'Because I need to know...' I couldn't finish the sentence.

Sara lay huddled at my feet, whimpering and crying. I looked down at her. It was all the convincing I needed. The way she lay there, curled into herself, protecting herself as women do when they are frightened of being attacked. And it was the high voice, the beseeching hands, the piteous cries of distress, the air of helplessness... In fact, it was everything about her. I wondered why Thuban had lied.

I reached down and pulled her to her feet. I tilted her chin so I could look into her face. Everyone was standing in silence, waiting to see what I would do.

'Go away, all of you. I'll talk to Sara on my own.'

Reluctantly, they all went away. And when they'd gone, I walked Sara over to a secluded area outside the town wall. No one else was there to see what happened. I told her not to resist, not to speak, and not to worry. Gently, I removed her clothes. She looked away, tears running down her cheeks, while she shook and shivered so badly I almost failed to get the last of her garments off. But finally, she stood naked on the grass in front of me, her eyes shut tight, hands fluttering in acute distress around her body.

A boy's body.

Joseph was making a good recovery, though without his spectacles he couldn't see too well. Aldara was assiduous at looking after him, and his wounds were healing. Thuban, though, seemed to be slipping.

'What's actually wrong with him?' I asked Rastaban as we sat on the riverbank eating apples and cheese, and drinking the rough wine.

'Personne ne sait,' he said thickly, spitting out bits of food. The man is disgusting.

'How long has he had the illness?'

Again, Rastaban shrugged. 'As long as I can remember. *Et maintenant arrête de poser des questions.*'

I did. I stopped asking Rastaban questions. Not only is he uncouth, he quite clearly dislikes me and is unaccountably rude. We've learnt that a boat is expected within a day or two, and we've found lodgings in the town until then. It was Xurxo who suggested everyone have a swim in the river. The hot weather, the unrelenting sun and the long, dusty road have made us all dirty and smelly. Aldara and Rosa walked upstream and round a bend. Guido was in an agony of indecision, and then declared he would not bathe.

'You bloody well will,' I growled at him. 'You're not going to be the only bad smell in the boat.'

He took himself off downriver. So long as he gets cleaned up, I don't mind where he does it. The rest of us couldn't wait to get rid of our clothes and dive into the clear, cool water of the Vienne. All except Rastaban. Turns out he can't swim.

'And now is definitely the time to tell me whatever it is Joseph says I need to know.' We were sitting on the bank after our swim, and I looked from Joseph to Yehudah.

'*El Rey* has a plan.' This was Yehudah, who never says much.

'The plan involves your alchemist,' Joseph added in his scratchy voice.

'I know that,' I said impatiently. 'He wants Jabir to join him.'

'*El Sabio* wants Jabir to join his court,' Joseph said. 'That much you know already. He knows of Jabir and the Elixir of Life from other travellers. Many have spoken of him in great awe. But Jabir is more than his invention. He is a great alchemist, a reader of books, and an astronomer. *El Rey* and his court travel around Castile and the other subjugated kingdoms all the time. And he – that is, Alfonso – is a collector. What does he collect? He collects people. People with knowledge, wisdom and insight. People of many faiths. People like Jabir ibn Hayyan.'

'How is Jabir so special that his price is Alfonso's own daughter?' I asked sceptically. 'Alfonso's court already has many scholars. Jabir will just be another one of those, surely.'

'Yes and no,' said Yehudah, cryptically. 'Your alchemist's reputation exceeds everyone else's. Alfonso is curious to meet him.'

'What if Jabir doesn't want to go to Castile?'

'He will want to go.' They said it together. So there was still something they weren't telling me. After all that, I'd learnt nothing.

The next day, we saw the boat coming slowly down the river. She was shallow-drafted, narrow-beamed and propelled by oars, although with a favourable wind I guessed a sail could be hoisted. She had a crew of four. We were ready for her. Rastaban had directed the taking apart of the cart. The various components were simply slotted together, and in a very short time they were bundled up on the shore, lashed with a long hemp rope, the wheels by the side of it.

'What about Albert?' Guido was worried about our big packhorse.

'Albert will walk along the path by the river, of course,' Thuban told him with a smile. Thuban and Guido seem to be very good friends, and Guido does more than Rastaban for the sick man now. In fact, I can't see the point of Rastaban anymore. He's unpleasant and he clearly hates Guido. My intention is to send him back, and now I know how to dismantle the cart I shall get rid of him at the next opportunity. He doesn't know this yet, and I guess he thinks he has free passage through Europe with us. I paid the boatman for all ten of us, and a significant amount of money changed hands. All the more reason, I thought as I helped get Thuban on board, to dump Rastaban at our next stopping place, which I believe is Chauvigny, some forty miles downriver from Saint-Germain-de-Confolens.

The passage north is uneventful, and I blessed Thuban for suggesting this form of transport. Yes, you have to pay, but you can sit quietly, read, write, or dream your dreams, while you let the river and the gentle splish-splash of the oars carry you along. Our mules have been sold. I was reluctant at first, not because we've got attached to the beasts (only Aldara and Guido could honestly say that), but because we might need them later. Kit made a clear case for selling them, though, and the money will certainly help with the boat and ferry fares.

Rastaban is sitting by himself, one arm slung around the stumpy mast. So far, we haven't used the sail. It's rolled up around its yard, the whole lot pushed out of the way under the overhang of the larboard gunwale. The crew asked most of us to sit forward of the mast, although Guido and Aldara are aft to provide ballast there. Our baggage is scattered around, positioned by the crew to balance their boat as they want it.

'Aren't you worried about that boy?' Rastaban asked me just now.

'Guido? No.' I've no desire to make conversation with Rastaban.

The countryside glides past us, though from this low vantage point you can only see the spires of churches, the turrets of castles and the summits of hills. The rest is just reedbeds and sedge, filled with the sound of birdsong. Albert isn't walking along the path; he'd have needed someone to walk with him, and the boatmen pointed out that, in any case, the path only goes so far. It fizzles out after a few miles. So Albert has been stabled in Saint-Germain-de-Confolens, and Rastaban will be sent to fetch him at some point. He doesn't realise it, but that's going to be very soon.

'You should worry about him,' Rastaban says, picking his nose. He's not someone who can take 'no' for an answer, it seems.

I don't deign to reply. I'm writing my journal, and I'm enjoying sitting still and letting the crew and the river take me along. Our boat is called *Fauvette*. I didn't know the word, but I think it's a type of bird.

It's beginning to get dark. We won't travel at night; we'll make a camp by the riverside. There are tents on board for that very purpose. I'm quite looking forward to it.

'You should ask me why,' Rastaban continues, flicking his snot over the side, although some of it somehow manages to go in my direction.

I'm not going to ask him anything.

He leers up close to me, and I smell the wine on his breath, the unwashed stink of his body and clothing. 'Go on, *fils de pute*. Go on. *Ask me why!*'

I stay silent.

'*Très bien. Je vais en parler à tout le monde.*'

What is he going to tell everyone?

Rastaban had threatened to tell everyone about Guido, and I had to stop writing because of what happened next.

He stood up unsteadily, his arm still wrapped around the mast. In the stern of the boat, the skipper's head jerked up, surprised and annoyed. He flapped his hand in alarm. We'd already been told we mustn't unbalance the craft.

'Guido!' Rastaban shouted.

Guido, in the middle of an animated conversation with Aldara, also looked up in surprise.

'Guido! *Dis à tout le monde ce que tu es*! Tell everyone you are a piece of shit! *T'es une merde! Imposteur! Une fille dans le corps d'un garçon!* A girl in a boy's body! You have broken the laws of God! You should not be allowed to live! *C'est un blasphème que tu es. Un blasphème terrible contre Dieu. Tu ne mérites pas d'être...'*

'*Assieds-toi, idiot!*' the skipper yelled in consternation. And then everything happened at once. The *Fauvette* yawed wildly as the skipper let go of his steering oar and Rastaban lost his balance. As the boat turned side-on to the stream, Rastaban fell heavily overboard, causing water to cascade into our vessel, and Guido, clinging to Aldara, cried out. Thuban woke up, shouting that he needed to piss immediately, while Kit leant over the gunwale to try to help Rastaban, which caused the *Fauvette* to roll violently. The rolling made the barrels, boxes and bales all tumble about in the bottom of the boat, some of them rolling right onto Thuban as he lay helplessly on the bottom boards. The damned things are so heavy, I was convinced they'd crush the life out of him.

Writing about it now, I cannot believe the *Fauvette* didn't actually capsize. Rastaban was carried downstream, thrashing and flailing his arms, calling uselessly for help. The man couldn't swim, I remembered, and we all saw his head disappear as the river water closed over it. Eventually the boat was got back under control, and Kit and I rescued Thuban. He was unconscious, but alive, thank God, and in not too bad a condition, all things considered.

And now we were all ashore, miraculously at the place the skipper had originally chosen for our overnight camp. The tents were up: four of them, all large and roomy. Aldara asked that Guido share with her and Rosa, and I allowed it, as the boy was still badly shaken up. Everyone had had something to eat, and we were about ready to crawl into our tents, wrap ourselves in our cloaks and blankets and get some sleep. The next day we should reach Chauvigny.

'Rosa is your wife, isn't she?' Thuban asked me. He was lying in the tent we were sharing. Thuban is upset over his servant's death, and I was pleased he was talking about something else.

'We're married, yes. You're wondering why she isn't sharing my tent?'

'That is correct. You always sleep apart, you two.'

'There are good reasons for that, Thuban. The way home is tough enough without having a pregnant woman to worry about.'

He smiled at that. 'Ah, you noblemen! Always so sure your seed is potent!'

'Well, it might be,' I said seriously. 'It was once before.'

'You have a child already?'

'He died. And I thought you were also a nobleman, *Monsieur le Vicomte?*'

Another smile. 'For a while. Now it hardly matters.'

14

PUT THINGS RIGHT

I wake up in the night, bleary-eyed, and I see my father sitting between me and Thuban's sleeping form. I can just about see Kit, curled up on the other side of Thuban. I roll over to look at my father. I know he wants to ask me something.

Are you sure you told your friend the truth?

My friend? Oh, you mean Thuban. I didn't know he was a friend. Yes, I told him the truth, although I don't really know what you're talking about.

I'm referring to your wife. Your alleged reasons for not sleeping with her. It's not pregnancy you're afraid of. We both know that.

Quickly, I roll over onto my other side. I don't want Father to see my face.

Look at me, boy. But it is said gently. *Let's get to the bottom of this together.*

So I turn back to face him, and in his eyes I see compassion.

What is it, Father? What am I afraid of?

Perhaps that you don't like her?

It isn't that. I don't have to like her. I need a wife, and now I have one, so everything should be fine.

Are you comparing her to Kathryn?

I can't compare anyone to Kathryn. She is incomparable.

He nods. *I thought you would say that. Then there is only one thing left.*

I wait, my fists clenched by my sides, wishing Father hadn't come to me in the night so that I'm naked in front of him.

You are in love with someone else, Father says.

There's no one I'm in love with. After Kathryn, there has never been anyone and there never will be. Father knows this.

But he's speaking again. *Look into your heart. Find out what lies there, boy. You don't believe me now, but you'll find I'm right. And by the way, are you happy that your new squire is spending so much time with your new wife*? As he speaks the last few words, he gets up and sweeps the hair from his eyes, the gesture so familiar to me I half choke. Then the tent flap moves, and he's gone.

'What's wrong with you this morning?' Kit asked, chomping on a small crab apple.

'I had a bad dream.'

'Ah. You saw your father's ghost again.'

'It was just a dream, Kit. And hurry up, the skipper wants to leave soon.'

The tents had been struck, the fire was out, we were ready to go. I put my hand on Guido's shoulder. 'I want you to sit with me today, Guido. Leave the women to talk to each other in the stern.'

He bowed his head but didn't answer. I frowned. 'You should say, "Yes, lord," when I give you an instruction.'

'Yes, lord,' he whispered.

'Now lend a hand with loading the boat.'

It didn't take long for the *Fauvette* to be ready for the next leg of her voyage. I hadn't expected the same boat would take us all the way to Honfleur, and so, early on, I checked with the skipper how far he was prepared to go.

'J'irai jusqu' Honfleur, si vous allez me payer assez.' So I dived into my purse, handed over whatever *assez* actually meant, and heaved a sigh of relief. It would be a great deal easier to stay with the *Fauvette* than try to look for a different boat on each river.

I rounded up my party and realised Guido was missing. Cursing, I hunted for him, everywhere I thought he might be.

'Rosa, where's Guido?' The first time I'd spoken to her directly since my father's appearance in the tent last night.

'You will find Sara behind the farmhouse over there. She is being sick.' Rosa's tone was frosty, and I didn't care for it.

I shaded my eyes with my hand to look over at the farmhouse, a building at least half a mile away from the river. If he was feeling unwell, why had he gone so far away?

'Sara is not ill,' my wife informed me, 'just very unhappy. She knows you want her to behave like a boy, but she cannot do it.'

I did not want to confront this now. Out of the corner of my eye I could see the crew unrolling the sail from its yard. At last we have a good, strong wind from the south, and it's the skipper's intention to get all the way to Trogues today, if at all possible. Which, if the wind holds, it might be.

'The river turns to the north-west at Trogues,' he explained, spitting into the water to test the current. 'Provided we get there in time, we will spend tonight in Trogues.'

I said I'd be happy to get as far as that by tonight, but he ignored that. My happiness is of no consequence; what matters is keeping the *Fauvette* and her crew happy. They bloody well should be, considering the amount of gold I poured into the skipper's cupped hands.

'Vous êtes prêts? Vous tous?' He was looking around at the people mustered on the bank. But the boy hadn't returned.

'I'll go and get Guido.' I set off towards the farmhouse.

Xurxo caught up with me. 'You may need some help.'

I was glad of his help. Guido had been very sick indeed, and was slumped down against the back wall of the dwelling. A young woman was bending over him.

'Elle ne va pas bien,' she said, looking up.

'Let's get him to the boat.'

Between us, Xurxo and I lifted Guido and hurried away from the farm. I threw my thanks to the young woman, and we went as fast as we could, reaching the river to find the skipper impatiently holding his mooring lines, anxious to make the most of wind and tide.

I dropped into the boat, and Xurxo bundled Guido down onto the bench beside me. A quick head count ensured we were all aboard, someone shoved off with a boathook, and the sail was rapidly hoisted. It billowed out strongly, and we frothed down the river, giving the crew a well-earned break from rowing.

The wind held fair all morning. Normally, we stop at midday for the crew to have a break and for everyone to stretch their legs and take in some food and wine. Today we simply thundered on downriver.

Guido vomited twice more during that exhilarating run, and Rosa offered to look after him. I shook my head. *Are you happy that your new squire is spending so much time with your new wife?* If even Father thought it suspicious, clearly I should take note.

Kit scrambled over the rowing thwarts and came to sit beside me in the bows. 'Let Guido go to the stern of the boat with Rosa and Aldara.'

'No.'

'Look. For one thing, he'll be less sick in the stern. It's not so bumpy there. For another, you've nothing to worry about. Rosa thinks of him as "Sara" remember.'

But I can be stubborn when I want to be. Guido stayed in the bows with me, his slight form rolling on the bench with the boat's movement through the water, his face a nasty shade of green.

I changed the subject. 'You know why Thuban is coming to Hambrig, don't you, Kit?'

'I thought he'd arranged it all with you back in Aulnay,' Kit answered. 'I don't know, but I'm guessing it's something to do with Jabir and his laboratory.'

'That's right. I hadn't realised how far Jabir's reputation has spread.'

'Jabir had a reputation before he even arrived in Hambrig. That's the thing, isn't it? None of us knows much about him or his past, but everyone in Europe seems to have heard of him and his work. Perhaps because of his illustrious ancestor, or – more likely in my opinion – because he travelled through here on his way to Mallrovia. Jabir would have done everything he could to make an impression.'

'Then they've got very good memories,' I said caustically. 'He came to Hambrig thirty years ago!'

'Exactly. That's what I meant when I said, "that's the thing." We don't know what he did or said, or who he met on his way. Think about the continuing influence of the Greek philosophers, or – or Galen, the physician, or even Archimedes! Would you like to meet Archimedes, Rory? Suppose you could? Suppose you could sit down with him and discuss your watermill! How amazing would *that* be? If Alfonso of Castile, and even Thuban of Aulnay, know much about Jabir ben Hayyan, and if they or their fathers, say, met *our* Jabir on his travels through Europe, and if they now know about his laboratory and his work for you in Hambrig, well then! No wonder Thuban wants to meet him. Thuban is a troubled man. He has more problems than a mathematical textbook.'

The wind stayed steady and the day passed swiftly. Guido rallied in the afternoon and had no more sickness, but he looked wan and washed out and talked to nobody, gazing down into the bilges and refusing food.

'But she must drink!' Aldara cried. The two women irritate me with their use of 'she'. Aldara was right, though. The boy had to drink. Over the course of the afternoon, and into the early evening, I did my best to get Guido to drink from a flask of watered-down wine. Eventually I lost patience, not so much with Guido as with myself and the whole damned situation. For the umpteenth time, I cursed myself for ever taking him on. He's a complication I can do without. I looked up to find my wife staring at me from the stern of the boat.

'Let Aldara do it,' she called, and it sounded like an order. 'You are not getting through to Sara.'

'*Fuck,'* I muttered under my breath. Tall, stern Yehudah, sitting opposite, heard me and actually smiled. I swapped places with Aldara, the two of us scrambling awkwardly past each other in the middle of the boat.

'No one should be moving,' one of the crewmen said nervously, and I wasn't surprised they were edgy after Rastaban's performance. We muttered our apologies and hastily sat down in each other's places, which meant I now had my wife for company.

'There must be other boys who would make a good squire for you,' she said.

'I suppose so.'

'But you want Guido? Is that it? You have taken a liking to him?'

'Taken a liking to him? No, not at all. But I've said I'll take him. He could do well, that's the frustrating thing about it. He's deluded, Rosa. I feel sorry for him and I'm trying to help him, believe it or not.'

'He's rejecting your help. Or haven't you noticed?'

The *Fauvette* flew on down the river. We passed other boats, their crews pulling manfully against wind and tide, while our skipper grinned and shouted good-natured insults across the water. Clearly, he'd got it right and they hadn't. We slipped alongside a tiny landing stage in the village of Trogues just after dark, secured our boat with various warps and lines, and set up our small camp on the riverside. Wood was gathered, a fire built and lit, food was produced from various canvas bundles and wooden boxes, and someone declared it was supper time. We'd made such good time, the skipper decided we could have a day's rest tomorrow. Welcome news for everyone.

My group is splintering. It's been happening since we started this journey, but it's only now I've really acknowledged it. Rosa and Guido. Joseph and Aldara. Thuban and Xurxo. Yehudah on his own, morose and isolated. And Kit, who flits between the different pairings, never settling anywhere, like the gypsy he is at heart.

I've eaten what I wanted to eat, which wasn't a lot. I'm writing my journal by firelight, looking around at the faces that come and go as the flames flicker, and as people move or not as they choose. Rosa and Guido are a little way apart, further from the fire than the rest of us. They're talking in low voices, and Guido has, finally, eaten something. I look over at him, remembering the interview I had with him an hour ago.

He's not used to telling his story, and at first he couldn't put it into words at all. But with Rosa's chastisement ringing in my ears, I'd pulled the boy into my tent and told him to talk to me, and not be afraid to tell me the truth. I asked many questions, some of which I never thought I would ask anyone. I think he did his best to answer me, but he's obviously never had to articulate his feelings before. It was hard work for both of us, and very draining.

Afterwards, I wondered whether to lay it all before Aldara. Or Xurxo. But Aldara hardly knows the boy, and Xurxo would be of no help to me. Xurxo's sister was raped many times by a man I once thought of as a friend. Xurxo will not be sympathetic to Guido, not once he knows the boy's story.

Guido, I learnt, has always felt he was a girl. Even as a very small child, he knew his body was not as it should be. He tried to play with girls instead of boys, and he took his sister's clothes and wore them when no one was looking. The sister's name was Aysha and she was just one year older than Guido. When Guido dressed as a girl, he looked very much like Aysha. The other boys taunted him, and he was bullied mercilessly. The older he became, the worse it got. His father did his best to help, but his mother didn't understand; she scolded him constantly.

'One day you'll be a man,' she said angrily. 'You'll grow a beard, your voice will be deep and your muscles will be big and bulky. You won't be able to wear Aysha's clothes then!'

Guido burst into tears. He didn't want a beard or a manly voice or a bulky torso. He wanted to be feminine, dainty and beautiful. Lovingly, his sister told him he was all those things.

One day, Guido and Aysha went out to bring in fruit from the orchard. Guido was wearing some old clothes of Aysha's, and the two children giggled at how alike they looked. Some boys appeared out of nowhere, following and taunting them.

'You're a *boy*, Guido,' they shouted. 'Why are you wearing Aysha's clothes? You're a sinner! You'll go to hell! That's what happens to perverts!' And then, when there was no response, 'Do you want to make love to me, Guido?'

The usual crude gestures followed, making Guido shudder. But suddenly the teasing became something else. One of the boys threw a stone. It hit Aysha on the arm and she cried out in pain.

'Run,' she shouted, as more stones hurtled through the air.

Panicked, Guido ran, holding up his caftan, careering through the trees.

'Split up,' Aysha panted, pushing him away from her. 'You go that way.'

In desperation, Guido ran, while his sister raced off in the other direction. After what seemed a very long time, he stopped running. No one had followed him. Warily, he retraced his steps to the orchard. The boys had gone. He called for Aysha, but there was no answer. A few moments later, he found her body. She'd been stoned to death.

The look on his mother's face tormented him, but it was his father who made him cry. The man, who adored his children, was in terrible pain, yet he said nothing to Guido. Instead, he hugged him tight. There were no words of recrimination. His mother tore her clothes, screaming at Guido that he was to blame. If the two children had not looked so alike, the boys would have stoned Guido, not Aysha. They had not realised they were targeting the wrong child. Guido must be possessed by demons, a child of Satan, a dangerous and deviant aberration. Why had God seen fit to curse her family with such a child? Why had Satan entered their safe and loving home in this hideous way? And now they were destroyed. Damned for ever.

'Who is your father?' I asked at the end of the falteringly told tale.

'It does not matter, he is not here. I travelled from my home to France. The *Justiciers* found me and they took me in. They gave me food and a new home. And they made me spy for them. You know why? Because I am a child of Satan.'

'You believe that?'

'Yes.'

'And you still think you're a girl?'

'I am a girl.'

'You have a penis.'

He went chalk-white, pushed his knees together and closed his eyes.

'Who knows this story, Guido?'

'Only my family. And you.'

'You didn't tell the *Justiciers?*'

He shook his head.

'Do you think the boys who killed her knew it was her and not you?'

'I'm sure they thought they were chasing me, not Aysha. But later, when she was buried, then they knew.'

'And do you know who they are? Their names?'

'I know them,' he whispered.

'Were they punished?'

He shook his head. 'The priest would not allow it. He said it was I who must be punished. I am to blame for Aysha's death. And so I have been sent away from my family and from my village.'

The freedom he claims as his right to life can be the denial of someone else's. Thuban said that. Thuban knew of Aysha's death.

After Guido had finished, I became aware that I was shaking. He looked at me in surprise; he hadn't expected such a reaction. He didn't realise I wasn't shocked by the priest's willingness to blame Guido rather than the boys who'd stoned Aysha. It wasn't the priest's words that were making me shiver with emotion, but I wasn't going to enlighten the tortured child sitting on the ground in front of me. Even now, I can't allow myself to think of it, but the more I tell myself not to, the more I *do* think of it.

Into my mind had come the image of a dark-haired, brown-eyed little girl, my own sister, Tamsin, who died of the phthisis at the age of five, and my younger brother, Nicholas, who blames himself for her death. Their story is nothing like Guido's. Aysha and Tamsin have little in common, while Guido is nothing at all like Nicholas. And yet, the boy's sorry tale has brought Tamsin and Nicholas into my mind, and it's the thought of *them* that makes me feel so ill. Nicholas is in Somerset. Tamsin is buried in Hambrig. If my mother's Will had been known to us when she died, Nicholas would have been Lord of Treborough decades ago, and Tamsin – and *this* is the thing that makes my bowels turn to water – *Tamsin might still be alive*. My brother, so our faithful servant Eliza believes, could have kept that little girl alive.

Don't torment yourself, my father says sternly, walking up to the stinking, miserable ditch where I'm squatting unhappily. He puts his hand on my shoulder. I am embarrassed he's found me here. *You know Eliza is only guessing.*

Perhaps, I say desperately. *But what do you think, Father? Do you think Nick could have kept Tamsin alive*?

We will never know the answer to that, boy. And it's another error I made. I told you I didn't deal well with the deaths of your mother and your sister. I told you to do better than I did. Put things right, boy. That's the charge I give you, now as before. Put things right.

How can I put anything right? I shout at him. *It's too late! She's dead!*

You have failed to understand, as usual. Father shakes his head in disappointment. *It is this new child you must not fail. A disturbed and miserable child. Solve the problem. Fac Fiat. Put things right.*

My father walks away, groping through the dark night back to whatever ghastly place he inhabits when he's not talking to me. And I am left with my gurgling insides, my unreliable bowels, and absolutely no idea how to *put things right.*

15

AFTER THAT WE WERE DONE

On our rest day, I went to the market. I knew exactly what I wanted and it didn't take me much time to find and buy them. Back at the camp, I did very little for the rest of the day, having acquired a pulsing and painful headache. I finally approached Guido just before we damped down the supper time fire. On the grass I laid out my purchases: tunic and hose, his size as I'd judged it. Squatting down in front of him, I asked him gently if, tomorrow, he would change out of his gown and into these new clothes. Travelling would be easier for him that way.

Wordlessly, he shook his head.

'Well, Guido, you know you have a—'

'No!' he squawked in alarm. 'Don't say it, lord! Please don't say it again.'

'I was going to say,' I continued heavily, 'that you have a right to choose what to wear. That's all. I just wanted to make things easier for you.'

I realised then I was getting nowhere. The boy looked over at Rosa, as if she could magic his problems away.

'Sara appreciates your concern,' Rosa said calmly. 'But she is comfortable as she is.'

Drat the woman. That sort of remark helps nobody.

In the middle of the night I had to go for a piss. Walking back afterwards, I noticed a tent flap move in the breeze. I couldn't remember whose tent it was, but if someone else had also gone to relieve themselves, it was odd I hadn't seen them. The skipper and his crew have a large tent which they all share, although sometimes one or other of them sleep outside it. The other tents are smaller. Guido, Kit and I share one, Rosa and Aldara have another, Yehudah and Joseph share the third tent, and Thuban is in with Xurxo. I looked in my own tent and saw Kit curled up in his usual corner. I opened the flap of the second tent, startling Rosa and Aldara, who were awake and worried by the noises they'd heard. In the third tent I saw Yehudah, who was snoring loudly; but Joseph wasn't there, and it was this tent that had the loose door flap. In the last tent, both Thuban and Xurxo were fast asleep, Thuban uttering piteous noises of discomfort and pain. Xurxo seemed able to sleep through that, and I let the flap close.

The two women crept out to join me.

'Joseph is missing,' I told them. 'I'll look for him. Aldara, please wake Xurxo and tell him to come and help.'

'*We* will help you look,' Rosa said. 'We are already awake. And so is Sara – oh!'

I turned to see what had surprised her, and there was Guido, emerging from my tent, wearing the breeches and tunic I'd been trying to get him into.

I applauded him. 'Much better now you're not a boy dressed up as a girl.'

'Only now I am a girl dressed up as a boy,' he said quietly.

The four of us kept together at first, but really there was no need. We could search more quickly if we spread out, and I had no sense of anyone lying in wait or watching us from the trees. The bright moonlight would help us, and so we moved off in different directions.

A sudden shout from Aldara. A shout – and a sob. She was standing by a scrubby clump of bushes. Rosa, Guido and I quickly joined her.

'He's here,' Aldara said. 'He's dead, though. Someone has murdered him.'

She held back the stems of the bushes. I bent down to look at Joseph. He had been stabbed through the heart, but the weapon had been withdrawn. Pushed into the neck of his tunic was a note.

> *Anyone who is not for me is against me. This man deserved to die, and the Justiciers knew it. The woman who saved him is next in line. In the end, you will all die because you are all against me.*
>
> *The Mudéjar*

'Who is "The Mudéjar"?' asked Rosa angrily, her hand on her heart. 'What does it mean? Is this man going to kill us all?'

'I don't know who he is,' I answered truthfully. 'I don't

even know what the name means. I shall find him, though, you can be certain of that. And there will be no more killing, Rosa.'

'I'm next,' Aldara said. 'I am "the woman who saved him".'

'I cannot think why anyone would want to murder this man,' Rosa said angrily. 'He was an astronomer in my father's court. He was a good man, knowledgeable, and dedicated to creating my father's works. There will be great sadness in court when they learn of this.'

'We must not lose any time,' I said. 'Get back to the camp and rouse everyone. We need to set a watch for the rest of the night.'

Rosa picked up a metal griddle and banged it loudly with the tongs. Bleary-eyed people poked their bewildered and indignant heads out of their tents.

I forestalled the questions. 'There has been a murder. Joseph has been stabbed.'

On my orders, everyone mustered in a line and I checked them off. Thuban is becoming more and more of a worry. He can barely stand, even with Xurxo supporting him. I read out the note from 'The Mudéjar' and warned everyone to be on their guard, then sent them back to their tents.

Guido and the women were waiting for me.

'I intend to stay outside your tent tonight,' I told the two women. 'Aldara needs protecting, and you are both vulnerable.'

'What about me, lord?' Guido asked.

'You stay with me.'

So the camp settled down again, but the atmosphere was tense and miserable. Yehudah was upset. Thuban was thirsty and almost drank the river dry, meaning Xurxo wouldn't get much sleep for the rest of the night. As for 'The Mudéjar' and his cryptic message – who knew what any of it meant?

In the morning I found out.

'The Mudéjar? He'll be a man from the south of Castile,' Yehudah told me tersely.

'You know him then? I've not heard of this man. Who is he?'

'No, that is not what I meant. The Mudéjars are Muslims from al-Andalus. King Alfonso's father conquered them and moved them on, but many of them were bitter about losing their homes and their independence, so there was something of an uprising. It's all over now. *El Rey* got them to surrender in the end.'

'When did this happen?'

'Not long ago. It was all settled at the start of this year. Their ruler, Muhammad, signed a treaty, and Muhammad is now a vassal of *El Rey*. Don Alfonso's army were supported by troops from Jaume of Aragon's garrison. Of course, you must know that King Jaume of Aragon is Alfonso's father-in-law.'

'What does "Mudéjar" mean?'

'It is an insult. It means they have been tamed. Forced into submission.'

'So our Mudéjar is a disgruntled rebel, who, misguidedly, holds us responsible for some reason?'

'He killed my friend,' Yehudah said nasally. 'That was no accident, Lord Rory. I believe you now know who we are?'

'You are trusted and respected intellectuals in the court of King Alfonso of Castile. You are neither his servants nor his henchmen.'

I'd deduced all that some time ago, when Joseph had first lectured me on the stars, and when Yehudah, aloof and disdainful, was content not to join in the search at Aulnay. These men were neither servants nor warriors. A strange escort, but Alfonso was a clever man; he'd have his reasons. And now we've lost both Isaac and Joseph. Bad news for Alfonso and his research into the stars.

The rest of the night was quiet. The women slept, and Guido slumbered next to me, twitching and shifting from time to time. As I kept watch during the night, I wondered about Joseph's killer, who had signed his note 'The Mudéjar', as if I should know who he was and understand his reasons. I thought this was significant. And since the Muslims have been conquered by Castile, I decided that Rosa, the only Castilian in our group other than the three Jews, would probably know something about it.

After a quick breakfast, we dealt with Joseph's body. Yehudah conducted the ceremony; everyone attended; it took two hours to dig the grave and bury the man; and after that, we were done.

16

ALFONSO WILL BE DELIGHTED TO SEE HIM

'What is our destination today?' I asked the skipper, who had set his men to rowing again.

'Chinon by midday.' His tone was surly. He wasn't thrilled he'd had to wait around twice before my group was ready to embark. Yehudah had now lost both his colleagues, but he didn't seem to be in mourning. I look at him in suspicion from time to time. He's done nothing obviously wrong, but he's a strange, greasy-haired man in his long black gown, and a hat that obscures large parts of his face.

I turned again to the skipper. 'And after Chinon, *mon capitaine?*'

He shrugged and spread his hands. *'Ça dépend.'*

But on what, he did not say.

In Chinon we tied up at a substantial landing stage. This is a busy, bustling French town, with a large market. Rosa and

Aldara begged the skipper to give them enough time to explore the stalls. He wasn't immune to their charms, and agreed we could spend a couple of hours in Chinon.

'Please, lord, may I go too?'

'You want to buy a nice new gown, Guido?' sneered the skipper.

The boy flushed, but he lifted his chin and waited for my answer.

'You can go too, Guido.' On an impulse, I pressed a florin into his hand. 'Buy something you like.'

He sent a wide smile in my direction and scrambled ashore to run after Aldara and Rosa.

'You should sort him out,' the skipper growled to me, as he secured his boat to the bollards. 'He's making a laughing stock of himself, and he'll make one of you too, if you don't take him in hand.'

'He's my responsibility, not yours. I will do whatever I decide to do, and at the moment I've decided to leave him be. So please do the same.'

The man gave a Gallic shrug, shoulders lifted to the ears. I don't even know the man's name; he's just *le capitaine* to his crew and to all of us too. What do I know about him? Absolutely nothing. It's conceivable he's the Mudéjar. Isn't it?

For the next two hours I observed *le capitaine*. Did he act like a follower of Islam? Did he seem hostile to anyone? It was inconclusive. He is certainly hostile to Guido. He's shown some compassion to Thuban, and seems ambivalent to the rest of us. I haven't seen him leering at the women or ill-treating his men; as far as I can tell, he's just doing his job. And his comments about Guido, though unsolicited, were natural. He only said what I've often thought myself.

I whiled away the afternoon by practising my gittern for

a bit and going for a short walk to stretch my legs. Chinon is a pleasant town, but I kept well away from the shops and its market. I didn't want to bump into Rosa, Aldara or Guido. Despite the skipper's words, when I consider it carefully, I think the two women are a good influence on my squire-to-be. And I noticed with approval that he was still wearing his tunic and hose when he chased after them. Perhaps, when we get home, I'll find I can train the boy to be a useful squire after all.

The three of them returned laden with parcels, chattering and laughing together, so clearly it had been a good afternoon. Mortifyingly, though, Guido stepped onto the quayside in a new and pretty gown.

'Don't be angry,' Aldara said, as I helped her into the boat. 'Sara saw it, fell in love with it, and I bought it for her.'

'I gave her some money,' I said, then, annoyed, corrected myself. 'I mean, I gave Guido some money. Didn't he spend it?'

'Oh yes. She has a new hat, purchased with your money!'

Xurxo chuckled mischievously, which didn't help.

Rosa and Yehudah were talking together in the stern of the boat, careful to speak so quietly they couldn't possibly be overheard.

'Do you know what's going on?' I murmured to Xurxo.

He followed my eyes. 'Those two? They are planning or plotting something. What it is, I do not know. I am more concerned for Thuban at the moment.'

I believe the captain is aiming for Saumur this evening.

The River Vienne has become the River Loire, and, as the waterway broadens, we're seeing more and more craft travelling along it; more people, more traders, and more difficult rowing conditions. When a sailing vessel comes by, her wash sweeps past the *Fauvette* and causes her to pitch and roll, so our oars catch only air on one side, and are buried under water on the other. The skipper curses, raises his fist and hauls on the steering oar to bring us back on course. This has happened several times now. Poor Thuban doesn't respond well to being thrown about, and Aldara asked the skipper if we can rearrange the cargo so as to wedge the sick man in place.

'*Non, Madame. Cela déséquilibrerait le bateau. Laissez la cargaison là où elle se trouve.*'

I was unsurprised he didn't want his boat unbalanced.

Instead, Aldara asked each of us in turn to donate what we could. I took my spare jersey out of my pack, Yohudah and Xurxo gave up their thick cloaks, Kit found a couple of blankets, and Guido proffered a bundle of clothes.

'Now I have my lovely new gown,' he said in a loud voice, intended for the skipper's ears, 'I shan't need these *boys'* clothes anymore.' And he had the cheek to wink at me.

Aldara took all these offerings gratefully and arranged them around Thuban.

'He doesn't need to pee so much now, does he?' Guido said to Aldara. 'He used to need it all the time.'

'His body's shutting down,' Xurxo said gruffly. He'd grown fond of the Frenchman.

'What do you mean?' Guido sounded scared. 'I don't understand what that means.'

'It means he's going to die,' I said. Just to save anyone else from saying it.

Guido looked terrified, Xurxo glared at me, and Aldara blinked back tears.

And so the rowers pulled us through the water, while the skipper steered his vessel, keeping his gloomy, taciturn thoughts to himself, and eventually the sun went down. I expected us to stop in Saumur, but we didn't. Even when it grew quite dark, we were still moving on the River Loire, black water rippling down the hull. The traders and other rivercraft had all moored up for the night somewhere, although occasionally a larger sea-going boat, her sails set and lanterns aloft, glided past in the middle of the fairway. The *Fauvette,* with her shallower draft, kept to the left bank.

Yehudah was snoring again. Rosa was half lying on the aft side-bench, her head pillowed on her hands. Aldara kept watch over Thuban, giving Xurxo a chance to get his head down. Kit sat by the mast, leaning his back against it, his knees humped, looking up at the stars. Guido, beside him, was pointing them out and explaining which was which. I couldn't decide if Kit was kindly letting the boy prattle on, or if he was actually listening. I was reminded of Joseph's lecture, but I didn't want to think of the corpse we'd found, the blood dark and dry on his chest and clothing, the legs awkwardly bent, the fingers clawed in death. Or the callous message from his killer. *The Mudéjar.*

'Guido!' I called softly, and he crawled across to me. 'Do you know a lot about the stars?'

'A bit, lord. Someone once told me that I'm like the Pole Star. If you want to know which way to go, just look for me and I'll show you.'

I stared at him. The confident sentences, the assured statements? They weren't at all like poor, frightened little Guido.

'I mean, lord,' he hurried on, 'what I mean is, I know I'm different from anybody else. So when you're lost, even if there are hundreds of people around you, if you can see me, you know where you are. I'm the odd one out.'

'Do you want to be different, Guido?'

'No, lord. But I am, and I can't do anything about it.'

'When you're my squire—'

'I can't be your squire,' he interrupted, his voice suddenly squeaking. 'People have always tried to find ways to "cure" me of my problem. There is only one cure, and I hope to find it in Hambrig. So I can't be your squire. But – if you can find a use for me – I would very much like to join your household.'

I was astonished. Even through the squeak, the confident tone had not disappeared, and the boy seemed quite clear about what he wanted. But one thing was *not* clear. 'What's this "one cure", then?'

'I need to be castrated. I'm so frightened things will happen, and my voice will change, before this can be done. Back home, I tried to get the – the priest to agree, but he would not. My father wouldn't go against him. But in Mallrovia you have the wonderful Jabir—'

'The wonderful Jabir!' I snorted loudly, almost waking Xurxo. 'He's no surgeon. We'll need to find Sir Stephen of Corby.' As the words came out of my mouth, I realised what I was saying. Had I just agreed to having this boy castrated? Without permission from his family?

'Sir Stephen of Corby!' Guido exclaimed excitedly. 'He sounds exactly what I need! Where is Corby? Is it near Hambrig?'

'Shut up, Guido,' I said, sickened. 'This conversation is over.'

The boy looked crestfallen, but I had my own problems to deal with. My nausea was intensifying, and with it came the usual pressing need for a latrine.

'Are you all right, lord?' my not-to-be-squire asked.

'No. Get me a bucket.'

He was good, I'll say that for him. Not only did he somehow procure everything necessary, but he supported me throughout the whole damnable, ghastly business, and even swilled the bucket out overboard afterwards, earning curses from the skipper at the dreaded *déséquilibre du bateau.* I lay on my back, staring up at the stars and wondering about Guido's confident speech, his 'one cure' and his desire to meet Sir Stephen. Although the other stars moved around, some spinning disturbingly fast, others moving in and out of sight, or even just fading from the sky as I watched them, one of them stayed constant. Polaris, the Pole Star. Polaris was always there, always showing the way north. *If you want to know which way to go, just look for me and I'll show you.*

As the sun rose on our left-hand side, the exhausted oarsmen pulled into Angers. The skipper declared a day off for everyone. We'll not move from Angers until tomorrow.

'There are good places to eat here,' the skipper said to me, though he'd never vouchsafed any information about any of the other stopping places. 'Good taverns. And women. If your men want women, I can recommend where to go, and you won't be ill afterwards.' He guffawed at his own joke, but then he moved in, his greasy face up close, and he spoke quietly. 'There is also a hospice. *L'Hôpital Saint-Jean.* Take your sick companion there. You will have to leave him, but at least his last days will be comfortable.'

It was a good plan. We reconstructed the cart and laid Thuban in it. Xurxo and I pulled it through the town until we came to L'*Hôpital Saint-Jean.* It was, of course, run by monks and lay people, and Thuban was accepted into their care. Xurxo insisted on staying with the Frenchman, though the monks said it wasn't necessary. For the rest of us, I was determined to find a tavern with enough beds. None of us had slept in a bed for many nights. I sent Kit and Guido to find a suitable hostelry, and Guido came skipping back to say that one such had been found, after which everyone spent the rest of the day in the hostel getting some sleep after our long night on the river. I didn't join them, but wandered instead through the town. As I walked along the river for a stretch, I had a chance meeting with the *Fauvette's* captain. A plump woman was walking along with him.

'Ma femme,' the skipper said gruffly, and I bowed to her. It was now clear to me why we had stopped in Angers, and why we'd rowed through the night to make the fastest passage possible. The woman simpered a little and adjusted her bonnet; she took her husband's arm and they walked on.

Our tavern isn't at all bad: a room for Aldara and Rosa, and another for the rest of us. Guido is on the floor, and Kit, curse him, has vanished. But Yehudah and I are sharing the bed, and it's luxury to be on dry land and off the ground for once. Guido fussed around, concerned I might be ill again. I tried to explain that the 'illness' is something to do with my state of mind – or so I've been told.

I feel fine now, as I sit on the bed and write my journal,

the last quarter inch of a meagre candle flickering in its holder in the window. We've eaten well in this tavern, though Yehudah refused the sausage, like a good Jew should. The 'Mudéjar' epithet could easily be a bluff. I don't trust Yehudah an inch.

'I want to talk to you. Come with me.' I was speaking to Yehudah after breakfast, and I led him to a small paddock behind the hostel. 'The letter King Alfonso gave you. Where is it?'

'I have it safely.'

'I want to see it.'

'It is addressed to Jabir of Hambrig and his lady. It is sealed with the king's personal seal. Would you have me break that seal?'

'No, I'll break it myself. Give me the letter, I want to see what it says.'

He felt inside his robe and pulled out a thick packet, which was indeed sealed with a large Castilian disc of embossed wax. Without a word, he handed it over. I had no wish to break it open in front of him, so I slipped it inside my shirt.

After an uneasy silence, Yehudah asked, 'Will we be embarking on the *Fauvette* soon?'

'Yes. And we'll not be keeping *le capitaine* waiting this morning. So go and rouse the others and send them to the jetty at once.'

I watched him go, knowing I knew no more about him than when we first met. I don't like him, and now I have the letter, I intend to tell Yehudah he need come no further with us. He will return to Castile, and I'm sure Alfonso will be delighted to see him.

17

IT IS COMING FROM BEHIND OUR CAMP

The *Fauvette* was getting herself ready for the next leg of the voyage north. Rosa, Aldara and Guido appeared, wearing their new gowns and wimples. We stowed our baggage as usual, and Xurxo begged me to help him bring Thuban from the hostel to the boat.

'No, Xurxo. We're leaving him here. He'll be more comfortable, and I've arranged it with the brothers.' I didn't add that I'd also paid the brothers to cover their costs.

'He's rallied a little, though,' Xurxo said. 'He wants to come with us; he's convinced Jabir will cure him. He even took some broth last night. And he slept quite well.'

'Which means you got some sleep too?'

He gave a slight smile. 'I can catch up with sleep later.'

Everybody thinks Jabir can cure their problems. Guido and Thuban are both desperate for help; they see Jabir as their saviour, the last chance they'll get. Reluctantly, I gave in, and we hurried across to L'*Hôpital Saint-Jean* to retrieve Thuban. We arrived at the landing stage, lifted the makeshift stretcher and lowered it down onto the bottom boards. As we did so, Thuban cried out something, but I didn't catch the words. I did see Kit look up, startled; but I was concerned with getting Thuban into position and not jolting him too much, so I took no notice.

Le capitaine took me on one side. 'We go west to Nantes, following the Loire. Then you can get a sea-going boat from Saint-Nazaire. We'll be in the *Duché de Bretagne* then, but you don't need to worry about that. A boat from Saint-Nazaire will, if you're lucky, take you to England.'

'I arranged with you to take us to Honfleur, *monsieur.* I would prefer that. It's further north, and—'

'Further north, perhaps, but the Loire does not join on to the Seine! So there is an overland part, and the *Fauvette* is not so good at that!' He spat derisively into the water.

The skipper of the *Fauvette* had fulfilled just half his side of the bargain, yet he had *all* of the money he'd asked for. But when I challenged him about that, the Gallic shrug was much in evidence: the money had been spent, or paid to the crew, and there was nothing he could do about it. I did not want to take up his Saint-Nazaire suggestion. It would be a circular route home, and who's to say there'd be a ship ready and willing to take us, or a fair wind to blow us north? In my opinion, it wasn't worth the risk.

'What shall we do now, lord?' Rosa had been by my side, listening to the skipper blowing our agreement apart. She was not pleased.

'We'll need beasts to ride, and we must put the cart together for Thuban.' I inspected my purse, which was a lot lighter now. I had not anticipated this.

'Let me help.' Yehudah held his own purse out to me. It was full of gold coin; I did not refuse his offer. It was uncharacteristic of this uncompromising Jew to offer anything, so he must have his own reasons for doing so now;

whatever they were, I was grateful. But I could not now send Yehudah home. He, and his gold, would come with us.

Angers, thank goodness, is a large town, and it wasn't hard to find what we needed. What's more, we discovered if we sent Guido, wearing his new gown, to do the bargaining, we saved a great deal of money. 'Sara' has winning ways, and 'she' procured the asses at a good price.

'Good boy, well done,' I said, pleased.

We set off as soon as we had Thuban settled in the cart, surrounded by our baggage. I've saved on the cost of one mule by deciding that one person should ride in the cart and keep Thuban company. Aldara's going first, but we will all take it in turns. Finding a decent animal to pull the cart was harder; there was no draught horse like Albert, sadly. So we hired two donkeys, who will be returned with someone travelling south once we arrive in Honfleur.

As the days pass and the miles with them, we grow more light-hearted. Whoever the Mudéjar is, his had clearly been an empty threat. He killed poor Joseph, though we still don't know why, and now, thankfully, he has disappeared.

Yehudah keeps to himself, riding alone at the back of the group. Aldara and Kit have been talking and laughing together. Rosa mostly rides with Guido, whom she insists on calling 'Sara'. It's a good guise when we need it, but we don't need it now. Occasionally, Rosa and Yehudah ride together. I remind myself that the two Castilians know each other well, and perhaps they discuss Alfonso and his scholarly quest for knowledge. Or perhaps not.

As for taking it in turns to ride in the cart, that hasn't worked out. Xurxo is the only one who really understands Thuban, and Thuban is at his happiest when Xurxo is looking after him. So Xurxo travels with Thuban in the cart, and that leaves me, the cantankerous old man of our group, to ride by myself, usually at the front, sometimes at the back, rarely in conversation with anyone.

Of course, by now I'd read the letter.

In it, Alfonso invites Jabir to come to Castile and work there, his 'wife' also. The Lady Joan is not Jabir's wife; well, leave that aside for now. They are requested to travel to Seville, where special workshops have been, or perhaps are being, constructed for them. They are enticed there by the promise of perpetual sunshine, unlimited funds, superior facilities, and the opportunity to work on huge, ground-breaking projects. The style of the letter is effusive and warm. There isn't a lot of information in it, just promises of a new and wonderful way of life. Why would they say no, I ask myself? They won't say no. Nobody would. Alfonso makes no mention of his three compatriots who set out on this journey with us. What was Alfonso's plan for them? Whatever it was, it's probably doomed, now both Isaac and Joseph are dead. So as we made our usual camp for the evening, this time in a village called Vimoutiers, I called Yehudah over and I took him behind the tents.

'Who are you?' I asked him when I was sure no one else could hear us.

'You know my name,' he said without emotion. 'It is Yehudah ben Moshe. I am a Jew.'

'But who are you? How do you serve Alfonso, and why are you here?'

'Why ask these questions now? We're nearly at the coast. We are a long way from Castile—'

'Just answer.'

'Very well. My name is Yehudah ben Moshe. I am a physician, an astronomer and a linguist. I am also a rabbi, and a member of the School of Translators. I have been translating important works from Castilian into Latin. Isaac ben Sid is – was – an astronomer and an inventor, and also a member of the School of Translators. It is King Alfonso's dearest wish to compile tables of the positions of the heavenly bodies through the year, and to translate from the original Arabic into Castilian all the astronomical and medical treatises of Islam. To that end, we three were helping him.'

I was angry. Not with Yehudah but with his king. 'Why didn't Alfonso tell me who you really were? Isaac and Joseph are dead! Good men, clever, scholarly men! None of you should have been sent on this precarious journey.'

'Do not blame yourself. King Alfonso knows what he's doing. He has a mission, and we were part of it.'

'No. *I* could have delivered the letter to Jabir. Does Alfonso think Jabir won't come unless he sees with his own eyes the men he will work with in Seville? Does he think Jabir will need convincing by the high-level conversations he could have had with you and your colleagues? Is that it, Yehudah?'

'It is, perhaps, some of it. There is more, but that is not, for the moment, relevant.'

His calm tone should have been reassuring, but I felt the nausea rising like a disgusting slug in my gullet. 'Yehudah, if I had known who you were, all three of you, I would not have left Isaac in the clutches of the *Justiciers.* I'd have protected him better.' And Joseph too, I was thinking.

'Yet you did not protect them.'

'I wish I'd been able to. But I did not know of the *Justiciers*, nor the Mudéjar. And I had an important mission of my own.'

'And your mission, Lord Rory? What was it?'

But, swallowing the slug, I had to turn away. 'As you said. It is not, for the moment, relevant.'

Reading Alfonso's letter changed nothing, nor did talking to Yehudah. Hitching the donkeys to the cart in the morning, I found Rosa by my side. My wife is a lovely woman, with the sallow complexion of her race, high cheekbones, black hair and eyes that gaze haughtily into mine. She is no more than average height, but she carries herself well and, whatever she's wearing, she looks good in it. Yet again, I wondered at Alfonso allowing her to become my wife. I am a very insignificant person in comparison to the great Alfonso X of Castile.

'Lord, you are troubled,' Rosa said. How her English has improved on this journey! Very early on, it was decided that English would be the only language we would use among ourselves, and the Castilians and Smanderinos have acquired various levels of fluency.

'It's nothing,' I said, adjusting the breechings, and checking the two outside shafts were balanced, so as not to put pressure on the donkeys' necks.

'It is not nothing. You talked last night with Yehudah,

and after that you were angry and Yehudah went to his tent. Tell me what it is about, lord. I am your wife.'

I wanted to ask her how being my wife gives her the right to question me; I wanted to tell her that being my wife does not entitle her to know everything I say and do; I wanted to point out to her that I don't need to share my every thought with her, simply because she's my wife. Nor did I care for her tone of voice or the frown that creased between her eyes.

'Rosa,' I began. And then stopped.

'Is it because I am not yet your wife? Although we are married, it does not count with you?'

It wasn't that at all; but it would do. I nodded.

'I am sorry you feel this way.' She sounded more disdainful than sorry. 'It was *your* decision not to consummate our marriage. But I could be of help to you, so if you wish to talk to me I shall be happy to listen.'

After a few awkward moments she walked away, her head held high, her gait straight and dignified. Like all Castilian women.

We couldn't start on the next leg of our journey because Aldara was taking her time to return from her ablutions in the stream, so we hung about, the fireplace scattered, the donkeys ready to pull the cart in which an ever-weakening Thuban lay, exhausted, on his rugs. Clearly, we should have left him to die in *L'Hôpital Saint-Jean*. But Xurxo had been convinced Thuban was getting better, and I'd wanted to give him his last chance of life at Jabir's hands. Xurxo had not yet climbed into the cart, but Kit, Yehudah and Rosa had their mules prepared and were already in the saddle. Guido's mule was ready too, and he'd also looked after mine while I was busy with the donkeys.

'I'll go and find Aldara,' Guido said, scampering down to the stream. We'd all bathed in it this morning, since it was another bright day and would soon be very warm.

Kit was talking with Rosa, and Yehudah was silent as usual, when Guido suddenly catapulted himself into our group, out of breath, his shoes and the hem of his woman's gown sodden.

'Someone has attacked her!' he gasped.

I raced down to the stream, Kit at my heels. We found Aldara lying on her back, and at first I couldn't see how she was hurt. I knelt down beside her.

'He jumped on me as I came out of the water.' Her voice was weak.

'What did he do to you, Aldara?'

'He hit me on the head. I think he must have used a rock from the beach. I fell. He must have thought I was dead. He ran away. I heard him crashing through the trees.'

I was feeling the back of her head. She had been gashed with the edge of something sharp.

'Who was it? Who did this?'

'I didn't see him. He was behind me.'

Thankfully, Thuban and Rastaban had not stinted on the size and robustness of their cart. Kit and I carefully lifted Aldara into it. Yehudah, whom I now knew to be a physician, examined her.

'It was a glancing blow,' he concluded. 'She perhaps turned just as he struck her. Had she not done so, the rock would most certainly have killed her.'

'I expect he thought it had,' I said soberly. The Mudéjar again? He had threatened to attack Aldara.

'You think this Muslim has followed us?' Yehudah was reading my thoughts.

'I suppose he must have done. Unless it was someone else, but nobody would attack a woman in that way. She wasn't raped, was she?'

'No. The attack was swift and powerful, but ultimately unsuccessful. She will have a sore head for a week, but apart from that she will be fine.'

So now we believe the Mudéjar is following us, but we don't know how or why he's doing it, and we still don't know who he is. Or who is to be his next target.

'Perhaps he'll attack me again,' Aldara suggested that evening, as she sat propped up against a boulder, a large bandage wound around her head.

'He will not,' I said at once. 'From now on, no one goes anywhere alone. Not even for a piss in the woods. We go everywhere in threes. Kit, you're to stick like glue to Xurxo and Thuban. Yehudah, you're to stay with me and Guido. As for the two women, they will be accompanied everywhere by me. And I mean everywhere.'

I looked round the circle of faces in the firelight. We'd made our camp a few miles north of Lisieux this evening. Good progress, but our confidence had been knocked by this morning's attack on Aldara.

The women nodded. Guido gulped, and I looked over at him. 'I'd like to volunteer to help look after Lady Rosa and Lady Aldara,' he said, and for the second time I heard a squeak in his voice. A tiny sign of his future. He looked suddenly terrified.

'Sara, you *can* help us,' Rosa said, pulling him towards her so his head rested against her shoulder. I shifted uneasily. There's plenty for me to be concerned about without the complication of this Guido-Sara business. I felt uncomfortably suspicious that my wife was doing this to undermine me in some way. She was resentful towards me, perhaps because of the non-consummated marriage, or perhaps because I didn't talk much to her.

I gave my orders. 'The men will take turns to be on watch all night, though not you, Xurxo. You have enough disturbance during the night with Thuban.'

It was true. Thuban is rarely conscious now, but he calls out in a kind of delirium at all hours of the day and night. He has also become incontinent, so Xurxo has his work cut out looking after him. But that left Kit, Yehudah and me. I looked doubtfully at Yehudah.

'I can keep watch,' he told me impassively. 'Just because I can calculate the position of the constellations on any night of any year, and just because I can work from Arabic to Castilian to Latin and back again, does not make me less of a man, nor does it make me incapable of staying awake and alerting you, should I see or hear anything.'

'So be it.'

I made a watch list, in which each of us would be on duty for two hours and off duty for four. Putting myself on watch first, I told everyone to get their heads down and sleep. Aldara looked exhausted, but found it hard to get comfortable. I thanked God for Guido then, who gathered a vast amount of bracken and piled it into a pillow for Aldara's sore head. Xurxo made Thuban as comfortable as he could and Yehudah crawled into his tent. After a short pause, his stentorian snoring began. Kit sat up with me for a while, whittling a stick into some sort of pipe he could blow into. But I soon sent him to his tent. I wanted him properly awake and alert when he came on watch.

I've settled down, wedging myself between the trunks of two ash trees. To my left, I can hear the River Touques burbling away to itself. To my right is a field of cows, though the animals have also settled down for the night. The cart is a vague solid shape in the dark, and the mules and donkeys are loosely hobbled, resting from their weary day's journey. Will the Mudéjar come tonight? I find I actually hope he does, and while I'm on watch too. I want to know who he is, what he wants, and why he says he's going to kill us all. In the middle of writing my journal, I pull out Alfonso's letter to Jabir, and squinting in the near-dark, I can make out the usual flowery greeting. And then:

> *Because we know you are well versed in the arts of astronomy, astrology, mathematics, science and medicine, we wish to offer you the most superior and creative place in which to study, work and progress our knowledge. To this end, we are having constructed a building, which we believe is to be called a 'laboratory', in which you will be free to carry out experiments and pursue your own ideas to prove or disprove your theories and philosophies. Whatever equipment you desire will be supplied, and you will have all the time you require to work. In addition, if you need to test your ideas on people, there will be no shortage of men and women willing to advance the sum of human knowledge by putting themselves entirely in your hands.*

I wonder what Jabir, and indeed Joan, will say to this proposal. Thinking about Joan, all the way back in Hambrig, makes me yearn to be home. I have been too long on the road, and it hasn't even helped. I did not retrieve my honour, and I'm beginning to doubt I ever will.

I wonder if Ben is running the castle as it should be run. Do my household listen to him? Is he, in turn, listening to them? Most especially, he should be listening to Rachel and Eliza. And how are Jonathan and Tessa settling in? Sitting here in the Norman countryside, I ache to be home again.

But all thoughts of home vanish when I hear a faint sound. It's not the beasts. It is not Thuban calling out, nor Aldara moaning slightly, though both those things happen from time to time. This noise is a kind of scraping, sliding sound, and it is coming from behind our camp.

18

HE NEVER DOES ANYTHING NAKED

Journal stowed away, dagger in my hand, cap pulled down low, I crept round towards the River Touques, skirting the silent tents. An owl hooted from the nearby copse. Then a tendril of music, as from a distant flute. The moon appeared briefly, before clouds covered it again, and in the quick burst of moonlight I dropped to my stomach and scanned the area as far as I could see. It could have been an animal I'd heard: fox, badger or rabbit. But I knew it wasn't. I saw nothing, heard nothing. Keeping very still and listening hard, I decided someone else was also doing exactly that. I inched forward, and then a bit further. To my left, the sound of canvas scraping against canvas. A tent flap was moving. I raised my head, and pushed myself up into a squatting position. It was the women's tent, and the flap was open. A man emerged from the tent, crawling through the opening and standing upright.

I launched myself across the open space and hurtled right into him. I grabbed him by the throat. He was quite short, and I forced him to the ground, my knee on his chest, my dagger to his throat.

'Rosa! Aldara!' I shouted. 'Are you all right?'

Kit appeared.

'Go into their tent,' I told him, keeping the Mudéjar pinned down.

Rosa peered out at us. 'I'm am all right. What is happening?'

'What about Aldara?' Kit demanded, trying to see past Rosa.

'Aldara has just gone out. Who is that on the ground?'

'That's what I'm about to find out.' I hauled the man to his feet.

He swayed in front of me. I shook him. 'Who the hell are you? What are you doing here?'

When there was no reply, I punched him hard, and he fell over. Then, once again, the moon floated out from behind the clouds, and its silvery light shone onto the bandage around the intruder's head. Except it wasn't an intruder. It was Aldara. Wearing Guido's clothes. *I shan't need these boys' clothes anymore.*

'Rosa!' I bellowed. 'Rosa, come out here!'

She appeared at once, followed by Kit, who was trying to tell me that all was well in the women's tent, and in an instant they both realised I had felled Aldara. Rosa exclaimed in Castilian and ran to her friend, kneeling beside her. 'What have you done, lord? Oh, what have you done?'

'I didn't know it was Aldara! How could I know in the dark? Why's she wearing Guido's clothes, for God's sake?'

Yehudah came at the run, thinking Thuban had died in the night. He brought Aldara round, gave her some wine to drink and patched up her wound again. Kit fanned our fire up to a good blaze, and once Aldara was safely back in her tent and sleeping, we sat round the warm glow. Just the four of us.

'Why is she wearing men's clothes?' I asked Rosa. I was still shaken by what had happened. I might easily have killed Aldara.

'For safety of course! She's been attacked once. She thought she would be safer if she looked like a man.'

No, I'd attacked her *because* she looked like a man.

'Why were you there anyway?' Kit asked, turning to me. 'We had a rota, and you were supposed to be keeping watch here.'

'I heard a noise. And I don't think it was Aldara who made it.'

'Someone is still out there?' asked Yehudah in his careful English.

'It's possible.'

'Then why have we left Aldara on her own?' Rosa asked, staring at me. 'Someone should be with her.'

Kit was the fastest, sprinting back through the circle to the women's tent, throwing wide the flap and pushing his head inside.

'It's all right,' he called back. 'She's all right. I'll sit here, just outside, until morning.'

'No,' Yehudah said, getting up and stretching. 'I will do that, your Grace.'

I decided we would all be on watch for the remainder of the night. Yehudah would stay outside the women's tent, Kit would wait behind the camp and I'd take up station in front of it. We devised a signalling system in case any of us heard or saw anything suspicious.

'I'll tell you what's suspicious,' Kit whispered to me after Yehudah had settled himself down. 'Why's Xurxo not here? He must have heard all the rumpus.'

A good point. I went to the tent Xurxo shares with Thuban. They were both there, and both fast asleep. There had been no reaction from Guido either. But when I looked to see if he were also asleep, I didn't see him at all.

'Guido's missing,' I said to Kit.

'He's maybe just gone into the trees for a bit?'

'Go and see. I'm not leaving the camp. Wait, I'll get Xurxo.'

I roused Xurxo from a very deep slumber. He was reluctant to leave Thuban, but Thuban didn't look like he needed anything, so I ordered Xurxo to get some clothes on and help Kit hunt for Guido. 'Unless he's back by now,' I added. Which he probably was, if Kit were right and the boy had just gone to relieve himself. But there was no Guido, and Kit looked worried.

'This was in your tent,' he said, holding out a folded piece of parchment.

I read it out.

> *Anyone who is not for me is against me. This boy deserves to die, but if you come looking for his body, you will also be killed. The woman who survived will be next. In the end, you will all die because you are all against me.*
>
> *The Mudéjar*

'Oh my God,' Xurxo said, crossing himself. 'That poor lad. Do we dare go looking for him?'

'Of course we bloody do!' I said. 'But we can't leave Rosa and Aldara without a bodyguard, nor will I leave the rest of the camp unguarded. Yehudah is outside the women's tent. Xurxo, I want you to stay here and keep watch. Kit and I will go and look for Guido.'

No one argued, and while Xurxo took up his post on the

edge of the camp, a stout stick in one hand and a sharp dagger in the other, Kit and I conferred on where to look first.

'We're looking for a corpse?' he asked.

'We don't know. Guido was alive when that note was left in my tent. He may still be.'

'One thing puzzles me,' Kit said slowly.

'We need to go, Kit. Puzzles can be solved later.'

'No, listen. How does the Mudéjar know that Guido's a boy? He doesn't look like one and he doesn't act like one. But the Mudéjar knows. How?'

'No idea. Perhaps he just lifted up Guido's gown. I don't know, but we need to get on with looking for him.'

'Does he sleep naked?' Kit persisted as we set off for the woods at a trot.

'No. He never does anything naked.'

19

TRULY AND PROPERLY MARRIED

In the woods we hunted as far from the camp as anyone would voluntarily go, even a boy who couldn't bear for anyone to see his genitals. Kit was right to draw attention to this fact, but it's not just Guido the Mudéjar knows; he knows us all. He knew about Joseph being wanted by the *Justiciers.* He knew that Aldara saved Joseph's life in Saintes. How does he know us? And why does he want us all dead?

These thoughts scurried round my mind as I systematically quartered the ground, covering it all just in case the boy's body had been left lying in some leaves, or kicked into a ditch. And after an hour, Kit and I came back together, aware we'd wasted valuable time looking in the wrong place.

Kit jerked his thumb towards the water. 'The river? Perhaps the Mudéjar has drowned the lad.'

My stomach flipped queasily at the thought. I have damned nearly drowned twice, both times in the dangerous and fast-flowing River Hurogol near my home. Both times were terrifying. But the Touques isn't the Hurogol; it's a small stream, nothing more. We raced down to the bank, but in the dark the water was black and we could see nothing.

'So what *does* he wear when he's sleeping?' asked Kit.

I looked at him in disbelief. 'What the hell does it matter?'

'It matters,' he said calmly, 'because it would help to know if we're looking for something light-coloured or something dark. If he doesn't sleep naked, he must be wearing something. What colour is it?'

'Oh. I see. He takes his gown off and just wears his shift, I think. It's probably white.'

'Good. White will be a lot easier to spot.'

Assuming the Mudéjar was considerate enough to let Guido preserve his modesty, I thought morosely, as I parted reeds and stirred watery puddles with my foot, inching my way along the riverbank. Kit was muttering something about 'dragging the river', but I took no notice. One thing we'd ascertained at the start was that the beasts were all present. The Mudéjar had not stolen an animal from us, and, if he were on foot, which he must be or I'd have heard the chink of his harness, then he hadn't gone far. Guido had definitely been in my tent at the start of my time on watch, and that was three hours before we discovered he was missing. Another hour was spent hunting for him in the woods, so he'd been gone four hours at the most. Enough time for an able-bodied man to make his escape, but not enough to get far if encumbered by a prisoner.

'He's not encumbered,' Kit said when I put all this to him. 'He's killed the boy and dumped his body somewhere. And no, I can't bear the thought of that either.'

We all like Guido. He's a peculiar child, but he tries hard and he's brave, cheerful and willing to do anything. The thought of his pathetic little body lying on the cold ground somewhere nearby filled me with rage. I looked up at the night sky. Polaris shone down, doing its job of keeping us heading north for home. *If you want to know which way to go, just look for me and I'll show you.*

I turned to Kit. 'We're going to find him.'

'You know this could be a trap, Rory? This crazy Muslim wants to kill us all, so he kidnaps and kills the youngest and weakest one and leaves us a note that makes us think Guido's still alive. He knows we'll try to find the boy, so he lies in wait for us.'

'Maybe. And maybe not. Either way, makes no difference. We have to find him.'

It's more than likely the Mudéjar has baited his trap with Guido. But I can't let that change anything, because I feel so guilty at having assaulted Aldara, thinking she was the intruder, while all the time the Mudéjar was making off with a vulnerable child.

I stopped in my tracks, my thoughts spiralling. What if Aldara was part of the plot? What if she dressed up in Guido's clothes to lure me away so the Mudéjar could take the boy? It had seemed odd at the time that the man hadn't killed her down at the river. The Mudéjar wouldn't have left an intended victim alive, would he? Not unless she wasn't *actually* an intended victim. I grabbed Kit.

'What do you know about Aldara? You grew up with her! Can we trust her? Or is she working with the Mudéjar?'

He looked at me as if I'd gone mad. 'Working with the Mudéjar? We don't even know who he is! And how can she be? She's in the camp with a sore head, not made any better, I might add, by your attack on her this evening.'

I told him my theory. Too vague to be called a theory, I suppose, but I told him anyway. Our search was a failure, and we returned to camp, where, unheralded, I entered the women's tent, leaving a startled Yehudah outside.

Rosa sat up in alarm. 'What has happened now, lord? Did you find the Mudéjar?'

I told her of Guido's disappearance; then I read her the note and described the fruitless search for the boy.

'What do you know of this, Aldara?' I asked, turning to her.

There was little light in the tent, the canvas walls dark, barely penetrated by the moonlight. But I'd seen her eyes gleaming.

'I know nothing about it.' Her voice sounded stronger than it should have, considering what she'd been through. Perhaps the earlier attack had been a fake. If so, it had been a convincing one.

'So it was just coincidence that you happened to be coming out of this tent, dressed up like an intruder, while the Mudéjar was stealing Guido out of *my* tent? He wouldn't have been able to do that if I'd been there. But I wasn't there because I heard a noise and I was trying to find out what, or who, had made it. And then I saw you, apparently a man, coming out of the women's tent. While I was grappling with you, Guido was being abducted. And possibly killed.'

Aldara gave a cry. It sounded genuine, but it's not hard to pretend to be distressed. I thought Rosa would have been equally distressed, but if so, she didn't show it. Instead, she got up from her bedding roll.

'I shall go out and search for Sara,' she announced.

'You will not,' I said at once, catching her by the wrist. 'It is far too dangerous.'

'Too dangerous? It wasn't so when you and Kit were hunting through the woods.'

'That was also dangerous. But it would be far more so for you, Rosa, so you're staying here.'

She twisted her arm, but I had her in too firm a grip. 'You are hurting me, lord.'

I let go, apologising, but also insisting she stay in the camp.

'And what of Sara? Are we to ride on in the morning, heading north to Honfleur? Are we to leave her behind?'

'Go back to sleep, both of you,' I said. 'We'll talk more in the morning, and it will be easier to search for Guido in daylight.'

Early this morning, as soon as it was light, I resumed the search. Kit came with me, Yehudah guarding the camp. We decided to head north, since we'd explored the other directions last night.

'There will be tracks,' I said firmly. 'Guido is not nearby, so he's been dragged along or forced to walk. We'll see evidence of that.'

We set out to look for such evidence, but found nothing. The morning passed, and we returned to the camp. It would normally be packed up by now, and we'd be well on our way to the next stopping place. But we'd the boy to find, and I wouldn't move on until that was accomplished. Which prompted a showdown with Xurxo.

'Thuban needs to get to Hambrig,' he insisted, distressed. 'We have to go, Lord Rory. We have to get to Jabir. Thuban needs the Elixir of Life!'

'Thuban's dying and you know it,' I said roughly.

'Guido's young. Dead or alive, he needs to be found. And the fucking Mudéjar too, whoever the hell he is. He's not going to get away with this.'

I turned the camp upside down, on the premise that often the thing you're seeking is under your very nose. Could the Mudéjar have hidden the boy in the camp itself? But he had not. I saddled my mule and rode off, circling the area, dismounting frequently to poke around in the undergrowth and the bushes, scanning the lush Norman fields as the sun rose high in the sky and the day dragged on, Guido-less.

I widened my circle, going ever outwards from the camp by the River Touques, my mind filled with Kit's doom-laden words, *Perhaps the Mudéjar has drowned the lad.* I pictured the man flinging the boy's unconscious, or already dead, body into the black, gurgling waters of the Touques, the ripples closing over his head, his dead eyes staring at the night sky above. Or perhaps he'd been conscious, fighting for his life, calling for help, struggling to stay afloat until the waters claimed him, while the Mudéjar callously held him under. *As Nicholas did to Felix.*

On an impulse, I plunged my hand into the pocket of my breeches and withdrew a small bone attached to a dark blue ribbon: the collarbone of Joseph of Arimathea. You have to hold it only by the ribbon, although I've been guilty of touching the bone a few times. I swung it by its ribbon and solemnly I intoned, *Ut Artorus Rex dare nos gloriam.*

The man who'd bequeathed me the relic thought this a powerful invocation. It didn't save his life, though, and it might well be too late for Guido's. It's been my last resort for months, and, in truth, I've never known it work. My friend, Rabbi Baruch, has gently pointed out to me that if you want an article of faith to do its job, it helps if you actually have faith in it. So much for that, then.

I stuffed the useless bone back in my pocket, briefly fingered the cockleshell of St James which hung around my neck, and dismissed it as a trinket. I kicked my mule to make it go faster. It took no notice. It's a single-speed mule, this one, plodding through life as it plods across the plains of Normandy. Frustrated and angry, I shouted at the sky, raising my fist, calling Guido's name in an agony of despair. And, as if in response to my prayers, out of the clear blue distance to the east came another rider. He hurtled towards me, his mule from another stable entirely, as the rider coerced it to a gallop, and, its hooves flying, its head tossing, it came slathering and slithering to a halt just a few feet away from me.

The initial shock wore off, though it took several moments of an incredulous coming-to-terms-with-what's-just-happened to do so. Those few moments seemed to last a lifetime. Rosa had slid down from her mule before I came to my senses, and the two of us gently lifted Guido down from where he'd been flopped over Rosa's saddle. He was unconscious but alive.

I could hardly believe what Rosa had done. Against my orders, she'd left the camp, taking her own mule, something I never even noticed when I was saddling mine. She'd ridden east. Why east, I asked?

'There is a castle on a hill. I saw it before. I wouldn't have thought of going there, but your despair drove me to do so.'

Yehudah tended Guido as Rosa talked, all of us sitting by the fire. Xurxo emerged from his tent, carrying Thuban, who looked grey and waxy, his eyelids barely fluttering, his body limp and weak. But he was conscious, and even able to speak a little. Xurxo put him down in the shade of the trees and sat next to him. Nobody said anything about Thuban's condition, or the sad expression on Xurxo's face. Thuban babbled to himself, dribbling from both ends. I spared him a glance, then brought my attention back to Rosa.

She hadn't known, of course, that she'd find Guido in the castle on the hill. But she did think it would be an obvious hiding place. She'd approached the fortress cautiously, leaving her mule tethered to a picket fence.

'But how did you get in?' Kit asked. Rather ambitiously, he was baking bread at the edge of the fire, having crushed some barley into a coarse meal, mixed it with water from the river and shaped the resulting dough into a dozen bannocks. Resourceful, I'll say that for him.

'I claimed to be a victim of robbery and violence on the road to Santiago das Cunchas,' Rosa said. 'The rest of my party were killed, but I hid from the attackers, and now I needed help. I put many details into my story.'

'And to whom did you tell it, lady?' Yehudah asked, looking up from Guido. The boy will live; he's not badly hurt at all. *Concussed* is what Yehudah told me. Concussed, knocked about a bit, slightly bruised on his arms and legs, and with the faint mark of a whip or lash across his back. But it was not serious, and nothing to endanger his life. Relieved beyond measure, I was happy to sit and wait for Rosa's story to unfold and for Kit's bannocks to be baked in time for dinner.

'I simply knocked at the gate,' Rosa said. 'A man came to

find out who I was and what I wanted. He told me I was at the *Chateau de Boutemont*, a fortress with a strong garrison. "And are you the *seigneur* of this place?" I asked him. "I am not," he told me. "But the *seigneur* himself will want to see you." I was taken inside the fortress—'

'You acted damned dangerously,' I growled. 'You should have told me before doing any of this. You should have had someone with you.'

'If I had had someone with me, I would not have been able to rescue Sara. As you will find out, lord, if you allow me to continue with my story.'

Kit looked up from his baking, his eyes wide. Rosa, of course, is a Castilian princess, the daughter of the all-powerful King Alfonso X. But her instant retorts in their sharp tone, even though she calls me 'lord', are not at all how you would expect a wife to address her husband.

'Lady, please continue.' I kept my tone level.

'I told the man at the gate I would be happy to talk to the *seigneur,* but first I needed to find the other member of our party, a young girl who had been taken from us and might be injured. Had he seen the girl? At first he didn't answer, but I pressed him, explaining that after our misfortune we were now two women travelling alone on pilgrimage to the sacred shrine of St James the Apostle. If my friend Sara were being held here against her will, the Holy Mother would be displeased. Pilgrims should always be treated well, as everybody knows. At this, the man crossed himself and told me to wait. He went away but quickly returned. "If I bring your friend to you, and you both hurry away from here, the *seigneur* will not know of your coming. Last year I made the pilgrimage myself. When you get to the shrine, pray for me, sister." And he showed me a small cockleshell. I told him both Sara and I would pray for him all the way to

Santiago. The man told me to wait at the side of the gatehouse. But while he was gone, I hurried back to the fence, untied the mule and brought it to the gatehouse; I thought I might not have long to get Sara away, and if it was actually a trick, it would be better to have the mule ready for a rapid escape.'

At this point, the bannocks were ready. Kit speared each one with a sharpened reed from the riverbank and moved it away from the heat. He broke the first one open to see if it was properly baked, then had to lick his burnt fingers. The bread, if you could call it that, smelt very good. Rosa asked for a drink, and I passed her the flagon of wine we're all sharing. Yehudah sat back on his heels.

'This child will make a good recovery,' he pronounced. 'But much sleep is needed. I recommend we do not move from this place until tomorrow.'

I had no intention of shifting our camp until tomorrow anyway. Moving on at this time of day would be unnecessarily dangerous, and everyone needed to get a good night's sleep. Having had nothing to eat all day, I was looking forward to Kit's barley bannocks, stuffed with olives, and the small fish Kit had also netted from the river while I'd been out hunting for Guido. A good supper and an undisturbed night. That's what we all needed.

Aldara chose that moment to emerge from her tent. She crawled over to the fire and flopped down next to Yehudah.

He glanced at her. 'I will examine you next, lady.'

A look passed between them; I caught it, but did not understand it.

Rosa finished her wine, set the flagon down on the ground and continued her story. 'It wasn't a trick, though. The man with the cockleshell came out carrying Sara in his arms. He helped me secure her over the back of my mule.'

'Did he say anything about the Mudéjar?' I asked. 'Is the Mudéjar the *seigneur* of the *Chateau de Boutemont*?'

'I believe he is.' Rosa's tone was confident. 'The cockleshell gatekeeper's name is Raoul. He wanted me to know so I could pray for him by name. Raoul said I must take Sara away quickly and not come back. We must hasten on our pilgrimage, he told me, since the *seigneur* is an infidel who prays daily to God but in a different way and in a heathen tongue. I believe that the Lord of Boutemont is indeed the Mudéjar.'

'Well, we will certainly pray for Raoul,' I said, meaning it. So the Mudéjar is just a few miles away from our camp, and apparently the lord of a military fortress, guarded by a garrison. But since Rosa saw neither the lord nor his soldiers, perhaps the fortress is not as strong as it appears.

Yehudah will not allow me to question Guido until the morning. 'The child must sleep. The child must recover. In the morning, *then* you may ask your questions.'

He examined Aldara next and was pleased with her progress. 'Though you are not in good spirits, and I wish to know why. This will hinder your recovery.'

'I am not in good spirits,' Aldara explained, 'because Rory believes I am a spy. I know he thinks I'm in league with the Mudéjar.'

I decided to speak to Rosa about this. We walked alone in the copse.

'Of *course* she's not a spy,' my wife said roundly. 'I cannot imagine what made you think she might be. She is as much a princess as I am, and she's the woman you might have married. I've no idea why she cares at all what you think of her. If you had rejected *me* in favour of another, I would have walked away from you and never wanted to see you again. Aldara is different. And she knows what she wants.'

'And what does she want?'

'Can't you see it for yourself? Why are men so stupid?'

I drew Rosa to me and I kissed her. And then, in the half-light of the shady copse, I removed her gown and laid her down on the woodland carpet. A short while later, we were truly and properly married.

20

IT MADE A KIND OF SENSE

'Did you see the man who took you?'

'No, lord. He hit me and tied me up and then he threw me over his shoulder. He was big and strong and he didn't speak a word. I'm really sorry I can't tell you any more.' Guido looked close to tears.

'It's all right, you can't help it if you didn't see him. What happened then?'

'He walked for a long time, but I think I blacked out, so I don't know where we went. I did try to work out the direction, but I was face down and couldn't see the stars. I was awake when we arrived, though. I heard some bolts being shot and a door opening. Then I was put down on a mattress. I still didn't see anything, but my hands and legs were untied, and then the man left and I was on my own. I wasn't frightened, lord; I just wanted to find a way to get out and get back to the camp.'

'What did you do?'

'I tried to look round the room, but then I realised why I couldn't see.'

'You'd been blindfolded?'

'Yes. I managed to take the blindfold off though, and then I saw I was in a room high up in a turret of a fortress, and through the window I could see the stars and the sky, and I saw the fortress was on a hill, but I didn't know where.'

'Did anyone bring you food or drink?'

'Nothing. I did fall asleep for a while, and when I woke up it was bright daylight, and then someone came into the room. He told me he was taking me to freedom, and he said my friend had come to get me. But then he picked up the timber that had barred the door and he hit me with it. I don't know what happened after that. Thank you for rescuing me, lord.'

'It wasn't I who rescued you, Guido. It was Lady Rosa.'

'Then I owe her my life. I will go and thank her.'

'Yehudah doesn't want you to go anywhere yet,' I told him, getting up. 'But there are things I have to do. Aldara will bring you some food, and you must get some more rest.'

'I'm not hungry, lord.'

Yehudah was waiting for me outside the tent. 'Did you get the information you need?'

'Not really,' I said, wearily. 'And he says he's not hungry. Is that a bad sign?'

'It's normal. The child will eat soon, have no fear.'

'Why do you keep calling him "the child"?'

After a few moments' silence, Yehudah said, 'This may not be the right time to discuss these things. You have much to deal with. This "Mudéjar", for a start. You are going to seek him out?'

'Yes. It's clear someone is following us; making violent threats; taking, injuring and killing. I have to put a stop to it, Yehudah.'

'We will discuss "the child" later, then.'

I was surprised to see the humour in his eyes.

Before I left the camp to go to the *Chateau de Boutemont,* I spoke to Kit. 'Find an opportunity to speak with Yehudah. He works for Alfonso, and this Mudéjar business must be something to do with him. Alfonso is responsible for what happened to the Muslims in al-Andalus. If our Mudéjar has a grievance, it'll be with Alfonso.'

'Why's he picking on us then?' Kit asked morosely. He'd been fishing again, but caught little, which put him in a bad mood.

'That's what I want you to find out. Tell him about his future, or whatever the hell you like, but find out everything you can about the Muslims of al-Andalus and what Alfonso's been doing to them.'

'I can tell you that.' Aldara's clear voice rang out as she suddenly appeared and dropped down onto the ground between Kit and me. She was still wearing Guido's male clothes. Oddly, they suited her. 'Actually, Kit knows all about it too. Castile has tried to take Smander. Alfonso wants to conquer the entire peninsula. We who live there know this. Your lady will tell you the same. It is the *Reconquista*.'

'The "Reconquest"?'

'Exactly. It began, oh, centuries ago! But, more recently, they took Córdoba and Seville, and the Muslims were left with Granada and nothing else. Your friend, Jabir, is a Muslim from Persia. You should feel sympathy towards the Moors, Lord Rory!'

'It makes no sense,' I countered. 'Alfonso wants Jabir to go to Toledo and work for him. How can he be against the Muslims? He must be power-mad, like all kings and rulers.

Kit, speak with Yehudah and find out everything you can about this. I am going to the *Chateau de Boutemont* to find the Mudéjar.'

'On your own?'

'On my own.'

True to Rosa's description, as soon as you climb out of the river valley it's easy to see the fortress, perhaps two miles away. In a haze of afternoon sunshine I saw dour, turreted stone walls on top of an old-fashioned motte, and as I drew nearer, an old wooden gatehouse became visible. There was no one at the gate, and no answer when I called for Raoul. So I rode the mule into an overgrown bailey where wild flowers grew among the ancient flagstones and around which crumbling walls gave little to no protection. The *Chateau de Boutemont* is hardly worth the name. Heavily garrisoned fortress? It didn't look like it to me.

'Raoul!' I shouted, leaping down from the mule's back. Where was the damned gatekeeper? Where was the Mudéjar? And where were the soldiers who should be guarding this so-called castle? Birds sang in the nearby trees, crickets called from the grassy hillocks, and no one answered my summons. Ahead of me was an ancient wooden keep, where, presumably, Guido had been imprisoned by the Mudéjar. Here, there was a new door, with a new lock on it. Here, then, was habitation. But the lock wasn't in use, and I was able to swing the door wide open. Carefully, I edged inside.

An hour later I was back with the others.

'Strike the camp,' I ordered. 'We're moving on at once. Xurxo, get Thuban comfortable in the cart. Yehudah, decide how you want Guido to travel. Get these tents down, load up the cart, saddle up the mules and let's be off.'

'But why?' they all bleated at me. 'It's mid-afternoon! It'll be dark in a few hours.'

They all know my rule. We don't travel at night; it's too dangerous. But sometimes other dangers are worse. Tersely, I told them of Raoul, his body at the foot of the spiral stairs, his neck broken, his cockleshell thrust between his teeth, and the Mudéjar's latest message in the dead man's stiff fingers.

> *Anyone who is not for me is against me. This man deserved to die. He betrayed me. Do not think the boy will escape justice. In the end, you will all die because you are all against me.*
>
> *The Mudéjar*

I did not read the note out. But they saw my expression, they understood the urgency from my tone, and within half an hour the camp was struck and we were on our way.

Guido had been pronounced fit to ride, and he jogged along beside me. The afternoon became evening, and the sun slowly sank on our left, casting long shadows across the meadow. The golden disc disappeared completely, leaving us in the twilight. An hour later, it was dark.

'Are we following it, lord? That star?' Guido's gaze was directed up at Polaris.

'No, Guido. We're following the road.'

He chuckled, but it turned into a croak and then a cough. And then silence. I tried to engage him in further conversation, but he was mute.

I calculated we'd be at Honfleur well before dawn. The road was well marked, but we were hampered by the cart, which travels only slowly. It almost ground to a halt on the uphill stretch into the Saint-Gatien woods. This was the part of our route I'd particularly wanted to negotiate in the daylight.

On my way south, I was aware of the dangers in the forest, but in spite of that, I'd been attacked twice, fighting off a lone robber the first time, and a startled wild boar a day later. The thought of traversing this place in the dark with a swaying, slow-moving wagon, a sick man, an injured woman and a vulnerable child made my blood run cold. But somewhere, and it wouldn't be far away, the Mudéjar was keeping pace with us. Possibly on foot. *Probably* on foot. But I didn't think he'd make his next move until we stopped somewhere. That's been his pattern all along: attack a lone member of the group while we're at camp, relaxed and off guard. I do not intend to be off guard anymore, not for one single moment.

'Where is he, do you think?' Kit came alongside on his mule, just as we entered the sinister Forest of Saint-Gatien.

'The Mudéjar? I've been wondering that. Keep your eyes open and your wits sharpened. This is a dangerous place.'

'Then let's wait until morning,' he said edgily. 'Why not, Rory? We can make camp here and continue tomorrow.'

I told him to shut up and keep going. Behind me, the cart creaked and rattled, the donkeys pulling valiantly. They must have been wondering why they weren't allowed to rest overnight. An owl hooted. Every step my mule took was a step nearer to coming out of this disagreeable place, while every crack of a twig or rustle of leaves set my teeth on edge. Who was there? Robbers? Vagrants? Or the Mudéjar himself? When an animal screamed just ahead of me, my heart pounded and my stomach cramped painfully. And then, from behind, there came a shout.

'Stop! We must stop at once!'

The column behind me came to a halt, the cart no longer creaking. I turned my mule around.

'What is it?'

'It's Thuban!' Xurxo cried. 'He's much, much worse. This is a terrible journey for him. He can't take any more!'

Yehudah said something which I didn't catch, and then I heard him talking with Xurxo. He clambered into the cart to examine Thuban, and I joined them. I figured we had about reached the middle of the forest, the thickest, densest part. The very worst place to stop.

'Can we do this when we're out of these woods?' I asked through gritted teeth. 'We need to keep going.'

'I have to help this man,' Yehudah said. 'His pulse is very weak.' He looked sharply at me. 'I can't examine him properly in the dark, so I need to know the truth. As I understand it, we are taking this man to your alchemist, a Muslim healer called Jabir. And the claim is that Jabir has discovered, or invented, the so-called Elixir of Life. Is that true, or is it wishful thinking? Are we subjecting this invalid to such an ordeal to good purpose?'

I swallowed hard. I could still taste the bile which had risen when I heard the animal scream, still feel the clammy sweat on my forehead. 'Yehudah, I don't know. I set out on a pilgrimage over six months ago. I don't know what Jabir has achieved in that time. But before I left, I can tell you that Jabir had not discovered the Elixir of Life.'

Xurxo gave a cry. '*Not* discovered it? But I thought he had! I thought that was the reason Thuban and his servant were coming with us! It is what they said! They were convinced…' His voice trailed away. He looked stricken. Not for the first time, I wondered why he cared so much.

'But you think there is a chance the alchemist has made progress with his research?' Yehudah persisted.

'There's a chance, I suppose. He has built a – well, as you know, we call it a laboratory. A word invented by Kit. It's bigger and better than the one he had before.' And I recalled, not just the original observatory in Sir Bernard's house, but the old Liberty Hut, a ramshackle wooden cabin on the banks of the River Shamet, where Jabir had worked himself into the ground to create the famed Elixir which he hoped would cure Rupert of a grotesque and life-destroying disfigurement. It did not cure Rupert, and Rupert is now dead. The new laboratory, equipped to Jabir's exacting standards, is nothing like the Liberty Hut. That scene of his failure will haunt him for the rest of his life; I know that because he's told me so. Perhaps the new laboratory has made the impossible possible. Perhaps.

'What are we going to do?' Aldara asked, her voice low. 'Will Thuban make it to Hambrig, Yehudah?'

'I do not think so,' he said, turning to her. 'Better to let the man live his last day or two in comfort. We should continue on our journey and find a hostel where he may stay, and arrange for his burial when the time comes. Alas, that time is soon.'

'Good, we'll do that,' I said, relieved. 'Let's press on then.'

Yehudah took over from Xurxo in the cart, and I think Xurxo was glad to hand over his charge, though he said nothing. Finally, we emerged from the Forest of Saint-Gatien, and although the night was still dark and the way still unclear, all our hearts lifted at being out of the trees. It was as if we could breathe again, feeling the fresh breeze on our skin and in our lungs.

'I can smell the sea,' Aldara exclaimed. It was true. We were finally nearing the Normandy coast, our departure point for England.

'What's wrong with Guido?' I asked her.

'What's wrong, lord, is that Guido doesn't want to be Guido. And, inexorably and against her will, Sara is turning into Guido.'

After a few moments' silence, I said, 'We will look for a hostel for Thuban.'

I acknowledged then that I'd failed to confront the Guido-issue. Aldara was being honest, and that was all Guido had ever been. But I was unwilling to accept these things. And I still am.

I had an abbey in mind, a place where I'd stayed after crossing the Narrow Sea from England to Normandy in early March. It was a bit to the east of our road, but only five miles out of our way. Once we'd left Thuban there, where he would be comfortably cared for, we could simply track westwards to the port of Honfleur.

I'm not worried about the Mudéjar now. Our party will stick together. We'll spend one night at the *Abbaye Notre-Dame de Grestain,* where we will be perfectly safe, and then we will embark on a boat for England. The Mudéjar's threats are empty ones. So far, it seems he's managed to kill Joseph, and of course Raoul, but he didn't kill Guido or Aldara, although he could have done so had he wanted to. Once we're in

England, it'll take us no more than two weeks to get to Hambrig and home. And thank God for that.

We approached the *Abbaye Notre-Dame de Grestain,* and, although it was now nearly midnight, I spoke to the abbot, who remembered me, and I told him about Thuban.

'Your friend is seriously ill? Do you have any idea what is wrong with him?'

I misunderstood at first. 'I don't think you need worry, Father. Not one of us has become ill during the whole time we have been travelling with this man.'

'That is not what I meant. I do not fear for myself or for the brothers. Have you heard of Herluin de Conteville? He founded this abbey, and he did so because the blessed Virgin Mary told him to bathe in the river here. Having done that, he found himself cured of leprosy. Your friend is suffering from some other illness, to be sure, but the waters of the Carbec have a powerful effect, especially when combined with sacred visions or artefacts.'

'We must hope Thuban finds his cure here, then,' I said with all sincerity. 'I haven't heard of Herluin de Conteville, but he must have been a man of great faith.'

'He was,' the abbot agreed. 'And it was in the year of his death that his stepson, King William the First of Normandy, conquered England.'

He called to some of the brothers who were detailed to show us to the male and female guesthouses. My heart sank as I envisaged yet more trouble with Guido. It's been good to have camped every night in the countryside; I've not had to put up with his nonsense. It would count for nothing here, though, I knew. However much he might insist he's a girl, I'll make sure he's sent to the men's guesthouse. No one will listen to his squawking.

Yehudah stayed to direct the moving of Thuban into the infirmary. With the abbot's words on 'sacred visions or artefacts' in my mind, I tucked the collarbone of Joseph of Arimathea into the open neck of Thuban's tunic. Then I caught Guido by the scruff of his ridiculous gown and hauled him along with me. Xurxo and Kit followed, while Aldara and Rosa were led away in a different direction.

'An extraordinary thing has happened,' Yehudah said the next morning. 'And it is hard for me to accept. Neither Thuban nor I share your Christian faith, Lord Rory. So why would your dead friend's relic work?'

'It worked?' I cried incredulously. If so, it'll be the first time that wretched bone has done anything useful.

'The abbot of this place made me undress Thuban and carry his naked body to a stream. He followed behind us, holding the bone you gave Thuban and muttering incantations and prayers. I was told to enter the stream, still holding Thuban in my arms. I protested at this, but the abbot told me you sanctioned the business. I see from your face you did no such thing, yet the abbot was quite clear that you did. So I complied, and I lowered Thuban into the stream and let it wash over him. The abbot held the bone by a ribbon and swung it over Thuban's head, while continuing to pray. I noticed no difference in Thuban's condition, although the cooling water took the heat from his body. After nearly half an hour of this, the abbot gave me permission to bring Thuban out of the water and dress him in a special robe, after which I carried him to the infirmary.'

'Did you stay with him?'

'I did. And for the first time in a long time, Thuban slept well. This morning he is much better than he has been for many weeks. He even took some food! And he is speaking, albeit slowly, holding short conversations! The abbot, needless to say, is unsurprised, and cited some relation of a long-ago king—'

'Herluin de Conteville,' I murmured.

'—who was apparently cured of leprosy in the same way. But you told me your friend's relic has never worked.'

'Perhaps it was waiting for the right moment,' I suggested. 'The right person to help. Perhaps my, er, friend, was never that person.'

'Hmm. Rejected by a bone? Well, you know better than I how these things are meant to work. I am just delighted that Thuban seems to be recovering at long last.'

'So do we leave him here or take him with us?'

'If we could stay here a week, I will know by the end of that time,' Yehudah said, and I, rather reluctantly, agreed to that. But I hadn't missed Yehudah's strange statement. *Neither Thuban nor I share your Christian faith.* I had not known that Thuban was a Jew, but perhaps that's why he was so keen to come with us and escape the vengeance of the *Justiciers* back in Saintes. It made a kind of sense.

21

IN THE MORTUARY

The *Abbaye Notre-Dame de Grestain* is a calm and pleasant place to stay, and by the third day we arrived at a routine consisting of attending at least five of the eight offices, taking two meals a day in the refectory and walking by the river. The weather has mostly been fair, although we have had some light rain as well the last day or two, which I have found refreshing. I feel I can wait out the next few days here while Yehudah monitors Thuban's progress, and then we will go to Honfleur, get aboard a cog or a hoy, and within a day we'll be in England. Once there, we're almost home.

Aldara spends a great deal of time with Yehudah, the two of them attending to Thuban, who is definitely, and incredibly, growing stronger by the day. Rosa and Guido are often together, Guido looking sad and wan. He hardly eats anything these days, and he is not sleeping well. If I wake during the night and look for him, he's often not in the dormitory. Yet he doesn't seem to be ill.

There was time for me to talk with Yehudah about Guido.

'The child has a disturbed mind,' Yehudah said in his nasal voice. 'It is a medical condition. The child is not well.'

'It isn't that at all,' protested Aldara, who was sitting in the refectory with us. 'Sara isn't ill. She just wants people to realise she is a girl. That's all. Her mind is perfectly sound, it's her body that is wrong for her.'

Yehudah did not acknowledge Aldara, but continued to talk to me. 'Sometimes children have bad things happen in their lives. It can cause them to become disturbed. It can make them do things they would not have done. It can change them. I use the term "the child" because I do not believe we have here a male or a female. The child's brain and body are incompatible.'

I don't know what to think. I continue to call him 'Guido', and to think of him as a boy. And I truly believe that's for the best, since nothing will stop his developing into an adult male.

Kit has borrowed my gittern and spends large parts of each day in the orchard, sitting under an apple tree and playing his music, his fingers rippling over the strings, and the silvery sounds wafting through the abbey gardens. I wanted Guido to sing with him, knowing what a lovely voice he has, but the boy has refused and I don't feel like forcing him.

As for Xurxo, he is delighted to see Thuban making such good progress, but, to my surprise, he doesn't seek me out to discuss this or anything else. I've grown fond of the younger man, and I'd hoped to spend some time with him, but everyone seems to be either paired up already, or else they're content with their own company. So this is where, in the privacy of my secret journal, I confess to feeling lonely. Why is no one talking to me?

On day four of our pleasant break from the relentless travelling, I found out why.

'Yehudah wants to perform an operation,' Aldara said carefully, just after terce. 'A surgical operation.'

'On Thuban?'

'On Guido.' Aldara never calls him 'Guido'. I didn't pick up on this at first, but later I realised the use of the boy's name was to get me to agree to the 'operation'. It also took me a few moments to work out the nature of the surgery, during which Aldara waited quietly, watching my face.

'Oh no!' I said, as soon as I realised what they planned to do. 'Absolutely not. I'd have to seek permission from his parents.'

'He belongs to you, lord. You can give permission.'

He does belong to me, but in the capacity of my squire-in-training, and that training, that whole *life,* would not be possible once this butchery had taken place. As for his parents, I have no idea who they are.

'No, Aldara. I can't give my permission for this. He has been given to me so he can train to be my squire and then become a knight. If Yehudah mutilates him, he'll be nothing.'

'Lord, there are many cases of boys being castrated—'

'There are, and for many reasons, but Guido does not qualify. And that's an end to it, Aldara. In any case, I thought Yehudah's views were fundamentally different from yours. What's changed?'

'Nothing has changed. In the end I agreed with him that Sara's mind and body are incompatible. Yehudah realised, as I do, that there is a way to change that. To align them, as he calls it.'

Oh, does he.

Rosa was the next to approach me, and after I'd dealt with her arguments I envisaged a procession of do-gooders, each with their own similar-but-slightly-different persuasive reasoning for Guido getting butchered by Yehudah. When I argued for waiting until we arrive in Hambrig, where, perhaps, other physicians could give their opinion, I was told that time is not on Guido's side.

'Her voice has started to change already,' Rosa informed me, as we stood in the cloisters just before dinner. As if I hadn't noticed that for myself. 'Other things are starting to happen. Manly things. You would know. But Sara cannot bear it.' Her direct gaze and condescending tone issued that challenge again. I understand it better now. It's a challenge to my authority.

When Alfonso first offered me his daughter's hand in marriage, I found it hard to believe he would choose me as her husband. I'm still in the dark about that, but I am beginning to realise who Rosa really is. The daughter, legitimate or not, of the great Alfonso, is a proud woman. She can be arrogant and supercilious. She understands the natural order of a wife being subordinate to her husband, but Rosa seeks to manipulate every situation so as to overturn this natural order. I have allowed this to happen once or twice, mostly out of sheer surprise, occasionally because it has not been too bothersome.

But this situation is different, and whatever Rosa's opinion, or Aldara's for that matter, I will not change my mind, and that's the end of it. Guido will remain intact, I told my wife. Then I turned and walked away.

I sought out Kit in the orchard, hoping to hear some of his beautiful music, but he laid the gittern on the ground and invited me to sit with him.

'Do you know what Thuban's name means?' he asked.

'I assumed it was just his name.'

'Thuban is the name of a star. It's in the constellation Draco. And I very much doubt it is our Thuban's original name.'

I digested this. Why Thuban would assume a false name, I had no idea.

'So Thuban is a star,' Kit continued. 'But not just any star. Well, to be fair, it *is* just any star now, but that wasn't always the case. You've heard of the great pyramids of Egypt?'

'For God's sake, Kit! I was *in* Egypt! I fought the infidel there for four years.' I was baffled. First our sick Frenchman, then a nondescript star, now the great pyramids! Where on earth was this leading?

'When the pyramids were built,' Kit said, 'about three thousand years before the birth of Christ, the night sky looked very different from how it looks to us now. If you wanted to travel north, as we've been doing, you wouldn't have followed Polaris. I'm supposing you've been following Polaris on our way home?'

'Not really. I've been retracing my steps along the *Camino de Santiago*. I came this way, and I'm returning along the same route.'

'The thing is, Polaris wasn't always the north star. During the time when the Egyptians built their enormous pyramids, the star nearest to the north was Thuban. Thuban was the north star then, the guiding star for all travellers and mariners.'

'How do you know all this, Kit?'

'Joseph explained it weeks ago. He was a very clever astronomer, tasked with charting the skies for Alfonso of Castile. It seems the sky moves, although very slowly. Or, at any rate, that's what Aristotle thought. But Joseph read the works of a Persian scholar called Tusi, who argued that it might be the other way around. Perhaps it is the earth that spins around, while the stars stay still. Either way, we have to accept that the earth and the stars line up differently as the years go by, and that, some four thousand years ago, it was Thuban and not Polaris that showed which way is north. Which means, of course, that at some point, some other star will take over from Polaris. But apparently we don't have to worry about that for another three thousand or so years!'

Having delivered his punchline, Kit waited. He's a patient man, knowing it often takes me a few moments to join everything up and make the necessary connections.

'Why do you think Thuban has taken the name of this former north star?' I asked, trying my best. 'Did Joseph speak of that as well?'

'He did. And he spoke to Thuban about it. And that night, he was murdered.'

'Yet this is the first time you've mentioned it to me?'

'It's the first I've heard of it myself, Rory. Don't blame me, blame Aldara. Joseph spoke first to Aldara. He intended to marry her, and she would have been happy with him. Aldara, as you know, is very anxious to help Guido turn himself into a girl. And all of *this* is relevant to *that*.'

Again, I took a few moments to think about it, and, slowly, I worked it out. 'Aldara was in love with Joseph, and he told her about this connection. Joseph was murdered by the Mudéjar. Are you saying there's something going on between Aldara and Yehudah now? The Jew told me Guido's brain and body are mismatched, but now he wants to carry out this mutilation of Guido and turn him into Sara. Aldara must be behind it all. Though I don't know why.'

'Aldara has many secrets,' Kit said cryptically. 'Don't forget I grew up with her. I remember her as a distant older sister who couldn't be bothered with grubby little boys. She was like her mother, and, actually, I think her father was scared of them both. Aldara has always had a mind of her own, and she doesn't care what people think of her. She does exactly what she wants to do. She always has done.'

'Did she do anything to you, Kit?' I was wondering at the bitterness in his voice. 'Or to Joy?'

He gave a crooked smile. 'To my mother? Oh yes. Aldara kept my mother working day and night in the laundry, even when her skin was raw and her fingers numb, and even though her son was living in luxury in the royal nursery.'

'But I thought it was Queen Valentina who kept Joy in the laundry! You've always told me that.'

'Does it matter, Rory? They're both the same. They hated both me and Joy. They couldn't touch me, because King Xisco liked me, but they let my mother live in poverty, and they allowed Gyalak to be raised by the man in the moon, and then to—'

'They didn't know who Gyalak was! Nobody knew, not even you.'

Kit looked furious, but I was thinking of something else. 'Aldara can't be the Mudéjar. She's not strong enough.'

'Don't you believe it.' Kit's tone was scathing. 'She's stronger than she looks. *And* she could easily have put Guido's clothes on, like she did the other day—'

'No, Kit. With or without Guido's clothes, Aldara is simply not strong enough, and in any case, she was in love with Joseph; she would not have killed him. I came to you to ask your opinion on turning Guido into a girl.'

'Oh that!' From surly to dismissive. 'He's already a girl. Chopping his balls off won't change anything.'

'You are wrong,' said a soft voice from behind us. 'It will change everything.'

Out of the fruit trees stepped Guido himself. He was wearing his shirt and breeches, and his long hair hung loose around his thin face. 'May I talk with you, lord?'

Kit levered himself up, thrust my gittern at me and strode off without another word.

'All right, Guido,' I said. 'I came to Kit for counsel and got none. Probably I should have chosen to speak to you in the first place. Say what you want to say.'

'Can we sit? It's easier for me than looking up at you all the time.'

I smiled at that, and we both sat down under Kit's shady apple tree.

I think he took heart from my expression. His smile was uncertain but hopeful.

'Yehudah has offered to change my life, and it's what I want more than anything. I don't want to be a man, but I'm turning into one. Since we set out from Saintes I have changed a lot and I hate it. Please will you allow Yehudah to help me?'

'Guido, it may be too late. Your voice has been cracking and there are many other signs of —'

'Lord,' Guido interrupted desperately. 'Yehudah says it isn't too late, but it will be very soon! He wants to operate on me here in the abbey. There's a good infirmarer here who will help, and Aldara will nurse me.'

'Has anyone spoken to the abbot?'

He fiddled with the laces in his shirt. 'No, lord. I would be very grateful if you would speak to him.'

'Why are you making yourself look like a boy this afternoon, Guido? Do you think I'm more likely to listen to you if you dress in those clothes and keep your hair loose?'

'It was Aldara's idea,' he whispered. 'She said you would treat me with more respect if I looked like a boy. She says you're not susceptible to womanly charms.'

'I hope I'll always treat you with respect, Guido, whatever you're wearing. All I can say for now is, I'll consider the matter and I'll give you my decision tomorrow morning.'

Disappointed, he got up and trailed away through the trees, and I went to find Yehudah. I had some extremely specific questions for him.

'Do you just remove the testicles? What, exactly, will he lose?'

'Everything. He will lose everything.'

'This can't be safe. There will be a lot of bleeding, surely.'

'It is not safe, and yes, he will lose a great deal of blood. He knows it is dangerous, he knows he could die.'

But I know Guido well enough by now. I know what he would think: better dead than male.

'How long will he need to recover before he can travel further?'

'A week. More, if he develops a fever.'

'If he develops a fever he stays here with Thuban. I'm not waiting more than a week. The weather will change and the boats may not sail. Do the thing tomorrow, Yehudah. And don't fuck it up.'

I am in my bed in the guesthouse, and I've finished my log of today's events. I can see Kit and Xurxo in their beds on the other side of the dormitory. They're both asleep, Kit curled into a ball as usual, Xurxo on his back. In the bed to my left is the boy who wants to be a girl, so this is his last night in the men's house. Tomorrow night, and for many nights after, he will be in the infirmary. Or in the mortuary.

22

THERE WAS NEVER ANY ANSWERING CALL

I was riding Blue, my wild mustang. Over the mountains we flew, over rivers and seas, their white-capped waves churning beneath our hooves. And then Blue was galloping across a vast desert, so arid and bleak my eyes watered and my hands shook. I nearly lost my grip on reins and stirrups, but Blue turned to look at me. *Don't let go,* she commanded. *This is much too important. We need to get there so as to have a proper view of things.*

Where though? Where are we going? I don't recognise any of this.

Of course you don't, Blue said. *You've never been here before.*

The terrain became more difficult, and I hoped Blue would soar into the air again, but she didn't. Her hooves pounded across rocks and stones, and I was nearly unseated. It was painful, bouncing in and out of the saddle. I was crying with the pain, but Blue took no notice, and I wondered if she were deliberately giving me the hardest ride she could. And then, when I was about to let go of everything, we began to slow down. Ahead of us I saw a shimmering palace, and surrounding the palace were glittering fountains and trees with golden fruit hanging from low branches. Blue trotted serenely under a rose-covered arch, stopping in a pretty cobbled courtyard. Water cascaded from an elegant fountain, and a man sat near it, playing a flute. He looked up at me. I slid down from Blue's back, barely able to stand, let alone walk.

Look at the bowl of the sky, the flautist commanded. I didn't know that expression, but he was pointing with his flute, and I looked up obediently; strangely, the sky was now dark, and pinpricks of stars were appearing everywhere. The ethereal music of the flute had calmed my mind and, somehow, also soothed the pain. I was able to focus my eyes on the stars while the flautist put his instrument to his lips and played the music of the heavens.

Blue's head was also tilted back. She was looking for her friend Pegasus. *Where is Pegasus?* she asked imperiously, her small ears moving forwards and back, waiting for my answer.

I don't know, I don't recognise anything. This doesn't look like the sky I used to watch from Grandfather's shoulders!

Well, I know I can't see Pegasus, Blue said crossly, tossing her head a little. *But I think that might be Draco, the dragon.* She was looking at a big pattern of stars, and I could see the huge tail of the sky-dragon.

Draco? I queried. *Where have I heard that name before? Oh yes! Thuban's here, isn't he!*

I certainly am, Thuban said, and I watched him hop off a star and stand on nothing. He didn't look particularly pleased to see me. *The bone you put in my tunic is a powerful healer,* Thuban went on, his voice echoing around the heavens. *Without it, I'd be dead by now. It wasn't the river that cured me, although the abbot is sure it was. But this must have been a bone from Islam! No wonder it did nothing for your*

Christian friend, of whom I have heard. No wonder it has done nothing for you either. But it has worked for me, and that is because it is a bone from one of the prophets, one of the Messengers from God. It has given me life!

Blue whinnied, and Thuban spun dizzily, then vanished, a trail of stardust arcing across the vault of sky, while the stars in his constellation applauded him. Blue was dancing. I fell to my knees. The stars whirled madly in space. Blue cavorted among the fruit trees, kicking up stones which hit me in the face and bounced off the cockleshell, dangling on my chest.

That's your badge of honour, Thuban taunted from the skies. *That cockleshell! Why aren't you proud of it, Rory?*

But I wasn't proud of it. The thing mocked me as much as Thuban did.

I vomited violently onto the pretty pink path.

I woke up on the cold, hard floor of the dormitory. I had been very sick indeed. A cold breeze was blowing through the unglazed windows, and it helped clear my head. I sat up, wet hair clinging clammily to my face, so I pushed it away and tried to stand. Stretching out my arms in the darkness, I somehow clawed my way to my bed and subsided onto it, my head in my hands.

When I next looked up, it was nearly dawn. Peeling off my stinking, sodden clothing, I decided to head outside to the river for a thorough wash. Across the dormitory, Kit and Xurxo still slept; they'd not wake for another hour or two. To my left was Guido's bed. I'd promised to give the boy an answer today, but yesterday I'd told Yehudah to perform the operation, so the decision seems to have been made. But, as I stood naked in the dormitory, the stench of vomit in my nostrils, I was haunted by my dream. The excruciating pain in my testicles, soothed by the music of the flautist in the Paradise Garden, was surely a sign. A message that I must not allow the boy to suffer such agony. The meaning of my dream was, in that moment, revealed to me.

I glanced over at Guido, but my confused mind took a few moments to register the bed was empty. I stumbled outside and picked my way through the abbey grounds to wash in the river. The brothers would be at lauds, having processed to the church using the night stairs; they would not pass me to question my mad and soiled appearance. The one person I did hope to meet was Guido, and I looked for him in the latrines and at the river, but there was no sign of him. I hastened back to the dormitory and pulled on my spare breeches, shirt and jersey. My gittern lay on the floor under my bed and I left it there. I wasn't concerned for Guido; he'd probably just wandered off by himself and would be back for food in the refectory. Yehudah had spent the night with Thuban in the infirmary, and the thought of Thuban made me shiver. In my dream he had been powerful. Almost a demon.

It has taken the entire day for the dream to re-make itself, first in my head, and then on parchment. I've had to piece it together as I write my journal with shaking hands in a strange farmhouse in the middle of a darkened field, a good few miles from the abbey. Anyone reading this account may think the description of my dream is how I instantly remembered it on waking. Nothing could be further from the truth. It was Thuban I recalled first, though not his appearance, nor the sound of his voice. Later, I remembered he'd spoken of the *bone from Islam.* At about the same time, I noticed my gittern lying underneath my bed; it shouldn't have been there, but I didn't register that at the time. I keep it in a leather bag propped up against the satchel which holds my clothes and my journal. And it was only after I'd spent the entire morning hunting fruitlessly for Guido, asking people if they'd seen him, which nobody had, that I returned at last to the men's guesthouse, convinced I'd solved the puzzle.

All morning, a suspicion had been forming in my mind, and I could see the scene play out. It was clear to me that Yehudah and Aldara were already performing the operation on Guido, so that by the time I made my decision known it would be too late. In my head I saw the surgeon's knife, felt it slice through the boy's penis and scrotum as if they were my own. I smelt the blood and sensed Aldara's urgency as she made haste to staunch the flow and keep the boy from losing his life force. The boy? No, no longer.

Angrily, I reached under the bed and pulled my gittern out. Wedged between two of its courses of strings was a folded parchment. With an oath, I wrenched it free. So convinced was I that I would be reading Guido's confession of his disobedience, or perhaps a clinical explanation by Yehudah for his actions, that I had to re-read the bloody thing three times before the words and their meaning penetrated my brain.

Anyone who is not for me is against me. Didn't I tell you the boy deserves to die? I know you didn't believe me, because when you found him he was alive. You thought yourself clever to have rescued him, but with your every move you are playing into my hands. Each one of you is marked for death. It's just a matter of when, where and how. So far three are already dead by my hand, first the too-clever Jew, then the pious gatekeeper, and now the satanic boy-girl. But in the end, you will all die because you are all against me.

The Mudéjar

I gave a roar of anguish mixed with fury and stormed out into the cloisters, startling two monks who were passing. Leaving them shrinking against the cloister wall, I ran towards the infirmary. I took the steps in one bound and crashed into the building. My chest heaving, my stomach in free-fall, I stood in the entrance, gazed frantically around and took in firstly that there were no patients in any of the beds, and secondly that there were in fact two of my party in one of the beds. Yehudah leapt away from Aldara, reaching desperately for his clothes. Aldara stayed where she was, heedless of the sheets falling away from her nude body.

'*What is happening here*?' I shouted. 'Where the hell is Thuban?'

Yehudah, hurriedly pulling on his hose and long black cloak, stumbled down the corridor between the beds. 'This is an unfortunate situation,' he said softly. 'We had wanted to keep it quiet.'

'I'll bet you did. Where are your patients, Yehudah? Where are Thuban and Guido?'

'Guido is not yet my patient, and I have not seen him since yesterday. Thuban is being taken out for a walk by your wife. She would have spoken to you earlier, but she couldn't find you.'

'How very convenient. And how very convenient for you and Aldara that the infirmary is now empty of patients.'

'We have done nothing wrong, except, perhaps, in your eyes. Aldara is the woman you rejected, Lord Rory. Do not forget that.'

'I am in charge here, Yehudah. Do not forget *that.* I need your help to find Guido. He has been taken by the Mudéjar, and I don't know where he is.' I didn't mention that, according to the Mudéjar, Guido is already dead.

'Again? Taken again?' But Yehudah's nasal voice was almost drowned by a cry from Aldara, who leapt from the bed, wrapping the sheet around herself.

'Is it true? Do you know it, or are you guessing?'

I handed the parchment to her. As she read it, tears flowed down her cheeks. Yehudah fetched Aldara's gown and draped it around her shoulders, but she took no notice.

'What are we going to do? Sara is like a sister to me. She *cannot* be dead!'

'Something strange happened last night,' I said, some of it returning to me as I spoke. 'I had a terrifying dream. I am sure Thuban is involved somehow—'

Yehudah swore in some foreign tongue. 'We must go at once! Your wife is with him, and she will be in danger!'

We ran, Yehudah and I, leaving Aldara to get dressed. I flung out some questions. I don't remember them now, but it was something like, *Which way did they go? When did they start? Did anybody see them or go with them?* But Yehudah either knew nothing or was so out of condition he couldn't answer while he was running. I soon left him behind anyway. Running made me feel better, somehow, and the last of the muzziness cleared my brain as I raced along the riverbank. I had no idea if I were going in the right direction.

Further and further from the abbey I ran, along the bank of the stream, and I found myself heading westwards alongside a much larger river, on which there were many vessels. It was a busy scene, dangerous for a murderer perhaps, since someone would be sure to see him. Sweat poured into my eyes and I could barely see. Every so often, I shouted my wife's name.

'Rosa! Rosa, where are you? Rosa! Rosa!'

There was never any answering call.

23

UNTIL MORNING

A couple of miles further on I came to a channel which cut across the mudflats. I was approaching the estuary of the great waterway. Ahead of me, just across the narrow creek, stood an old church with a thatched roof and a short tower at its west end. Exhilarated and exhausted, I stopped to catch my breath. Thuban and Rosa couldn't have come here; it was much too far.

But a movement caught my eye, and I saw someone coming out of the church. There was something about the figure that I recognised, something in the walk, perhaps. I dropped down behind the reeds fringing the little channel and watched carefully. The person walked the length of the church from east to west, stooped to pick something up, and retraced their steps. Then I lost sight of them. They must have gone back inside the church. I waited a few moments, but there was no further activity.

I removed my boots and jersey, and keeping the movement of reeds to a minimum, I lowered myself into the water. It wasn't deep, but the bottom was mud, and I couldn't stand on it without sinking, so I trod water where I was, formulating a plan of sorts, and then swam mostly underwater. Before I knew it, I was tangling myself up in the reeds on the other side.

I lay in the reedbed, half in, half out of the water. Parting the reeds, I peered up at the church, but there was no sign of the person I'd seen. It had been too tall and burly for either Rosa or Guido, and too mobile for Thuban. Or had Thuban been pretending all the time? All these weeks? Was that possible? And why hadn't I thought of it before? Had he pretended to be so seriously ill that we would agree to take him with us? His apparent deterioration in health would then delay us in the *abbaye,* after which would come the miraculous cure, allowing him to leave the infirmary and seize and kill Guido. Even if all that were true, I knew this person was not Thuban. Thuban may or may not have been pretending he couldn't walk, but he did not have the physique of the figure I'd seen coming out of the church. And that person had *not* been pretending, for he didn't know he was being watched.

I crept further out of the reeds. The church was a couple of hundred yards away. I got to my feet and charged the length of the building to where I'd seen the figure go in and out. The door stood open and I rushed in, weaponless, clad only in my breeches and a thin shirt. The interior was very dark, but at the far end there were two tiny pinpoints of light. Candles on the altar. I kept to the shadows behind the door and listened for the sound of someone breathing. No sign of a hidden murderer, but, strangely, and from far off, the thin reedy notes of a pipe. A lone shepherd in these watery French meadows?

I explored deeper into my shadowy corner. Moving my hands along the bumpy stone wall, I expected to follow it to the edge of the door. But the wall stopped abruptly, a long way short of the door, and there was a space. An alcove, maybe? But as I moved into the space, my feet met the beginning of a flight of steps, and I understood. I'd seen the stumpy tower from the outside; this, then, was the way up the tower. And I knew with certainty that the person with the familiar gait was at the top of those steps. Was he waiting for me? Sword, axe or club in hand, he'd send me tumbling to my death. I shook my head to clear it of such thoughts. I was positive I had not been seen.

I dodged back outside, eyes smarting in the sudden glare of daylight. In haste, I hunted for a weapon, but there were no trees, no fallen boughs, and no handy baulk of timber to latch the door. Inwardly cursing, I went back in. Bare hands it would have to be then. Bare hands and bare feet, my native wit, and the experience of nearly twenty years of combat. I crept soundlessly up the tower steps, winding to my right, listening acutely for the sound of anyone coming down.

The problem with spiral steps is you never know how far you've got to go. The tower had looked a stubby little thing from the outside. Inside, treading carefully, step by step, it seemed to go on for ever. But I knew I was nearing the top when I heard noises. There must be a room, or perhaps just a landing; whatever it was, someone was there. I stopped climbing and pressed myself flat against the wall of the tower. The noise came again, a whimpering sound. Then sniffing. Sobbing. A woman was crying in that room. *Rosa.*

I raced silently up the remaining few steps and found myself outside a closed door. I pushed at it, and to my surprise it opened. The room was circular and very small. Above was a planked roof, and in the far wall were two arched windows. But Rosa wasn't there. Under the windows crouched someone else, a girl in a pale shift, her hands to her face, her shoulders heaving. I strode over, pulled her hands away, and found myself looking straight at Guido.

He gave a startled cry and jumped to his feet, tugging his ludicrous gown into place around himself.

'Are we in danger?' I hissed at him. 'Who else is here?'

He gulped. 'The Mudéjar.'

I grabbed his hand, bundled him down the tower and we ran like fury back to the channel. Hoping he could swim, but undeterred if he couldn't, I threw him into the water and propelled him as fast as I could to the other side, where the two of us floundered out onto the bank. To my great relief, my boots and clothes were waiting for me.

'What's going on?' I asked the shivering Guido as I tugged my boots on. 'Who is the Mudéjar and how did you end up here?'

'He promised he'd help me,' Guido said through chattering teeth. 'I believed him. I was waiting for him when you found me.'

Dressed, I grabbed the boy again and we sprinted away from the channel and back to the path that ran alongside the River Seine. As soon as I found some cover – a dilapidated farmhouse in the middle of a field – I hustled Guido over to it and we crouched down out of sight.

'Now. Tell me everything.'

'He spoke to me weeks ago. He said he knew what I needed, and he understood how urgent it was. I *have* to have them removed before my voice breaks and my face gets hairy and – and…' Copious tears ran down his face and he made no attempt to stop them.

'*Who* spoke to you?'

'The Mudéjar. It was before Joseph died, though. I didn't know he was going to kill anyone, I swear it!'

'Guido, listen to me very carefully. You know who the

Mudéjar is. Perhaps you have always known. He's dangerous and he wants us all dead. I want you to tell me his name. Right now.'

The boy looked terrified. 'I can't, lord. If I say his name, he'll kill us both.'

'There's no one here but us, Guido. He can't kill us if he's not here. *Now, what is the Mudéjar's name?'*

But the boy shook his head. 'You don't understand, lord. He *is* here, the Mudéjar! He's here right now, he's always with us. *And he will kill us both!'*

For a brief, terrifying moment, I believed him. The mysterious Mudéjar, who has somehow followed us on our entire journey through Castile and France, never seen, never heard, always with us. But where? I looked frantically around. There was no one. I looked at Guido's frightened face, the hem of his gown scrunched into his hand, his body shaking with fear. Whatever I might think, Guido genuinely believed the Mudéjar was here and ready to carry out his threat.

'It's late afternoon, Guido.' I hoped my tone was reassuring. 'We're a long way from the *abbaye.* Come on, we must get back.'

Again, the boy shook his head. 'No, lord. Please go back without me, and forget me. Just forget I ever existed. I have to go back to the church.'

The desperation in his voice, and the plea for me to forget his very existence, touched me in a way I'd not known before. I stayed silent though. I judged it to be an hour or so before vespers, and I realised I was exhausted. Struggling back to the abbey with a terrified Guido, darkness falling, did not seem a good idea after all. I told him we'd wait until daylight.

'We'll have a look inside this farmhouse,' I said. 'If possible, we'll stay the night here.'

Not trusting him an inch, I grasped his wrist firmly and found the door to the house, a door almost off its hinges, and a house that had not been lived in for a long time. Not by people, that is. Rats scurried across the floor, bats lined up on the rafters and something larger shot out of the door as we entered. A smelly hovel, but better than the cold air outside. There was a rickety table by the far wall, and in a drawer I found a tallow dip and the means to light it. By the light of the dip, I looked around.

'There's a fireplace!' I exclaimed. It was in the middle of the room, and there was no chimney, so we'd have to contend with a smoky interior; that's if we could find any fuel to set fire to. Mutely, Guido pointed to a corner, where a small stack of firewood had been piled. I stood by the door so there was no chance of the boy making a run for it, and I directed him in the art of fire-lighting. After several failed attempts, he managed it, and immediately dropped down on his knees, holding out his hands to the blaze.

I wanted to dry his clothes, but he hugged his gown to him. 'Guido, I know you are self-conscious. But you can't stay in wet clothes, you'll be ill.'

'I don't care,' he muttered miserably.

'I care. Now remove your clothes.'

I draped all our clothes over a stool in front of the fire. Guido hugged his knees to his chest and refused to look at me. I was concerned about the night. How could I ensure the boy didn't get out while I was asleep? There was no way to bar the door and keep him in. I resolved to tie the two of us together with the laces from my shirt, though I said nothing of this to Guido.

'I'm hungry,' the boy said in a small voice.

'The Mudéjar was feeding you well?'

He nodded.

'I've been thinking about it all.' I tried to keep my tone light and neutral. 'You weren't taken from the *Abbaye Grestain* were you? You came here of your own volition.'

Again, he nodded.

'The Mudéjar arranged it all beforehand? He told you where and when to meet him?'

Another nod.

'Guido, you can tell me something about that, surely. You don't have to say the Mudéjar's name. Just tell me how he arranged to meet you, and what he's been doing to you.'

'I had to meet him outside the abbey near the road. I had to wear my girls' clothes and hide my hair under a cap. He had a cart with a canvas sheet, and I had to get into the cart and hide under the sheet. I didn't know where we were going, but he told me that when we got there he would see I got help.'

'What sort of help?'

'The surgery. Removing things from my body.'

'But you'd asked me about that, Guido! You knew I was going to give you my answer today! Is the Mudéjar a doctor? Could he do this as well as Yehudah could?' Though as I said the Jew's name, all I could see was him copulating with Aldara in the infirmary. Perhaps he isn't a doctor either. He didn't cure Thuban....

'The Mudéjar told me you would still say "No". He said you would never agree to it. He said he was my only hope and I believed him. Lord, *have* you changed your mind? What answer were you going to give me today?'

'The Mudéjar was right. I was going to refuse to allow it.' I spoke heavily, but it was the truth, after all. 'That other time,' I said slowly. 'When you were rescued by Rosa from the *Chateau de Boutemont*. Had you gone there willingly as well?'

'Oh no, lord! I was taken from the camp. Everything happened as I told it to you. Yehudah had to treat me for my injuries!'

'That is so. So why agree to go with him this time?'

The boy didn't answer.

'The Mudéjar killed the gatekeeper at the *Chateau de Boutemont*. He's a murderer, Guido. Why would you believe anything he says?'

'Because he's my only hope. I *am* going back to the church, you see. He'll be there, waiting for me. He knows I'll come back. I have to.'

I had no food with me, and both Guido and I were hungry. But the fire was warm, and the day had been long and tiring. Slowly, the boy's head slumped onto my shoulder. I tied his wrist to mine and I put my arm around him, and though he slept fitfully, I stayed wide awake. At some point during the night, he woke, needing a piss. I took him outside, still attached to me. It was a clear night, and, before we went back to the farmhouse, Guido pointed to the north star. 'We *could've* got back tonight. The star would've guided us.'

There were dangers other than losing one's way, I could have pointed out. As I looked at the sky, my dream returned to me in all its full, rich colours. Once again I saw Blue dancing in the garden, heard the splish-splash of the fountain, saw Thuban standing and sneering at me among the stars of the Draco constellation. *Thuban is a Muslim,* I thought. *I didn't know that before. Why has he never told us?*

We went back to the farmhouse, and I stoked up the fire, then sat down, leaning my back against the rough mud wall. I pulled Guido down, and again his head lolled onto my shoulder. With some difficulty, I extracted my parchment and quill from the pocket of my breeches and began to write about my dream last night, and the strange things that have taken place today.

Guido is sleeping as I write. He stirs and moves from time to time, his sleep disturbed. And I begin to see why, if it's going to be done at all, he needs to have his operation as quickly as possible. Looking into the fire you see strange shapes sometimes in the moving, living flames. This time, I see Thuban again, mocking me. He's brandishing the collarbone of Joseph of Arimathea, and my hand strays to my neck to touch my lanyard and feel the hard-edged shape of the shell that represents Saint James the Apostle. I wonder if Saint James is testing me. I have so many questions. What is the right thing to do for this poor boy by my side? How do I tackle the problem of a killer in our midst? Can I be sure I will bring my group safely home? Why does my wife ignore and despise me? And where the hell is she? If Saint James knows any of the answers, I beg him to reveal them to me. I hold his little shell in the palm of my hand, and I close my eyes to pray.

Guido moves again, and his head is heavy on my bare chest. I look down at the naked boy, and his problem is clear to see. It's not that I don't want to help him, I tell myself. Thuban dances angrily in the fireplace, clutching the bone that cured him. *Not the collarbone of Joseph of Arimathea,* he laughs. *Oh no, Lord Rory, you are very much mistaken. This bone is from Islam, from one of the many Messengers of God, perhaps from the Prophet himself, 'alayhi as-salām.*

I look away from the flames and from Thuban, who's not really there anyway. I'm trying to make sense of things, but I have only my unanswered questions. Guido cries out, his voice cracking. Mostly, he controls it. In his sleep, he cannot, any more than he can control his nightly ejaculation. Immediately afterwards, he wakes, deeply and desperately distressed. I am unable to comfort him.

'Is the Mudéjar a doctor?' I asked Guido in the darkness, and it was Yehudah I meant. Yehudah, the strange, taciturn Jew. Would he have murdered Joseph? And if so, why?

'I don't know, lord.'

'You don't know? Yet you will trust him to cut you up?'

'It's as I said, lord—'

'He's your only hope. Aren't you scared?'

'I'm terrified.'

'Guido, you are not going back to the church, and you are not going back to the Mudéjar.'

'But—'

'Listen to me. I will allow Yehudah to do this for you. We will start off for the abbey as soon as there's enough light to see by. And soon you will have your operation. But the Mudéjar won't be doing it.'

Guido said nothing. Tears splashed onto my hands, and the boy was speechless, but resting his head on my chest again, he slept well until morning.

24

GET HIM TO BLOODY TALK TO ME

I would not let Guido leave the farmhouse until I had checked everywhere. I looked over at the church beyond the creek – no sign of anyone. Birdsong indicated no cause for alarm either. Back in the farmhouse, Guido was huddled into a corner.

'I'm so hungry, lord, I can't think properly.'

'We'll get food from somewhere, but in the meantime you must not only think, you must also speak. I need to know what you meant last night, and you'll explain it all to me as we walk back to Grestain.' I hauled him to his feet, thinking what a ragamuffin he looked. The ancient shapeless gown was torn down one side and filthy all over, and he had no shoes. Well, there was nothing I could do about that. No doubt someone at the abbey would produce soap, needle and thread when asked. But walking even a couple of miles would be painful for the lad.

We set off straight away. Guido was valiantly silent about his sore feet and his grumbling stomach.

'Last night, Guido,' I began as soon as we were out of sight of the church, 'you told me the Mudéjar was here. You said, “He’s here right now, he’s always with us, and he’ll kill us both”. What did that mean?’

‘I’m not allowed to say.’

‘Look, I’m taking you away from that place, away from the Mudéjar and from the threats he made to you. And I’ve promised you the treatment you want so much. Yehudah will operate on you, I swear it. So tell me!’

But he looked down at his feet and shook his head.

‘What on earth are you afraid of?’ I asked, exasperated. ‘The Mudéjar can’t hurt you now; you’re with me! You’re safe, don’t you understand?’

He stopped walking then, so I had to stop too, and he looked up at me.

‘It is you that does not understand,’ he said carefully. ‘The Mudéjar is always with us. *Always.* And I’m grateful to you for agreeing to let me have the surgery, but it won’t change anything. The Mudéjar is going to kill us all in the end.’

He stood very still, allowing me to scrutinise his face. ‘I can see you don’t believe me,’ he said at last. ‘I can’t tell you any more; I can only repeat what I’ve already said: the Mudéjar is here, he’s here right now, he knows what we’re saying and what we’re doing.’

‘Tell me this one thing, then,’ I said eventually. ‘If he’s going to kill us all, why are you so anxious to have this operation?’

‘I was born a boy. I want to die a girl.’

We carried on walking. Some fishermen on the banks of the Seine sold me some bread and a few shellfish, and Guido ate it all ravenously.

‘Your daughter, monsieur?’ The fishermen were just making conversation, but I felt Guido tense up beside me.

'The daughter of a friend,' I answered, staring at the sea. As soon as Guido had eaten, we hurried away.

The thought of the Mudéjar being with us everywhere was spine-chilling. But how could a man be with us, yet invisible? How could he have travelled with us for so many miles without our knowing? And who the hell *was* he? We arrived at the *abbaye* an hour before noon, Guido practically dead on his feet. I carried the boy to the infirmary, where the infirmarer helped me to strip him and lay him in one of the beds. There are four beds, two on each side of the building, and as I looked up, I saw that two of the other beds were occupied, and one was screened off.

'It is your wife,' the monk informed me hastily. 'Unfortunately, she has been taken ill, and she has been here since terce yesterday.'

I hurried to her bedside, shoving the screen away. Rosa was awake. Her face looked ashen.

I knelt beside her and took her hand. 'What has happened? What's made you ill?'

'I do not know. I cannot keep any food down. There must be something wrong. I think I'm dying, lord. I am so sorry.'

My heart raced. I have had one wife die. I knew I must get better help for Rosa. 'Has Yehudah seen you?' I don't like the man at all, but he's supposed to be a physician.

Rosa shook her head. 'I need a bowl,' she said urgently, but it was too late, and she vomited onto the floor.

Seriously alarmed, I told the monk to summon Yehudah. 'I don't care where he is or what he's doing. Get him here now.' The man ran, and while he was gone I found a mop and a bucket of water. I sluiced the floor and cleaned everything up as best I could. Rosa, her hair clinging clammily to her face, was barely aware of my actions. She looked as if she were going to be sick again, so I kept a bucket, mop and cloths to hand.

Yehudah entered, hatless for once, the long, lank hair looking greasier than ever. He followed me to Rosa's bed. She'd vomited again, and my heart sank. No one can survive if they can't take nourishment. And without water she will soon die. Yehudah checked the colour of her tongue. He felt her forehead and tapped at her temples. He asked to examine her urine.

'We will see how she is tomorrow morning,' Yehudah pronounced, getting up. I knew what that statement meant: *I don't know what the matter is, and I won't know tomorrow either. That's if she even survives the night.*

Yehudah went over to talk to Guido. I stayed with Rosa. She fell asleep, looking pale and washed out on the pillow. I hadn't looked at the other occupant of the sickbeds, but saw now that it was Thuban. His eyes were closed, his breathing ragged.

Yehudah joined me. 'He does not have long.'

The famous waters of the River Carbec, together with the bone, whether it be from Joseph of Arimathea or not, had seemed to help him. But perhaps I hadn't had enough faith after all.

'And Rosa? Are we burying them both here in Normandy, Yehudah?'

He didn't answer me, and I felt real fear. I pulled the cockleshell out of my shirt, and eased the lanyard over my head.

'Do you want to pray over that?' Yehudah asked. 'For your wife and for this man?'

'If I do, they will be Christian prayers.'

'Of course. That is why I was asking. I can leave you, if you wish.'

But Thuban, according to my dream, is neither Christian nor Jew. '*You* pray for them,' I said roughly, ripping the cockleshell off the lanyard and thrusting it into Yehudah's hands. 'Saint James and his brother John were known as the "Sons of Thunder" during Christ's lifetime, because they were impetuous, rough fishermen. But God changed them into different people. He made them into saints. Use this icon, Yehudah. Change God's mind about Thuban and Rosa.'

I couldn't look at any of them, not Yehudah, nor any of the three desperate patients in that sad room. I had to leave. The infirmarer had not returned; presumably he thought Yehudah's presence sufficient. I could only hope he was right.

Xurxo and Kit were waiting for me in the abbey. They were full of questions. 'We don't know what's been happening! You disappeared, you came back with Guido, who's sick. Where did you go? What's going on?'

'I'll tell you. Let's go somewhere quiet.' We went to Kit's favourite apple trees and sat in the orchard for nearly two hours while I filled them in. Hearing myself recount the finding of Guido in the church tower and his belief in the Mudéjar's ability to make him into a girl, sent shivers through me.

'And Thuban's a Muslim?' queried Xurxo. 'What makes you think so?'

'I dreamt about him,' I explained again. 'And that damned constellation was in my dream as well. Draco and Thuban, they were both in the sky, and my warhorse, Blue, was talking to them.'

'Your warhorse was there?' Xurxo asked, doubtfully.

'She was looking for a different set of stars, the constellation called Pegasus. But we never found it. Instead,

Thuban said the collarbone of Joseph of Arimathea cured him, which meant it's *not* the collarbone of a Christian saint after all. He said it must be an Islamic bone.'

'This was all in your dream.' I heard the scepticism in Kit's voice and turned sharply to face him.

'It was in my dream, yes, but it was vivid and real, Kit. Somehow it led me to the church where Guido was waiting. *And* he knows who the Mudéjar is!'

'I reckon he's known about the Mudéjar all along,' Kit said. 'Guido is not what he seems.'

'What do you mean by that?' Xurxo said. 'Has he been pretending to us? He's been pretending to be female—'

'Oh, there's no pretence about that,' Kit said at once. 'Guido is convinced he should have been a girl. But where the Mudéjar's concerned, I think Guido has definitely been stringing us all along. He knows the man's identity, that's for sure.'

'What about Aldara?' I asked. So far, I have not told anyone that Aldara and Yehudah are lovers.

'Aldara is a woman who's trying to escape her destiny,' Xurxo said, as if he'd known this for a long time. 'See how it is for her? She thinks it is all settled, she is going to marry you and be Lady of Hambrig. This is very satisfactory for her, because, at nearly thirty-one years old, she's still unmarried, and likely to remain so. Then what happens? Far from her home, to which she cannot return without being shamed, you reject her and you marry a Castilian princess. This princess comes with a price tag, and it's a high price as well, yet you are willing to pay it, and you are willing to incur the wrath of Aldara's father. So she deduces, correctly, that this marriage is worth a great deal to you. But does she go back to Santiago? No, she continues her journey to Hambrig! Why? Because she still hopes for a future there, even if it is a very different one from that which her father planned for her.'

'She'll marry someone else?' Kit's tone showed lively interest. He always loves it when people talk like this.

'She will have to,' Xurxo said, nodding. 'She cannot live the rest of her life as a spinster, and her father is hoping to hear she has married Lord Rory in Hambrig. If King Xisco hears it is not Lord Rory, then the news, though unexpected, must be equally welcome.'

'Then who's she going to marry?' Kit asked, his eyes dancing.

'Joseph asked her, and she accepted. But that plan came to nothing when the poor man was murdered. There is now someone else I believe.'

I clicked my tongue in disgust. 'All right, enough speculation about Aldara's future. We need to get Guido to tell us who the Mudéjar is. He won't tell me. Any suggestions?'

'He will talk with the women. *The women,'* Xurxo repeated emphatically. 'Guido relates to them. Either Rosa or Aldara must get him to speak the truth about the Mudéjar.'

'Rosa is sick,' I said morosely, pulling up blades of grass from under the trees.

'Sick?' Kit sounded surprised. 'Are you sure, Rory?'

'I've seen her. She's very ill indeed.'

'Then it will have to be Aldara,' Xurxo said, 'and we must pray that your wife's health improves, Lord Rory.'

'I've left Yehudah with her.'

They looked at me as if I'd gone mad.

We found Aldara wandering by herself in the cloisters. She's taken to wearing the 'boys' clothes' most of the time now. Guido despises them, so Aldara may as well use them, I suppose.

'Have you seen Yehudah?' she asked.

'He's in the infirmary. And so is Guido, and I want you to talk to him.'

'Her. Not him. And her name is Sara.'

I ignored that. 'Get him to talk to you about the Mudéjar. We have to know the man's identity. He's got some sort of hold over Guido, so the boy feels too frightened to say what he knows. Get him to tell you, Aldara, and come straight back here.'

With an odd look at me, she walked off to the infirmary.

Kit said, 'Xurxo was right, Rory. Aldara knows time is not on her side. She may wish to marry, but it'll have to be soon.'

'Do you think Thuban is the Mudéjar?' It's been on my mind, ever since my dream revealed to me that Thuban's a Muslim.

'How can he be?' Xurxo cried in disbelief. 'Thuban is completely out of action, and has been for weeks!'

I didn't mention my theory that he'd only been pretending to be ill; in my heart I knew it was nonsense. The man can't possibly be the Mudéjar. But who the bloody hell *is* it then? Guido *has* to tell me. I can't simply rely on Aldara.

I have to speak with Guido myself. Call him 'Sara' if necessary, but get him to bloody *talk* to me.

25

TODAY I BECOME MYSELF

'Sara,' I said firmly.

The boy turned his head and looked at me in surprise. He pushed himself up onto his bony elbows and sat up properly. 'Is everything all right, lord?'

'No, everything is far from all right. My wife is ill, probably dying. Thuban is also dying. Joseph is dead, murdered by someone *whose identity you know.* And you are going to tell me who the Mudéjar is *right now.*'

Yet again, the boy looked terrified. 'Lord, if I could tell you I would, I really, really would! But I cannot. If I break my word to the Mudéjar, something awful will happen and it will be my fault. That's why I can't say anything.'

'What awful thing will happen, Guido? Sara, I mean.'

'The Mudéjar will kill you, lord. He has told me how he'll do it, and I believe him. I cannot be the cause of your death.'

'I can take care of myself, Guido. You should know that by now. The Mudéjar can try his luck, but I don't give him much of a chance.'

The boy shook his head. 'No, lord, you don't understand. He will and can do it. It's you who wouldn't have a chance.'

I frowned at him. How could he be so sure? What has the Mudéjar told him to make him believe these lies?

'I can tell you don't believe me,' Guido began, but he got no further. From the far end of the infirmary came a heart-rending cry which ended in a scream. I ran for the canvas sheet that screened off my wife's bed and flung it away. Rosa was leaning over the side of the bed, vomiting violently.

'Oh God, please help me,' she moaned, clutching her stomach with one hand and her head with the other. 'I just want to die. Please just let me die.'

'Guido!' I yelled. 'Get up and fetch someone!'

I did my best. I tried to soothe her; I fetched cool water and bathed her head, neck and wrists. I held her head as she retched. And I despaired.

The infirmarer came running, wringing his hands, bleating something about the abbot.

'He'll be here soon, lord,' the man said, skidding to a halt beside Rosa's bed. 'To administer the Last Rites to your lady—'

'No!' Guido appeared suddenly, flapping his hands. 'Not that! She isn't dying, sir. Lord Rory, your wife isn't dying, she isn't even ill!'

I swore at him. Rosa moaned in my arms, her face wet with tears and sweat, her body limp and unresponsive.

'Lord, I know what this sickness is.' He picked up the hem of his torn and useless gown and hurried to my side. 'The sickness is because your lady is expecting a child.'

The infirmarer's mouth fell open, and, after a moment of complete silence, he ran from the building.

I swung Guido round to face me. 'Are you sure, boy? Are you absolutely sure?'

'Yes, lord. I have seen it in my hometown many times. And...' he hesitated, blushing '... the women trust me, lord. They talk to me. I know how they are during the first few weeks of a pregnancy. Some don't feel bad at all, but many others are sick, some as bad as your lady. It lasts different lengths of time. Then they feel a lot better. And then they get big bellies.'

I hugged Rosa closer to me and she settled her head into my chest, her eyes closed, her breathing slowly steadying. I sat with her for hours, as it grew dark outside. No one disturbed us. There was no visit from the abbot after all, and the infirmarer stayed away too. Rosa slept peacefully, and there was no more vomiting.

As I held my wife close, Guido busied himself with clearing up. He disappeared outside for a short time, returning with a basket of rose petals, which he scattered on the floor around the bed. He produced a bowl of rose water, dipped his fingers into it and flung droplets into the air, scenting it with summer fragrance. Gradually, I lowered Rosa's head to her pillow. Guido and I changed the soiled bed covers for fresh ones pulled from one of the other beds. My wife slept peacefully on, and I tiptoed over to Thuban's bed to look at him.

'Guido, do you know much about Thuban? Do you know what's wrong with him?'

'Lord, I loved it when you called me "Sara". It made me feel strong and confident.'

Strong and confident! I was baffled. How could a girl's name do that? He'd have to be both strong and confident to be my squire, and ultimately, to be dubbed knight. Yet that was not the future he wanted. 'Sara, then,' I said heavily. 'What can you tell me about Thuban?'

'I can tell you just one thing. His real name is not Thuban.'

'I had a dream, Sara. In my dream, Thuban told me he's of the Islamic faith. Do you know if that's true?'

'It is so. He is a Muslim.'

'But he is not the Mudéjar?'

'No, lord. Thuban is not the Mudéjar.'

'Is he going to die here, Sara? In this abbey?'

'I can't foretell the future. But it is important he does not die here. We must take him to your country, and we must keep him alive until he gets there.'

'And how do we do that?'

'Aldara is a good nurse. Let her care for Thuban, and he will have the best chance.'

'Did you know Aldara is Yehudah's lover?'

'Yes, lord. Lady Rosa knows it too. Aldara hopes to marry Yehudah.'

'Does Yehudah love Aldara?'

'I do not think so, lord. I think Yehudah loves his work. I do not think he loves any woman. But he should marry Aldara, and the sooner the better.'

I looked sharply at Guido. He made a sign of his belly growing larger.

'Aldara? She's pregnant as well?'

When I asked him how he knew, he said Aldara has also been sick, but nothing like as bad as Rosa. I left the infirmary and found Aldara, who unapologetically confirmed Guido's story.

'How could you?' I raged at her. 'This is a complication we do not need!'

'Yet you do not blame Yehudah,' she observed. 'Is it my fault alone I am expecting a baby?'

'Oh, for God's sake!'

And I still don't know who the Mudéjar is! I had been determined to make Guido tell me, but instead he'd told me both the women are pregnant and Thuban's name is a false one. Guido stopped Rosa's sickness by telling her what was wrong with her. I have to be grateful to him for that. As for Thuban, he's a Muslim, but not the Mudéjar. I am no nearer the truth.

This morning I looked for a ship to take us across the Narrow Sea. At the port of Honfleur there were many fishing vessels, none of which was prepared to carry us to England. Sick men and pregnant women are unlucky passengers; nobody wanted us on board. On my way back to the *abbaye*, I met Guido hurrying towards me.

'Lord, we don't have to sail from Honfleur,' he panted. 'There are other places where we can find a vessel.'

'I daresay,' I acknowledged irritably. 'But they'll all say the same thing as these fellows, I imagine. We are not propitious cargo.'

'Try the boats at Fécamp. It's worth asking, isn't it?'

'Why Fécamp?'

'One of the monks mentioned it. I think they may use that port instead of Honfleur when they sail to England.'

'They sail to England? I didn't know that. Well, I'll give it a go.' But I was hot and tired from tramping to Honfleur and back, so I decided to leave it until the next day. I've taken Guido's advice with regard to Thuban, sacking the infirmarer and putting Aldara in charge of nursing him. Aldara's opinion is that every day we can keep Thuban resting in bed gives him more chance of making it alive to Hambrig. As for Aldara herself, she seems happy and more at peace now it's known she's pregnant by Yehudah. Yehudah is as stern and unsmiling as ever, barely talking to anyone and no longer interested in Aldara, now it's known she's carrying his child.

On Thursday morning Guido and I took a couple of mules and rode to Fécamp, a good thirty miles away. It took all day. We had to cross the Seine, and finding a bridge took us out of our way by about ten miles. So it was after vespers when we arrived.

'Let me negotiate our passage,' Guido offered, as we clopped our weary, dusty way to the harbour.

'As a girl?'

He didn't answer that, but slid down from his mule and ran barefoot to the quayside. I watched him animatedly talking with the fishermen there, and saw one of them pointing to a larger trader anchored in the sound. Guido nodded enthusiastically and pointed at me, where I still sat on my mule, my legs dangling almost to the ground. I waited, wondering how much I was going to have to pay for our voyage on that fine-looking ship.

'It's all arranged, lord,' Guido said with a grin, taking back the reins of his mule and leaping up onto its back. 'We're sailing on that ship there in four days' time. We can stay in the inn tonight, ride back to Grestain tomorrow and get back here with everyone, including Thuban's cart, by high water on Monday. Have I done well?'

'You *may* have done exceedingly well,' I said to him. 'But

you haven't yet told me the price of all this. I hope you drove a hard bargain. I am running out of funds.'

'Er, well, we don't actually have to pay anything. Only our board and lodging for tonight.'

I didn't believe him. Why should the master of that large and impressive-looking ship take us all to England for nothing? Guido shrugged. 'He says he's going there anyway; he has a cargo of wine to sell to English wine merchants. He's short-handed, and I've promised that you and Kit and Xurxo will help crew his ship.'

He hurried off to find us a room in the inn, which turned out to be both reasonably priced and reasonably comfortable, so all-in-all a good day's work. As we prepared for bed after a tasty supper in the inn, I congratulated the boy on his achievements today.

'And you *are* going to keep your promise, aren't you, lord?' he asked anxiously. 'Yehudah is going to operate on me soon?'

'I don't know how soon,' I hedged. 'We have to take ship for England in four days' time, haven't we. Then we'll be journeying north-east to Mallrovia, and—'

'Lord, I can't wait that long. You know I can't. You remember what happened in that farmhouse? It happens almost every night, and I can't bear it. And when my voice changes, it'll be too late. I want Yehudah to do it as soon as we get back to the abbey.'

'That won't give you long enough to recover.'

'I'll be all right. I can travel with Thuban in the cart until my wounds heal.'

I told Guido to blow out the tallow dip, which was the only light we had in the room, but he refused. He confronted me again with his demand, invoking my promise to him. So I agreed. As I lay on my back, unable to sleep, I thought it more than likely Guido would die under Yehudah's knife, and would never make it to England, much less Hambrig. And if that happened, I might never know the identity of the Mudéjar.

I blew out the flame and crossed to the window. It faced out to sea, and the waves were silver in the moonlight. With the cold wind ruffling my hair and fingering my bare chest, I made a decision for the morrow.

I woke up late. Guido was already awake and out of bed. He was organising a rough breakfast of oatmeal slops and rye bread. Rough – but filling. He looked eager to go, and he couldn't stop smiling.

'What are you so pleased about?' I growled at him.

'It's today, isn't it.' He beamed. 'Today I get rid of my boy parts. Today I stop becoming a man. Today I become *myself*.'

26

A CROOKED GRIN

The ship is nearly ready, and we've been told a boat will put out from her and pick us up from the beach in a few hours' time. We're all here now, and last night we camped on the shore. In spite of everything, we've made it to the French coast, and we're now a stone's throw from England.

As everyone slumps around the campfire, I take out my journal, and I look at each person in turn. Starting with my wife.

Rosa is feeling much better now. Yehudah, unsmiling, told me it's her mind that has cured her; her mind has told her she isn't ill, simply pregnant. She's still sick from time to time, but she no longer believes she's dying, thank goodness. I'm grateful to Yehudah, I suppose, though he didn't diagnose her pregnancy. It was Sara who did that.

Sitting next to Rosa is Aldara. She doesn't let being pregnant stop her riding her mule and bantering cheerfully with everyone. She's a survivor. And now I wish I hadn't written that, for someone I respect a great deal once told me Rupert was a survivor, but it turned out he wasn't. Yehudah is still regularly taking advantage of Aldara.

Thuban lies in the cart, sometimes awake, more often asleep, but still, somehow, alive. Aldara tends him, and so does Xurxo. They are both devoted to him and are determined he will make it to Hambrig. I wouldn't put money on it.

Kit, sitting on the other side of the campfire, is withdrawn. He's not usually like this, and I wonder what's the matter with him. He spends a lot of time alone, playing my gittern, singing softly to himself. Sad songs, always.

I look around for Xurxo, and I see him talking quietly with Sara. Xurxo, I've come to realise, is one of the most sensible men I have ever met. He knows when to speak and when to keep silent. He cares for Thuban with genuine compassion, and he boosts everyone's spirits with jokes and light-heartedness.

Yehudah is unpopular with everyone except Aldara. He's only here because his money has paid for much of our accommodation on this journey, and because his skills as a physician have been needed. But I'd much rather I hadn't needed him for either of those things. Now we're so nearly in England, I think we can do without his gold. As for his medical skills – well, more on them later. Suffice to say we can definitely do without those as well. Before we get on board the ship tomorrow, I'm going to tell him to head back to Castile. In fact, I'll do that as soon as I have finished my writing.

And what of Sara, whose face is permanently contorted in pain? I will relate exactly what happened to the boy, Guido. First he was stripped and made to lie on his back on a table in the infirmary, his body tense with dread, his eyes full of hope. Under Yehudah's directions,

Xurxo, Kit and the infirmarer held the boy's legs and arms to keep him still. But just as Yehudah was sharpening his knife, the abbot came in and demanded to know what was going on. When he saw Guido's naked body on the table, he made his own deductions, and, in a rage, he ordered the whole lot of them out of the infirmary. Xurxo and Kit let go of Guido's legs, and Guido sprang up, clutching some garment to his loins, while the abbot ranted about acts of sacrilege in God's holy temple. They decamped to a barn on the other side of a small field, but the infirmarer, under the abbot's orders, naturally refused to go with them.

I'd hoped not to have anything to do with the grizzly business, but it was at this point I was roped in to help. So there was Guido on some makeshift table; Kit, Xurxo and I holding him down, and Yehudah looming over him like the Grim Reaper. I had to look away, and later I learnt that the others couldn't watch either. So none of us witnessed Guido lose his manhood, but we all felt him shudder and shake, and we heard his screams. Guido suffered for his emancipation from maleness. He passed out, and Yehudah continued in silence, flinging bits of Guido's flesh into the hay and dabbing at the child's body with the hem of his dirty robe. Finally he took a needle and a length of thread, which he ran through his teeth before suturing up the wound. Then the tall Jew strode from the barn, no doubt pleased with his butchery. I forced myself to look down at Guido. The whole groin area was a mess. There was blood everywhere, and fragments of flesh clung to the edges of the wound. Yehudah had not cut cleanly.

'How will he piss?' Xurxo whispered. He was also gazing down at the chaos, tears running down his cheeks.

'I don't know,' I said thickly. 'This has been a disaster.'

'Why the *hell* wasn't I involved in this?' Aldara stood in the barn doorway, her eyes blazing. 'Why did nobody tell me what was happening? I should have been here! I would have made sure Sara was all right!' She stalked into the barn and approached the table. I wanted to shield her from the sight of poor Guido's mutilation, but she pushed through all of us.

Xurxo and I fell back, but Kit stayed where he was, his hand on Guido's brow, smoothing and soothing. Around his shoulder was the strap of my gittern. He touched it and raised an eyebrow at Aldara. She nodded. Kit unslung the gittern, pulled up a small stool and sat down. He began to strum the strings and then to sing. The song was sonorous and strong, not soothing, quiet or pretty. There was no break between songs, either. When Kit finished one song, he simply began the next straight away, and hours went by with this music in all our ears. While Kit played and sang, Aldara worked. She told Xurxo and me exactly what she wanted. Yehudah's knife was discovered tossed into the hay, and Aldara retrieved it. I asked if she needed fire to hold the blade in. I have seen Sir Stephen do this.

Xurxo and I made fire using friction sticks, letting the sparks fall into a small heap of hay that we piled inside a ring of stones. As the fire took hold, Aldara held the knife blade in it until it glowed red. Xurxo, under Aldara's instructions, leant over Guido's chest, keeping the child still, while at the same time ensuring he couldn't see what was happening. Aldara gave me the worst job of all, and just writing about it has made me spew again. It was I who had to pull at the fragments of flesh so that Aldara could cut cleanly through them. The remains of a young boy's genitals had to be cut free and then tidied neatly away. I can't say I didn't disgrace myself, but Aldara said nothing; she could see I was doing my best. More stitches were inserted, and this time the needle was also heated in the fire. Yehudah's embroidery was either removed or improved. By the end, Guido's body was red and raw, and I still didn't know how he'd be able to urinate.

Aldara, still grimly furious, said she'd sit with him all night. Kit also stayed. There was no sign of Yehudah, and Xurxo and I needed to get some fresh air. The two of us stayed up all night talking in the refectory; there was no way we could have slept. We avoided talking about the boy in the barn, discussing everything else, so long as it wasn't that. Rosa joined us at some point during the night and offered to get food for us. I didn't think I'd ever be able to eat again, but when the cold meat and pickles arrived, I found I was ravenously hungry.

We were sitting at one of the trestle tables, and after a while we must all have fallen asleep, our heads on the table. I was shaken awake by one of the brothers and came to with a start. Then I remembered. It was just daylight, and I ran from the abbey, heading out to the barn. I was convinced Guido would be dead.

Kit was asleep, my gittern lying carelessly in the straw. The fire had gone out. Aldara sat by Guido's head. There was a rough linen sheet over the boy's body, and I couldn't tell if he were alive or dead. Wordlessly, I looked at Aldara.

'Sara will survive this,' she said carefully.

I tried to read between the lines. Sara will survive this. Not, Sara will be all right. And definitely not, Sara's doing well and making a great recovery.

'Will she be able to be – to be a normal girl?' What a

stupid question, I thought angrily as soon as I'd uttered the words.

'A normal girl? Depends what you mean by that. She'll never be able to have a child. She won't even be able to have sex with a man. But she doesn't have boys' genitals anymore, so she won't *become* a man. And that, I think, will be enough.'

The question had to be asked. 'How will she piss?'

'She will have to work that out for herself. A hole has been left, and I've made sure it won't close up. But it won't be easy for her to adjust, and it will be very painful at first.'

Guido travelled the thirty miles to Fécamp in the cart with Thuban. He's in constant pain, yet he's told me he's happy, and when he's not crying, he's smiling. He is ridiculously grateful to Yehudah; at some point I'm going to tell him exactly how much he owes Aldara.

I've now spoken with Yehudah, who is chillingly adamant he's coming with us all the way to Hambrig. I know why, of course. He has to make sure I deliver Alfonso's damned letter to Jabir, and that Jabir and Joan do actually begin their journey to Alfonso's court in Seville. I snarled something at him, but he shrugged it off with his usual severe expression and walked stiffly away.

'He doesn't care,' Kit observed, sauntering across the beach to join me. 'He only cares about his stars, constellations and cosmic bloody algorithms. Alfonso pays him a fortune, you know. King Alfonso X wants to go down in history as the man who made the first set of accurate, usable astronomical tables, and Yehudah is going to make that happen for him. What you or anyone else here thinks of him doesn't matter in the slightest.'

'He's no physician then? I thought he was! It's why I let him loose on Sara with a knife!'

'He knows about anatomy. But his experience of doctoring is pretty limited, I'd say. Did he know your wife was pregnant, Rory? No, I didn't think so. An experienced physician would have known straight away.'

'The infirmarer didn't realise either,' I said bitterly. 'Only Sara knew.'

And now we're ready to cross the Narrow Sea; the master's beckoning and a small boat is scudding over the waves and crunching her keel on the beach. Time to stop scribbling.

I mustered my group and we made our way to the boat. Sara and Thuban were lifted aboard. The rest of us had to wade in up to our knees; further, in the case of Aldara, the shortest of us. I carried Rosa in my arms and laid her carefully on one of the boat's side-benches. As we pushed off from the shore, I looked back at the coast of France. We've sold our mules and our donkeys, and our possessions that have travelled all this way in strong saddlebags are now packed in canvas bundles and leather satchels. Yehudah's belongings are in a wooden crate that has been with him from the beginning. As for the cart, we sold that too. I'll have to buy another when we get to England.

There are roughly eighty miles of water between Fécamp and Hastings. Already, though, Sara looked green and Yehudah was clenching his teeth. We'd barely set sail, but the wind was stronger than I'd thought it would be, the water was choppy and the ship was heeling hard over. The sea hadn't looked this bad from the shore; I remembered sunshine glinting off the water, the waves appearing small and harmless. Now we were in the big trading ship, and the waters mounted menacingly, the vessel heaved and rolled, while the sky had darkened and rain looked imminent. I'd never known such a sudden change in the weather.

I looked down at Rosa. She was sleeping, a damned good thing. Yehudah was seasick, not just once but many times. When I looked for him, I couldn't see him, and I guessed he was spewing his guts out in the stern of the ship. Kit is hardy, not given to seasickness, but even he looked unsure of himself. Aldara was the worst affected. She leant over the leeward rail and moaned in distress, clutching her stomach. The green waves swirled beneath her, the ship bucketed alarmingly and Aldara's feet kept leaving the deck. I secured her to the rail with the fall of one of the halyards, tying it around her thickening waist. That line saved her life a dozen times, as the poor woman's clammy fingers slipped off the rail and she fell to the deck.

Sara could do nothing for herself. The misery of seasickness, added to the pain of her wounds, made the passage torture. She lost consciousness, and I kept her beside me. One of the seamen threw a tarpaulin over her.

'The lass looks cold,' he said quietly. 'You've chosen a bad day for this passage to England. And an unsound, leaky vessel to make it in. Let's hope we get to the other side.'

I looked at Thuban. He had my cockleshell around his neck; Yehudah must have fastened it there. Thuban was not in such a bad way as some of the others. Because he was so obviously ill, he'd been made comfortable and had been protected right from the start. He had bundles of waterproof canvas stashed around him, and he was wedged into a safe place just abaft the mizzen mast. I leant down and pulled the cockleshell off him. Clutching it, I found the rough edges biting into my hand oddly reassuring. On the weather side, Xurxo looked like he was enjoying himself. A sailor wearing a greasy apron had brought out a dish of potage earlier. Xurxo was the only one of us who accepted a portion of the stuff, and he drank it down, smacking his lips in satisfaction. The smell of it set all the sufferers off again, and they hung grimly over the side and emptied their stomachs into the sea.

I gripped the cockleshell of Saint James while I prayed. I prayed we would make it to England, because that sailor had been right. This ship, though she'd looked so fine at anchor, leaked like a sieve. High above me, the mast creaked and moaned. The wind howled through the rigging, and around my feet swirled a great deal of water that shouldn't have been there. When Aldara's fingers slipped off the rail again and she dropped like a stone to the deck, the bilge water closed over her head. Kit sprang across and lifted her out of danger.

'Captain!' I cried out, standing on the dangerously heaving deck, my arm wrapped tightly around the mast. 'Are we sinking? We're taking in a lot of water!'

He took no notice.

Kit looked across at me, Aldara's limp body in his arms. I shouted to him to stay on the leeward side. I had to bellow to be heard over the noise of the screaming wind and the surging of the vessel through the waves. But she was definitely settling.

Xurxo noticed it too. He put down his tankard of potage, and now pointed to it. 'Look! When I first set this down, the water barely touched the bottom of the tankard. Now it's halfway up! We're sinking!'

I pulled Rosa closer to me. We must surely be nearly halfway across by now. I tried to ask Xurxo if he thought so too, but it was a waste of breath. The winds had risen again, the gale shrieked through the rigging, and my words were shredded as soon as I'd uttered them.

The storm raged on, and the wretched ship sank lower in the water with each mile we covered. When I looked astern, I could not see France at all, and when I gazed ahead, I couldn't see England either. Steep, grey, solid-looking walls of water travelled unrelentingly towards us, breaking as we crashed through them, surging on past, then vanishing. Rain fell relentlessly, the drops like tiny daggers, penetrating every item of clothing we wore and stinging our skin as they did so.

'Can this possibly get any worse?' I muttered.

'Oh yes,' said the sailor who'd covered Sara with the tarpaulin, and though his voice was quiet, I could hear him clearly. He was right in front of me, bending down to check that Sara was covered securely. 'Yes, it can get worse, and it probably will. Do not expect everyone to survive this crossing, Lord Rory.' He was standing again, looking straight at me. I thought I saw honesty as well as compassion in his eyes. Someone shouted to him from forward in the boat, and he turned. A sail had to be got in. The seaman cast off halyards from a belaying pin nearby and let the rope out hand over hand. They were hard, calloused sailor's hands, good at their job. But something was sticking out of his closed fist, and I gasped. He flashed me a crooked grin.

27

THE ROAD HEADING NORTH

The sail was handed, and the boat rocked back to a more even keel. But then one of those rogue waves came along, a mass of grey water, hitting the boat amidships, pushing her over till she was lee rail under. And, to my horror, Rosa rolled away from me. I was certain I had a strong hold on her, even when the wave struck us, but it couldn't have been strong enough. As my wife rolled down the sloping, uneven deck, cracking her head on the mast-step and bruising her body on ring-bolts and metal fastenings, she cried out. The water rose over her head.

I launched myself forwards, falling onto my face on the heaving deck. My arms were flung out, my fingers stretched to their limits, reaching for Rosa. They closed only on cold saltwater, water which filled my lungs, so I could not breathe. Groans, creaks and horrible-sounding bangs echoed all around. Surely the ship was breaking up? I turned my head, gasping for air. Strong arms lifted me and flung me to the side. It was the same sailor.

'My wife!' I spluttered, pointing down the deck, unsure if Rosa were even still on board.

'He's trying to save her!' a voice yelled in my ear. It was Kit, his hair plastered to his scalp, water cascading everywhere, sluicing down the sails and bubbling up through the deck. 'That man's trying to save Rosa. Pray that he succeeds!'

I could not make out what was happening. There was too much water everywhere, and far too much noise. The master was directing the crew, and the crew, who were short-handed, couldn't cope.

We should never have put to sea. Never. Why did the master agree to sail? Surely he must have known we were in for a storm. I have never experienced a storm like this one. Perhaps he hasn't either. And that sailor is right. We won't survive this.

Kit was clinging to the guardrail, and I tried to tell him to find something more solid to hold on to.

That rail will go; it will simply vanish into the sea.

And no sooner had I made Kit transfer his grip to the mainmast, than that's exactly what happened. There was a splintering and cracking from bow to stern. The guardrail disappeared, leaving the flooded decks exposed, and showing that the deck planking was level with the sea itself.

'I have lashed her to the mast,' the sailor said to me, suddenly by my side again. 'She is alive, though only just.'

I grabbed his fist and pulled his fingers open. Surprised by my action, he reacted too slowly to stop me. So I was able to retrieve the collarbone of Joseph of Arimathea from his grasp.

'How did you get this?' I shouted, almost beside myself. We were all going to drown in the Narrow Sea, so what did anything matter now? 'This is a sacred relic! How did you come by it?'

He shook his soaking wet locks. I blinked water from my eyes, but the sailor wasn't there anymore. I slumped down onto the deck, letting go of the mainmast, not caring now if I were washed away. Next to me, Kit's legs were slowly buckling, and he too slid down the mast.

'Look!' Kit shouted, his eyes raised to the sky.

It was clearing. Around us, the waves subsided and the storm blew itself out. Within an hour, our unseaworthy vessel was wallowing in a greasy calm.

The master strode along the deck, checking his crew, his equipment and his ship. When he came near me, he said, 'What did you do?'

'I? Nothing!'

'*You* caused this storm and all the damage it has wrought. I would never have set sail if I had known of these conditions. This is *your* doing. You are bad luck to us all!'

He turned angrily away, sending his sailors on their various missions to repair the ship, while I untied Rosa from the mast and held her tightly to me. The unknown sailor had saved her from drowning, but it was the collarbone of Joseph of Arimathea that had quelled the storm. I had absolutely no doubt about that.

The ship rocked gently on the calm surface of the Narrow Sea. I looked around for my group. Kit was nearby, massaging his arm which had been badly knocked when the sail came down. Xurxo sat on a side-bench. He held Thuban in his arms.

'How's Thuban?' I scarcely dared hope the sick man had survived such a beating.

'He is still with us,' Xurxo said forlornly. 'But the lee guardrail broke, and Aldara was washed over the side.'

Poor Aldara.

And poor Xisco, who has now lost two daughters because of me.

'Guido?' I asked, looking wildly around for him. I knew

he'd been with Aldara, the two of them hanging limply over the lee rail in agonies of seasickness.

'I am here, lord.' Guido slithered over the wet deck, tears streaming down his face. 'Aldara is dead! I tried to hold on to her, but I couldn't! The wind was too strong for me! I can't bear it, lord. I can't bear it.' He broke down completely.

Xurxo beckoned, and Guido crawled over to crouch on the bench next to him. We were a sorry-looking lot. Our clothes were ripped, leaving us with only fragments of cloth. Our hair was wild and our eyes wilder. We were soaked to the skin. Xurxo had lost his boots, and I couldn't imagine any of our carefully hoarded possessions had survived.

'You don't ask after me, but I am here still,' said Yehudah's nasal voice from behind me.

I twisted round and stared up at him. He still had his clothes *and* his boots. How he'd managed to stay looking so complete was a mystery. 'Yehudah! I'm glad you have survived this terrible storm. Where were you when the waves lashed us all to pieces?'

'Where was I? I was in the hold, taking care of our belongings.'

In the hold! What a place to be during such a tempest! How would you cope below decks, unable to see or know what was happening? He must have heard the terrible groaning noises all ships make, but which are vastly magnified when the ship is in distress. He'd have been thrown violently about, crashing into the ship's sides, perhaps breaking bones and sustaining terrible injuries. He'd have been in the pitch dark the entire time, not even knowing which way up he was. How could he have been 'taking care of our belongings'?

'When I realised the storm was going to be of life-threatening proportions,' Yehudah announced pompously,

'I made the decision to go below and keep hold of my instruments. They are valuable in themselves, and extremely precious to me. I speak of course of my astrolabe, my Arabic treatises and my quadrant and sundial. These I have carried with me all the way from Toledo, and I do not intend to be parted from them. So, in the ship's hold, I first located my crate of instruments and then made sure it was protected from harm. Then I sought and found the bags and bundles that belong to the rest of us, and I used them to cushion my precious crate. I lashed everything securely to the bolts and fastenings I found below deck, and finally I tied myself tightly to the whole unwieldy parcel. And thus I ensured that, if we went to the bottom of the sea, I would at least be with my beloved astrolabe. But if we did not, and the storm abated, all our possessions would be saved from loss and damage.'

I scrambled to my feet, aware of how sodden and wrecked I must look compared with Yehudah. I couldn't like the man, but I admired him. It was Kit who told him, gently, about Aldara. But Yehudah scarcely blinked. He bowed his head in acknowledgement of the news and carefully sat down between Xurxo and me.

'How is the Muslim?' Yehudah asked, looking at the man in Xurxo's arms.

'Alive,' Xurxo said shortly.

'You have done well to keep him so.'

It was another two days before our ship limped into Hastings harbour. In that entire time, the master didn't utter a word to me. Kit, Xurxo and I helped with the ship as much as we could, Xurxo reluctantly leaving Thuban in Yehudah's care. Guido was constantly tearful and upset.

'He did this, you know,' he sobbed. 'He did it. The Mudéjar. He killed Aldara.'

'No, Sara, it was the storm,' Xurxo said gently. 'Aldara was weakened by seasickness, and she was swept into the sea when that giant wave hit us.'

'But it was the Mudéjar who made the wave come! He killed Aldara!'

Xurxo looked over Guido's head at me and shrugged. We all know Aldara was Guido's friend. Aldara helped Guido more than anyone else.

'Others lost their lives too,' I pointed out. Two crewmen were washed overboard at the same time as Aldara.

'The Mudéjar doesn't care about them. He's picking us off one by one. I told you he would, Lord Rory!'

I looked at my group standing on the quayside. Thuban was lying on various bundles of our things. Xurxo, looking like some ne'er-do-well in his ragged clothes, stood protectively next to him. Yehudah gazed aloofly at the distant hills, his long black robe billowing in the English breeze. Rosa had regained some strength, but she couldn't stand for long, so she sat on Yehudah's precious crate. Her gown was ripped in many places, and her hair had straggled out of her wimple and lay in a tangled mass down her back.

Kit was hunting for carts, ponies, anything to get us home. I'd briefed him and given him money. He looked more presentable than either Xurxo or me; he's resourceful and has a way with words. Guido wouldn't leave Rosa's side. But he was also in pain.

His tear-streaked face looked up at me. 'Lord, I don't think I can ride. I know you'll say I've brought this on myself, and it's true. But it hurts so much there, it hurts all the time.'

'You won't have to ride,' Rosa said to him. 'Lord Rory has told Kit you need to travel in the cart with Thuban and me.'

Kit returned with a group of four farm lads who brought three horses and two sturdy wagons, one larger than the other.

'The wounded and the sick ride in this cart,' Kit said, indicating the larger wagon. 'The smaller one takes all our stuff.'

All our stuff. Yehudah said he'd guarded it, but that hadn't stopped it getting sodden. I had carefully dried my gittern, not letting it get too much sun on it, and hoping the glue hadn't completely dissolved in the seawater. Morosely, Kit told me not to expect to play it ever again. As for our other 'stuff', there's little of it, to be honest. A few bundles of clothes, which we'd hung on the rigging to dry during the two days we sailed to England in brilliant, hot sunshine. And Yehudah's crate of course, a large wooden box, encased in stitched, waxed canvas, so the contents will be dry and unharmed. Or so he tells us.

The money I'd given Kit wasn't enough, apparently, so I paid the farmhands what they wanted, and we began to load the wagons, Xurxo and I passing boxes, parcels and bundles up to Kit.

'Hey, what's this?' Kit called down. I'd just handed him my gittern in its leather case, and Kit was holding it in one hand, while in the other he held out a piece of parchment.

My blood ran cold. The words screamed inside my head: *Anyone who is not for me is against me.* I'd seen those messages too many times not to recognise this one.

'It was sticking out of your gittern case, Rory,' Kit called again.

'But that's impossible!' I cried, scrambling up into the cart. 'I just gave you the gittern to pack, and there was no note sticking out of it!'

'Perhaps you didn't see it?'

Didn't see it? Does he think I'm blind or something? I yanked the note from his hand and tore it open.

> *Anyone who is not for me is against me. The plain-looking woman from Smander was getting too nosy, that's why she had to die. Nonetheless, she was not next on my list, so you will be punished for interfering with my plans. But it does not matter because in the end you will all die because you are all against me.*
>
> *The Mudéjar*

I didn't read it aloud. I didn't need to. Everyone knew it was from the Mudéjar. How *could* this note have got into my gittern case? I was looking at the thing only a few moments before I handed it to Kit.

'Show me exactly where you found it.'

The soft leather bag that my gittern lives in has a drawcord at its neck. Kit showed me how the folded parchment had been protruding from the neck of the bag.

'But that means the cord had been untied, and then retied around the note. How could that have been done *after* I passed it to you? I'm certain the parchment wasn't there when I handed the instrument up to you, Kit. This whole thing is impossible!'

'Wait,' Kit said, sitting down suddenly on Yehudah's crate. 'You passed it to me. I put it down over there while I moved these packages around; I wanted to make a space for the gittern where it would be safe in case we hit a rut in the road. I only laid it down for a few moments though. Hardly any time at all…'

'But it was *enough* time,' Xurxo declared. 'You put the gittern down on the other side of the wagon, Kit. We were all looking at *this* side of it. A man standing on the other side could have managed the knot, slipped the note in and tied it up again. We would not have seen. He must have been very quick—'

'—and very good at knots!' I finished angrily. 'That sailor! The one who helped Guido—'

'Which one was that?' Kit scanned around. But Hastings is full of sailors. Our man looked nothing special.

'He had the collarbone of Joseph of Arimathea,' I told them urgently. 'I don't know how he got hold of it, but I took it off him. And straight after I did, the storm abated and the waves calmed down.'

'And the ship was sound again,' Kit said quietly, as if to himself. But he was right. The ship, which had seemed to be breaking up all around us, once the wind and sea had calmed, had somehow managed to continue her voyage and sail into port.

'Where is the relic now?' Xurxo asked.

I had it with me, but a more important question occurred to me. 'Where is Yehudah?' I was suddenly convinced again that Yehudah must be the Mudéjar. He'd had the opportunity to push Aldara into the sea, *and* the opportunity to put the message into my gittern bag.

'Yehudah's not our man, Rory,' Kit said quickly. 'He's over there, look.'

I followed Kit's pointing finger and saw Yehudah standing next to Guido. He was stroking the boy's hair in a way that made my skin crawl. Yehudah couldn't have put the message into the bag, and now I was convinced the sailor from the ship's crew had done this thing. Also, I reasoned, if it had been Yehudah who pushed Aldara to her death, he would not, in the message, have blamed me for it. The Mudéjar has a clear agenda on the order in which we must be killed.

I told Kit and Xurxo my theory about the sailor. But Kit responded quickly. 'It's not necessarily him. Maybe the Mudéjar told the sailor to put the message into the gittern bag. Maybe he was just doing as someone asked.'

'Well, let's just get going as quickly as we can,' Xurxo cried, unsettled by the whole business. And I wholeheartedly agreed with him. We finished loading in double-quick time, got Thuban, Rosa and Guido comfortable in the big wagon and hitched the ponies up. Xurxo was driving the smaller cart; Kit and I, the larger one. And as the sun sank behind the high ground to the west, we rolled onto the road heading north.

28

THE TRUTH ABOUT THE MURDERER

It's my intention to find hostels, inns or monasteries for our lodgings each night. Camping under the stars is all well and good when everyone's hale and hearty, and when the nights are warm. This time of year the weather's getting colder, the nights are distinctly chilly, and, moving northwards, you really feel it. Add to that the fact that Thuban is dying, Guido is in pain and Rosa is pregnant. Those three need comfortable beds to sleep in.

The first night was no problem. We were still close to the port, and we easily found a house where we could rent two rooms and where the beds weren't too flea-bitten. We had some sort of supper in the tavern, the food being plentiful and filling. A good start to this final leg of our journey, and I was thankful for it.

Thuban, Xurxo, Yehudah and Kit took one of the rooms, but I don't believe Xurxo got any sleep, for he sat up all night tending to Thuban, who's drifting in and out of consciousness. When he's conscious he's very demanding. He can't help it, we all know that, but it's Xurxo who bears the brunt. Thuban is clinging on to life until he meets Jabir.

This is what sustains him, the knowledge that my alchemist from Persia is waiting with the miraculous Elixir of Life, which, once administered, will make Thuban whole again. It makes more sense to me now I know Thuban is a Muslim. His faith is sustaining him, together with the knowledge that his deliverance will come from a fellow Believer.

In the other room, Guido and Rosa shared a bed, and I lay on a straw palliasse. All night long Guido moaned and shifted. Sometimes he screamed in torment, and guests in other rooms banged angrily on the wall. I gritted my teeth. When the third bout of screaming started, I jumped up and went to him; he was hot and feverish.

'Guido, in the morning Yehudah will look at your wound,' I said, hoping he could hear me. I put my hand on his forehead; he was burning up. I began to think the Mudéjar's prediction was right; in the end we will all die before we get home.

'Yehudah?' Rosa sat up and stared at the shaft of moonlight coming through the narrow window. 'Remember Yehudah did not manage the operation well. It was Aldara who patched Sara up.'

'Well, Aldara can't look after him now,' I said. 'And Yehudah is the best we've got.'

'I disagree,' my wife said. 'I *strongly* disagree. But the wound does need treating. Xurxo is good with illness. You must fetch him. You must also stop thinking this is Guido, a boy. This is Sara, and even you are going to have to accept this.'

'I'll speak to Xurxo in the morning,' I said wearily. I thought Sara was dying. Sara. Not Guido. Born as a boy, died as a girl. That was what she wanted, wasn't it?

'The morning may be too late,' said my wife, firmly. 'Get Xurxo here now.'

'Rosa, how is the baby?' I asked suddenly. Since Sara told me Rosa was pregnant, I had not mentioned the baby once. If she'd miscarried, I wouldn't have known. Rosa would have coped with the loss by herself. Perhaps she would have confided in Aldara or in Sara. But not in me. Not in her husband.

Her dark eyes widened. 'The baby? Lord, this is a strange question for the middle of the night.'

'I wish to know if you're still carrying our child.'

It wasn't how I'd meant to say it, but before Rosa could respond, Sara screamed again, thrashing around, and the screams went on and on, piercing the night, setting up yells of anger from the adjacent rooms, for the mud walls were no barrier to sound. Indeed, someone in the next room threw something at the wall and it almost gave way.

I leapt to my feet. 'I'll get Xurxo.'

We were a grim party of four at breakfast the next morning. Thuban and Sara were still in their rooms, both finally asleep. Xurxo managed to procure some sort of balm and rubbed it onto the ugly red scarring that was giving Sara so much pain. He also put something on her lips which he said would make her sleep. He made Thuban comfortable, telling us he'd be all right for an hour or two. Rosa was also in the bedchamber, catching up on missed sleep, so Kit, Xurxo, Yehudah and I sat down to a meal which none of us relished. We were a fractious, ill-tempered gathering.

We got back on the road as fast as we could. I remembered, as I arranged our overnight belongings in the cargo cart, that Rosa had not answered my question about the pregnancy. Considering everything she'd been through, it would hardly be surprising if she'd lost the baby. I also found myself thinking about Aldara, who would have looked after Sara and made her feel better, and could have reassured me about Rosa as well. *The plain-looking woman,* the Mudéjar had called her. Plain-looking she may have been, but she was worth her weight in gold. I clenched my teeth. The Mudéjar. It seemed he was in England now. *He's here right now*, said Guido's voice on the banks of the River Seine. *Here right now, here right now, here right now...*

We rumbled down the cart track onto the lowest slopes of the High Weald. I told Yehudah to take Xurxo's place with the invalids, and sent Xurxo to ride in the baggage cart.

'Get your head down. Get some rest'

'I don't trust the Jew.'

'You'll have to trust *me* though, won't you,' I replied savagely. Nobody trusts Yehudah, but we've no choice. And Xurxo will be no use to anyone if he's dead on his feet. Reluctantly, he did as he was told. Yehudah insisted on the transfer of his precious crate to the large wagon, partly so he could sit up high in lordly comfort, and partly so he could be near his valuable astrolabe.

'I do not altogether trust that Smanderino,' he said in his soft serpent-voice.

'That's odd. He's just told me he doesn't trust *you*.'

Yehudah gave me a contemptuous look, then settled himself on his crate, arranging the long black robe around it. He had a book in his hand.

'You're here to keep an eye on the sick and injured,' I reminded him. 'Don't get too engrossed in your book, Yehudah.'

We made it over the Weald in one day, arriving at Mylkehouse this evening. It's been a good day, with no mishaps, thank goodness. The hostelry here is basic, and the women are sharing the single tiny room, while the men have been sent to a nearby smithy. Yehudah picked his way through anvils and firepits to make a nest for himself in some straw at the far end of the building. Xurxo is even more anxious about Thuban; he seems delirious, his mind wandering, his speech unintelligible.

'Perhaps he hasn't much longer,' I suggested quietly, and not for the first time.

'Don't say that,' Xurxo hissed at once. 'He just needs to make it to your alchemist. I have to keep him alive until we get to Hambrig.'

Everybody seems to think the so-called Elixir of Life is neatly bottled in Hambrig, and the moment Thuban arrives, the cork will be pulled, Jabir will dose him up to the eyebrows, and the man will be instantly cured. But Jabir's claim to fame is based on – *what,* exactly? Two failed attempts to make the magic potion? The dubious and unproven assertion that he's the descendant of one Jabir ibn Hayyan of Persia? A meddling in things so far beyond his control that he created a monster which turned into a fireball which blew up a house and caused near-fatal injuries? I shook my head at Xurxo, but I didn't say anything. Let the man clutch at straws. After all, there was nothing else to hold on to.

So I asked Xurxo a different question. 'Why are you so concerned for Thuban?'

'He asked me to look after him, Lord Rory. Right at the start, when he could walk and talk, when he seemed unwell but not seriously so, he told me things were going to get worse for him – much, much worse. And I made him a solemn promise, which I intend to keep. I promised to do my utmost to get him to Jabir in Hambrig. This is what's keeping Thuban going, when by rights he should have been dead weeks ago. He is holding onto the promise of a cure, and he's relying on me to get it for him.'

'What if the Mudéjar doesn't let him live?'

'You believe the Mudéjar is out to kill us all?'

'We *are* gradually losing people.'

'I will not let any stranger near Thuban. Even the Mudéjar can't murder him while I'm here.'

We settled down for the night, but I was wide awake, and so was Kit. He was playing my gittern softly in the far corner of the forge.

Rosa das rosas e fror das frores.
Dona das donas, sennor das sennores.

Odd to hear my wife's name in one of the cantigas Alfonso has written, but then she *is* his daughter. I remember, as I write these words, that Sara is the only one of us who knows the Mudéjar's real identity. Tomorrow – *tomorrow* I must force Sara to divulge this information. I've said this before, and I've not been able to make her tell me his name. How will I force her? *Can* I force her? What if she still out-and-out refuses? But she must not refuse. It's time to know the truth about the murderer.

29

INTO THIN AIR

In the morning, I raced across the shingle yard to the inn, and spent an uncomfortable time waiting for the latrine to become available. Rosa called my name. Fearing my wife was ill again, I hurried up the short flight of steps to the little chamber.

'Are you all right, lady?'

'I am, lord,' she answered from just inside the doorway. 'But Sara has been taken! A note has been left for you.'

'Taken? When? By whom?' But of course, I knew. And the expected parchment was thrust into my hand. The letter was longer than usual.

Anyone who is not for me is against me. This boy is mine, and you will understand why very soon. Now that we are in England, it is time to show my hand a little. You are an educated man, and you know by now that Thuban's name is not his own. His real name is Husain. Thuban is the name of a star. Ask the Jew the significance of this. The boy is not who you think he is. He is the son of an influential man in Murcia. He is worth a great deal. You may continue your journey, and you won't know

> *if the boy is alive or dead, but it won't matter to you. There is no point whatsoever in your looking for him, so do not waste your time. Continue to Hambrig. The man you know as Thuban must see Jabir ibn Hayyan. This is your mission, Lord Rory. Do not fail in it.*
>
> *The Mudéjar*

I re-read the damned message. Several times. Then I called Kit and told him to muster our group, together with the wagons and the animals. The innkeeper brought bread and some fruit wrapped in pastry. We bundled it all on board, and I helped Xurxo lift Thuban into his cart. Rosa's face was grim, though no one else yet knew what had happened. I quelled their questions, refusing to answer anyone. In silence, we clambered on board one cart or the other and drove the ponies over the shingles and onto the road. Once round the first bend and out of sight of the inn, I called a halt, jumped down from the driver's bench and hauled Yehudah down with me.

'What does the name "Thuban" mean, Yehudah?'

'It's the name of a star.' Tall and imposing, he stared over my left shoulder. His voice was austere. Uninterested in the question.

Kit had already told me about the moving sky when we were at the *Abbaye Grestain,* but Yehudah didn't know that I knew. I moved closer to him, and he backed away. 'What star? What does the name mean? Tell me everything you know about it.'

'The star Thuban is in the Draco constellation. It is not the brightest star in that constellation, and it looks inconspicuous.' He paused.

'Go on.'

'At the time of the building of the pyramids in Egypt, Thuban was the north star. The Egyptians built their beautiful constructions so they could observe Thuban through the entrance. Mathematically, the Egyptians were superb, and they knew how to work out the angles, distances and geometry of their massive buildings. Thuban was their north star.'

'Do you mean the direction we call "north" was different then?'

'Of course not. The direction we call "north" is always the same. But the stars in the sky change their positions. It is a very, very slow change; nonetheless, it happens. The star Thuban used to be the north star.'

'Why didn't you tell me this before?'

I'd always known Yehudah was hiding something. I was more suspicious of him than ever now. He had known Thuban's name was false, right from the start. Yet again, I thought it likely Yehudah was the Mudéjar.

He continued to stare over my left shoulder, his large black hat shading his face. He did not respond to my question. So I read the Mudéjar's latest letter out to everybody.

'What are we going to do?' Xurxo asked into the appalled silence.

'We are going to find her.'

Xurxo bit his lip. 'If we stay to look for Sara, I doubt Thuban will survive the journey to Hambrig. He's on borrowed time as it is.'

'We've been here before, Xurxo. Now you're telling me I have to choose between Sara and Thuban?'

I'd put the choice into words, but no one wanted to face up to it.

'What do you think we should do, Yehudah?' I asked, swinging round to him.

'It is not my decision. But – there are many here who wish to finish this long and weary journey, and only one who is, perhaps, in danger. Although perhaps not. Perhaps the boy is already dead.'

'Do not call her "the boy",' Rosa commanded imperiously, standing up in the cart. 'She is a girl, and her name is Sara. Do not forget it, Yehudah.'

Yehudah shrugged disdainfully. 'Even the Mudéjar calls him a boy. Besides, removing the genitals does not change a boy into a girl. If it did, many soldiers who have suffered castration in battle would now be women. This is not logical.'

I made my decision. 'Thuban is already sick. He may or may not survive. Sara needs our help. Kit, Yehudah and I will search for her. Xurxo, stay here with Thuban and my lady.'

I think Sara is still alive. The Mudéjar has killed before, and he's left his ghastly *Anyone-who-is-not-for-me* messages on the corpse. He has also enticed Sara away before and has not killed or even harmed her. The letter goes a long way to explaining why.

'He says Sara is worth a lot,' I reminded Kit, as we started to hunt through the undergrowth by the side of the track. 'He won't kill her, not if he can use her in some way.'

'Do you think the letter tells the truth?' Kit asked. 'We have always assumed Sara was from peasant stock. And that she's French. The Mudéjar must know Sara pretty well,

Rory. Which means Sara knows *him* well too. Something very strange about all this, don't you think?'

'I was aware Sara knew the Mudéjar's identity. But you're saying they actually *know* each other? Maybe they're both from Murcia.'

'What do you know about Murcia?'

'It's in the north-east of al-Andalus. It keeps changing hands between the Muslims and the Christians. About two years ago Jaume of Aragon, together with Alfonso, took it back under Christian rule. They resettled the Muslims into other regions, but the Mudéjars stayed. At great cost to their culture and their livelihoods. Aldara explained it all to me weeks ago.'

'So our Mudéjar is holding Sara hostage? Is that what you think?'

It was exactly what I thought. The Mudéjar said Sara's father is 'influential'. How influential, I wondered? Influential enough to turn the tide for the Murcian Muslims? I told Kit about the church on the Seine estuary, where I'd found the boy at the top of the tower waiting for his operation. 'He thought the Mudéjar was going to turn him into a girl.'

Kit looked at me strangely, holding his hands out. '*Suppose he was?* Suppose that was the idea all along?'

'What the hell do you mean, Kit?'

'Now we know that Sara, or rather Guido, has power and wealth to his name, that changes everything. Obviously the Mudéjar has been luring Guido away in order to use him. The promises of surgery were the bait. That's what I think.'

'Then why not do that to start with? Why all the threats about killing us all?'

'The other thing is,' he said weightily, 'you say Guido has always known who the Mudéjar is. He's clearly helping him.

We never see the man, do we? We don't know how he travels, how he knows where we are or who we are. Well, we know now. Guido's an informer.'

I shook my head. 'Guido's frightened of the Mudéjar. I mean, *really* frightened. He thought the Mudéjar could help him, so he went to meet him when he was asked to. And Guido's best friend was Aldara, remember. There's no way the boy would have helped someone kill *her*. I think Guido actually hates the Mudéjar. Especially now Aldara's dead.'

'What about Thuban then? The Mudéjar knows Thuban and he wants him cured by Jabir. What was that bit? Something about Jabir ibn Hayyan?'

'Thuban must see Jabir ibn Hayyan. This is your mission, Lord Rory. Do not fail in it,' I quoted.

'So he's got his facts wrong. Jabir ibn Hayyan lived in the eighth century!'

'Enough talking,' I said. 'We need to widen the search and find Sara. I mean Guido. If we don't find him soon it won't matter if the Mudéjar's killed him or not, he'll die from his wounds.'

We separated, giving ourselves two days and two nights. We arranged to meet at the cart at sunset on Sunday, but if one of us found Guido before that, we'd get him to the wagon and make haste for Hambrig. The other would have to catch up as best he could.

'And Yehudah?' Kit asked pointedly.

I shrugged. Yehudah, I was fairly sure, had no intention of hunting for Guido anyway. I only included him in the search party because I didn't want him anywhere near Rosa. I trust Xurxo to look after my wife. Yehudah, I do not trust at all.

I tried to think what the Mudéjar's plan might be. He'd surely expect us to mount a search for Guido. So where might he have hidden him? If it's true that Guido's father is a powerful man in Murcia, then the Mudéjar is in a strong position now. Provided he can keep Guido alive. And keep him alive, he must.

I remembered he'd first imprisoned the boy in the deserted *Chateau de Boutemont,* while the second time he chose an isolated church. So I looked for buildings in remote areas. They are plentiful here, just north of the High Weald. The area is not densely populated, so I entered churches, barns, farmhouses and manor houses. Sometimes I knocked, hoping to hear an answer. Sometimes I pushed the door and tiptoed in unannounced. Mostly the buildings were empty of people, although plenty of cats, rats and bats greeted me in their various unwelcome ways.

I wandered through a great deal of woodland, discounting it as a place of concealment. The Mudéjar wouldn't hide his hostage among the trees. The forest seemed to go on forever, and the sky was darkening. I quickened my pace, anxious to be out in the open before nightfall. And as day turned to dusk, I emerged from the woods and found myself staring at an old monastery surrounded by fields. I hardly thought Guido would be in the monastery itself, but there might be, almost certainly *would* be, outbuildings the Mudéjar might use, and in any case there was no harm in asking the gatekeeper if he'd seen anything.

There was no gatekeeper. The gate itself, almost off its

hinges, swung in the cool night wind, creaking mournfully. Inside, the cloisters were eerily silent. No bell tolled, no monks shuffled across to vespers, and the church loomed in front of me, a dark, brooding building with a squat, square tower.

As a rule, I'm not afraid of ghosts. But this was surely the most haunted place I'd ever come across. My feet made no sound on the flagstones of the cloisters, and I couldn't even hear myself breathing. *Was* I breathing? I stared at the church, the darkness of the night descending over everything like an enveloping cloak, the sky beginning to show pinpricks of light, which dutifully arranged themselves into the familiar constellations.

'Who are you?' I bellowed into the furthest reaches of the abandoned passageways. 'Mudéjar! Show yourself!'

A rustling movement from behind made me swing round, my heart in my mouth. A rat ran across the flagstones. I breathed again. Crept forward. Stopped. Was there another sound? Not an animal this time. Someone following me, keeping well behind, sticking to the deepest dark of the cloister walls. I pulled my dagger from my belt and circled slowly.

'Who's there? Show yourself!'

The faintest sound of music. I stood still. But it had gone. Nothing moved; no one spoke.

I moved forward again, aiming for the church. If Guido were here, he'd be in that church, I knew it. My insides were misbehaving chronically; I ignored their protests. Sweat plastered my hair to my head and my hands were clammy. I tightened my grip on my dagger. The church came nearer. One long side of it stretched away from me; the tower was nearest. I put out my hand and touched the rough stone. Real stone and a real church. I felt my way around the tower, hoping to find a door. When I did, I nearly fell through it; it was wide open. I groped my way inside, cursing myself for a fool.

My father curses me too. *Who,* he asks sarcastically, *goes into an unknown, enclosed space in the dark, knowing it may well contain an enemy and that you are only lightly armed? No one but a fool. Go back. Get help. Wait until daylight.*

But by then it may be too late, I protest. Though I stop, nonetheless, my heart pounding, my dagger's hilt slipping in my sweating hand.

And you will at least be alive, boy, my father points out.

I peer into the darkness. I think I can just about discern his shape. Like me, he's tall, but he's thinner. He's grown thin in his old age, I suppose, as some men do, while others get fat and fleshy. It's hard to make him out though, and I really, really want to see him. I wish, as I will never cease to wish, that he'd lived long enough for me to greet him on my return from Crusade. He'd be in his sixties now, but when I last saw him he was forty-five and I was nineteen. His ghost comes to me often, and I've always wanted to approach him. To touch him. Once I tried. It was in my library in Castle Rory. He was sitting in the leather chair by the fire, and I reached out to him, falling forwards, desperately needing to be with him. I passed out and woke just a few moments later to find myself alone.

But here, in this remote and silent English church, perhaps here there is a chance. I've forgotten all about Guido and the Mudéjar. I've forgotten the reason for my being here in the first place. I just know my father has come to me, that he's waiting for me, leaning against the tower wall, half hidden in the darkness, but *there.*

Can I come closer, Father? I ask. It has suddenly occurred to me that perhaps I need permission. This isn't my safe and private library at home; I can't risk passing out here. Better check it will be all right.

I'd like that. Father's voice is warm and inviting. He looks up then, and I see his eyes glinting in the starlight. Where are the stars? Aren't we inside a church? I follow Father's gaze, tilting my head back, and I see the sky where the roof should be. I catch my breath.

You didn't realise? Father laughs gently. *This church is a ruin. The whole monastery is ruined. It is an ancient and sacred place, and said to be haunted, but no one worships or lives here anymore. It is falling down, boy. Falling down. It could collapse at any moment; in fact, it probably will.*

I'm breathing too fast, my heart thumping, not in my chest where it belongs, but high up in my throat. My legs are shaking, and my dagger slips from my hand. I hear it clatter onto the stone floor. I move towards Father, groping with my hands, just as I did last time. I tell myself I will not faint; I will not mess up. Father and I will be reunited. We will meet, touch each other, hold each other. I stretch further towards him.

You're not here yet, Father says. He sounds sad, but it's true. I think I've taken several steps, but I am as far away from him as ever. I try again, forcing my legs to move. After all, the tower isn't that large. Just two or three steps should do it. They are pitiful, those steps. It's as if I am standing still.

But then Father himself reaches out to me. I see him move towards me. I call out to him. *Father! Take my hand!*

I feel the touch on my sleeve, then a hard grip around

my arm. Father bends down and retrieves my dagger. But he holds the hilt of it himself and touches its point to my chest. I shake my head, confused. The dagger's point pierces my jersey and my shirt, nicking my skin, drawing blood. Suddenly I can't breathe, and my legs buckle. Father holds me up, but he presses against the dagger again, and the sharp pain of it makes me cry out. He leads me away from the tower, through a small door and into the nave of the church, which is also wide open to the sky. He pushes me down onto a bench under a window.

I look at him in horror. His robe has a deep cowl, shadowing and hiding his face. I peer at him, but the starlight no longer glints in his eyes. I can't see his eyes at all. As I shiver and sweat on the bench, staring at the man who holds me at dagger point, it finally dawns on me.

This is not my father.

'You are seeking the boy.' It was a simple statement. It brought me back to my senses and my mission.

'I'm looking for Sara. Who are you?'

'Surely you know by now.' The tone was mocking.

'You're the Mudéjar?'

The blade twisted slightly.

'What's your real name?'

'Well, again, I thought you'd have worked that out already.'

I was silent. If I was meant to have worked it out, did that mean I knew the man? Did I recognise his voice? I couldn't place it. 'Where is Sara?'

'The boy? He's not here. But your friend Kit is. I have

managed to acquire both of you, though I neither want nor need you. Still, it is not yet your turn to die, Rory. And you can replace a minstrel a hundred times over, I am sure.'

I clenched my fists. Did that mean Kit was dead?

The Mudéjar laughed. 'You won't find his body. Nor do you need a letter this time. You must know their style by heart. So, no Kit to play his music on the last part of your journey home. And no whingeing boy to torment you with his deluded fantasies. I will let you go, Hambrigger, and you will continue to take Husain to Jabir ibn Hayyan, you and your wife, your Smanderino friend and the Jew you despise. Four of you will get a bit further, before you become three and then two. Two of you will make it home, and yes, you are one of the two. The other?' He laughed again. 'Don't tempt me. The killing has been too easy, and maybe two survivors are one too many.'

The dagger twisted again. Trickles of blood ran down my chest.

'Did you kill Aldara?' I asked. For none of us had thought the Mudéjar did that.

There was a pause, and the tip of the dagger was withdrawn slightly. 'I did not kill her. She took her own life.'

'Took her own life?' I exclaimed. 'She was swept away in a storm at sea—'

'She was not swept away.' He turned his head away from me. 'She deliberately let go of the rail. She had decided to take her own life. If you do not know why, you are a bigger fool than I thought.'

'Because she was pregnant?'

'She let the Jew abuse her, and you let her let him abuse her. She was desperate to marry and she thought her pregnancy would force it. It did not. I blame you, and you will pay dearly. I will not tell you how, but you will regret to the end of your life that you did not put a stop to the Jew's lust for Aldara.'

Shocked at his words, I wanted to keep him talking. 'I didn't know about it. I found them together once, but by then it was too late...'

'That is so. Yet you should have known; it was your duty to know. The Jew does not control his lust, and you will do well to remember that for as long as I let you both live. You have left your wife to come looking for the boy. Do you know where the Jew is now, Hambrigger? Is he with her?'

I jumped to my feet, swinging my fist, but something caught me on the side of my head and I fell to the ground. He kicked me. And then he laughed.

'So now you will forget about the boy. You will hurry, hurry, hurry, back to your wife, to see if she has been assaulted by the Jew. And if she has, then you will kill the Jew and save me the trouble. If she has not, you will make haste to take Husain to Jabir ibn Hayyan. You must not waste any more time, for Husain will not survive if you do. Once he is dead, I shall have no more use for any of you. Now get out of here.'

I rose to my feet, thinking to find some weapon from somewhere. I had to get this man and either kill him now or take him prisoner. The Mudéjar was right there, talking to me, and I was sure I could beat him, dagger or no dagger. But as I stared wildly around the forgotten, ruined little church, I realised I was, once again, alone. There was nobody there. No Mudéjar, not even in the shadows. I searched the entire building, tower and all, but he had simply vanished into thin air.

30

WHAT ELSE COULD WE DO?

You should find Kit before it's too late.

My father is sitting on a bench by the door to the tower. I frown. He wasn't there a moment ago; there was no one in the church at all.

Before it's too late?

Remember what I told you before? The church is falling down. It could collapse at any moment. That's why I stay near the tower; I'll be able to get out quickly. But Kit won't escape, not unless you find him first. The Mudéjar intends him to die, crushed and suffocated by the collapse of this building.

Where is he, Father? Where's Kit? And where's Guido?

I'm trying to look around, but the moonlight and the starlight are too weak, there are too many shadows, too much darkness. And, in truth, I'm frightened. My boots seem fixed to the spot where I stand, and I can't move.

My father clicks his tongue. *Now is not the time to take fright, boy. You need to save your musician's life. As for the boy who wants to be a girl, you surely don't think the Muslim has hidden him here in this condemned building? Save the minstrel and yourself. Get out as fast as you can. You do not have long.*

What about you, Father? I cry. *Where will you be?*

He laughs. *You've managed well enough without me for many years. Now hurry!*

I did. My boots unstuck themselves from the floor and I raced to look in all the possible places Kit might be. There weren't many. I called his name, over and over, but there was no reply. Something made a sound though, and as I swung round, I saw the north wall begin to crumble. Stones cracked and split. Small pieces of sandstone fell to the ground, clattering all around me. The church was breaking up.

The walls were crumbling, rocks showering onto my head, and it hurt. I slipped and stumbled in the sandy dust now covering the floor. I kicked at the stones and pebbles that rolled and jumped around me, but soon big rocks were thundering down, and I ran with my hands over my head. How was this happening, for God's sake? What was making the church disintegrate right now? I called Kit's name again, choking on the dust which suddenly clogged my throat and lungs, forcing me to stop moving and bend over, coughing, gasping for air, desperate to breathe, grit stinging my eyes. Covering my head and face, I sank to the ground, while stones that had stood solid for centuries rained down all around me.

I retched on the debris in my mouth. Was it all a lie? Maybe Kit wasn't here at all, and it was I who would die in the rubble. It was piling up around me and on top of me. I choked, struggling to get air into my lungs. I couldn't move from my knees.

What else could we do?

He's over here, Father says crossly. *Over here, boy, but make haste! You've so little time left!*

I looked up, my eyes smarting. Over where, for heaven's sake? Everywhere was dust, and I couldn't see more than an inch in front of my face. There was a massive rumble like thunder, and more enormous stones crashed down, shattering on the hard stone floor. Behind me, the tower began to crumble, and I crouched down further, my arms over my head, my eyes squeezed shut. I didn't hear my father leave, but I knew he had. The moment I felt the cold emptiness of his absence was the lowest point in the day. He'd left me. He'd given up on me. He'd told me to hurry, but I hadn't moved.

I launched myself upwards and forwards. At the east end of the church, through a haze of dust, I thought I saw Father; perhaps he hadn't left me after all. I pushed through the fallen stones. Father was showing me where to find Kit, and I needed to get to the altar.

As soon as I touched the holy table, Father vanished. But there, lying unconscious under the table, was Kit, bound and gagged. I dragged him out. The altar table had protected him, but now we were both in danger of being submerged by falling masonry. I heaved Kit up over my shoulders, and, at last, my strength returned to me. Bent over to try to shield my head, I lurched back down the nave.

The tower had gone, and its fallen stones blocked the doorway. In horror, I scanned what was left of the building. There seemed to be no way out. The walls were half their previous height, but they were still high.

And then, silence. No more stones tumbled and shattered; no more rubble bounced up from the floor. The church, it seemed, was not to fall completely. I set Kit down on a pile of stones and went to look for a way out. I chose the lowest point in the south wall, which seemed to have suffered the most damage. Could I climb it? Possibly, if I first piled more stones at its base. That didn't take long. But climbing up onto my heaped-up rubble was more difficult. It kept shifting. Stones slipped and tumbled down the little hill, my boots skidded, and by the time I reached the top of the pile, it was a lot lower and less useful than I'd hoped. I tried again, shoring the stony construction up with lengths of timber from the wrecked benches; but they also simply fell away. The only way to do this was to drag the entire altar table through the rubble-filled nave to this point where the wall was at its lowest.

It was exceedingly heavy, that table. And first I had to clear a way through. Those planks of wood came in useful for that; I used them like shovels, driving the loose stones away, pushing them to one side or the other and creating a pathway for the altar. After a couple of hours, I had the altar table in place. Day was on its way at last, the sky lighter now, though dawn was still some hours away.

I climbed onto the table, high enough now to be able to see over the jagged edge of the wall, and there was no Mudéjar lying in wait. I jumped back down, hauled Kit onto the table, where he looked like an Old Testament sacrifice. I scrambled up next to him and tried to think how to do this. I couldn't just drop him down over the wall – he'd probably break his neck. Bell ropes, I thought with sudden inspiration. There might be bell ropes in the tower, and I could use them to lower Kit gently to the ground. But I looked with consternation at the huge pile of masonry that had once been the squat tower of this little church. If there ever *had* been any bell ropes, they were no longer accessible. Could I carry him? Impossible. I was in despair. I'd found Kit, I'd dragged the massive altar to the right place, and now I was stuck.

For lack of any other ideas, I hauled myself onto the top of the wall, trying to avoid the worst of the jagged, broken stones. Perching uncomfortably there, as dawn broke, I looked around the bleak Kentish landscape. It was fairly flat, forested in the near distance, but farming country mostly. Something caught my eye, some tiny movement. I stared, rubbed the remaining grit out of my eyes and blinked in the dawning of another chill, sunless day. There it was again, something moving, snail-like, along the horizon. I waved. Waved again and again, wanting to stand up to be more noticeable, but I didn't dare, for fear of losing my balance. I tugged my jersey off, and then my shirt. Frantically, I waved it over my head.

The movement stopped. Started again. Stopped again. And then began to travel towards the monastery. I continued waving my shirt, and as the person came nearer, I shouted. 'Help! I need help!'

He picked up his pace and stopped some fifty yards from the broken-down wall. A Kentish peasant in a smock and leggings, a woollen beret on his head, some kind of crook or staff in his right hand. He looked maybe fifty or sixty years old. He was out of breath, panting and gasping.

I waited a moment for him to look up at me. 'I'm trapped here. I need to get an unconscious man over the wall. Will you help?' Though, my heart sinking, I doubted he could, really.

'Dunno. How much is it wert?'

Damn. I'd left my money with the wagons, Xurxo in charge of all our belongings. 'I've nothing to give you,' I admitted. 'But I can make it up to you later.' What that meant, I'd no idea, but I'd think of something.

The man seemed to consider. 'Werry well,' he said. 'Bwing your fwend to da top o' da wall.'

I jumped back down to the altar table. Kit was still lying there with his eyes closed. I'd taken off the gag and the bindings, and now I heaved him up, somehow getting him onto the wall.

'Now,' called the aged peasant from below. 'You must 'old 'is wists and dandle 'im down. When I say da word, you must dwop 'im.'

It sounded dangerous, if not lethal. How could this old man catch Kit?

'I'm not sure...' I began warily.

'You want my 'elp – but you don't want it. Werry well. I'll be on my way.' He turned to go.

'I'll give it a try,' I called down hastily. 'It's just this man weighs quite a bit, and you don't look young.'

'Please yourself. I c'n go, or you c'n trust me. It's your own choice.'

But there was no choice. I did as he said. I hooked my feet around the jagged stones and inched my way towards the edge of the wall, dragging Kit with me. I grasped his wrists as tightly as I could, manoeuvring him so he was almost at the edge. I couldn't quite get him to go *over* the edge though. I tried to explain all this to the peasant.

'You're not twyin' 'ard enough,' he said unhelpfully. 'Give 'im a kick.'

Unhooking one foot, I swung my leg and gingerly kicked Kit in the side. He moved, but not enough. I kicked harder and only just had time to hook my foot securely back again, when Kit fell over the edge of the wall. The wrench on my shoulders was painful, but I somehow held on to his wrists. Now he was dangling down the wall at the full stretch of his arms and mine.

'Wait dere. Not long.'

It'd better not be long.

'Now. Just dwop 'im.'

Holding on to Kit was hard enough, but dropping him was harder. I couldn't see below me at all. I had no idea where the peasant was standing, or what his true intentions were. I didn't know what kind of ground lay directly below the wall. But, just as before, there was no choice; I couldn't hold Kit for much longer anyway. So I let go.

I heard a thud. Then nothing.

'Your turn now,' the man called up to me.

I hung by my arms, kicked out from the wall and dropped like a stone. But I landed on a feather bed. Well, it wasn't actually a feather bed. It was a huge pile of bracken and fern fronds, soft and giving. I clawed my way out of it, brushed the stuff off me and looked around for Kit and the Kentish farmer.

'Thank you.' It seemed inadequate.

'Your fwend is all wight. In fact, 'e's woken up.'

Now I was on the ground, I could see my helper more closely. He was a short, wizened man, even older than I'd first thought. His gnarled hand on the stick shook with an aged tremor.

'Who are you?' I asked.

'My name is Eltanin. I work some land 'ere. 'Ow will you make it up to me?'

'Make it up to you? Oh, yes. I remember. I don't know, I—'

'I have money.' Kit's voice. He was sitting on the ground and looked bemused, but in reasonable shape. 'I have money. I'll pay this man for his help.'

Kit pulled a purse from his pocket and gave the peasant some coins. Interesting to find out that the Mudéjar is no robber.

Eltanin bade us a dignified farewell, and I watched him lope back down the track to his fields, his stick doing much of the work for him.

'I wonder what he grows there,' I said. 'The harvest must be over by now.'

Kit stood, swaying a little. 'I feel a bit wobbly. But I think I'm all right.'

'What happened to you?'

'I thought Sara might be in this monastery. I didn't realise until I got to it that it's nothing but a ruin. When I was just inside, someone hit me on the head from behind. I never saw him. Next thing I knew I was on the ground here with that old man standing over me. How about you?'

I filled him in, but all the time my mind was thinking about Eltanin, his sudden appearance and his empty fields. Odd that he'd come into view at the very moment I needed help. Nobody else had turned up, or had even been seen on the horizon. And the man looked too old to be a farmer. Too old – and too convenient. He must have piled the soft vegetation at the foot of the wall, but when? It would have taken an hour or more for all that springy stuff to be piled up there. So he must have done it beforehand. Or *someone* had.

Kit and I walked back towards the road where we'd left Xurxo, Thuban and Rosa. I voiced my thoughts on the

Kentish peasant, but Kit hadn't seen him appear out of nowhere as I had. He was inclined to dismiss my puzzlement. 'We were lucky, that's all. Very, very lucky. As for the bracken and all that, perhaps it was just there anyway. Maybe nobody piled it up.'

It seemed the only explanation.

'So,' said Kit when we were making our way through the woods, 'what about Sara?'

'We can't spend any longer looking. I need to get Rosa home before the baby's due. We're going on, Kit.'

Xurxo would be pleased for Thuban, and Rosa would be angry, but what else could we do?

31

SURELY WE'LL BE ABLE TO GET HELP

Kit and I came out of the forest and I heaved a huge sigh of relief. I'd half expected our carts to be gone – or if there still, their occupants murdered, mutilated or missing. But when we emerged from the trees and saw not only the carts, but the ponies as well, with Xurxo sitting on Yehudah's crate, Rosa leaning against him for support, I ran the last few yards.

'Xurxo!' I called out. 'We didn't find Sara, but we're ready to—'

I got no further. Rosa turned an accusing gaze on me. 'We have Sara here. Yehudah found her. But both of them are in a bad way. We wanted to make haste to an abbey to find a priest, but Xurxo insisted we wait for you, and now it may be too late.'

I climbed up to look in the wagon. Lying on its floor was Yehudah, one of Rosa's gowns balled up and strapped to his side. Blood was seeping through it. I saw no sign of Sara.

'Sara is sleeping in the other cart,' Rosa told me. 'We moved Thuban as well. We needed this larger wagon for Yehudah. Xurxo thinks his wound is serious.'

'What happened?' Kit asked grimly. He'd climbed onto the wheel and was hanging over the side.

'Early this morning we heard a shout from the trees,' Xurxo said. 'I didn't want to leave Lady Rosa or Thuban, but Lady Rosa insisted I find out who needed help. I thought it might be a trap. I wish now I'd done what Lady Rosa said, but I did not. I stayed here, in case the shout was to lure me from the cart in order for some terrible fate to befall the lady. But if I had gone, I might have been able to save Yehudah, for eventually he emerged from the trees looking exhausted. He carried Sara in his arms. When I saw them, I went to their aid, and Yehudah collapsed onto the ground. He had been stabbed, and the dagger was still sticking out of his side. He was wise not to have pulled it out, for then he would certainly have bled to death.'

'He was brave,' Rosa said. 'So very brave. He somehow carried Sara all the way here, though he must have been in such great pain.'

'Do you know what happened to Sara?' I asked. 'Do you know where and how Yehudah found her?'

Rosa shook her head.

Xurxo looked suddenly angry. 'Lord Rory, I think Yehudah may have had a fight with the Mudéjar. I'm sure I heard him say, "The Mudéjar did this" before he fainted. I have removed the dagger and have done my best to staunch the bleeding, but I fear he will die anyway.'

'Show me the dagger.'

I knew what I was going to see even before Xurxo reached behind, pulled something out and put it in my hand. *My* dagger. The one the Mudéjar, masquerading as my father, had taken from me. I felt sick. 'It was the Mudéjar. Yehudah was right.'

'Let's bind this wound up more effectively,' Kit cried,

leaping into the cart and pulling off his tunic. Rosa had tried to stop the Jew's bleeding, but Kit did a better job, using both my wife's gown and his own tunic, tearing the gown into long strips and wrapping them tightly around Yehudah's body. While he did so, I climbed into the other wagon. As Rosa had said, Guido was asleep. He lay curled in a corner of the little cart, while Thuban, still somehow breathing, lay on his back beside him. I shook the boy. He moved a little, but did not wake. I tried again, calling his name.

'Hello,' he said sleepily.

'Sara, I need you to wake up properly. I need to know what happened.'

'What happened? What do you mean, lord?' He yawned and stretched.

'Did the Mudéjar take you? Or did you go to him again of your own volition?'

'Oh, that! The Mudéjar told me to meet him. I got up in the middle of the night and I did as he said. At first he was nice to me, but then he said I had to go back to my father, and when I told him I didn't want to, he twisted my arms and that really hurt. I was frightened, but the Mudéjar told me it would all be all right. He said he would cure the pain in my – you know? Where my thing was? He promised he could make it all better. He said he had some ointment to put on it, but first I should eat something. He gave me some delicious food and wine. The wine made me fall asleep though.' Guido paused, rubbing his eyes, clearly still drunk and unable to think straight.

'Kit!' I called. 'We must go now. Xurxo must drive the large cart, and you must come and drive this one. I don't want to spend any more time here.'

Kit finished binding up Yehudah's wounds and hurried

over to take the reins of the sturdy little pony who pulls the smaller of our two wagons. We began to roll forwards. It's a miracle we are all here. I shook Guido out of his lethargy and told him to continue his story.

'When I woke up, the Mudéjar had gone and Yehudah was with me. Yehudah said I had to come with him, and he'd take me back to you. That was what I wanted, but I was too sleepy to walk. Yehudah said I was drunk, and he was annoyed with me. He said he'd carry me, but then the Mudéjar came back, and when he saw Yehudah he was furious. He pulled out a dagger and he stabbed Yehudah over and over. I was terrified and I screamed. But you didn't hear me, and then there was a horrible, vicious fight between Yehudah and the Mudéjar. Yehudah had a knife, a wicked knife. He tried to stab the Mudéjar. I think he managed to stab him quite a bit, but the Mudéjar inched round to Yehudah's side and he plunged his dagger into him. Yehudah screamed in pain. He was lying on the ground with blood pouring out of him. The Mudéjar told me to go to sleep and he would see me later. Then he limped away; I think Yehudah had injured him badly.'

'Well, go on,' I said grimly, as he stopped again. I was not liking this story at all.

'Yehudah had only been pretending to be unconscious. As soon as the Mudéjar had gone, Yehudah got up. He told me we had to run to get back to you, but I couldn't. I was so sleepy and I couldn't even stand up without falling down again. Yehudah picked me up, even though he was so badly injured. Carrying me in his arms, he ran as fast as he could. That's all I remember, lord.'

'Yehudah was a brave man,' I said. 'He may well die of his wounds. If he does, the Mudéjar will have killed him, and Yehudah will have sacrificed his life to save you. For that sacrifice not to have been in vain, you now need to tell me who the Mudéjar is.'

I was anticipating resistance and refusal. Instead, Guido said, 'I know. I know I must now tell you. The Mudéjar has killed too often. Lord, his name is Eltanin.'

It was as if someone had struck me a great blow between the eyes. Eltanin! How could that possibly be? I felt the pony stutter as Kit also reacted to the name.

'Are you sure?' I cried. 'Eltanin? You're sure that's the Mudéjar's name? What does he look like?'

'It is his name, lord. He wants me, he *always* wants me.'

'Why does he want you?'

The boy flushed a deep red. 'It's because of who I am, lord. Who I *used* to be, I mean.'

'You are the son of a powerful man in Murcia,' Kit called from his driving seat at the front of the cart, though he did not look round.

'How do you know?'

'The Mudéjar told us,' I said. 'In his note. He calls you "the boy" every time he refers to you. He doesn't seem to recognise that you are now female.'

Sara looked down at her lap. 'He knows I'm a girl. He helped to make me one.'

I didn't see how Eltanin could possibly be the Mudéjar. He was too old, and he'd helped Kit and me escape from the wreckage of the church, although my father had said the Mudéjar intended Kit to die there. I had to admit, though, it was very odd the church had stopped collapsing when it did, and soon after that, Eltanin had appeared like a guardian angel, guiding Kit and me to the only safe place to drop from the top of the ruined wall.

We rattle uncomfortably along. Thuban barely stirs. The man looks already dead, and if it weren't for the faint rise and fall of his chest I'd be convinced we should stop forthwith and bury him, though what prayers would be said I could not decide. Thuban's faith is Islam, and we are an assortment of Jew and Christians, although the Jew, also, may die. But, for the moment at least, no funeral is needed. I am keen to get to Dartford by nightfall. I had planned to cross the River Thames today, but the search for Guido has eaten into the daylight hours and my intention now is to find lodgings in Dartford, and tomorrow, a barge or lighter to transfer our beasts and wagons to the northern side of the river. Between Dartford and the river lies marshy country, and I have no desire to get stuck there in the dark. Still, from Mylkehouse to Dartford is nigh on thirty miles, a long way to go in a short autumn afternoon. It'll take us six hours at least.

'How long have you known the Mudéjar?' I asked Guido.

'He's friendly with my father. I have known him for years.'

'And the Mudéjar was introduced to you as Eltanin?'

'I never knew his name. He wanted help, I remember that.'

'Did he get it?'

'I don't think so.'

'Where is he now, Sara?'

The answer was as expected as it was unsatisfactory. 'He's with us, Lord Rory. He's always with us. I told you that before.'

I looked around. The cart was an ordinary one, and in it were the four of us: Sara, Thuban, Kit and me. Ahead of us was the larger cart, and in that were Rosa, Xurxo and Yehudah. Yehudah had saved Sara. And he was a Jew, not a Muslim. Neither Rosa nor Xurxo could possibly be the Mudéjar. I turned to Guido, meaning to point all this out, but, remembering how the murderer keeps pace with us wherever we are, I changed my mind.

'Who is next on the Mudéjar's hit list?' I asked instead.

'I don't know. But he won't let all of us get to Jabir. Thuban and you must survive, and he says one other will survive. But he didn't tell me who it would be.'

'So it could be you?'

'I will survive, Lord Rory. But I won't make it to Hambrig. Remember? The Mudéjar wants me. He will take me.'

'Sara, you keep going to meet him! Stop doing that and he won't be able to take you.'

'You don't understand, lord. I have to go when he calls me. I have no choice.' He lay down next to Thuban, his head on a canvas bundle of somebody's things, and went instantly to sleep.

'Odd isn't it,' Kit remarked conversationally from the driving seat above me. 'What do you think she means when she says she has no choice?'

'I don't know,' I said crossly. 'Surely that old man who helped us can't be the Mudéjar.' I haven't yet told Kit that I saw the Mudéjar inside the church. His face had been hidden by his cowl, but he'd neither looked nor sounded like the elderly Kentish peasant. He'd been taller and younger. And he'd sounded *exactly* like my father.

'And even if the old fellow *is* the Mudéjar,' Kit continued, 'he's certainly not here now. How can he be?'

We fell silent and made good progress along the bumpy track. But it got bumpier, and then the left wheel of the cart dipped into a sudden pothole, and we lurched to the side.

Thuban cried out in distress. '*Ayn 'ant? 'ayn 'ant rashid?*'

Kit turned in surprise, pulling on one of the pony's reins, and inadvertently hauling his head round. The pony objected, and Kit quickly soothed him, but the whole business had made the cart wobble violently, its wheel still stuck in the rut. Thuban rolled over and crashed into Guido, who woke up and crawled away. That made Thuban roll even further, until he struck the far side of the cart, the side with the stuck wheel. We all heard it: his head cracking hard against the wooden washboard.

'Ouch,' exclaimed Kit, involuntarily.

Guido crouched by the driving seat, moaning to himself, and I was alarmed to see that the lower portion of his skirt was stiff with dried blood. Kit jumped down from his box, and I knew he was going to help Thuban.

I had to stop him. 'No! If you move your weight to that side, we'll capsize; the cart will be wrecked. We have to stay on the high side of the wagon to balance it, you, me and Guido.'

So Kit stayed where he was, and we all watched Thuban.

He turned himself round and faced us. '*ayn rashid?*'

I didn't understand the words, but his voice was weirdly clear and strong. And then he sat up, rubbed his head, blinked a few times and struggled up onto his knees.

'Don't try to stand, Thuban,' I warned, astonished to see him so recovered, but alarmed at what might happen if he moved too quickly. Out of the corner of my eye I saw Xurxo running towards us. He'd stopped his wagon as soon as he realised we were in trouble; it was twenty yards or so ahead of us. Xurxo had sense enough not to unbalance our cart, which was teetering and wobbling. It was creaking too, and a horrible crunching sound had begun.

'The axle's giving way,' Kit said quietly. 'The whole thing's going to subside into the road, I reckon.'

'We must get out. You help Guido. Climb over this side. Xurxo, help them.'

I had to get to Thuban before the cart overturned on top of him. I called to him, and he managed to inch his way up towards me. The ghastly creaking continued, and I was just able to lower the sick man into Xurxo's waiting arms and jump out too, when the axle split with a resounding crack and the cart fell into the road. Kit hurried to release our distressed little pony. But we were all safe. I looked around at my group. Rosa had joined us, and she stood next to Guido. Thuban, though supported by Xurxo, was standing. I couldn't believe it, but there he was.

Guido was in torment. No position gave him comfort. Normally Rosa took care of Guido, but Rosa was also uncomfortable. She'd been having some pains, and there were other problems she wouldn't discuss with me. And Xurxo had his hands full with Thuban. So that just left me. I picked Guido up in my arms and strode forwards to the other cart.

'We will go on to Dartford,' I said. 'We'll have to squeeze together, that's all. Xurxo, get Thuban on board, then help me with the bags and bundles. Kit, you sort out the pony.'

It took a while, but eventually everything and everyone was in the large wagon, the pony had been hitched up so both animals could walk in line and we set off. I wanted to know what Thuban had been saying.

'It is Arabic,' Guido said drowsily.

I spoke to Thuban in French, and he rambled incoherently about someone called Rashid. I couldn't make out who Rashid was, or why he was important. After a while, I gave up.

I've been getting my journal up to date. Dartford lies just a few miles ahead of us now. I'd wanted to make it by nightfall, but it's dark already. We need to get help for Yehudah, which will delay us yet again. I'm no longer optimistic that we'll cross the river in the morning, but I do believe now that Thuban may survive until we reach Hambrig, and I'm hopeful that whatever ails Rosa is not serious. The people who worry me most now are Yehudah and Guido. Both are bleeding. Yehudah's wound has bled right through Rosa's gown *and* Kit's ripped up tunic, while Guido's clothing is now soaked in blood. He keeps a hand between his legs all the time, trying, unsuccessfully, to dull the pain. We need to get to Dartford. And there, surely, we'll be able to get help.

32

IN OUR CAMP IN DARTFORD

After an uncomfortable night on the roadside, we managed to find an apothecary, thank God. He seemed a knowledgeable and competent man. We discovered his shop in a street full of different merchants, recognising it by the signs hanging over the door. Kit jumped down and went inside. He returned saying the apothecary had time to see us and would take a look at both our patients, though he'd charge more for his services as it was Sunday today.

He came out to the cart, a distinguished-looking man with dark hair and a beard. I explained our long journey from Santiago das Cunchas, and gave a rough description of Yehudah's and Guido's injuries. The apothecary told me he had all the plants and herbs he would need. His medical knowledge was impressive. He went to look inside the wagon. When he'd inspected the site of Yehudah's dagger wound, he gabbled off the Latin names of the medicinal plants he would use. The prognosis seemed promising. Then he looked at Guido and openly sneered at him. My heart sank.

'You've got a weirdo here, then.' He made the sign of the cross against himself.

'She's nothing of the sort.' Rosa's tone was imperious, but the apothecary leered at her and her tender belly, before lifting Guido's skirt, taking a good look and then holding his nose. I wasn't surprised at the nose holding. Guido's wound had begun to smell bad, and I knew very well what *that* meant. Bad-smelling wounds are said to fester. Festering wounds make a person very sick indeed, and, mostly, they die.

'Neither a he nor a she,' the apothecary noted, apparently to himself, before getting Kit to help him lift Yehudah. He left Guido in the cart.

Rosa thought we should not let this man treat either of our injured people. 'He is a charlatan,' she said derisively.

'Well, he's all there is,' I told her. 'And he seems to know his stuff.'

'Didn't you see the way he reacted to Sara?'

'Well, it's too late now.' It *was* too late; the apothecary had taken Yehudah into his shop. Rosa pointed out that the apothecary had recognised Yehudah was a Jew, which meant he'd immediately tripled his fees, even over the Sunday premium.

After helping the apothecary, Kit disappeared, hopefully to get food, since we had nothing to eat. Rosa wasn't hungry, but I knew she should eat or she would also fall ill. She was sitting next to Guido on the floor of the wagon, bathing the boy's face and hands with cool water; at least the apothecary had been able to provide that. I decided our wounded needed rest. We would make camp here for the night.

It's some hours later and the apothecary is still treating Yehudah. He has not yet come to get Guido. Of course, Yehudah is very badly wounded. It's bound to take a long time to patch him up properly.

Xurxo is edgy. 'I am going to see what is happening,' he announces suddenly. 'I know he said we weren't to disturb him, but we should find out what he's doing.'

Xurxo has already declared he won't let the apothecary look at Thuban. Thuban, after rallying when the cart broke its axle, has gone downhill again. He sleeps fitfully, wakes for short, incoherent bursts of speech, then lapses back into semi-consciousness.

'The Mudéjar wants us to take Thuban to Jabir,' Xurxo has reminded me several times, though I'm in no danger of forgetting.

But why does the Mudéjar care? What's the connection between Thuban and the Mudéjar?

Before Xurxo can go in to challenge the apothecary, the man comes out of his shop, wiping his hands on a rag, heading for our wagon where we are all tensely waiting. Xurxo stands up and adopts a defensive position in front of the wagon. Rosa stops bathing Guido's forehead. It's time for me to put away my journal.

Rosa got her questions in first, accosting the apothecary and demanding to know what he'd done to Yehudah. The man gave her his suggestive smile and told her not to worry. He said Yehudah was doing as well as could be expected; he needed rest, and must not yet be moved. It sounded like good news. The apothecary then slid his hands under Guido's slight body and began to lift him out of the cart.

'No!' Rosa laid her hands on Guido. The boy groaned, and beads of sweat appeared on his face.

The apothecary's grip tightened. 'Lady, would you have this creature die here?'

'Creature? She's no creature! She's a young girl, for God's sake!'

'And it's God's blessing it will surely need, and you too for sanctioning this mutilation. This apology for a body once belonged to a young and healthy boy. What is it now? A creature of some sort, you might say, barely alive, unable to reproduce, which is, perhaps, a blessing. You may call this thing a girl, but it will not be accepted as such in any normal place or abode. Perhaps it is better dead, wouldn't you agree?'

I did not agree, and I said so. What's more, I told the apothecary to finish treating Yehudah, but Guido would remain here.

Thuban slept, gabbling in Arabic from time to time. Kit did not reappear. Rosa sat unmoving in the cart, unwilling either to look at or talk to me. Xurxo sprawled on the grass, pretending to be resting, but in reality as tense as the rest of us.

Eventually, of course, my own tension showed itself the way it always does. I bolted for the apothecary's shop, hoping to find relief. The door was locked. I hammered loudly on it, but there was no response. Xurxo joined me and the two of us banged on the door as hard as we could.

Someone came out of the butcher's shop next door.

'Stop your hammering, there's no one there. The apothecary was taken sick last week and he died. Couldn't heal himself, could he!' The man laughed at his own joke and disappeared back into his shop.

'So who is this so-called apothecary?' Xurxo asked, appalled. 'Who the hell *is* he, Lord Rory?'

We put our shoulders to the door and forced it open. Inside, the shop was dark, but we made out Yehudah's shape on the floor. He lay in a huddle, his long black robe swathed around him. He was undeniably dead. Towards the back of the shop, a door banged in the breeze. There was, of course, the usual note.

Anyone who is not for me is against me. This Jew should have died yesterday, but he had a knife up his sleeve, and though I should have foreseen that, I did not. He got the better of me for a short time, but I am happy it was your own dagger, Hambrigger, that killed him in the end. So now I have evened the score a little. You have learnt something about me from the boy, I believe. You are beginning to make connections. Your main problem is that you are so ignorant of essential knowledge of al-Andalus. The boy has that knowledge, but so do others in your group. No matter. The boy will now continue to travel with you. You are, I know, doing your best to get Husain into the hands of Jabir ibn Hayyan. But the boy must also receive treatment. Get him the help he needs. Do not waste any more time. You must continue with this mission, it is vital for your survival.

I will give you some more advice, advice which you ignore at your peril: Do not leave your lady's side. She may give birth before her time, and that is dangerous for both mother and child.

You asked the boy who will be next to die. I will tell you. It is your minstrel. I saved him last time, didn't I! What a surprise!

You did not expect me to save him, not after I'd been to so much trouble to destroy the church and bury him in it. Well, I have my reasons for changing my mind, and they don't concern you. Next time, though, I will not change my mind. Next time, the minstrel will die.

But then, as you know by now, in the end you will all die because you are all against me.

The Mudéjar

'What does he want?' Xurxo cried. 'What is all this *for?*'

'I believe it's about land, power and control. The Mudéjars lost their home, the land which they call Murcia. Jaume of Aragon and Alfonso of Castile took it from them. They want it back, and they want control of their homeland.'

'Yes, but this *one* man, with this *one* child, can't achieve all that, surely!'

'He believes he can, Xurxo. The Mudéjar believes Guido will give him the power to take back Murcia.'

'Do you think she will? How can she be so important that whole territories could change hands because of Sara?'

'It's not Guido who's important, Xurxo, it's his father. We know his father is influential and powerful in Murcia. He will be a Castilian or an Aragonese, part of the *Reconquista* that Alfonso is engaged in. He may have warriors at his disposal, and almost certainly a castle or a fortress. The Mudéjar needs Guido's father to agree to his terms. And this move of his tells me that Guido's father cares very much for his child and will want to get him back alive and whole. The Mudéjar can threaten to castrate the boy if he doesn't get his way.'

Xurxo whistled. 'Yes, of course. The mutilation can be the threat. Mutilation, and then murder. Unless Castile and Aragon agree to his terms. The Muslim is a clever man.'

'He's a very clever man. He disguised himself as a peasant farmer in Mylkehouse; now he's disguised as a Dartford apothecary, and we did not know him either time. And I now believe the sailor who helped Sara on the ship must have been the Mudéjar in disguise as well.'

'Which would explain how he managed to get hold of your relic,' Xurxo said, and I realised he was right. Perhaps Guido had taken it from my pocket and given it to him. Even though I snatched it back from him, it was a clever ploy to make me doubt my own mind.

'What are we going to do?' Xurxo continued in despair. 'Should we question and search Sara? Find out more about her father, and, of course, the identity of the Mudéjar? Or do we get on our way and cross the river as planned?'

'Neither, Xurxo. Our first job is to find Kit. Before the Mudéjar finds him.'

I didn't mention it to Xurxo, but there was something different about this latest message. It was longer than the others, and the writing was spikier. But the opening and closing sentences were exactly the same, so I mentally shrugged and added the venomous little parchment to my collection.

Rosa listened to our tale with increasing anger. Not distress, as most women would have shown. Rosa is not a woman who sits around and waits for the men to make all the decisions; she has decided many things so far, the most recent being that I was a fool to have let the so-called apothecary take Yehudah into his shop. And I agreed with her. Xurxo had already gone from the camp, searching frantically for Kit.

I sat in the cart with Rosa, Guido and Thuban. Guido

was awake, but Rosa wouldn't let him get up from the floor of the wagon. Thuban was conscious as well. He stretched out a hand, reaching, most probably, for Xurxo. The hand fell dejectedly back by his side, but he said nothing. I was aware we were an even more vulnerable group now. Rosa, pregnant. Thuban, dying. Guido, in great pain. As for me, although my dagger rested by my side, for the first time I was not convinced I could defend us all from harm.

'I have been thinking,' Rosa said, stroking her belly. 'The Mudéjar mentioned al-Andalus.'

I'd shown my wife the letter, though I hadn't wanted to, since it referred to bad things that might befall Rosa and our baby.

'You had that dream about the dragon constellation,' she continued. 'You saw Thuban on the dragon's tail. But when you had the dream you didn't know his real name is Husain. Do you know the names of any of the other stars in that constellation?'

I shook my head. I know the stars my grandfather used to talk about. I don't know much about the others, and the dragon constellation never featured in his stories. 'The answer is in the stars then?' I asked Rosa. 'Is that what you think?'

'It's what the Mudéjar wants us to think,' she said obliquely. It was a Kit-answer.

With huge relief, Rosa and I saw Xurxo and Kit returning together, running through the Dartford streets. They were laden with parcels, which they threw into the cart. There were even oats for the ponies, together with other food that would sustain us for a couple of days at least.

With provisions on board, I made my decision. 'We're moving on tonight. We won't cross the river here, it's too dangerous. We'll go west to London and use the bridge, then head north. We'll travel through the night.'

'That is not going to be good for either Thuban or Sara,' Rosa observed. 'They need to rest here for the night. That was the plan, was it not?'

'I've changed the plan,' I said shortly.

'Then change it back again.'

Xurxo, settling Thuban's head on a soft bale of rugs, looked up, his glance moving slowly from Rosa to me and back again.

Who was in charge here? Was it the Lord of Hambrig? Or was it his pregnant wife?

In fact, it was Thuban. Conscious, awake, lucid and ready to talk, Thuban kept us in our camp in Dartford.

33

WE WERE UNAWARE OF IT

'Who is he, Husain?' Xurxo's voice was soft as summer rain.

Thuban's eyes were open. Xurxo held a small cup of water to his lips, raising his head so the man could drink. He smoothed Thuban's wispy hair back from his face, then leant over so the Muslim could see him clearly.

'Husain? Can you hear me?'

'I can hear you.' The words were little more than a croak. Kit, who'd been ready for my order to depart, swung himself round, the reins slack in his hands. I did not move from my seat on Yehudah's crate, but my nerves were taut as my gittern's strings.

'Good,' Xurxo said calmly. 'That's good, Husain. You are very sick, but we are taking you to a healer. He will make you well again.'

'It will be a miracle. I have the wasting sickness, you see.' Thuban turned his head and water dribbled onto his neck. I'd never heard of the wasting sickness, but it's well named. Thuban's limbs were like sticks. There was no flesh on him.

'This healer is a miracle worker, Husain,' Xurxo said. 'With his help, you will regain your strength.'

Thuban turned his head slowly again. We could all see the pain it caused him to move any part of his body. 'How do you know my name?'

'Your friend told us. But we don't know *his* name. Is he Rashid?'

I caught my breath. Rashid! The name Thuban called out in Arabic when he was flung to the side of the wrecked wagon.

'Rashid. Where is he?' Thuban's tongue tried to lick his dry lips, and Xurxo held the cup to his mouth again. But it took too much effort for Thuban to drink; he sank back onto the rugs, exhausted, his eyelids fluttering down.

'No, Husain, not yet.' Xurxo spoke more firmly. 'You must stay awake just a little longer. Who is Rashid?'

'Rashid,' Thuban whispered. 'Rashid is my son.'

I wanted to get down off the crate and ask my own questions, but Rosa put a hand on my arm. Xurxo did not need my help.

'Where is Rashid now?' Xurxo asked, almost as if it didn't matter.

'I do not know. I have not seen him for many days.'

Still Xurxo did not ask the vital question. Frustrated and anxious, I had to listen to him dance around it a little more. 'Did you travel with him, Husain? You and Rashid together?'

'Of course. It was hard crossing the mountains.'

'Into France, you mean?'

'Into Aquitaine. We were chased by armed men.'

'Do you mean the *Justiciers*?'

A slight nod of the head.

Xurxo looked up at Kit, still sitting on the driver's box. 'Food! We need food for Thuban.'

Kit slipped across to one of his packets and produced bread and a hunk of cheese.

'No,' Rosa called firmly. 'He cannot eat that; it will choke him. Something soft, Kit. A broth or a gruel is needed!'

'No broth or gruel here, lady,' Kit growled. 'I purchased food we could take with us on the road. But I have wine, and the grapes it's made from.'

Rosa slipped down off the crate and burrowed into one of Kit's packages. 'Not wine,' she muttered, 'that will merely send him to sleep. But grapes will work, if we can split them and remove the stones...'

Rosa and Kit worked together, passing soft, seedless grapes to Xurxo who hand-fed them to Thuban. I sat on Yehudah's crate and prayed we would get the information we needed. *Go on, Xurxo! Ask him. Before he falls asleep again. Before he gets suspicious. Before anything else happens...*

Thuban gummed the grapes, swallowing them down, then opening his mouth for more. And in the end Rosa agreed to let him have wine, watered down. The questions resumed.

'Where did you go, Husain? You and Rashid?'

'To Aulnay, of course. Rashid said I must pretend to be a *vicomte*, a French nobleman.'

'So it was in Aulnay that you changed your names?'

My heart lurched. At last we were coming to it.

'Rashid chose them. Star names, because we were following the stars. The Egyptian north star, that's my name. Our Egyptian ancestors built the pyramids in the desert.'

'But you have not travelled from Egypt, surely?' Xurxo asked in mock horror.

Thuban almost laughed. Wine dribbled over his grey stubble. Night fell, and Kit lit two clay oil lamps. He'd spent his money well, I thought, as I saw the jar of oil he'd bought, together with splints and char cloth. The small flames glowed fiercely but cast strange shadows over Thuban's face. He opened his mouth and Xurxo fed him another deseeded grape.

'No, not from Egypt,' Thuban croaked, once the grape had gone down. 'From Murcia. Rashid and I live there. Though now, we cannot. The Christians have made it their country and they have cast us out.'

'So you travelled from Murcia, through Castile and Aragon, over the mountains and into Aquitaine! That's an amazing journey, Husain!'

'Oh, but it would not have been possible without my son. I was very sick. Rashid had to carry me. Then we bought a donkey, and that made it easier. Rashid is taking me to an alchemist we know. He is the only one who can cure me of my wasting sickness.'

'What is the alchemist's name, Husain?'

'He is from Persia. His name is Jabir ibn Hayyan. He has made a powerful potion, the Elixir of Life. It will make me well again. But Rashid has left me. I will not get the medicine I need.'

'We will take you, Husain. We will get you safely there. What's Rashid's star name?'

So subtle, so by-the-way. You would never have known the vital question had just been asked. Did Thuban know? Did he realise? Even now, I doubt it.

'Rashid? He called himself Rastaban. And now I remember. Poor Rashid is dead. He drowned in the river.'

Xurxo made Thuban comfortable, and the Muslim fell asleep. I rummaged frantically through Yehudah's crate, with Rosa patiently holding one of the oil lamps to allow me to see. I found the Alfonsine Tables, as Yehudah seems to have labelled them, somewhere near the bottom. An incredible book. There were charts of the stars, meticulously drawn; tables for the rising and setting of stars, planets and the moon at all times of the day and night; and the most beautiful drawings of the constellations.

It took me a little while, with the flame from the lamp flickering and fading occasionally, but I found what I needed. The Draco constellation, showing its main stars, among them some familiar names. Eltanin, Rastaban and Thuban. I sat back, appalled at the deception of these two men, and at the length of time it's taken me to uncover their true identities.

'Rastaban only pretended to drown,' I briefed Kit, Xurxo and Rosa. 'He's alive, and he's calling himself the Mudéjar. No wonder he wants us to get Thuban to Jabir. He's Thuban's son! We thought he was a servant, but they're father and son.'

'But why does Rastaban want Sara?' Rosa asked.

'He will use Sara to buy back Murcia,' I said. 'That's his plan. Guido, the son of the most powerful man in Murcia, will be held captive until that land is restored to the Mudéjar Muslims. Rastaban, or rather, Rashid, wants to deliver his father to Jabir and his country back to his people. All in one go.'

Rosa frowned. 'Perhaps. But why kill Aldara? Why kill Yehudah? How do their deaths help him do either of those things?'

'It has to be something to do with Sara,' Kit said at once. 'Sara is in his power. But it was Aldara and Yehudah who castrated her and changed her into a girl. Maybe that's why they had to die?'

'What if Sara is working with the Mudéjar?' Xurxo suggested slowly. 'Maybe each time Lord Rory has rescued her, that was part of the plan?'

There was a stunned silence at that. All of us have assumed up till now that Sara is 'one of us'. *Anyone who is not for me is against me.* But perhaps Sara is for him and against us.

I look round at my little group, their anxious faces lit or shadowed according to the positions of the two small oil lamps. The sky is now completely dark. The ponies are once more released from their traces, hobbled, but free to munch grass. The six of us sit or lie on the grass outside the apothecary's shop. Yehudah's body is still inside, exactly as we found it. Exactly where the Mudéjar flung it once he'd finished what he'd started, I presume. I'm thinking about that. Yehudah rescued Guido that time, not me. Was Yehudah meant to do that? Guido has been in such pain, such distress. Is that also part of the Mudéjar's plan? But I can't answer any of my own questions, and I have no wish to ask the others what they think, not tonight, anyway. I'm too exhausted. I'll stuff my journal into my jersey again, and I'll tell Kit to snuff out the oil lamps. The night is cold but dry. We can all get some sleep under the stars tonight.

I am tired out, but I can't sleep. I lie on my back and stare at the sky. They are all there, those stars of the Mudéjar's. Rastaban, part of the Draco constellation. Sometimes he calls himself Eltanin. A master of disguises. No wonder Guido said *the Mudéjar is always with us.* Of course, Guido has always known that the Mudéjar is Rastaban, and that he is Thuban's son. Guido knew this. Guido took himself off to the church at the mouth of the Seine and allowed himself to be 'rescued' by me, though there was no sign of the

Mudéjar, and he could easily have got out by himself. Later, Guido took me to Fécamp so we would sail on the ship where Rastaban was disguised as a sailor. Guido 'negotiated' the deal for me, whereby we paid nothing. I have been set up time and time again by Rashid and Guido. But that *still* doesn't make sense. If Rashid is using Guido in his power play, then surely Guido won't willingly help him defeat his own father.

I sat up; I had to know. With a great deal of difficulty, I lit one of the oil lamps, then climbed into the cart to find those Alfonsine Tables again. I took them back to our camp and huddled into my blanket to read, setting the clay lamp down by my elbow. I'd looked only for the Draco constellation before, but now I began to read the whole booklet. It was a detailed and precise work, and must have taken many years to complete. The drawings were intricate, carefully labelled, and the tabulated data were impressive. I didn't read every line; mostly I looked at the drawings, trying to discern some connection between the three Jews, the Christian Don Alfonso and the Muslim who had killed so many of us, and who was still at large. We hadn't set a watch for the night, but I'd positioned myself between Kit and Rosa, while Xurxo was protecting Thuban. Thuban? No, I must remember to call him Husain from now on.

After an hour or so of squinting at the booklet, I found what I was looking for. In the margin of one of the pages near the end, where there was a complex table showing the moon entering and leaving different constellations, there was an inscription in a different hand. *Now is the best time for surgery to remove the genitals. Waning Moon in Scorpio.* There was my connection. A booklet written by Yehudah for Alfonso, annotated by someone else, possibly Rashid, referring to Guido's operation. I didn't know what it meant nor how it changed anything, but it had to be significant. Worn out, I extinguished the flame, tucked the Tables into my jersey and pulled the blanket up to my ears. These English nights are cold.

A sound caught my attention. Something was rustling in the trees to the side of the road, and it wasn't the ponies. They were on the other side, whuffling occasionally in their sleep, but otherwise quiet.

I pushed the blanket away and sat up silently, then shook Kit awake, my hand over his mouth so he couldn't say a word. He understood and disentangled himself from his coverings. We each grasped a dagger. Silently, Kit pointed in the direction of the sound, and I nodded. He made some other gesture, and I shook my head; whatever he was suggesting, I didn't want to do it. We had to stay exactly where we were. In fact, I made Kit lie down again, and I did the same. If the Mudéjar were creeping around our camp, I wanted him to think we were unaware of it.

34

ALL ITS CELESTIAL FRIENDS

'Was that someone calling for help?'

Kit whispered the question into my ear. I thought I'd heard a voice as well, but I'd dismissed it as a faraway owl. But if Kit had heard it too...

We listened, our ears out on stalks. I heard it again, and Kit's grip tightened on my arm. Definitely a human voice, louder – or nearer – than before.

'I'll go,' Kit mouthed in my ear.

But I couldn't allow that. Not with the Mudéjar's death threat hanging over him. I told him I would investigate, and he must stay near Rosa. It was a gamble, and one I did not relish. As much as I didn't want Kit to go off on his own and get the Mudéjar's knife in his back, I didn't want to leave him here either – for exactly the same reason. And the cry for help could easily be a trap.

I sprinted towards the hedge, body low to the ground, head down, dagger in my hand. Away from the safety of the camp, I felt very exposed. Who could be calling for help in this deserted street in a small riverside town? The further I got from the camp the more convinced I became that I was being tricked. Someone wanted to lure me away.

At the halfway point, I turned. I could make out the wagon, though only just, and the ponies, who jostled a bit as I watched them. The moon went behind a cloud, and I could see nothing. I waited, willing the cloud to pass, the moon to reappear, the camp to be bathed in its soft silver light.

'Help! Please help me!'

I spun round again, but the dark made me lose my bearings. Which way was the camp now? Was I looking towards it or away from it? The cry for help had come from a different direction this time. Surely it should have been behind me? It came from somewhere ahead. I felt with my hands, my dagger moving forwards. Nothing.

I waited.

The owl hooted again – if it had been an owl in the first place. But surely it had been someone calling for help? I'd heard the words, hadn't I? Suddenly I wasn't at all sure.

From my right now. It had to be a trick. Someone was circling around, making bogus calls for help, using the dark of the night to confuse and disorientate me. The sound changed again. A snatch of a tune on a flute or pipe. Perhaps it had always been that, not an owl at all. It was behind me. No, to the side again. I didn't know which way I was facing, and I knew I'd made a terrible mistake. I had to get back to the camp.

I ran, stumbled, fell, got up and ran again, straight into a tree this time. Reeling, I tried the opposite direction, and at that moment the cloud shifted, and glorious, welcome moonlight shone down. Staring wildly around, I saw I had indeed run into the trees instead of back to the street. I pounded across the grass, onto the track, heading for the distant wagon, now clearly visible. Back to the camp. Back to Kit and Rosa. But they weren't there.

My wife had gone, and so had my minstrel. Guido was asleep, curled around his pain. Xurxo was sleeping next to Thuban. Both looked as if nothing would wake them. But I shook Xurxo awake, demanding to know what had happened. It was all too obvious, though, and I'd been so very, very stupid. Having lured me away by the sham call for help, the Mudéjar had crept in and had taken both Kit and Rosa.

Xurxo knew nothing, of course. He had heard nothing; he'd been asleep. But he was as alarmed as I was. Could we risk leaving Thuban by himself? The Mudéjar wouldn't hurt Thuban, we knew that now. We were on the point of splitting up to search the area, when we heard voices.

'Who's there?' I shouted.

'Just us.' Kit came into view in the moonlight, Rosa on his arm.

'Where the hell have you been?' I asked furiously, lowering my dagger.

'Lord,' Rosa said acerbically, 'just occasionally your wife needs to relieve herself. The duke would not allow me to go off on my own, but I can assure you he was very discreet. And now we are returning. Is all well?'

'No, all is not well.' I told them what had happened. When I said I'd heard music, Kit swore in Smandego.

'I heard that flute too,' he said grimly. 'Just before I was hit on the head in the ruined monastery. But we still don't know if someone really needs our help, or if it's a trick, so perhaps we should put it to the test.' And from inside his tunic he brought out some small devices. I knew them well. His firecrackers.

'I thought they were spoilt in the storm,' Xurxo exclaimed.

'They were. These are new ones, Xurxo; I made them today. You know I went to the market? I bought food, but also the ingredients I need for my firecrackers. They're not hard to make if you know what to do.'

'Throw one into the trees,' I said quickly. 'Lob it as far as you can, Kit.'

I made everyone lie face down on the ground, and Xurxo flung himself over Thuban. I felt the wind as Kit's arm sliced through the air above me. I knew what would happen next. Barely a moment later, the bang came. Not big, but sharp and explosive. The effect was immediate. Something crashed through the trees and we all heard the sound of flying hooves. And then silence. I checked on the invalids. Both asleep. Thank God for that.

It took us barely half an hour to get back on the road. Thuban was bundled into the wagon and I lifted Guido in myself. Kit took on his usual job with the ponies, while, having settled Thuban, Xurxo helped Rosa aboard. I collected up all our possessions, repacked the boxes and secured the bundles, then threw everything into the cart. Kit leapt up onto the driver's box, Xurxo crouching down low to reassure Thuban who'd just woken up and was disturbed by all the movement and noise, while Rosa sat, as instructed, in the bottom of the cart, her gown spread around her, a look of fear on her face. I registered the fear, but I didn't know the reason for it. I also sat on the floor of the cart, Guido on my right-hand side. The boy had woken. When someone tried to explain to him what had happened, he seemed to crumple.

'The Mudéjar,' he whispered. 'He's come for me again.' And he burst into tears.

It made no difference that I assured him I would not let the killer anywhere near. When Guido heard that Yehudah was dead, there was no consoling him. Yehudah had saved Guido's life in Mylkehouse, just as Aldara had saved him in Grestain. And now both were dead. At first the boy cried jerkily, but then he began to scream.

'It is the pain,' Rosa said distantly, though she did not move to comfort Guido, which surprised me. 'It is not the death of the Jew that has upset Sara, but her own pain. It is good we did not let that fake apothecary take her. Don't you agree?'

I felt the barb of the question. Rosa knew I would have allowed it had we not found Yehudah's body first. And *that* had only been because of my treacherous intestines.

'Stop your screaming,' I commanded Guido. 'The Mudéjar wants us to take you to Jabir in Hambrig. He wrote another of his messages. You are to receive treatment for your injuries, Guido. I'm instructed to get help for you.'

Guido's tear-streaked face looked up, though the moonlight was weak now and I couldn't see him well. I let him lean against me, and, in time, he fell asleep.

I shouted to Kit to make haste, and he drove those ponies hard. We were out of Dartford in the blink of an eye, heading west.

'Make for London Bridge,' I called out, and by the time we reached it surely day would have dawned, and perhaps the weather would even warm up a little. Sitting in the cart in the dark, I felt bitterly cold. I eased Guido's weight off me, laying him down on a pile of rugs and cloaks. And then I crawled forwards to speak with my wife.

'Rosa, is something wrong?'

'I fear it may be. I am bleeding.'

I held Rosa close and felt my shirt grow wet with her tears.

'I can't lose the baby,' she whispered into my chest. 'I can't lose it. Please, God, save my baby. Will you pray too, lord?'

I did, most fervently. I wrapped my arms around Rosa, somehow hoping that the closer I held her the more I could protect our baby.

And so we rattle through the night. Kit sits high on his box, driving the ponies on and on, westwards to the great city of London and its beautiful stone bridge across the River Thames. Occasionally he lets the ponies slow down, and once we stopped so they could rest and drink from a stream.

I'm trying to think of Thuban as Husain now. Husain has woken up and is speaking with Xurxo. Their voices are low, and I can't make out the words. I call to Xurxo to tell me everything as soon as he can, and he gives me a thumbs-up sign. My parchment rests on Rosa's shoulder, and I'm trying to write with it like that, but it's not easy. I don't suppose anyone will ever be able to make out this scribble. Never mind, there's nothing I can do about that.

Guido moans and cries out frequently, in constant pain. The noises he makes are unbearable for all of us, to say nothing of the stench of his wounds. But I am determined to outwit the Mudéjar this time. He will not get his hands on Kit, Rosa, Xurxo or Guido. Not now I know he disguises himself so well. Not now I know he's Husain's son, Rashid, whom we used to call Rastaban, and sometimes goes under the name of Eltanin, one of the brightest of Draco's stars.

And now we're here, rattling and bumping over London Bridge itself, having wended our way through the city's dank and narrow streets. Out through Aldgate in the north-east part of the city wall. North of the river and north of London, which feels good, and my spirits begin to lift a little. The road deteriorates a lot though, and Kit has to slow the wagon down. We can't risk another broken axle. The sky is beginning to lighten, and now Xurxo is crawling across to me, careful not to disturb my wife, who's fast asleep in my arms.

'I'll tell you what Husain has been saying,' Xurxo begins.

I stow my journal away. I must give all my attention to Xurxo.

'Husain has told me more about the Mudéjars,' Xurxo began. 'But, more importantly, he's told me about Sara and about Jabir. Jabir spent quite a time with Husain and his wife and children when he was on his way to Mallrovia from Persia. He got to know them well, and after that they've all kept in touch.'

'Kept in touch?' Kit called incredulously from the front of the cart. 'How?'

'Letters, of course. Jabir has sent them letters over the years—'

'Wait a moment,' I interrupted. 'How many years are we talking about?'

'Thirty. Or thereabouts.'

Thirty years of letter writing between Jabir and the two Muslims?

But hang on... 'Rashid must have been only a child thirty years ago!' Kit and I said it more-or-less together.

'He was,' Xurxo confirmed. 'He was five years old when Jabir first arrived, and he thought the Persian was fabulous. He adored him. Jabir taught him a lot—'

'But how old was Jabir then? Surely only a young man himself!' This was Rosa; our conversation must have woken her. She struggled to sit up, leaning against me. I grabbed a blanket and wrapped it round her.

'Husain says Jabir was fifteen or sixteen,' Xurxo continued, 'and already very sure of himself. He'd made his own way from Tusa in Persia, arriving in Murcia sometime in the spring. This was in the eighth year after Ibn Hud conquered Murcia, which I've worked out must have been the Year of our Lord, 1236. Husain and his wife opened their doors to Jabir, and he stayed with them around twelve months, during which time he made a very good impression on the whole family. And since then, his letters have told them of his many discoveries and inventions in the court of "King Rory of Hambrig", and, of course, the wondrous Elixir of Life.'

'The court of King Rory?' Kit scoffed. 'What king? What court?'

I shook my head in disbelief at this utter garbage. Not only that, but the man has *not* found his long-sought-after Elixir.

'Then if he has not done any of these things,' Rosa said spiritedly, 'what *has* he done?'

Kit looked round, made a face, shrugged and spread his hands in a parody of ignorance. Kit has never been very impressed with Jabir.

'The other thing I should tell you,' Xurxo said quickly, 'is that Jabir introduced himself to his new friends as Jabir ibn

Hayyan. Husain truly believes Jabir to be the legendary alchemist.'

But I wanted to answer Rosa's question. 'He created the *takwin*. That was a monster, but it *was* alive, and it was made by Jabir.'

'He created life? Truly?'

I thought she'd be appalled as I had been, but Rosa sounded intrigued.

'I don't know, lady. I thought the *takwin* was truly alive, but when I saw it I was—'

'You were what, lord?'

I'd been about to say that I was drugged. And then I didn't want to say it. Drugged I had been, through no fault of my own, and the hallucinations induced by the Liberty Cap mushrooms had involved people transforming into dead bodies, and seductive sex with a goddess. The truth is, I still don't know what those drugs did to my brain and my body, nor exactly what I did under their influence. I remember only fragments of that time, and have no wish to relive it. I'm also quite certain I do not want my wife to know anything about it.

'You were what, lord? What were you going to say?' Rosa gazed searchingly at me.

'I was terrified,' I finished lamely. 'Yes, lady, the *takwin* was frightening, as frightening as it was deadly. In the end it nearly killed me, and it crippled a friend of mine.' It was stretching the point to call Richard a 'friend', but it would do for now.

Rosa will not talk about her baby. There has been more bleeding. So much blood. I feel her start to grieve. I have to stay distant from this. If I also become caught up in grief and loss, I will not be able to see this journey through.

I no longer think or care about the letter from Alfonso to Jabir and the Lady Joan; it has lost its relevance. The don's three henchmen are no longer with us, and Castile seems a long way away. My sole thought is to get help for Guido, Husain and Rosa. We who are uninjured must deliver these three sufferers to those who can care for them; this is our mission now.

On the edge of my consciousness hovers the Mudéjar. At each new turn in this long journey home, I've thought him gone; but he surfaces every time, then disappears again, leaving misery and death behind him. Sitting in the wagon, travelling through the monotonous English countryside, I look around me. How can that man be here? It isn't possible. Yet I've thought that before, and then found his sordid, wretched note on the corpse of one of my companions. And Guido's words haunt me still. *He's always with us.*

We arrived in Bedford, a market town in the English midlands, passed the ruins of Bedford Castle, and made our way to the market square. I'd intended to climb down from the cart and go about finding lodgings, but Rosa, asleep and leaning heavily against me, was disturbed as I moved. She turned an unpleasant shade of green and vomited violently. Kit and Xurxo looked at me in alarm. Guido was moaning, a constant background now to everything, but it was getting worse. And Rosa was losing more blood. I could see it and smell it. In a heartbeat, I changed the plan.

'Drive on,' I said tersely to Kit, supporting Rosa and trying to soothe her. 'Can't be more than thirty miles or so to Corby from here.'

'The ponies —' Kit began.

'—will have to cope,' I finished for him. 'And so will we. We need to get to Corby. Drive on.'

Xurxo bit his lip. He knew about Sir Stephen; God knows we'd spoken of him enough.

'Isn't Hambrig closer?' Kit's voice was suddenly tight and strained. No one's been relieving him on the driver's box, and it's hard work driving, driving, without a break. Xurxo had his work cut out with Husain, and I'd been tending the other two. We were at our limit, and we knew it.

'I don't know, Kit. Maybe. But I trust Sir Stephen.'

The ponies were struggling, night was coming on, and we didn't know the way. That became more obvious when we came to a fork in the road. At this hour, there was no one to ask, and no sign of which track to take. Xurxo looked at me, and, no doubt seeing indecision in my face, put his head in his hands. I looked away. If Xurxo were weeping, things were bitter indeed. But Husain was his weakest yet, and Xurxo had been counting on a good night's rest for him. Jolting and bumping along in the cart does him great harm, although we've tried our best to cushion his bony body with our rugs, blankets and bundles of clothing.

'It'll kill him,' Xurxo whispered.

'Look at the stars,' I said suddenly. Guido would have thought of that immediately. 'Head north, Kit. Follow the pole star and go north to Corby.'

The night was clear, the stars bright. High above us was Ursa Minor, and all its celestial friends.

35

THE CORBY LIVERY STABLES

'The Phoenicians used the pole star to guide them,' Grandfather says, perching me more comfortably on his broad shoulders. 'One day, Rory, you'll read the works of Aratus, a wonderful poet from antiquity. He describes the constellations in verse! Zeus, of course, is the father of all, at least according to Aratus. Now look, can you see Ursa Major? Ursa Major is one of the few constellations that we can see at any time of the year. Ursa Minor and Draco are also always visible. Remember that, Rory, if ever you get lost. Not that you will!'

'I want to stay with you for ever, Grandfather,' I tell him, gazing in awe and wonder at the heavenly display above me. 'Anyway, who were the Phoenicians?'

'A sea-going empire from a very long time ago,' Grandfather explains dreamily. 'Look for the pole star, Rory. Can you see it clearly?'

He is determined I will be able to find my way about the skies, and I want to please him, so I obediently point to Polaris.

Grandfather reaches up and pats my knee. 'That's the one', he confirms, pleased. 'Now, Aratus tells us that the Greeks used Ursa Major to navigate the ocean, but the Phoenicians used the Little

Bear, which, although smaller and less bright than the Big Bear, is a more accurate way to steer, since its stars move less in the sky. And the pole star, Polaris, is right at the tip of the Little Bear's tail. That's how you find it, Rory.'

Kit was tilting his head back, seeking the star we needed to guide us home. The right-hand fork lay directly under the pole star, and he flicked the reins. Through the night we rumbled, Kit driving our poor, exhausted ponies on and on, while Rosa, her face sweating and her hands clammy, lay in my lap. Between her legs the blood pooled, and there was nothing I could do about it. There was no one to cradle Guido's head or reassure him, and I had no words for either of them. I feared the worst for both, and for Husain too. Xurxo was constantly trying to get him to drink, but the man turned away from the cup. He used to drink gallons, needing to urinate every half hour or so. Now he neither drinks nor pisses.

Whenever there was a turning, a fork or some decision to make concerning our route, we looked up at the stars, and there were the comforting, unchanging shapes of the ancient constellations. Draco gazed down on us, its enormous tail carving out a huge portion of the sky. Thuban, Rastaban and Eltanin were all there, and once, I now know, Thuban guided the ancient navigators. I wondered why Husain had chosen that name. And why he'd pretended his son was his servant. What was the reason for the false names? I was sure Guido had the answers to my questions. Aldara, Kit and even Yehudah had all told me Guido knew far more than he ever admitted to.

As a small boy, I learnt from Grandfather that the stars don't actually go anywhere, but are still there in the daytime. Grandfather showed me that things can be hidden from sight, but it doesn't mean they cease to exist. I was awestruck. All those stars, all that glory, hidden by the sun!

'Even if it's a cloudy day?' I ask doubtfully.

'Even then,' Grandfather says solemnly. 'The sun's light is still there, isn't it? Otherwise it would be night-time! The stars are always with us.'

Always with us. Like the Mudéjar. I shivered, remembering Grandfather's words. What if the Mudéjar were like the stars? Hidden in some way, but still there?

Just before dawn, Guido awoke. 'Where are we, lord?'

'Nearly in Corby, I think. We're going to get you some proper help, Guido.'

'I'm sorry, lord. I've caused you a lot of trouble.'

'Rosa needs help too,' I said. 'And so does Husain.'

'You know his name?'

'Yes, Guido. And I know the Mudéjar is his son, Rashid.'

'Rashid wanted to help me,' Guido whispered. 'But it all went wrong.'

The ponies, almost dead on their feet, came to a stop in the village of Corby, not in the centre where we'd usually finish up, but by the side of a meadow through which ran a clear-flowing stream. Kit leapt down, unhitched our two valiant little beasts and turned them loose in the meadow. I couldn't begrudge them one blade of grass, nor one swallow of fresh, running water; they had done us proud. But I needed Kit to find Sir Stephen, and he knew where the physician lived; he'd been to his house before. Although he was almost as tired as the ponies themselves, I sent him running.

'How long will he be?' Xurxo's voice cracked with the strain.

'Not long I hope.'

Xurxo said nothing more. The three patients continued to make their various noises of distress and pain, and I was all too conscious of the unpleasant smells in the cart.

'I'm going to go and see what's happening,' I said suddenly, unable to bear it any longer. I desperately needed to stretch my legs and breathe some air that wasn't foetid and foul.

'You're going to leave me with these three?' Xurxo looked up.

It wasn't fair on him. But I had to. I clambered over Rosa and Guido and swung myself down to the ground. 'I'll be as quick as I can.'

Stephen's house, I knew, was a mile beyond Corby. My feet pounded along cobbles, which gave way first to an uneven flinty road and then became a wide grassy strip leading into a paddock, beyond which stood a large grey-walled house with a tiled roof.

Stephen was at home. He was very surprised to see me, and no, he had not had a visit from Kit. I sank down onto a wooden stool in his hall, a feeling of dreadful certainty filling me, my stomach contracting painfully. *It must have happened.* Somehow, God knows how, it must have happened. It had been written in black and white, and the ghastly thing was still in the pocket of my breeches. I pulled it out.

> *You asked the boy who will be the next to die. I will tell you. It is your minstrel. I saved him last time, didn't I! What a surprise! You did not expect me to save him, not after I'd been to so much trouble to destroy the church and bury him in it. Well, I have my reasons for changing my mind, and they don't concern you. Next time, though, I will not change my mind. Next time, the minstrel will die.*

After I'd re-read the horrible letter, the sickness overcame me. A concerned Stephen was owed an explanation. I did my best, but the tumultuous journey from Santiago in Smander to Corby in England couldn't easily be condensed into a few sentences. Stephen is an intelligent man, though, and his sensible questions helped me tell the tale. After a little while, he knew most of it, and he latched onto the most urgent facts.

'Your wife is pregnant?'

'She thinks she's lost the baby.'

'Guido's wound is festering?'

'It's ghastly.'

'Husain is dying?'

'By now he may be dead.'

'And this Mudéjar Muslim has probably captured Kit, and may have killed him?'

I put my head in my hands.

'You said the Mudéjar uses disguises,' Stephen went on,

thoughtfully. 'That's interesting. When would he have arrived in Corby? He must have got here before you did.'

'He gets everywhere before I do,' I said bitterly. 'We have injured and dying passengers in a lumbering great wagon pulled by a pair of ancient ponies. We have to keep stopping, and our pace is slow at the best of times. I don't know how the Mudéjar gets about, but it's got to be faster than we do.'

'He'll be on a fast horse. But you don't see his horse, do you? You've never seen it, though you probably heard it in Dartford when Kit frightened it with his firecrackers. The man stables the horse somewhere, he has to. We'll go to the livery stables first, it's the obvious place.'

I followed Stephen out of the manor house, and we collected two palfreys from his barn. I'd seen no sign of his wife and daughters, but I didn't comment on that. At the livery stables, Stephen motioned that I should stay mounted. He jumped down and talked to the groom, a wall-eyed man with long straw-coloured hair. He came back and told me, 'Someone left a horse here two days ago. He left a name, too. Eltanin.'

'That's him!' I exclaimed. I hadn't gone into the details of the Draco constellation, the star names, the Egyptian pyramids, or the Alfonsine Tables, but I nodded vigorously.

'Master Eltanin did not give a date for his return,' Stephen said. 'Apparently he's paying by the day and will settle up when he comes back here. I doubt he'll come back before you leave Corby. So the way to catch him is for you – or some of you – to leave. Then our man comes back to collect his horse, and we nab him.'

'Meanwhile, Kit dies?'

'He's probably already been killed, Rory,' Stephen said softly. 'We are dealing with a ruthless and desperate man.'

My mind wouldn't accept it. 'No. We have to look for him. We have to try and save Kit.'

'We may miss the Mudéjar altogether then. If he knows you're after him, he may just disappear. You may never catch him.'

'I have to try.'

'I think it's a mistake—'

'I don't care what you bloody think!' I rounded on Stephen, my face suddenly on fire.

'And your sick and injured people who are waiting for you? Waiting for *me,* in fact? What of them? What of your wife?'

'You go to them. I'll search for Kit and the Mudéjar.'

'Rory—'

'Just go, Stephen. Please try to save Rosa.'

He gave me a strange look, not a pleasant one, snatched back his reins and drove his horse out of the stable yard. I'd told him where we'd put the wagon; he would find it. And my heart was suddenly full of relief at the thought of Stephen taking charge of Rosa, Guido and Husain. Xurxo would help. I would not be needed. I called my thanks to the groom, who raised a hand and stared after me as I galloped out of the gate.

I had no idea where to go. In my mind was the image of Rastaban, Thuban's so-called servant. He'd seemed exactly like a rough French servant would be. He'd spoken coarsely, laughed at his own obscene jokes, got drunk in the gatehouse and, later, he'd made fun of Guido. But the Mudéjar could play any part; he'd been convincing as the stalwart sailor, the gnarled old farmer and the surly apothecary. Oh, and my father's ghost. Rashid's disguises were so clever we never recognised any of his characters. Had he also been in disguise as Rastaban, when we first met him in the *Chateau d'Aulnay*? It was likely, and if so, it meant none of us had seen the man as he really was. I rode around Corby. It's not a large town, and I rapidly covered it.

I asked everyone I met if they'd seen two men, one obviously in captivity to the other. Every time, I drew a blank. I retraced Kit's likely route from the meadow where the cart was stationed to Stephen's manor house, and saw no sign of a scuffle or a fight – and no sign of Kit.

In despair, I went back to the stables. Perhaps the groom would remember something more? Perhaps the Mudéjar had said something that would help me? It was a desperate long shot, I knew, but it was all I could think of. I turned through the gate. The groom wasn't there, but a girl came out of one of the looseboxes, a pail of horse dung dangling from her hand.

'Girl,' I called. 'Can you tell me where to find the groom?'

'The groom, sir? He's away on business.'

I asked how long he'd been away, and the girl was quite clear on that. The man left a week ago. I flung myself down from the saddle, grasped my dagger and went looking for the wall-eyed, fair-haired man, who was probably none of those things in reality.

How did he do it? How did he fool us all so easily? It must take some nerve to stand here and talk to Stephen about the Mudéjar stabling his horse and paying by the day, with me just a few yards away, and all the time he was the very man we sought. With fury in my heart, I hunted the Mudéjar through the Corby livery stables.

36

A TREE BY THE BROOK

I'd seen the 'groom' showing Stephen the very stable where the Mudéjar's horse was being kept, his hand waving towards the loose box on the end of the row, though no horse's nose hung itself over the stable door. I'd seen Stephen stride across the yard and look into that same loose box, after which he had come loping back to where I sat, holding the reins of his palfrey as well as my own. I'd heard Stephen describe the horse that had been left by the man who had given his name as 'Eltanin' – a very nice chestnut roan, apparently, not large, but long and strong in the withers. In other words, a fast mount.

I approached the loose box. The girl followed me, but I motioned her back. It would be dark inside, and the horse would be in the way, but that, whether it were an advantage or a disadvantage, would apply as much to him as to me.

He was pressed to the back wall of the stable. He was not tall, so I couldn't see him over the horse's shoulder. I saw the man's legs first. Only there were four legs. Kit was there too, and unless dead men can stand, he was alive.

'Rashid!' I called from the doorway. 'I know you're there.'

'Of course you do.' The voice was high-pitched and the English good, with no trace of an accent. I recognised none of his previous personae in that voice.

'Come into the light, then. I can't see you properly.' I'd thrust my dagger back through my belt, not wanting the cold October sunlight to glint on its blade.

'The issue is,' said the voice from the gloom, 'I'm willing to bargain with you, but I'm not willing to be killed or captured by you.'

'Bargain? You've never wanted that before.'

'You're wrong. It's what I've always wanted. But I had to get you here first. Now Sir Stephen is with my father, I'm willing to do a deal with you.'

'I thought you wanted your father to be treated by Jabir ibn Hayyan.'

'That is what *he* wanted. I went along with his fantasy because it was of no consequence. I can offer you this man's life in return for what you can do for me, Rory. But you'll need to listen carefully, and you'll need to give me your word of honour.'

I curled my lip at that. I made my pilgrimage to the shrine of Saint James the Apostle in order to retrieve my honour. I acquired the ubiquitous cockleshell, a simple symbol of the journey, and then I dishonoured Aldara, daughter of the King of Smander, who counted himself my friend. I don't think my honour's worth a great deal these days. Still, perhaps this Muslim didn't know that, and in any case, his was worth even less. He had blood on his hands.

'Go on then. What's the deal?'

'In return for the minstrel's life, you give me the boy and your woman. I expect you'd be willing to trade the boy for the minstrel, but perhaps, when I include your wife in the deal, you're thinking I'm asking too much. Look at it this way. You can marry again. It won't be hard for you to find a wife, you're a respected member of the aristocracy. That particular woman has been nothing but trouble to you. Because of her, your progress home has been slow and difficult. Because of her, you gave up a far more suitable match. Had you married and slept with the Smanderina princess you would have been home by now, she would be nearing her time, and everything would be looking good for you. Nor would you have made an enemy of the King of Smander. But you threw her over and married the Castilian, and for that you have paid a heavy price. And it will be a heavier one if you don't agree to my terms.'

'Let me see Kit,' I said at once. I'd seen his legs from the knees down, that was all. And in the dark too.

'Sing one of your songs, minstrel,' I heard the Mudéjar say softly.

'*Rosa das rosas, e fror das frores. Dona das donas, sennor das sennores.*'

My heart jumped into my throat. 'Are you all right, Kit? What happened to you?'

'I haven't been hurt. Not yet. This fellow fooled me with his disguise. He lured me here, saying Sir Stephen was tending a sick horse. He has a knife to my throat, Rory. I think it may be Yehudah's knife. Just so you know.'

Well, of course. I'd assumed that was the case. 'What makes you think I put such a high price on the minstrel's life, Rashid? Why do you think I'd swap my wife for him?'

'I think you'll swap your wife for him because he's valuable to you. He knows the past and the future. The woman's just a woman, for all she's Alfonso's daughter. This man is far more valuable. He is a source of knowledge, and knowledge makes men powerful.'

'Just take the boy, Rashid. You've wanted him all along. Hand Kit over and I'll give you the boy.'

The Mudéjar laughed. 'Even you can't think that's much of a deal. The boy has been mutilated. He's neither a boy nor a girl. He's no use to anyone. But you seem to like him. If I leave him with you, you must promise me that if Sir Stephen can't help my father you'll take him to Jabir ibn Hayyan, so he can receive the Elixir of Life. I will accept your word as a nobleman of honour.'

I am not a nobleman of honour, but I did not tell Rashid that. 'Guido also wants to see Jabir,' I said.

'Oh, of course. If the Persian alchemist can cure the incurable, then he can also do the unthinkable. Stands to reason.'

'Your father's illness is incurable?'

Silence for a moment, and then the rasp of a blade against flesh and a strangled cry from Kit.

'Rory,' Rashid said softly, 'such words are dangerous. You should take more care.'

'Tell me about your disguises, then,' I invited, moving slightly closer to the stallion. 'We never once recognised you, not after you disappeared in the River Vienne. What were your disguises after that?'

He laughed again, sounding genuinely amused. 'You think to trick me with flattery? You won't succeed. I was in disguise long before the river trip, Rory. I was Franco in Saintes. In Aulnay I was Rastaban, Thuban's bad-tempered servant. In the *Chateau de Boutemont* I was Raoul, the gatekeeper, though not, of course, the man you found with his neck broken. There were two different Raouls, but nobody ever saw both of them. On the ship I was a sailor. I took good care of you all in that storm, didn't I? We only lost one of you. In Mylkehouse I was your father's ghost. I hope you think I did a good job of being him. After that I was Eltanin, a peasant farmer who helped you and Kit get out of the ruined church. In Dartford I was an apothecary, though that didn't go too well. Here in Corby I was the groom in these very stables. In none of these guises did you know me, and you still do not know me.

'If I were to come to you now, in the broad light of day, would you know if you were seeing me, or if I were yet again in disguise? I can almost hear your mind working on this, Rory. You cannot believe that it wasn't your father you saw in that ruined church. You're devastated that I saw you at your most vulnerable. You forget I have seen everyone at their most vulnerable. I've watched you having sex with your wife, and I've seen you groaning in misery as your bowels discharged into a ditch. I've seen Yehudah frantically consulting his astronomical data so as to know when to operate on the boy, for though he knew nothing of surgery, he wouldn't admit it. And, speaking of the loathsome Jew, I've seen him masturbating until he reached a sexual frenzy, before fornicating grotesquely with the fat Smanderina. As for the boy, I've watched him in his own pathetic disguise, fooling no one but himself, desperate for an outcome that's way beyond reach. That boy is a killer, did you but know it. And finally, I have seen the Smanderino, whose precious sister was abused by the man to whom you gave your protection. I have spared the Smanderino, you will notice. He has never been threatened. He has taken good care of my father, and for that reason he survives.'

'You haven't mentioned Rosa. Nor Aldara.'

He sighed. 'Too long a list. But they were not forgotten, I promise you.'

'Why did you kill Joseph, Rashid?'

'Joseph was a clever man. He knew Rastaban hadn't

drowned. And he knew, somehow, that I was Franco. You won't believe me, I know, but I did not kill Joseph.'

'You're right, I don't believe you. What about Yehudah? You killed a wounded and unconscious man in cold blood.'

'Too many questions, Rory. Do you want me to slit your minstrel's throat or are you going to redeem him?'

Neither, I was thinking. I'd been keeping the Mudéjar talking, which bought Kit extra time and gave me a chance to assess the situation in the stable. My eyes were used to the darkness now.

'One more question, Rashid,' I said, looking at the stallion and wondering how I could use him to overpower this murderous man. 'One more question. Why did you tell Guido you could operate on him in France?'

'I can wield a knife just as well as that Jew could. I would have had his balls off in one clean swipe, but you interfered. A shame for him, because I was going to show him how to change his appearance completely so he could fool the whole world into thinking he was a woman.'

'And is that what you're going to do if I hand him over to you?'

'I hardly think what happens then concerns you.'

I didn't think Guido was going to get lessons in disguises. I thought he'd be killed immediately, and his body left to rot in an English ditch.

She'd crept up softly behind me. I felt her touch me lightly on the back. Carefully I turned round, noting how she'd positioned herself so the Mudéjar couldn't see her: an intelligent girl. She held out the pail and I took it, wondering. How could I use horse dung? Clearly, the stable girl thought it would be useful; she was gesturing, silently pointing to the end wall of the row of boxes. She began to creep along it, disappearing around the corner. She had a plan. Trouble was, I'd no idea what it was.

'Kit, I'm going to have to bargain with this man. You understand that, don't you?'

'Do whatever you have to do.' His voice was muffled. I imagined him with his head tipped back, the blade touching his throat, his Adam's apple bobbing nervously, his eyes on the rafters.

Rafters! I looked up at them. Could I reach? I decided I could. But I didn't move. The girl was somewhere behind the stables now.

'Rashid, why did you and your father use the star names?' I hoped to keep the man talking.

'We found our way across the continent by way of the stars. My father chose the name "Thuban". It was once the pole star.'

'Oh yes. In the time of the Egyptians, I believe. But how did you know that?'

'Jabir taught us a lot. About the stars and many other things. I've never forgotten what he taught us.'

'Us? Who else did he teach?'

'I had two sisters then.'

'What happened to your sisters, Rashid?'

There was no answer. Instead, there was a loud rumbling from somewhere behind the stable block and two sharp bangs. Daylight suddenly shone through from the far side of the barn. Leaping up, I seized the rafters with both hands and swung my body forwards, kicking out with both my feet. I hit the stallion's side with force, and he reared up angrily, his front hooves threshing the air. He came down heavily, but by then I'd already swung forward again, this time catching his neck with my left foot and kicking up into his belly with my right. As he reared up again, whinnying furiously, I dropped to the ground, grabbed the pail of manure and charged into the stall.

The stallion was moving, and behind him there were three people all tussled together. But I knew which one was the Mudéjar. He wasn't Kit and he wasn't the girl, so whatever his disguise this time, I knew him. I flung the stinking horse shit all over him, leaving the wooden pail stuck over his head. Of course he tore it off at once, but his feet were floundering in the muck and he couldn't see. The stallion trampled everywhere until he realised he could run freely through the ruined back wall of his stable. Hooves pounding, he flung himself out of the stall, knocking the Mudéjar over as he went. Kit and the girl had already removed themselves at top speed, and I saw them in the distance, hand in hand, running like the devil was after them. My instinct was to fling myself aboard my palfrey, charge out of the gate and get quickly back to the rest of my group. But there was still the Mudéjar. I stayed where I was.

The man was sitting in a pile of horse shit, his back to the wall, what was left of it, his legs stuck out straight in front of him. The empty wooden pail stood beside him. The knife was on the ground. I picked it up.

'Cut my throat,' said the Mudéjar.

'What was behind it all?' I genuinely wanted to know.

'It was my last chance. We tried before. A whole lot of us, with Ibn al-Aḥmar in charge.'

'Ibn al-Aḥmar?'

'From Granada. It's part of al-Andalus. Ibn al-Aḥmar is the ruler there, an emir, we call it. He has never liked Castile. Alfonso...'

‘What about Alfonso?’

‘It doesn’t matter. Ibn al-Aḥmar started a rebellion. We joined it. Most people joined because the Christians have taken our country and we want it back.’

‘But not you? Your reason was something different?’

‘Yes. But again, it doesn’t matter, not anymore. Is Husain dead?’

‘I don’t know. It may be that Stephen can save him, or it may be too late. You should have let Kit fetch Stephen. He’d have got to your father earlier then.’

Rashid shrugged. ‘Nothing matters now. Are you going to kill me?’

I looked at my dagger in my right hand, Yehudah’s lethal-looking knife in my left. I have once killed a man in cold blood. It was something I had to do, and it was for him, not for me. This was not an occasion like that one, and I had no intention of killing the Mudéjar just because I could. ‘You’ll stand trial,’ I said heavily, knowing he would not. ‘You have murdered innocent men and women. You’ll be tried for your crimes.’

Through the layers of horse dung, he gave me a sardonic look. I smiled briefly. ‘Stand up. I am going to secure you and take you to your father.’

‘I would like to wash this muck off first,’ he said, looking down at himself.

But I’m not that easily fooled. I made him stand and then used various bits of horse tack to tie his hands behind his back and to make a short leash for him. I left Stephen’s palfrey secured to a rail and I marched the Mudéjar down to the meadow. I was relieved to find the wagon parked just as we’d left it and our two little ponies munching happily in the meadow. As we drew nearer, I counted six heads. Six? Rosa, Guido, Xurxo, Kit, Stephen, Husain – surely not

Husain. He'd be lying down. The sixth person must be the stable girl. I had yet to thank her for making this possible. I hurried Rashid along.

Husain was still alive. Stephen shook his head at me though. The man had little time left, and there was nothing Stephen could do for him. Rosa was very sad. Stephen had examined her and was fairly sure the baby was dead. Yet Rosa was still carrying it. Stephen asked Rosa about the pregnancy, and my wife told him how sick she was at the start. Apparently Aldara had told her the sickness meant the baby would live and be healthy. Stephen shrugged. Whether or not the pregnancy was going well back then, it most certainly wasn't now.

The sight and smell of Guido's wound made Stephen recoil. 'Who did this?' he gasped. I explained, and he looked grim. 'I don't know if I can save his life,' he said harshly to me when we were out of the boy's hearing. 'I want to, but it may not be possible. Even if I do, the scar tissue will be disfiguring and uncomfortable. He will never be able to live a normal life, neither as a man nor as a woman.' Stephen was incensed.

'It was what he wanted.' It sounded pathetic. Aldara would have put it so much better.

Aldara. I miss her more and more. She was an exciting woman to be with, daring and different. Where Guido put on girls' clothes to hide his true identity, Aldara wore men's garb to make a statement about herself as a woman. She knew she was short and plain and no longer young. Guido's 'boys' clothes' suited her, and I liked her in them. But I didn't realise any of that at the time.

Stephen and I stripped Rashid and scrubbed him in the little stream which the stable girl tells us is called the Willow Brook. From the pocket of Rashid's tunic I pulled a small flute. I doubt it will play again; it's full of horseshit. We found Rashid some spare garments of Kit's and Xurxo's, and we tied him to a tree by the brook.

37

MUCH WORSE THAN THAT

The stable girl's name is Ellen. She's nineteen, older than I'd first thought. I was going to take her home, but she says she doesn't want to go back.

'Where do you live and with whom?' I asked her, frowning. We don't need any more lame ducks on this harrowing and protracted journey to Hambrig.

'Just in the town. By myself.' It was unsatisfactory. She opened up much more to Kit.

'She lives with her father, and she hates him. He wants to control her and everything she does,' Kit said afterwards. 'She's been working at the stables since she was twelve, but she hates that too. The groom tries to abuse her. Her father says it doesn't matter what the groom does, and he takes all her money. She doesn't want to go back. In fact, she wants to come with us.'

I felt like making some cantankerous retort, but I owe a lot to Ellen. If it hadn't been for her, Kit would have been another victim of the Mudéjar.

Stephen wanted to get Guido to a surgeon. But, he told me, there's no surgeon in Corby.

'Can't you do it?' Rosa asked him. It sounded as if she expected him to perform the operation there and then in the meadow.

'Sadly, lady, I cannot. I have the knowledge but not the equipment. The nearest reputable surgeon is in Leicester. You should hurry there at once.'

'But that's in the wrong direction!' Kit pointed out sharply. 'And we don't know who the surgeon is. We should go straight to Hambrig.'

Anger sparked in Stephen's eyes. 'The direction hardly matters, Kit. This boy's life is at stake. Leicester is closer than Hambrig. I insist you go there, or the child will die.'

'Will the surgeon be able to treat Husain?' Xurxo was anxious to know, but Stephen didn't think so. Husain is doomed, he told Xurxo, not mincing his words.

Stephen turned to go home. I told everyone to get ready for the road and instructed Kit and Xurxo to tie Rashid's legs together, bind his arms behind his back and chuck him into the cart. At last, at *long* last, the Mudéjar's reign of terror is over. I hurried after Stephen.

'Your wife and daughters,' I began.

'Gone.'

'Where?'

'I don't know. My wife decided to leave me and she took the girls with her.'

'But why, Stephen?'

'Reasons which I will not go into. However, I believe they are at Amelia's parents' house, which, ironically, is in Leicester, whither you are now bound.' His voice was strained, his expression haunted.

'Come with us,' I said impulsively. 'Come to Leicester and introduce us to the surgeon.' I didn't know if he'd loved his wife, but he'd been besotted with his two daughters. They'd meant the world to him.

The journey took the entire night, mostly because, of course, we had to stop several times for the needs of our patients. An hour before dawn we rumbled into Leicester. Stephen gave his instructions to Xurxo, and we skirted south of the town wall and passed through a turret gateway that seemed to connect with the castle, finally drawing up in the courtyard of a convent known as The Newarke. Here, Stephen informed us, we would find the surgeon whose skill was beyond compare.

'Your surgeon's a nun?' Kit asked disbelievingly.

Sister Magdalena was an austere, unfriendly looking woman. It was hard to deduce her age, but from her physique and her voice I put her in her early fifties. She was not the prioress, but she was clearly used to giving orders and to having them instantly obeyed. I told Kit to find stables for our ponies and a place to leave our wagon, while Xurxo and I moved the patients. There was, of course, a hospital wing in the priory, but I'd never seen one quite like it. Everything was scrubbed clean, everything was coloured white and everything was arranged in meticulous order.

No wonder Stephen approves of Sister Magdalena. He taught our Doctor Bethan the value of cleanliness when treating wounds, and Bethan practically worships the ground he walks on. Sister Magdalena greeted Stephen with a nod of recognition, and they spoke quietly to each other in Latin.

'Sister Magdalena is from Germany,' Stephen said, swinging round to me. 'We are very lucky to have her services, and luckier still that there are no invalids currently in the hospital here. There's plenty of room for our patients, and Sister Magdalena will be able to give them her full attention.'

Under the direction of both Stephen and Sister Magdalena, we got Husain, Guido and Rosa into bed in the hospital.

'What about Rashid?' Xurxo asked.

'Rashid stays with me,' I said, surprising myself. Why would I want the Mudéjar anywhere near me? He should be taken to the town gaol and kept there until we are ready to move on with our journey, But I didn't take him anywhere.

There was much I didn't understand about Rashid and his father. The main thing that interested me was their connection with Jabir, but I also wanted to find out exactly how the Mudéjar managed to carry out his crimes, and why he was so intent on destroying us. *In the end, you will all die because you are all against me.* Every single one of his letters ended with that sentence. I wondered why this man thought we were all against him, and why he wanted to murder us all, one by one. There would be no more murders, thank God. But he must have had some reason for hating us so much.

Ellen was taken to the lay sisters' dormitory. Kit, Xurxo, Stephen and I are being quartered in the gatehouse, but Stephen would, I knew, barely set foot in the place. He would be at the bedsides of our patients. Whether he assisted the nun, or she him, I didn't much care. I was just relieved beyond measure that we now had Husain, Rosa and Guido safely in proper beds, being cared for by a physician whom I greatly admired, and his friend, this straight-backed, stern-looking German nun.

I hustled Rashid into the gatehouse and shoved him down onto one of the beds, a narrow, rickety thing with a thin straw covering.

'Now explain it all to me,' I ordered, sitting on the bed opposite. 'You've told me about the uprising and Ibn al-Aḥmar who started it. But you had different reasons for joining the rebellion. What were those reasons, Rashid?'

'I told you it doesn't matter.'

'I think it does. And I need to know why you want to kill us all.'

'Not all. The messages said "all", but it was just some of you.'

'Did you actually fall off the boat? We thought you'd drowned. Was that the plan?'

'It was the plan, yes. To fool you. But I swam underwater and got out of the river. After that, everything was easy. Even my father thought I was dead.'

'Why, Rashid? Why did you do all these terrible things? Why did you kill Joseph and Aldara?'

He did not answer.

'I'll give you one more chance. Why did you murder those two innocent people?'

His eyes suddenly blazed with anger. 'Murder two innocent people? I didn't do that. Joseph guessed my secret.

But it was the *Justiciers* who wanted him dead. *They* are the ones who murder innocent people!'

'Joseph knew who you were.'

'He knew I'd survived, and he guessed the rest. He threatened me.'

'What about Aldara?'

'I did not kill her.'

'Your message threatened her though – this one.' I pulled a parchment out of my saddlebag and read aloud, '"The plain-looking woman from Smander interfered with my plans, although she would have been the next to die anyway."'

Again, there was no response. The man sat on the bed, his tired but intelligent eyes holding my gaze. Yet he did not refute the accusations. His guilt was clear to see.

'You have not yet explained the point of this whole business,' I went on. 'The disguises, the killings, the threatening letters... What is it all *about,* Rashid?'

'It is about the terrible things Prince Alfonso and his father-in-law did to my homeland, my friends and my family. It's about revenge.'

Prince Alfonso. He's not a prince now, he's the King of Castile, León, Murcia and many other places. He is – *El Rey*.

'What were you going to do to Guido and Rosa in the name of revenge? Whatever was done to your homeland and your family, Rashid, it had nothing to do with either Guido or Rosa, and you know it.'

'My mother and my sisters were likewise no threat to the Christian invaders. Yet they were raped and murdered.'

'And you were going to do the same to them?' As I said it, I felt the bile rise treacherously. Angrily, I swallowed it down.

But Rashid shook his head. 'No. I was going to do much, much worse than that.'

38

WE SET OFF FOR HAMBRIG

We are definitely not having a baby. Stephen's examination of Rosa by the Willow Brook had been the best he could manage, and he'd been fairly sure then that the pregnancy was over, but here, in the white, bright dormitory, with Sister Magdalena in stern attendance, the confirmation was complete and unequivocal. Rosa is white-faced and silent, which surprises me. Had she been so desperate for a child?

Xurxo has asked me how I feel. 'Everyone is looking after Rosa,' he said. 'Everyone knows she's desolate. But what about you? You must also be grieving.'

I don't want to go there. It's become another place which must be hidden away, like my love for Kathryn, my tears for Little Rory, and my knowledge of Tommy's existence. I could add to the list: Nicholas's drowning of Felix. Jonny believing me guilty of rape and murder. Mother dying while I was away at the court of King David. Father lying to me about Kathryn.

'I can deal with it,' I said to Xurxo.

Did Xurxo see through this? I'm not sure, and anyway it didn't matter.

I spend a lot of time with Rashid, which must seem mad to everybody else. Rashid is my enemy and my prisoner, yet I sit with him in the convent gatehouse, hour after hour. Stephen is in the hospital. Kit is with Ellen the stable girl, although no one ever sees them. Xurxo sits with Husain, holding his hand, and I think he's almost willing him to die. I do not want to be in that hospital. I know it's where I *should* be, helping Rosa get through this loss of ours, knowing she's carrying a dead child in her womb. But I can't do it.

'Tell me about your sisters,' I said to Rashid. He was reluctant, so we sat in silence together for an hour, each with our own thoughts.

'Their names were Shakira and Amira,' he said suddenly. 'Shakira was the eldest of us, and Amira the youngest. I was the middle child. They didn't like me. Or perhaps they did, but I never knew.'

'Guido had a sister,' I said, remembering his story, 'but she was killed by some bully-boys who thought they were killing Guido.'

'He is *mukhannath,*' Rashid said, his eyes suddenly flashing. '*Mukhannathun* have to be castrated. It's the law.'

'When did you first meet Guido?' I asked.

It took many hours. Rashid is not a man who's used to

making even light conversation, much less baring his soul. He didn't want to tell me anything. I said I could easily question Guido instead. Uninterested, Rashid shrugged. And it wasn't true – I couldn't talk to Guido. He's very sick, and Sister Magdalena is angry with me for allowing him to have been so damaged.

Immediately after nones, the nun asked me to join her in the infirmary.

'Lord Rory, this was a child in your care. Yet you allowed unscrupulous adults to exploit and hurt him. This is not easy to forgive. You have gone against God in what you have done.'

I gazed down at Guido, who was unconscious under a blanket. His long dark hair was spread over the pillow. *Mukhannathun have to be castrated. It's the law.* Islamic law. Which does not apply in a strict convent in the English midlands. And no excuse whatsoever that it was not I who wielded the knife. 'Will he die?'

'Stephen and I are doing our best to save his life. But what sort of life will it be?'

Her guttural German accent made her words sound even more severe. And she was right.

'Sister Magdalena, this surgery went wrong—'

'This was not surgery. This was butchery, by a man who knew nothing of medicine, nothing of human anatomy, nothing of the pain he was causing. If he did know of these things, but did this terrible deed anyway, we must question his humanity. I have been told the man who did this is dead. Is that so?'

I said it was so. Not only is Yehudah dead, but so is the woman who tried to patch Guido up after Yehudah had finished. I made an effort to explain about Aldara.

'I can see where she did her best,' the tall, angular nun interrupted. 'Yet she also had no medical training.'

I felt as if I were drowning in all this. I was to blame for Rosa's distress, that was certain. And, it now appeared, also for Guido's mutilation. I could not claim I'd had nothing to do with it, that it was what the boy had so desperately craved and that I'd made him a promise. I knew what this uncompromising German nun would think of such excuses. So I said nothing, while the austere woman standing in front of me seemed to search my very soul. I was unsurprised Stephen thought so highly of her.

'Is there anything you can do for him?' I asked at last.

'We have already done it,' came her unexpected reply. 'The boy will live. The fever is broken and he is recovering. As for the transformation you tried to achieve, as Stephen will tell you, it is perfectly possible to remove the male genitalia safely and successfully. But only by a skilled surgeon. You should have forbidden anyone to touch this child.'

I went to find Stephen, surprised he wasn't also in the infirmary, and I tracked him down in the kitchen, where he was talking to the cooks, a pair of elderly nuns.

'Stephen. I need to know what you and Sister Magdalena have done for Guido.' My voice sounded shaken; I hadn't meant it to sound like that.

He turned. 'I was instructing these cooks to make a special broth for him. Come with me.'

He took my arm and walked me through an arch that led into the cloisters. There was no one else there. Stephen leant against the stone wall. He looked shattered.

'You asked me earlier about Amelia, my wife. She became suspicious, Rory, and I should have known she would, because she's always distrusted me. She blamed you, since it was after our journey back from Sussex that I first met Sister Magdalena. It is irrational, but Amelia holds you responsible. Sister Magdalena and I are colleagues, but Amelia would not accept that. She believed that under your influence, as you stood accused of rape and murder, my own morals fell by the wayside. I should have turned against you too, since I lost not only my wife but my beautiful girls. But you came here seeking my professional opinion, and it's hard to walk away from that.'

I met Amelia once. A sharp-featured woman who made her dislike of me abundantly clear. Perhaps Stephen and his nun were colleagues; perhaps they were more than that. It wasn't my business. I touched his shoulder. 'I'm your friend, Stephen. And I hope you're still mine.'

'At this moment it is hard to know,' he said. 'But I will do what friends should always do; I will tell you the truth. Guido is delusional. He will never be a girl. He is stuck with a boy's body and a boy's mind for the whole of his life. Meddling in these things only causes trouble, and can be dangerous. Sister Magdalena is extremely angry with you. It is now impossible for Guido to have a normal life of any sort, and he will be in pain and discomfort until he dies. There is nothing we can do.'

'But I've just spoken with Sister Magdalena, and she said you'd already treated Guido. You must have been able to do something for him!'

'We've done what we can, which is precious little. We have inserted a small tube through which urine can exit his body safely. This on its own will make a big difference to his life. We have soothed the inflamed area with a balm. We have dosed him with camomile to help him sleep. Sleep is often the only and the best cure. When he wakes, Sister Magdalena and I will talk to him. We will explain that he must give up this dream he has of becoming female. We shall be gentle but firm, Rory. This is what the boy needs now.'

'Are you going to look for your wife now you're in Leicester?'

'No. And please don't mention Amelia to me ever again. Now I must go and check on your wife and on your Islamic friend, Husain. Husain does not have much longer, and it is truly a miracle he has lasted this far. Rosa will live, Rory, but she may not be able to bear you any children. Be prepared for that.'

This may turn out to be the worst day of my life. Stephen is near breaking point, yet he will not stop driving himself. He neither eats nor sleeps, but tends to his patients all the time. Sister Magdalena's dour face greets me when I go to sit with Rosa, but Rosa lies listlessly in her bed, unable to summon up a smile or a greeting. Indeed, she turns away when she sees me enter the room. I don't know if Stephen has told her she may now be barren. I don't raise the subject myself.

I sat with her for less than an hour, then wandered restlessly around the abbey, before returning to see if Husain was awake, which he was.

'I'm dying,' he said to me, coherent for once. 'It is the wasting disease.'

'How did you get it?' I asked him.

'I got it in my hometown of Mula. We were under siege and there was no food. We had to eat animals we would not normally eat, even those forbidden to us by the Prophet. Even such! Although the Prophet tells us "that which is necessary makes the forbidden possible". And it is no wonder so many fell sick afterwards. Yet I did not realise I was sick, not at first. I continued to farm my land and to raise my son. But they came again, the Christians. They came because we had dared to live in our own country and be our own people. They slaughtered us. Alfonso of Castile and Jaume of Aragon, they killed us, or they kicked us out. But Rashid, Sara and I escaped. We made for—'

'Wait a bit,' I cried. 'You were with Sara during the revolution?'

'Sara is special,' Husain said, his voice dwindling now to a whisper. His eyes were closing. Sister Magdalena came over to tell me off for tiring her patient. I stood up and stretched until my joints cracked. And I was thinking, *who, exactly, is Guido*?

At that moment there was a terrible, tearing cry from Rosa, and I sprinted across the room to her bed. But Stephen pushed me aside. The two doctors bent over her and I could see nothing. My mouth was open, my eyes staring, and I knew something terrible had happened to my wife. But no one told me what it was. They were busy with tubes, bags, splints, things I didn't recognise. I ran from the infirmary, down the steps, straight into Xurxo.

Xurxo steadied me and then took me to the refectory.

'What has happened?'

'I don't know. I hate this place. Nothing makes sense anymore. Guido is a wreck, Rosa can't have children, Husain is dying. Joseph, Isaac, Aldara, Yehudah – all dead. I haven't seen Kit all day.' I put my head in my hands. I usually have a plan, no matter what fate throws at me. Today I had nothing.

'We should go to Hambrig,' Xurxo said gently. 'We should take our sick, our wounded and our dying to Jabir. It is what I have wanted all along. Husain too.'

I suddenly knew he was right, and I raised my head. 'Tomorrow, then, Xurxo. Tomorrow we set off for Hambrig.'

39

AN IMPOSSIBLE ALTERNATIVE

He almost didn't let me. Stephen. With his warped mind, distraught at the loss of his daughters, he's not the man I remember. And, perhaps because of Sister Magdalena, he's angry with me. Confronting me on the steps of the infirmary, he spat his words into my face, asking me what the hell I thought I was doing. *Did I seriously want to kill my wife?*

'What happened, Stephen?' I had to shoot the question into the vituperative snarl. 'What happened yesterday when Rosa screamed?'

'My God, I thought you'd never ask. Rosa aborted the pregnancy.'

My heart seemed to stand still. Aborted the pregnancy? I thought the baby had already died!

'She did it herself, Rory,' Stephen continued, his voice quieter now. 'She used the wrong end of a ligula. Sister Magdalena had been using it only an hour previously to apply an unction in case Rosa were developing a fever. She left the ligula within reach, and Rosa – well, she used it inside herself to scrape out her womb. Excruciating. And extremely dangerous.'

I could not speak.

'We got to her in time, thank the Lord. She was bleeding profusely, but she will live. She was extremely lucky not to have fatally damaged herself. Do not take her from the abbey, though. She must rest here several weeks. Only then will she be fit to travel.'

I've always trusted Stephen. Anything he says, in his line of work as a doctor, is absolutely and without question the right thing to do. Yet today I went against him. He howled at me that *he* is the physician, not I. That I had no right. That my wife would die and I would have killed her. That I would be a murderer after all. I invoked my rights as Rosa's husband. I decide where she goes and what happens to her. Stephen has no authority; he can only advise. Then Stephen raged about Husain. The man must stay in Leicester.

'Why, if he's going to die anyway?' I asked. 'He can't be saved, you've already told me that. So let him come to Hambrig with us.' And again, Stephen had no power to stop me.

Nor could he prevent me from moving Guido.

I also took Rashid. But Stephen was uninterested in Rashid, and equally uninterested in Kit, Xurxo or Ellen. The healthy, he doesn't care about. The sick are his world. I was sorry for him, but I couldn't let his crazed despair at losing his family exert a hold over me. No doubt he would seek comfort from his grim German 'colleague'.

I gathered my group, the strongest carrying the weakest out of the infirmary, laying them as best we could in the cart, swaddled in blankets and cushioned by bales and bundles; Kit hitched up our stalwart little ponies and mounted the driver's box, his new friend Ellen beside him. Xurxo swung himself on board and helped me haul Rashid up into the cart.

'I spoke to Sister Magdalena,' Xurxo said, manoeuvring himself to sit closer to me. He and Kit have been taking turns driving, but I have not yet offered. I *will* offer, I tell myself. Soon.

Xurxo grew tired of waiting for me to ask. 'About Rosa.'

I stiffened. What right did the Smanderino have to talk to the nun about my wife? But I remained silent.

'She told me a great deal. I think you should know what she said.'

I shook my head, anger bubbling up inside me.

'Your wife wasn't trying to hurt herself,' Xurxo explained, as if to a child. 'She wanted to rid her body of—'

'The dead baby,' I said. 'I know.'

'It was your baby too,' Xurxo said after a pause. 'You're allowed to grieve—'

'No. You do not get to tell me what I'm allowed to do.' I was shocked to hear myself shouting. Who the hell did he think he was? Allowed to grieve? What did Xurxo know of grief for dead children? My stillborn brother, my little sister, my tiny baby son, even poor Felix... And now, more than likely, Guido to be added to the list.

Rosa was awake and she'd heard everything. 'It is true, lord,' whispered my wife. 'I could not face carrying the dead thing inside me. That is all.'

'Why didn't you ask for help, Rosa? Why did you do it by yourself? It was too dangerous.' But so was jolting along in this cart on these badly potholed English roads.

'Sir Stephen refused to do it. Afterwards, Sister Magdalena was furious with him. Xurxo knows. He was trying to tell you.'

More anger, this time directed at Stephen. My anger is

constant and all-consuming. It has become part of me, like another organ in my body; I cannot be separated from it. The baby, I tell myself, was scarcely even a baby. Boy or girl? Beautiful or deformed? Mallrovian-looking like me, or Castilian like its mother? We will never know, and none of it matters. It's dead.

'Don't cry, lord,' my wife said, reaching out to brush the tears from my cheeks. I hadn't known I was crying. 'We will try again. I will give you a son, I promise.'

What made me say it? 'Stephen says you won't. You may not be able to have children, lady.'

I felt Xurxo's consternation, but I didn't care. From around my neck I pulled my lanyard and ripped off the cockleshell of Saint James the Apostle, the proof of my successful pilgrimage to Santiago das Cunchas. For a moment I held the little shell aloft, aware that Rosa, Kit, Rashid and Guido were all watching, these broken, wretched companions of mine. Unsteadily, I stood up. The cart wobbled, and Xurxo looked round in alarm. Kit got onto his feet, crouching, ready to jump if necessary, but I wasn't about to throw myself to my doom. Instead, I hurled the useless shell away from me, heard it hit some stony obstacle to the side of the road. We rumbled past – the thing was lost.

Nobody spoke, but there was a sort of collective sigh.

The next day I asked Guido about his relationship with the Mudéjar.

'Rashid and his father wanted to travel with you, lord,' Guido said, his voice stronger now. 'They used me. They said they would offer me to you for training as your squire. And I had to lead you to them in the *Chateau d'Aulnay,* and then they would also tag along, and so we could all get to Hambrig. If I didn't do what they said, they told me they would make sure I didn't get my treatment.'

'But how did you meet the two Muslims in the first place, Guido?'

He frowned. 'Lord, please call me "Sara". You always did, until we got to Leicester.'

'But *when* we got to Leicester I discovered you will never be "Sara". You will always be male, with or without a penis. You have to accept this, Guido, though I know it's not what you want. When we get to Castle Rory I will find work for you, and you can be part of my household.'

'Will you still want me as your squire?'

'No. You are not suitable for that. But there will be something you can do, and you will have a good life in Hambrig.'

He nodded, fingering his clothing. Before we left Leicester, someone had found hose and a tunic for him to wear, and the disgusting, bloodied shift has no doubt been burnt. I looked at him. Even in male clothing, he is unconvincing as a boy. But I meant what I said. There will be kitchen or stable work that a young lad like him can do, and even with his effeminate ways, he'll shake down.

It took us a week to get to the Mallrovian border and another three days to arrive in the shire of Hambrig. Husain has remained stable, much to Rashid's relief. I have not bound Rashid since Leicester. He has no interest now in escaping or killing; he knows we are trying our best to get his father to Jabir.

Jabir and the Lady Joan live on the outskirts of Hambrig Town, north of the town wall. We approached from the north, having crossed the River Hurogol by the bridge at Wisbech, so we came to Jabir's house before we entered the town and long before I clapped eyes on Baudry Hill, at the top of which stands my home, Castle Rory.

Jabir had no money to build his home and workshops. I made it my business to fund the laboratory, but the house was built with Joan's money. She had it put by, a decent inheritance from her father. Her textile business has always made a fair profit, but since Mallrovia joined the Hanseatic League, Joan's business has grown. She now has three apprentices working for her in the 'factory', learning their trade at the wheel and the loom, and dyers too. Whereas Joan herself once handled the operation from start to finish, it's now divided into different jobs, each with its own specialist workers. This was Kit's idea. Joan thought it would work well, and, by all accounts, it has done. I've not seen it for myself. After Joan and Jabir moved out of Castle Rory, I left them to it. I told myself they needed to find their feet without my interference, but of course, it wasn't that at all; I couldn't bear to see Joan so happy away from the castle, when I was so unhappy she'd gone.

We clattered into a rough courtyard, and there was the laboratory on our left-hand side. Jabir's laboratory and Joan's workshop make two sides of a square, while the house they share makes a third side. Jabir has called the whole collection 'The College'. He really does have pretensions to scholarship! Our little ponies deserved a good rest, and both Xurxo and Kit jumped down to lead them to a solid-looking water trough next to one of the wells. A donkey poked his head out from a nearby stall. I climbed stiffly down from the cart.

Jabir emerged from the laboratory, but he was not the Persian alchemist I remembered. He always used to wear garish colours; wide pantaloons and long, flowing tunics with vivid, striped decorations. The Jabir I saw today had his slim, dancer's form encased in plain russet leggings and a shabby dark blue jersey, the kind the Lady Joan always used to knit for me. The jersey was belted around his waist, and his hose were tucked into plain leather calf-length boots. He looked very workaday, and I rather liked it.

He stood stock-still as he saw our cart in the middle of his courtyard, with Kit, Xurxo and me in plain sight. He cupped his hands around his mouth, threw back his head and howled for his lover. Just the one syllable. 'Joan!'

She came at a run. Again, there was that shocked standing-still moment; then Joan picked up her skirts and ran straight into my arms.

Two scenes will stay in my mind for ever.

The first is Jabir, bending over Guido who was sitting in the cart, his back against Yehudah's crate that we'd continued to carry with us. Guido, wearing male clothing, his hair tied behind him, boy-fashion, and just the very faintest sign of a downy growth on his upper lip, looked up at the Persian, hope shining in his eyes.

'Hello, young lady,' Jabir greeted him. 'And what's your name then?'

'It's Sara,' Guido said. And burst into tears.

The second picture I will never forget also involves Jabir.

We were all still in the courtyard, and Jabir was on his way to fetch something from the laboratory, but Rashid somehow vaulted out of the cart, landed on his feet and sprinted across the yard to halt Jabir in his tracks. Rashid went down on his knees, holding his hands out to the alchemist. The rest of us were transfixed. We all knew Rashid was going to plead with Jabir to save his father, and we all knew, because both Stephen and Sister Magdalena had told us, that there was no hope for Husain. So unless Jabir had truly found the Elixir of Life…

'Sir!' Rashid began, his high-pitched voice trembling a little. 'Sir, please hear me! I know you can work miracles. I know of you and your great works here in Hambrig. You won't recognise me, but many years ago you travelled in my country and you stayed with my family, and now I *implore* you to help me.'

There was no pretence and no disguise; this Rashid was for real. This was the man behind the innkeeper in Saintes, the gatekeeper at Boutemont, and so many other false identities. We waited for the Mudéjar to introduce his sick father.

Rashid continued, almost breaking down as he spoke. 'I am begging your honour to help the child in the cart become a girl. If you have the power, please, please do this. I have money. I will pay. This poor child is a girl in the body of a boy, but he has been mutilated by others and—'

'Enough.' Jabir held up his hand.

Kit, Xurxo and I were gazing at each other in astonished disbelief. All this was for *Guido?* Not for Husain at all?

'What the fuck?' Kit swore under his breath. 'What is going on?'

Xurxo had already doubled back to the cart. I knew why; he thought Husain may be dead already. Perhaps he had finally succumbed to his 'wasting disease', or maybe the Mudéjar had added one more to his tally.

Rashid was sobbing now. Jabir looked again for his lover, and the Lady Joan came to his side. Between them, they helped Rashid to his feet and the Lady Joan led him into the house.

Xurxo shouted that Husain was all right. So was Guido. Jabir went into his laboratory, and I followed Joan. I was not leaving the Mudéjar alone with her, no matter how tearful he might be.

Joan wanted to hear all about my pilgrimage. She was not surprised Kit has returned to Hambrig, and was pleased Joy will join him here. Ellen was introduced, and proved unexpectedly shy in Joan's presence; she stayed close to Kit's side the whole time.

I hate upsetting Joan. I didn't want to tell her about the murders, the storm at sea, the loss of life, the injuries and the illnesses, and I especially didn't want to tell her that Rosa had been pregnant and now she wasn't. I didn't want to mention the appalling vengeance of the *Justiciers,* or the ruthless crusade of the Mudéjar. I spoke about my pilgrimage, just a little, enough for it to make sense. Nobody knows my reasons for making it, so it wasn't necessary to mention that it did me no good whatsoever. I spent quite some time describing the splendours of the cathedral in Santiago, and Kit and Xurxo, who both know it well of course, were able to supply extra details. I mentioned my marriage, the prestige of the match, the new connection we now have with Castile. Ellen stayed silent, clinging to Kit, while we three men sounded, to my ears at least, falsely cheerful and far too glib. And it was stupid, because Joan is probably the most perceptive person I know.

'All right,' she said when we'd finished painting our own

gold leaf onto the cathedral's glorious portico. 'All right, Rory. I understand you've left out three quarters of the tale. I don't know why, but I expect it will come out sooner or later. I don't know who all these other people are, or how you acquired so many extra companions either.'

There had been even more companions, we could have told her.

'I know your mind is on other things,' Joan said. 'Your friends, who are being treated by Jabir. Tell me about them.'

'I cannot,' I said, getting up from the table. Looking about me, I could see that Joan has made a perfect house for herself and her Persian lover. The furniture is covered with rich fabrics, the walls are hung with Eastern tapestries, cheerful fires burn in every room, and some of the windows even have glass in them. The hall windows are glazed, and the whole place is cosy. Warm. Inviting. I no longer wonder at Joan moving to be here with Jabir. Castle Rory is a bleak, draughty place in comparison, although Joan's own little workshop in the bailey, her House of Colours, always looked as comfortable as this new house does. But the House of Colours, the *Egg* as we always called it, had been just a simple log cabin, a single room. Now Joan has a proper house. She has companionship and love; she has work to do and a loyal clientele. Joan is content and I should be happy for her.

I moved away from the table, but caught Kit's eye, and he followed me out into the courtyard.

'Kit, don't leave Rashid alone with anyone. I want him tied up. *Chained* up if necessary. Don't forget what he has done: the threats he's made and the murders he has committed. I charge you and Xurxo with imprisoning Rashid securely while we're here.'

I waited until I saw the three of them coming out of

Joan's house. Kit and Xurxo had Rashid between them, his head bowed, his arms once more pinioned behind him. They marched him to an outhouse, shoved him inside and turned the key. Satisfied, I walked over to the laboratory, took a deep breath and went in.

I was expecting to see the same apparatus as I'd seen first in Sir Bernard's great hall, and then, though it was much more rudimentary, in the Liberty Hut. But this new laboratory is nothing like the old ones. I stood in the doorway looking at everything Jabir has done, and I was stunned. He looked up from his work and saw me.

'Come in, O Lord of Immobile Stupefaction.' It was odd to hear the old epithets back in use.

'Not so immobile,' I answered, leaving the doorway and going fully inside. Husain lay on a wooden bench near the door. Jabir had undressed him and covered him with a thick blanket. But the laboratory was not cold; it was heated by two furnaces, one at each end of the building, which is long and low, and which also has glazed windows. From the far corner came an intermittent, familiar sound: the contented grunting of Sappo the toad. I walked across the room and found her squatting in a large wooden box lined with a dark red blanket, one of Joan's, of course. I greeted Sappo, and she chuntered back at me. We've had a few adventures together, Sappo and I. It was good to see her again.

'So what do you think?' Jabir asked me, his long, pointed fingers making shapes in the air around his head.

'I don't know what to think. What are you doing to Husain? And where is my wife?'

'I will answer all your questions, O Lord of Inquisitive Impatience, but first I want you to have a look at this child.'

I hurried over. On another wooden bench lay Guido, also stripped and covered by a patchwork blanket.

Jabir drew back the blanket. 'See? See the damage that has been done here? This child had male anatomy, but somebody has changed that. There are two problems, however – and do not worry, she cannot hear us; I have sedated her. Here, then, is the first problem. She no longer has male anatomy, but neither does she have a female body. This, though, is fixable, or perhaps I should say that to a certain extent it is fixable. The second problem is these changes are largely hidden from view. No doubt my corrections of this botched business will make Sara feel better in herself, and the pain will be gone, but the world will be unaware of her transformation, so what is the point?'

'I thought the castration would do it, Jabir. Doesn't it mean that her voice will not change? She won't grow a beard?'

'You are right, O Lord of Superior Wisdom. But there is more to a woman than a high voice and a hairless face. What of the female shape? Breasts, hips, the length of the long bones? Would she be allowed to marry? Will she ever be able to lie with a man? Can she bear children?'

'Well?' I rasped. 'You're asking a lot of questions. Do you have any answers?'

'Oh yes.'

I didn't believe him. Jabir always thinks he has the answer to everything. But he's been proved wrong. Other than the creation of the miraculous *takwin* – which I only saw through a drugged hallucinatory haze – I cannot think of a single successful experiment he's carried out since I've known him. So I am, as always, sceptical.

And he saw it in my face. 'You do not believe me, O Lord of Doubt and Distrust? Well, we shall see. And now, we shall look at the Lady Rosa.'

Jabir took me into a separate chamber which led off the

main laboratory. There, in a comfortable bed, wrapped up warmly, but sitting up and reading a book, was my wife. She looked up, then instantly looked away, closed the book and laid it on the bedcover.

'Lady Rosa tells me she lost a baby recently,' Jabir said. His words met with silence, but he was undeterred. 'This often happens with a first baby. It does not foretell future disasters. Lady Rosa, in my opinion, is ready to conceive again, and I have told her so. I shall leave you, O Lord of Great Good Fortune, to look after your wife and to create your family.'

Jabir twirled on his toes and danced out of the room.

I cleared my throat. 'What if it happens again?'

'Jabir does not think it will happen again.'

'Jabir thinks he knows everything. He doesn't.'

'Do we have any choice, lord?'

'Choice?'

'The alternative is that we sleep in separate beds for evermore, and that you never have an heir.'

An impossible alternative.

40

COME WITH ME AND I WILL SHOW YOU

The next few days were all the same. We stayed with Joan and Jabir, using various outbuildings and barns, although there was one room in the main house where Kit and Ellen were allowed to sleep. Nobody questioned or disputed this; we had more important concerns. I checked on Rashid every day. Though he was a prisoner, he was well fed and cared for. He asked occasionally after his father, but mostly his questions were about Guido.

'I just want him to have his dream,' he said sadly. 'It's so important to him.'

I didn't believe him. It wasn't a good enough reason for the elaborate disguises, the stalking, maiming and killing. The Mudéjar was hiding something. But the oddest statement he made was that he never killed anyone.

'I know you won't believe me,' Rashid said, as we walked one day through the field that adjoins Jabir's property. 'Nevertheless, I want you to know that I have not killed a single member of your group. Nor have I threatened anyone.'

I shook my head. I understand Rashid does not want to face trial for his crimes, and perhaps he thinks that because I'm keeping him here, rather than in the town gaol, and even letting him out to take a walk each day with me, he can talk his way out of it. I told him there was no chance of that. The sheriff has been sent for. Rashid can say his piece in a court of law, but I doubt anyone will believe a word of it.

Jabir isn't letting anyone into the laboratory, so nobody knows how his patients are faring.

'Why won't he let me see the boy?' I asked Joan, tetchily. 'I brought him here. I've a right to know how he's doing.'

'And I expect you will,' she said calmly. 'When Jabir is ready to tell you.'

'But why is he being so secretive?' I cried, and I kept Jabir back after supper that evening.

'You should not stop me from returning to my patients,' he rebuked me. 'They need me more than you do.'

Undoubtedly true, but I asked him to tell me, as concisely as he could, in words of one syllable if possible, how Guido and Husain are doing. And I reminded him that I'm Lord of Hambrig. I have the authority to walk into his buildings if I choose to do so.

'Very well, O Mighty Lord of Hambrig, I will tell you in words of one syllable.' And he ticked the words off on his fingers. 'They. Are. Both. As. Well. As. I. Hoped. They. Would. Be. At. This. Stage.' Then he skipped away from me and hurried back across the courtyard. Joan, still at the table, was laughing.

The sheriff will be here any day, and once Rashid has

been taken away, I'll be free to go home and to put this wretched pilgrimage behind me. And, of course, to introduce my new wife to my household. The thought of doing that does not fill me with pleasure.

I was sitting at the table in the hall, when through the open door, I saw Jabir heading towards the house, his head down against the wind. I assumed he'd be wanting Joan for something, but he came in, mounted the dais and sat opposite me. I waited for his opening 'O Lord of Puerile Pomposity', or some such insult. It never came.

'Rory.'

He never calls me that.

'I want you to see something.'

It could only be a death. But whose?

Jabir held out his hand, and I saw a piece of parchment. Rolled. I took it. Unrolled it.

'What is it?' I asked, unsure of what I was looking at.

'It is a deed of indemnity. To protect me from being sued if my patient survives but is not cured – or if my patient dies and has relatives who might blame me. I have learnt about this the hard way, so now I ask all patients to write and sign a deed of indemnity before I treat them.'

I looked up. 'Even Rupert?'

He nodded.

I looked again at the parchment. The writing looked familiar. I read each word carefully.

I indemnify Jabir of Tusa against any damage done to my body or my mind by the medical treatment and surgery he may perform on my person. Signed: Darakhshan bin Ibrahim

'Who on earth is Darakhshan bin Ibrahim?' I was totally at sea. I had never heard of this person.

'Darakhshan bin Ibrahim is a Muslim. His name means 'Bright, shining one'. He never uses this name, though. In France he chose a different name, a name which means "Guide".'

Guide? Not hard to make that into a Christian name. 'This document was written by Guido?'

'It was. And what do you notice about it, Rory?'

Still bemused, I pulled another parchment from the pocket of my breeches, and, with shaking fingers, I opened it. I passed it across to Jabir. I didn't know which of the many letters it was, but since they were all much the same, it didn't matter.

'"Anyone who is not for me is against me",' Jabir read aloud. '"This man deserved to die, and the *Justiciers* knew it. The woman who saved him is next in line. In the end, you will all die because you are all against me."'

He put the parchment down on the table and moved the deed of indemnity so it lay next to the letter, their edges touching. I stared at them. I could not believe it.

'These were both written by the same hand,' I said at last.

Jabir's long brown fingers kept the two documents together. He waited for me to say the next, the obvious, thing.

'Guido wrote them both. Guido wrote the Mudéjar's letters.'

'And so?'

'And so Guido is the Mudéjar. Not Rashid. Rashid was

telling me the truth. It was Guido who killed Joseph and all the others.' My lips said the words, but my mind couldn't accept it.

'Sara did the killing,' Jabir said heavily. 'And it is this child who has been threatening you all along.'

'But why?' My voice rose. 'Why did he do these things to us? We were trying to help him! This is why you wouldn't let me see him? You knew he was the Mudéjar?'

'It is the right question. Why did Sara feel the need to commit murder?'

'Sara!' I broke in, derisively. 'You mean – what was it again? – Darakhshan bin Ibrahim!'

'I made her sign her proper name, Rory. She did not want to, but I told her I would not treat her unless she wrote the document in her own hand and signed it with her proper name, witnessed throughout by me. You see how much this treatment means to her? She was even willing to admit to a male name. Have you ever known her do that? You have known her a great deal longer than I.'

'Have you made her a girl?'

He sighed. 'You do like your words of one syllable, O Lord of Banal Brevity. It doesn't always work in such a clear-cut way, much as we might like it to. Come with me and I will show you.'

41

WHAT IS GOING TO CHANGE OVERNIGHT?

And so, on Friday 14th October, I was finally taken to see Guido, who was really Darakhshan bin Ibrahim, and whom I now knew to be the Mudéjar. And who now truly *was* Sara.

She lay in her bed, sobbing quietly.

'I have told him,' Jabir said, sitting on the bed and stroking Sara's hair. She did not look up.

I had the questions ready on the tip of my tongue. The whys and the hows, the when-did-you-knows and the how-could-you-possiblys, the who-are-you-reallys and the what-was-it-all-fors. But the sight of Jabir gently stroking Sara's long hair, his face full of compassion, kept me silent. The questions could wait.

'Turn over, Sara,' Jabir said, and she did. Tear-drenched eyes gazed up at me, the sheet clutched to her chin. 'I am going to tell Lord Rory what we have done. You can join in, if you want to. But first, because there is such a lot to tell, we will get Lord Rory a stool to sit on.'

I looked around, located a stool in a corner and fetched it. When I'd sat down, Jabir nodded to Sara. 'That is good.

We shall not be disturbed as we tell our tale, you and I. Lord Rory has a right to know everything. Then he can make up his own mind about you, Sara. You must trust him, as I do. Do you understand?'

Jabir's eyes searched Sara's face, and Sara whispered that she would trust me. But it would have to be a damn good story to mitigate the Mudéjar's terrible crimes over the past few months.

'Everybody knows,' Jabir began, 'that I have long been searching for the Elixir of Life. But few know I have never found it. I have allowed rumours to travel across continents; rumours of my success and of my triumphs; rumours, even, of my glory, here in little Hambrig. I have told lies and I have suppressed the truth. I have sent false messages, giving false hope. I have built a famous and magnificent reputation on a gossamer of untruths. And the reason for this? It is not that I crave fame and fortune. No. It is that I wish to work with the best physicians, alchemists and astronomers. I wish to be accepted among them as an equal.

'I have built up in my mind a picture of what it would be like to walk with men of learning, men of scholarship, to discuss data and information with them, and to speculate on the unknown. This is my dream. For me it would be *paradise*. So. I know what my paradise looks like. But my paradise is not anyone else's. For example, it is not Lord Rory's wish to do these things. No, Lord Rory's paradise looks very different. Perhaps he will tell you about it one day, Sara, but I will give you one clue. For Lord Rory, paradise is being with the people he loves.'

I blinked. It was true, and I hadn't known it. But, somehow, this man from Persia had. I could never have put it into words.

'And now we can talk about your own, your very own,

paradise, Sara. This is where you can speak as well, because you know it better than anyone. You have walked in this paradise, in your mind, just as I have walked in mine. I have seen myself in animated conversation with the best scholars in the world. I have heard their words of wisdom, and I have treasured the respectful way they listen to my opinions. All in my mind, perhaps, but very, very real to me. Your paradise, Sara, like mine, and perhaps everybody's, is an *acceptance*. An acceptance of who you really are. By whom, though, must you be accepted? There is someone – someone special. There must be, or you would not have done so many desperate things and taken so many risks. Now, Sara, would you like to take up the story from here?'

Her eyes were fixed on Jabir. And then she spoke. 'You are right, Jabir ibn Hayyan. I have been seeking my paradise since I was five years old, when I played in my father's garden with Rashid's children. It was a wonderful garden, full of little paths and places to hide. We played there day after day. We grew up together, knowing each other well. I had no brothers or sisters, so they were my family. That garden was my paradise.'

'Ah, yes. This is an idea from Persia, my own country,' said Jabir. 'But there is more to this paradise, Sara. You are no longer five years old. You grew up, as you said, in that garden. But then something happened, and the paradise was destroyed. Tell us about that.'

She shifted under the sheet, but she was transfixed by Jabir's gaze. Her lips opened and she moistened them with her tongue. I saw that Jabir's hands, his long, spatulate fingers, were on Sara's shoulders. I hadn't noticed him placing them there, but there they were, and his malleable thumbs caressed the hollows of her neck. I swallowed. What was he doing to her?

'You are right, Jabir ibn Hayyan,' she said again. 'Something happened. I was thirteen years old, and Rashid, who worked for my father, was the leader of a rebellion against the Christian rulers of our country. But the rebellion failed, and Rashid and his army were defeated. It lasted two years, and I was fifteen by the time King Alfonso and King Jaume entered our city as conquerors again. Oh, how we had hoped never to see the Castilians or the Aragonese! It had been a dream, and it came to nothing. All our hopes came crashing down. We were punished severely for daring to want to practise our own faith in our own land.

'Many Muslims were killed, and others were exiled. Some stayed, subservient to our masters. These were called the Mudéjars. "Mudéjar" – it's an Arabic word, and it means "subjugated". When I signed my letters "The Mudéjar", I could just as well have signed them "The Slave". But although we became Mudéjars, Rashid was determined to escape, and to take his sick father to find help here in Mallrovia. Because they knew the famous Jabir ibn Hayyan! And they knew, because he had told them in his letters, that Jabir had discovered the Elixir of Life! Rashid told me his plans. He would hide his wife and his children in a safe place, and he would take Husain to find Jabir ibn Hayyan and beg him to cure his father. And then he would return to Mula, rescue his family, and make a new life somewhere else.'

'What part did you play in this plan, Sara?' Jabir asked softly, still caressing the girl's face and neck.

'I found them a good hiding place. It was I who hid Rashid's family. I know where they are. And nobody would find them, nobody!'

'How can you be so sure? The Christians are clever. They are devious. They—'

'I *am* sure! James wouldn't let it happen!'

Jabir sat back then, his fingers drifting away from Sara's neck. 'James. Tell us about James.'

Again, the moistening of the lips.

'Tell us about James, Sara,' Jabir repeated. 'I think we have arrived, don't you? James is your paradise, isn't he?'

Sara gave a sob. She tried to turn away, but in a heartbeat Jabir's hands were around her neck again. She couldn't turn.

Jabir leant over the girl, his face inches from hers. 'We need to know this part of the story, Sara. James is your paradise. Tell us about him.'

'He is the second son of Jaume of Aragon,' she whispered, her voice so quiet I had to lean in to hear her. 'He came with the invaders. He set up his camp near to where Rashid lives. I met him and I spoke with him. He is tall, with dark hair and kind eyes. He is a warrior, strong and manly, but he is also beautiful and full of gentleness. He took my breath away.'

'You fell in love with him?'

'And he with me!'

'You told him your name was Sara, and that you were Ibrahim's daughter.'

'Yes.'

'You told James that Ibrahim and Rashid were friends, and you were like a sister to Rashid's children.'

'Yes.'

'So even though Rashid had led the uprising, he and his family were spared.'

'Yes. Because James loves me.'

'James knows where Rashid's wife and children are hidden.'

'James and I chose the hiding place together. James will not let them be taken. Malik and Hanif are my brothers.'

'And your mother is with them. Although she is not your real mother.'

Sara's eyes filled up again, and the tears ran down her face, into her ears and onto her neck.

Jabir wiped them gently away. 'And so James waits for you to return.'

'He said he would wait for me. And then we shall be married.'

'He knows of the problems you have with your body.'

'He – he knows I am getting help. He wants me to get help.'

'He believes I can cure you. Make you a real woman.'

'We both believe it,' she whispered.

Again, Jabir pulled away. 'This is your paradise, Sara. A life with James the Christian, the son of a tyrannical invader, a man who believes I can work miracles and deliver him a pure and golden wife. And then you and James will walk forever in your own paradise garden.'

I wasn't sure I could listen to much more of this. I had never before seen Jabir in action in this way. The probing statements, not couched as questions but facts, the pathetic responses, the gradual revealing of the true story behind Darakhshan bin Ibrahim's life. I stood up. It was a signal, for Jabir smoothed Sara's hair one last time, and then he also stood.

'Sara, you may go to sleep now. Sleep well and deeply. You need time to heal. Come, Lord Rory, we shall talk outside.'

Jabir tucked the patchwork blanket around Sara, whose eyes closed quickly in sleep. In the far corner, Sappo shuffled in some leaves and grunted her approval.

On the way out, we passed the bench where I'd last seen Husain. But it was empty. My heart lurched. Had it all been for nothing? Had Husain died right here, just as he'd reached his hero?

Jabir read my expression. 'He is not dead. I have merely moved him. I will tell you more about him later. For now, we must discuss Sara. You have questions for me.'

I did, indeed. I wanted to know what Jabir had done for Darakhshan bin Ibrahim, and what the outlook was. I also wondered how on earth Jabir knew so much already.

'Oh, that part was easy,' he said. 'It was clear to me that Sara's perceived need for treatment stemmed from something that mattered more to her than anything else in the world. After that, it was easy to guess. As soon as she mentioned her lover, James, I knew how it must have been. So much medical treatment could be achieved if people would only look at the mind as well as the body. But do physicians do that? Very rarely. And surgeons, not at all. For them, it's all about the knife, the scalpel and the sutures. But the mind reveals all, Rory. That is where we should always begin.'

I thought of Stephen, the unhinged physician who'd been my friend, and the stiff, unbending nun who had looked at Sara's body and despaired. They would never have spoken to her as Jabir did.

'How did Sara get Rashid to do all those things, though? The disguises and the pretence? And who actually did the killings?'

'She manipulated him, it is true. And the killings? Well, Sara used threats to get what she wanted. And she was not afraid to be violent when she thought it necessary. Perhaps if she had confided in you from the start, none of it would have happened. But she decided she couldn't take the risk.'

'But why kill at all? And why make all those "anyone who is not for me is against me" threats? I don't understand why she felt she needed to kill us!'

'I thought Sara explained that very well just now. She had to get to me for help. James will not marry her unless she is truly a woman. Sara and James both believe I can accomplish this, and it is the most important thing in the world to that young lady. The threats were to make sure you brought her straight here. And she needed to carry out the threats, at least once or twice, to show you it was real. Only then, so she reasoned, would you race across Europe to find her salvation.'

I reflected on the sad loss of life. And remembered Thuban's words from long ago: *I am asking, no, Monseigneur, I am begging you to take this boy as your squire.* Of course he'd begged me to take Guido. The fate of his family – and perhaps even his country – depended on it. Later, Thuban had told me, *The freedom he claims as his right to life can be the denial of someone else's.* I'd not understood this at the time, but now it was clear. Others had to die so that Sara could save not only herself, but her marriage to James of Aragon, Rashid's wife and children, and all the condemned Mudéjar Muslims. Long ago, in the *Chateau d'Aulnay*, Husain had tried to warn me.

'What have you done for her, Jabir?' I asked, aware I'd been silent for some time. 'Can you help her at all?'

'I have already helped her. Could you not tell?'

'I meant—'

'I know what you meant, O Lord of Many Misapprehensions. I will be able to help her. But I needed to know her story first. I will do my best. And after I have done my best, I will tell you all about it.'

I had one more question. 'That reference to paradise.

And Sara's talk of a garden. When we were in Saintes, which is where I first met her, there was an actual Paradise Garden. It was in an abbey, a convent.'

'That is interesting. Did Sara know of this garden?'

'Oh yes. She was employed by the *abbesse* to spy on people. There was a clever spyhole in that very garden.'

'And they called it the Paradise Garden? As I said before, this is a Persian invention. It is not from Islam, but has been adopted by Islam. Sara, who is a Muslim, would know all about it, which is why I chose my words as I did. The Paradise Garden was originally nothing to do with paradise. The Persian word is "pairidaēza", which means a garden encircled by a wall. An enclosed garden. They are always very beautiful, and divided into four quarters, each one reached by a wide grassy or gravel path, and with a fountain or a pool in the centre. There are often channels of water running through the garden—'

'But it was *exactly* like that!' I exclaimed. 'The one in the *Abbaye aux Dames* in Saintes, I mean. How can a Christian convent have an Islamic garden in the middle of it?'

'Who was this *abbesse* who was so keen to employ a spy?'

'She was the sister of the chief of the *Justiciers*. And their mission was to kill Jews. She used her spies to listen to conversations in the Paradise Garden, and then she reported them to her brother.'

'Perhaps he had been to Persia. Somebody must have been, or there would have been no Paradise Garden in this convent.'

That evening, the sheriff and his men arrived at The College. I sent them away.

Rashid is not the Mudéjar.

He says he killed no one.

He says Sara killed no one.

Then who killed Joseph? He says it was the *Justiciers.*

Who killed Raoul? He says the gatekeeper had fallen down the steps and broken his neck before Rashid even arrived at the *Chateau de Boutemont.*

Who killed Aldara? He says she was swept out to sea by an enormous wave during the storm.

Who killed Yehudah? He says the man died of heart failure, brought on by loss of blood from his wounds. Who inflicted the wounds? Darakhshan did this, but only in self-defence.

Who threatened to kill Kit? He says that was neither him nor Sara. It was Darakhshan bin Ibrahim.

A week later we were ready to leave. I was anxious to get home. I left the wagon in the field behind the outhouse where I'd been keeping Rashid prisoner for the last ten days. As I manoeuvred it into position, close by the barn where the donkey lived, Joan joined me, clutching a bright orange shawl around her. It had been raining all night and was still doing so. I was already soaked to the skin, and shoving the wagon into place on my own was not easy.

'The ground's very boggy,' Joan cautioned needlessly. 'Mind the wheels don't get so bedded in we can never move the cart again. And don't startle Ismail al-Jazari.'

'Who?'

'The donkey. His name is Ismail al-Jazari.'

I told Joan I'd come back for the wagon in the spring, unless she wanted to keep it.

But she didn't want to talk about the wagon. 'Jabir told me about the Islamic garden you were in. It sounds beautiful.'

'It was.'

I decided to get some stones to wedge half under the wheels. That would make it easier to move the cart later. I found a couple of solid ones, flat and square. Bending down, I tried to drive one under the nearest wheel. Found I was kneeling in wet, sloppy mud. Realised I should have put the stones in place before getting the cart lined up. Discovered I could simply haul the cart forwards a foot or two to get the wheels properly positioned. Nearly tore my arms out doing just that. Caught the odd word Joan was saying – not everything, but I got the gist of it.

She wants to make a paradise garden of her own! In this very field. Somewhere peaceful, beautiful and private. 'Land is always *used* for something, isn't it?' she said earnestly. 'We build on it, or we farm it, or we make roads out of it. And the rest is just left wild. But I *love* the idea of making a garden that is just for walking in or sitting in and enjoying. What do you think, Rory?'

Happy that the wagon was now safe and secure, I stood up, squelching in the mud. Joan began to laugh. 'Look at the state of you!'

'Hmph. *You* try wedging stones under cartwheels in this weather. As for the garden, Joan, it's a lovely idea, but again – look at the weather.' I waved a filthy hand at the steadily falling rain. 'Those gardens were designed in Persia! And the one I saw was in the south of France. The climate's different. How will your pretty pathways and lovingly created flower beds look in the Mallrovian winter, do you think?'

'It doesn't matter, Rory. Even if I only get a few weeks' pleasure from it, it will be worth it. And it will be a gesture towards Jabir's own culture, won't it?'

Jabir never talks about his early life. Or not to me, at any rate. Perhaps Joan is right. Perhaps a Persian garden, thousands of miles from his birthplace, will make him feel more at home. I didn't realise Jabir was homesick, but Joan would know better than I about that.

Kit and Xurxo were organising three ponies to be saddled and ready to go in the morning.

'What about Rashid? He's travelling with us,' I said.

'Thought he was staying here,' Kit said. 'Now we know he's not the Mudéjar.'

I haven't told anyone about Sara's confession, but somehow everybody knows.

'Mudéjar or not, he was involved in everything, and he held you at knifepoint, in case you've forgotten. He comes with us.'

'And Husain?' Xurxo's voice sounded strangled. 'Would you separate the father and son?'

'Husain stays here, he's still receiving treatment. Sara and Rosa also stay here, but we will return for them. Now get this sorted out, I want to make a start.'

I walked away. My anger has returned, almost as if it had never left me. I stuffed my belongings into my bags and rounded up my hat and dagger. Thinking to say goodbye to my wife before leaving, I hurried across the courtyard to Jabir's laboratory.

But as I turn the corner, I run straight into my father.

So you're not going to wait for your wife to recover? You are so anxious to go home you intend to leave her here?

She's getting better, Father. She's improving every day. I'll be back for her in a week or two.

And the girl whom we are now calling Sara? You will be returning for her as well?

She is responsible for several deaths. She will be put on trial in Hambrig.

Before you do that, Father says sternly, *you should talk to the man whom you once thought responsible. Now you think him innocent. It is easy to make mistakes.*

But I—

Father had vanished. To my right, the laboratory door banged shut. Was that the wind? Or had my father just gone in? I whirled round, and the wind caught my hair and whipped it in front of my face, blinding me. I pulled my hat from my pocket and crammed it onto my head. Three strides, and I had the door wrenched wide open.

Jabir, standing by Husain's bed, looked up in surprise.

I scanned the laboratory. No sign of Father. 'Did someone just come in?'

'No. Please either enter or leave, but shut the door.'

'The door just banged shut, Jabir. Was that the wind then?'

Of course it wasn't. Jabir keeps the door shut. His patients must not get cold. So it *was* my father, and that meant he was in here right now. I looked everywhere.

But I only see him when I open the door to my wife's small chamber. I didn't think he would go into her room, but there he is.

'You're leaving, lord?' Rosa says. She is busy with some embroidery, but she sets it down on the bed.

'Tomorrow. How are you?'

I'm conscious of my father standing by the wall.

Take your time, boy, he says. *You have this opportunity now. Tomorrow everything will be different.*

'I am getting better,' Rosa says. 'I will soon be well. And I ask one thing of you. It is this: be kind to Sara.'

Why is her voice always so harsh when she speaks to me? Her request sounds more like an instruction. And surely her Castilian accent is stronger than it used to be.

Nonetheless, I respond. 'Sara murdered the three Jews.'

'Not Isaac. He ran home to Castile.'

'Two Jews then. It's a serious crime, Rosa.'

'Talk to Rashid. He may give a different story.'

'Have you been speaking with...?' But of course she can't have been speaking with my father, since I'm the only one who can see him. And why will tomorrow be different? What is going to change overnight?

42

NEITHER OF THEM HAS SAID A WORD TO ME

Xurxo, taking Rashid his breakfast, discovered he was missing. Naturally, Xurxo raised the alarm, and, naturally, I ordered a check on Husain, Guido and Rosa. Rosa was safe and well, Husain and Guido were absent.

Jabir, in whose locked laboratory Guido, Husain and Rosa were all being treated, was interrogated.

'How the hell did Rashid escape from your barn? He was locked up!'

'Yes. A mystery.'

'So Rashid somehow escaped and then *somehow* took Guido against his will—'

'No, not against her will, O Lord of Careful Deduction. Sara went willingly with Rashid.'

'How do you know that?'

'I will show you.'

It was like one of those moments when you're sure you've been there before. You know exactly what's going to happen, because you're reliving a previous experience. From out of his jersey, Jabir brought a parchment. He held it out to me, but I shook my head. I could almost recite it without ever having seen it. Jabir read it out.

> *Anyone who is not for me is against me. This is my final message to you, for I know you know who I am now, though you do not know my story. My story is Rashid's story too. I have to go back to Murcia, there are many lives at stake. If I do not go soon, everything will be lost.*
>
> *I am grateful to Jabir for treating me, and to Lord Rory for bringing me here. Do not try to stop me. This is my destiny.*
>
> *The Mudéjar*

I flung out my question. 'He says he's grateful to you for treating him. What did you do, Jabir?'

'I did three things for Sara. Firstly, I gave her soothing drinks, some of which contain a special substance that change the way you think. Secondly, I spent a long time with her, talking to her and listening to her. I affirmed who she was, over and over and over again. More than anything, she needed this. Finally, and perhaps least importantly, I treated her physical wounds with balm and with stitching. I was able to sedate her for this, so she felt nothing. She is no longer in pain, and she can pass as a female. I think she is more than happy with this outcome.'

'Tell me about the special substance that changes the way you think.'

He smiled. 'It is not the Liberty Cap mushrooms! No, it is actually several substances, which I mixed together in a particular proportion. There was black snakeroot, which is extremely hard to get hold of in this country. Still, I managed to obtain it. Together with that, I mixed some spearmint and some linseed oil. This I made into a paste, which I used on Sara's body, but I also made a physic, changing the linseed oil for spearmint oil and adding ground flaxseeds. This physic I asked the girl to drink four times a day, and while she drank it I stroked her hair and I talked to her about her life as a woman.'

But in the pocket of my breeches reside seven small scraps of parchment, all threatening the murder of innocent people. I reminded myself that this is not just about some child's confused identity. This is real. The Mudéjar Revolution is real. The subjugation and killing of the Muslim population of Murcia is real. And Husain…

'How is Husain?' I asked suddenly. 'Jabir, how is Husain?'

'He died last night.'

'Why the hell didn't you tell me?'

'I was going to tell you, O Lord of Indignant Accusations. But first I had to inform the son.'

The words dropped like tiny stones onto a hard floor. I felt them in my head, heard them echoing in the vault of my skull. *But first I had to inform the son.* Jabir had gone to see Rashid in the middle of the night. And in the middle of the night, Rashid had escaped from the locked barn. Except it hadn't been locked, had it. Jabir had unlocked it.

'You let him out.'

'They had to leave. They have to return to their homeland. There is much at stake.'

I was furious. Jabir had no right to take matters into his own hands. Whatever he thought of the Muslims' lost cause, and whatever his sympathies with it, he should have spoken to me first. I was so angry with him that, for the first time ever, I saw fear in Jabir's eyes.

'I will explain…' he ventured cautiously, but I was in no mood for his excuses. I sent Xurxo and Kit to find the Mudéjar and her assistant. I told them they had two days.

Two days of silence and bitterness, resentment, anger and fear. Joan kept Ellen with her, and they spent the entire time in the textiles workshop, keeping out of my way. Rosa stayed in her room and I did not visit her. Instead, I spent the days stalking the grounds of The College, and the nights scribbling in my journal and letting my angry thoughts seethe unchecked around my head.

Then Kit and Xurxo returned, having seen nothing, found nothing. Bitterly, I recalled how Rashid had tracked me for months without anyone knowing he was there, and how Guido had fooled me into thinking he was an innocent child and a victim, when all the time he was the so-called Mudéjar, the brain behind the whole bloody conspiracy. Jabir tells me I'm wrong about this. Just as Xurxo and Kit were given two days to look for the Murcians, so Jabir has had two days to try to convince me that neither Sara nor Guido is or was the Mudéjar.

'It is not Sara,' he said, earnestly. 'Sara is *not* the Mudéjar. And Guido? He never existed! He was an ephemerum, living for a short time only, and that only when required. Sara was in disguise as Guido, Rory, not the other way around. Just as Rashid disguised himself, so Sara disguised herself as a boy who was pretending to be a girl. Sadly, you were taken in by both of them.'

This talk made my head spin. How could a boy be a girl disguised as a boy? Jabir shook his head sadly. I still hadn't understood.

'Well, if the Mudéjar wasn't Sara, and he wasn't Guido and he wasn't Rashid, then who the fuck was he?' I demanded angrily.

'The Mudéjar was Darakhshan bin Ibrahim,' Jabir explained patiently.

I almost exploded with irritation. 'But that's ridiculous,

Jabir! They are all three the same person! Guido, Sara, Darakhshan, it makes no difference what you call him! He still wrote the letters, he still made the threats, he killed innocent people, he manipulated Rashid and made use of everyone...'

'Darakhshan did those things, that is correct.' Jabir's fingers tapped rhythmically on the table in his great hall, and the Lady Joan, probably at Jabir's request, sat in a shadowy corner by the fire, pretending to knit a woolly hat for her Persian lover. I felt ill at ease between the two of them. 'Darakhshan was the Mudéjar,' Jabir continued. 'He has admitted it. But Sara is not Darakhshan. Sara is a woman in love with James of Aragon, and she would never have threatened anyone. Do not forget, O Lord of Convoluted Conclusions, that it was Darakhshan who was responsible for the death of Rashid's only daughter. That was not Sara either. This is a case of confused identity, in which a single human being can have more than one self. It happens, and not only when there is gender confusion. It's important to recognise that Sara sees herself as innocent. Even a victim. She needed help to transform her body and to be recognised and accepted as female. When, however, the Mudéjar wrote his vicious and violent messages, you were hearing the voice of Darakhshan bin Ibrahim, the boy whose father is one of the wealthiest and most powerful men in the whole *taifa* of Murcia. And it was *this boy* who murdered your friends.'

I looked over at Joan. I wondered if she understood this gobbledegook any better than I did. The knitting needles clicked and clacked, and Joan never once looked up. I shook my head. Jabir should get his paradise one day, I thought. He's far cleverer than most of Alfonso's lot.

We have buried Husain. He hung on until the night when he finally realised there was no hope. Jabir had been tending him, much as Aldara, Xurxo and Guido had done, all through our long journey from Aulnay, and as Rashid must also have done before that. But on that fatal night, Jabir sat with Husain in the laboratory, and in the enveloping darkness confessed that there was no Elixir of Life.

'You told us you had been successful,' Husain whispered. '*Years* ago. My wife, Elmira, kept your letters. I have them with me. I brought them all with me on this long and terrible journey.'

'I know,' Jabir said sadly. 'I found them in your clothing. I read them, Husain, and I was ashamed. They were all lies. I do not work in a royal court. There is no Elixir of Life. I am not a famous alchemist who has done amazing things. And I am not ibn Hayyan.'

After that there was no sound except for the wheezing rattle of Husain's last few breaths. When he died, he was almost nothing. His bones had disintegrated, there was no flesh on him and his face was a skull.

I thought, as I watched Xurxo pick up the body, that the bones would just detach one from another and clatter to the floor. They didn't, but he weighed less than a small child. It was easy to dig a grave in the mud behind the laboratory, and there lies Husain, a Mudéjar Muslim from Murcia in al-Andalus. Jabir and I dug the grave and Xurxo laid Husain's body in it. Kit came along at that point, and the four of us stood around in the rain. I asked Jabir to say a prayer and was instantly reminded of the day we secretly buried my wife Begoña. There's a small marker with Husain's name scratched on it to mark the place. I cut out the wooden lath from one of the wagon's side planks. Husain had spent so many long days and nights rattling through the continent in that thing, I thought it fitting to mark his grave with a small piece of it.

'What did you do after Husain died?'

We were all sitting around the high table in the great hall of The College on the day Kit and Xurxo returned from their fruitless search for the runaways.

The fire was blazing in the pit, flames leaping up the wall. Joan had gone upstairs to bed, for it was late. But I knew the question was an important one, and I knew Jabir held the key.

He answered me. 'I went to tell Rashid that his father had died. I did not tell him I was responsible. That it was my failure to produce the Elixir that had killed the man. But I did say I knew his story, and Sara's too.'

'Stories you should have related to me.'

He bowed his head. 'You are right. I should indeed have told you everything. I made an error of judgement.'

'Tell us now then. Tell us Rashid's and Sara's stories.'

'Yes, go on, Jabir,' Kit urged. 'What is the *real* story of the Mudéjar?'

'The real story of the Mudéjar is a love story. There was once a boy called Darakhshan. He grew up in the city of Mula in Murcia. He was the son of an influential Muslim, a man called Ibrahim, who was very devout and also very rich. Ibrahim and his son lived in a large white-walled house with a courtyard and a very special garden. This garden had four quarters, each irrigated by a special channel, and in one channel flowed water, in another milk, a third contained wine and the fourth, honey. Or so it was said. Olive trees grew there in abundance, together with fig trees, date trees and beautiful pomegranate trees. It was lush and colourful, a place of perfect peace and sustenance. But Darakhshan was an only child, and he was lonely.

'On Ibrahim's estate was a farmer called Rashid, a man clearly of much lower status than Ibrahim and his son. Rashid was married with three children, two boys and a girl. Ibrahim decided to invite Rashid's children into his beautiful garden to play with little Darakhshan. The four children played together every day and became firm friends.

'As he grew, Darakhshan began to realise something important. He knew, beyond all doubt, that he was a girl. He discussed this with his three friends, and they were enchanted. "Not three boys and a girl," they cried delightedly. "Two boys and two girls! Much better!" With their help, Darakhshan chose a new name, Sara, and all the children began to use that name, and to think of their friend as a girl, as their *sister,* in fact. Sara began to wear girls' clothes. Slowly but surely, Darakhshan became Sara in every respect. Even Ibrahim respected this choice his child had made, and he bought her clothes and headgear that she liked. Sara's mother was dead, but Ibrahim loved his child and wanted her to be happy. An enlightened and compassionate man was Ibrahim. Sadly, Rashid's daughter died a few years later, stoned to death by some ruffian boys who mistook her for someone else. Sara became even more important as the only sister to the two boys.

'And then came news that the leader of Granada, a

country to the south of Murcia, was instigating an uprising. All Muslims subservient to Christians would band together and overthrow their rulers. In the town of Mula, Rashid, fired up with patriotism and religious zeal, led the revolt, and Ibrahim joined him, along with many others. The children were too young to take part in the fighting, and they watched in horror as their fathers' efforts proved futile. The revolt failed. The Murcian leader, Muhammad, sued for peace, and a treaty was drawn up. The Mudéjars of Murcia had been betrayed yet again, but there was nothing they could do. Jaume of Aragon swept into the country with a huge military force, showing the Muslims once and for all that they must never contemplate rebellion again. Alongside King Jaume rode twenty-three-year-old James, his son. As the town of Mula settled down to accepting it was yet again under Christian rule, somehow, James of Aragon met Sara of Mula, and the two fell in love. Yes, my friends, as I said, this is a love story.

'Hand in hand, James and Sara walked in Ibrahim's Paradise Garden, and James confided to Sara that, to set an example, his father intended to kill the leaders of the revolt in Mula, and their families too. He offered to hide Rashid and Ibrahim, together with Rashid's wife and twin boys. He offered to keep them fed and looked after. "And what must I do in return?" Sara asked, full of trepidation. And James, already her lover, cupped her face in his hands and kissed her on the mouth. "I cannot marry you," he said softly, "not while you have the body of a boy. You must truly become a woman. Then we shall be married. I will give you one year. Come back to me in a year, Sara." "And if I cannot?" she asked him. But there was no answer, so Sara knew her friends would pay with their lives.

'With James's help, Rashid, Husain and Sara got out of

the country and began the long journey north. Husain was dying, but Rashid had read my letters. He knew I had discovered the Elixir of Life. Rashid told Sara that the famous Jabir ibn Hayyan of Hambrig could make the changes in her body that James wanted. He showed her the letters I'd written to Husain and his wife, Elmira. Husain and Sara would both be made whole by Jabir ibn Hayyan. But the journey was a long and daunting one, and Rashid was unsure how he would manage with a sick old man and a girl. But then – *then* they heard there was already an expedition on its way to Hambrig. It seemed providential, almost too good to be true. But how could they join it?

'In Saintes, in France, they found an old, ruined chateau they could hole up in. But they'd spent all their money, so Sara went into the town to find employment. She was taken in by the *Abbaye aux Dames,* and the *abbesse* put her to work and paid her well for it. Because Sara was small and slight, young and fast, the *abbesse* knew the best way to deploy her. And so, ironically, Sara became a spy in the *abbaye's* own Paradise Garden. Every day she had to report to the *abbesse* everything she'd seen and heard, and the *abbesse* would pass the information to the *Justiciers*.

'You all know how the story developed after that. Throughout the journey north, Rashid and Sara were in constant communication. The deaths of the Jews and the Smanderina were either accidental, or they were carried out by other people, but Darakhshan made use of them. He invented a mysterious and frightening killer, whom he called the Mudéjar. He wanted fear to be the driver, pushing Lord Rory to move ever more quickly to Hambrig. Darakhshan knew time was running out. Sara had one year and no more. Rashid had a genuine talent for disguises, something he apparently picked up when he was a boy. Darakhshan told him what to do and he did it.

'Darakhshan bin Ibrahim, the son of the most influential citizen of Mula, was in charge of the whole Mudéjar operation, even when dressed as a girl. And Rashid was her puppet. Sara was not the Mudéjar, but Darakhshan was. He was the mastermind, he controlled Rashid, he wrote the threatening letters, he spread terror amongst the travellers, and he cared nothing for the loss of life. But his alter ego, Sara, was a different person, and she was the person you knew. Darakhshan became 'The Mudéjar', and Sara was terrified of him, but she could not escape him, no matter what she did or where she went.

'And so, eventually, they arrived in Hambrig. But by now the year was nearly up. Sara was frantic. There was almost no time left before she and Rashid must begin the long journey south again. She was distraught that there was now insufficient time for her to receive the treatment she had dreamt of. Sir Stephen of Corby, together with his lover, Sister Magdalena, did much to repair the tissue damage and to alleviate the pain, but there was still the broken mind.

'Gentlemen, I did what I could. I gave her various different and effective treatments, but, much, much more importantly, I talked with her and she with me. My Lady Joan has learnt not to question me when I do not come to bed at night. She knows I often work all the hours God sends, burning candle after candle, trying to get my work done. I stayed with Sara, night after night, soothing and reassuring her. Clearing her mind. Giving her hope and courage for the future. And now she and Rashid have gone home. Sara will make a new life with James, and Rashid will reclaim his family.'

As soon as Jabir finished, Xurxo spoke. 'This James. I

know of him. He is the second son of Jaume of Aragon. I now understand some of the things Husain said to me.'

'Go on,' said Kit, encouragingly. 'What did he say?'

'Husain had faith in James. He kept saying James would bring freedom to the country.'

'He must have meant his family, Xurxo. James has promised to free Rashid's wife and children when Sara gets back.'

'No, it was more than that. Husain kept talking about his country. Do you think it's possible? If Sara comes back to him, and if her body is acceptable, do you think James will make his father give Murcia back to the Muslims?'

'It's not a decision young James can make,' I said, looking from one to the other in the firelight. But I saw only two faces in the red and golden glow. Jabir had drawn back into the shadows, his face hidden.

'Jabir. What do you know of this?' I reached out and caught his wrist, wrenching it. He grunted at the pain, but I pulled him forward, forward into the light. 'You're keeping something back. What is it?'

'Would you have Husain die in vain?' he said, rubbing his sore wrist. 'There was no need for violence, O Lord of—'

'Cut that out. What else do you know about this?'

'The son of Iago is correct,' Jabir said in a suddenly clipped voice. 'James has promised to free Murcia from its Christian overlords. If Rashid and Sara get there in time, not only will they save Ibrahim, Jamila, Hanif and Malik, but they will restore their country to the Islamic faith and culture.'

'Wait a minute,' I said. 'Jamila, Hanif and Malik, you said. Jamila is Rashid's wife?'

'That is so. As I said, there was a daughter—'

'Aysha.' I remembered Guido's sad story. 'Stoned to

death by some ignorant boys after being mistaken for Guido in his girls' clothes. But Guido told me Aysha was his sister.'

'They were like sisters,' Jabir said. 'It was a terrible thing that happened to Aysha. Jamila and Rashid were heartbroken.'

'Those boys deserve to be punished,' Xurxo observed. 'In a Muslim country, the *Mukhannathun* are not blamed for the way they behave. They are respected.'

'That is so,' Jabir agreed. 'But Sara is not *mukhannath*. She is something else, and these boys realised that. Stoning anyone to death is illegal and carries the death penalty, Xurxo, son of Iago. It matters not who dies.'

'So Rashid blames Sara for his daughter's death?' Kit asked.

'He blames Darakhshan bin Ibrahim, Kit, Duke of Casuel, but at the same time he cannot allow harm to come to Sara, for in her hands lies the key to the survival of the rest of his family. If Sara instructs James to tell his father the hiding place, there will be no one left for Rashid to return home to. Darakhshan has great power, and that is because his father loves him so much. There is a new material, and it is called paper. This paper is time-consuming to produce, and therefore it is expensive. But Ibrahim has found a way to make paper at scale, and so it will be cheap, and this will change the world.'

Change the world? There's only one person to talk to about that, so I asked him.

'Does paper have a future, Kit?'

'Oh, yes,' he said. 'Paper will replace every writing material currently in use. It doesn't just have a future, it *is* the future. Of writing, at least.'

Jabir learnt a lot during Husain's last night on earth; the Persian had made his confessions, and that prompted

Husain to make some of his own. So Jabir learnt that Ibrahim designed, built and runs a paper mill in Mula. I had thought he must be a powerful warlord in command of an impenetrable fortress, but he's better than that. He is a merchant with a new and sought-after commodity to sell. As such, he commands the world. He has many employees, among whom are Rashid, Rashid's wife, and even their children. Ibrahim was spared from the revenge killings after the Mudéjar uprising was suppressed because of his value to Alfonso. Not only will Alfonso keep Ibrahim's mill in production, he wants more mills to be built as well. And who better to build them than Ibrahim, who already knows everything there is to know about paper milling?

'We'll never know,' Kit said sadly. 'We'll never know if Sara makes it in time. If James is still there, and Murcia is handed back to the Muslims.'

'Won't we?' Xurxo said suddenly, gazing intently at Jabir. 'You'll know, won't you, Jabir. *You* will know if Islam is restored to Murcia.'

He nodded. 'We must wait, and it will be many months before we know. But eventually, yes, we shall know if this has worked.' After a small silence, he looked sharply at me. 'You do not ask after your wife. She is recovering well, and in a month or so she may have good news for you, O Lord of Unrequited Love. But you should also ask yourself why your wife thinks you are a dishonest man. And now, since it has been many nights that I have not slept, I am going upstairs to bed with my lady. And I bid you all goodnight.'

Everyone stood, and Kit, Xurxo and I waited until Jabir had left. Tired as he was, he still managed to move like a dancer. The wooden stairs creaked a little, but after that there was no sound. Xurxo made his excuses and left to go to his bed as well.

The fire was still glowing, but it needed more wood if it were to stay alive. Kit bent down and threw on two more logs. We watched a small flame explore them, lick around them for a few moments before flaring into life. The wood caught, crackled, and settled. The table was littered with bowls and goblets; no one had cleared them away. I pushed them to the side and sat down.

'I know why she says I'm dishonest.'

'We both know. Where is it?'

'I'm not sure. Do you think Rosa told Jabir about it?'

'If she did, then Jabir's told Joan.'

'Neither of them has said a word to me.'

43

THE WORTHLESS COCKLESHELL BEARS WITNESS TO THAT

I wasn't lying. I could not remember what had happened to Alfonso's letter, written several months ago, in which he traded his daughter for Jabir and Joan. Kit was arranging himself on the bench against the wall. He pulled one of Joan's coloured shawls over himself, pillowed his head on a second shawl and closed his eyes. Flames danced in the firepit. Kit's breathing steadied and became filled with sleep.

My thoughts steadied as well, and I pulled parchment and charcoal from my pocket. I jotted down some notes. When did I last see Alfonso's letter? Alfonso gave it to Yehudah. But Yehudah gave it to me, reluctantly perhaps, but I remember insisting he hand it over. And I remember reading it. It said little other than issuing a tempting invitation to Jabir to travel to Seville and join Alfonso's extensive court. What did I do with the letter after that, though?

My saddlebags were leaning against the wall. Flipping them open, I rummaged through the contents: spare braies, shirts, a jersey. My dagger. My hat? No, wait, that was still in my pocket. Spare parchment and charcoal for my journal. Down at the bottom of the bag, my fingers closed on something hard. I brought it up, through layers of clothing, then opened my hand. I had to go back to the fireside to see clearly, because I needed confirmation of what I was looking at. And that was because it simply wasn't possible that I was looking at the cockleshell of Saint James the Apostle.

Slowly, I sat down at the table and turned the shell over in my hand. There was no mistake. It was my cockleshell, the one I was given when I walked out through the *Gloria Portico* of the cathedral of Santiago das Cunchas. How did I know it was the very one? Because of the small hole I made in the top of it, through which I threaded my leather lanyard. For weeks I wore the shell around my neck, feeling it against my chest, together with my keys. I removed it only twice. Once I gave it to Yehudah, with instructions to pray over it for the lives of Husain and Rosa. Yehudah hung it around Husain's neck, and I took it back from him as we crossed the Narrow Sea in all that foul weather. The second time I removed it was when I learnt my baby was dead, and that Rosa had done great damage to herself. On an English road near Leicester, I hurled the shell as far from me as I could, and then our wagon rumbled past it as it lay abandoned in a hedge. And now – it had returned to me.

'Holy Mary, Mother of God,' I whispered to the cockleshell. 'I do not know how you have returned to me, nor how you have found your way into the bottom of my saddlebag, when I had cast you away and abandoned you, but please help me, your humble servant, to do the right thing for my wife and for my friends. Please help me find the letter that Don Alfonso wrote to Jabir. Please help Rashid and Sara get back to Mula in time, and I pray that

James, son of Jaume of Aragon, will allow the Mudéjar Muslims to reclaim their homeland. Also—'

I looked up, mid-prayer, my eyes misty. Someone was coming into the hall, and I knew who it was by the footsteps. The Lady Joan.

'I knew you were still up,' she said quietly.

'I thought you weren't. You went to bed hours ago.'

'Then I awoke, and heard your voice down here.'

'Are you happy here, Joan?'

'Yes, Rory. Very happy. I am with Jabir. He does his amazing work, and I have my textile factory. I have more customers than ever. Everything is going well for us here. And William—'

'Tell me about William later,' I interrupted. William is Joan's son. He's a seafarer, and a good man, but I didn't want to talk about William just now. 'What if you could leave, Joan? What if you and Jabir could go somewhere warm and beautiful, where Jabir could work all day on new ideas.'

'But why, Rory? We have everything we need here. It may not be "warm and beautiful", but it's home to us. And Jabir is already working all day, and usually most of the night as well, on his new ideas. You wouldn't believe the things he comes up with! Oh yes, and I wanted to ask if you could spare some of your parchment and a piece of your charcoal. I'm keen to start planning my garden. I know it won't be the same as the one you saw. That's what you're talking about, isn't it? You think I should go to France and build my garden in the warm climate there? I wouldn't want to do that. I know the weather's often cold here, and it rains sometimes, and the winters can be bleak, but it's my home. I wouldn't want to live in the south of France.'

'I wasn't thinking of France. Castile in Spain. Seville, to be precise.'

'There's a lot of unrest in that part of the world,' she said uncertainly. 'Are you not happy Jabir and I have made our home here?'

'Joan, I am as happy as I can be about it. I loved it best when you were inside the curtain wall at Castle Rory, but here is second best to that.'

'Then why would you have us move to Castile?'

I explained. I told her what Jabir had said to Sara. His definition of 'paradise'. And paradise could be his. I no longer had the letter, but I tried to remember it as accurately as I could. 'There was something about a "superior and creative space in which to study". And Alfonso's built a new laboratory for Jabir to work in. He says he'll provide everything you and Jabir need, including people Jabir can try his experiments on. There's a letter, Joan. I'll find it. I can't remember where I put it, but I'll find it.'

Joan was frowning. 'Why is he offering this? Isn't Alfonso the most powerful ruler in Europe? Why is he interested in Jabir and me?'

'Alfonso's heard of Jabir, and he knows how clever he is. He's heard of your amazing shawls, too!' I pointed to Kit, who was lying on a light blue bundle of wool, while covered over with a pretty patterned number in pink and green.

Joan smiled without humour. 'I wouldn't have thought so, Rory. I think I'd like to go back to bed now. Will you lend me the charcoal and the parchment?'

'Of course. You're right to plan it carefully. The main thing about the Persian gardens is their design. The design is everything.'

I heard Joan repeating, 'The design is everything,' as she mounted the stairs to her chamber. She hadn't mentioned the cockleshell, although it had been lying on the table the whole time. I finished my prayers with a rapid *pater noster*. I wondered if the shell's power had been weakened when I gave it to Yehudah, who gave it to Husain. From a Christian to a Jew to a Muslim. But perhaps that added strength, not weakness. And does the shell have any power anyway?

I decided to go back to the laboratory. Perhaps Rosa would be awake. And if she were, perhaps she would talk to me. I put my journal away, but left out a good-sized piece of parchment and a new stick of charcoal for Joan. She would design her Paradise Garden, but whether she would build it in Hambrig or Seville, I did not know.

The rain had stopped, thank goodness. I took the oil lamp with me but was astonished to see a light glowing in the laboratory window as I crossed the courtyard. Who could have lit a lamp there at this hour? I returned to the house and picked up my dagger, then hurried to find out.

Sometimes it's not the worst thing you can think of. Sometimes it's the obvious and simplest explanation after all. Visions of Rosa being attacked by an intruder proved unfounded, as I entered the laboratory to find Jabir himself working by the light of two large oil lamps.

He looked up as I entered. 'You! Why are you here at this hour?'

I'm always suspicious when he doesn't taunt me with 'O Lord of Something-Or-Other'. He moved the oil lamps to the side of the bench, shadowing his face. He was standing in front of something, I realised. Something quite large, but it was in the shadows beyond the light cast by the lamps. The lamps had been moved, then, to hide the object behind him. I stepped towards Jabir.

He held out a hand, palm towards me. 'No further, Rory. This is my home. You are my guest. I wish you to stay away from the laboratory.'

'Do you? Why? I have a right to see my wife.'

'I am moving Rosa to the house tomorrow. You can tend her there. It will be more comfortable for her, now her recovery is progressing so well.'

'What are you hiding?'

'It is not your concern. I would ask you to leave now; we will speak again in the morning.'

I closed with him in one stride, my hand at his throat. I didn't intend to hurt him, just to see what he was hiding. He cried out. A curse, perhaps, or a spell. But I'd seen it. Yehudah's astrolabe – the entire contents of Yehudah's precious chest laid out on Jabir's bench. The Alfonsine Tables, on the cover of which I saw, newly inscribed, Jabir's own name. The books of alchemy, astronomy, magic and poetry.

I had no time to say anything. A bright light suddenly filled the laboratory, blinding me, stabbing into my head with a sharp pain, making me cry out and sink to the floor, my eyes tight shut, my hands to my face. Moments later, I opened my eyes and the light had gone, the laboratory again lit only by Jabir's two oil lamps. I leapt to my feet. On the workbench was spread a fringed scarlet shawl, which I flung to the side, expecting to see the books and the astrolabe hidden beneath it. But there was nothing. The shawl had been spread over the wooden bench. Everything else had gone.

'What have you done?' I growled at Jabir. 'Where the hell did that blinding light come from? And what have you done with Yehudah's things?'

Jabir spread his hands. 'You realise I shall deny everything? I shall tell you a little, just a very little. I am a seeker after knowledge. I wish to achieve my goal. You heard me talk of this to Sara. My goal is to walk with the greatest scholars and intellectuals of our age. To do that, I must—'

'Steal their work? Lie about your achievements? *That* will get you to heaven?'

'You do not understand.'

'No. I do not understand. Last year, I also told lies. I was guilty of great deceit and dishonour. It broke me, Jabir. It sent me on a journey of a thousand miles to try to find peace. I made it to my destination and was awarded my prize, the cockleshell of Saint James the Apostle, but that wasn't the prize I sought. You, though! You dishonour yourself, and you do it without a qualm. I would not have thought it of you.'

He answered me softly. 'You Christians have a very rigid idea of honour. For those who come from the East, it is different. The Prophet approves of paying one's way. He says: *Begging is right only for three people: one who is in grinding poverty, one who is seriously in debt, or one who is responsible for compensation and finds it difficult to pay*. I, myself, have been in grinding poverty. *And* I have been a beggar. But I have turned my two dirhams into ten dirhams. You, who have known *nothing* of such a life, do not judge me now.'

He turned away and took down a flask from a shelf above the bench. Then he put on his most sarcastic tone of voice, and spoke with his back to me. 'I have work to do, O Lord of Discourteous and Unwarranted Intrusion. Please forgive me if I do not spend any more of the night in this fascinating discourse.'

I left him to it, walked back to the hall, sat on the floor with my back propped against the wall and tried to go to sleep. At first it was impossible. The cockleshell of Saint James still lay on the table. I thought of my pilgrimage, and realised quite suddenly that Rashid, Husain and Guido had been pilgrims too. Their shrine was not mine, their reasons for going were different, but our various mystic journeys led us to travel far, and, in the end, get nowhere. It seems unlikely that Guido-Sara will get to Mula in time to ransom Ibrahim, Jamila and the boys. Even more unlikely that the wretched child can persuade Jaume of Aragon to release his hold on the territory. Whether Rashid will see his family alive seems doubtful, and poor Husain is already dead. The outcome of their pathetic pilgrimage is scarcely worse than that of my own, and the worthless cockleshell bears witness to that.

44

ROSA DAS ROSAS E FROR DAS FRORES

On the dais, Joan sat fingering the cockleshell. Kit was no longer lying on the bench. And I'd woken up with a headache.

'Where's Kit?' I asked.

'He said he would walk into town,' Joan replied. 'He had something to do there.'

'And Jabir?'

'I don't know.'

'I will check the laboratory.'

Jabir was not in the laboratory. Neither was my wife. Xurxo, Joan and I searched every inch of The College, but we did not find either of them. We reconvened at the table on the dais. Joan had news.

'I had no idea he was doing these things,' she said despairingly. 'I didn't know he was writing to Rashid and Husain all these years. I didn't know what they were planning.' In her hand was a bunch of letters, and she held them out to me.

They were all addressed to Jabir, and I knew immediately that they must be read aloud. We should all know their contents. Xurxo offered to read them out. Some were in Arabic script, others in Castilian, and Xurxo battled manfully with them all.

Not all the letters were from Rashid; some were from Husain, and there were letters written long ago from Elmira, Husain's wife, and even one from Shakira, whose immature handwriting professed eternal love and adoration for a youthful Jabir ibn Hayyan of Tusa. Shakira, I remembered had been Rashid's sister, raped and murdered by Alfonso's men. Every single letter was addressed to the Persian in the 'Court of King Rory', which has never existed.

'Killed more than twenty years ago,' Joan said sadly. 'Poor Husain. Wife and young daughters all lost. In the name of religion.'

Did she think to make me squirm? It was my father who sent me on Crusade. I feel plenty of guilt for my behaviour as a man, but none for my boyish efforts to help retake the Holy Land. I am not responsible for that.

Xurxo came across letters from Ibrahim too. The first few mentioned his son, Darakhshan. Later messages talked of Sara, his daughter. And there was a detailed description of a certain Persian Garden, in which Sara played with her friends – Hanif, Malik and Aysha. Hanif and Malik were twins, and a year older than Aysha. Sara was the youngest. The four children were inseparable, and the beautiful garden rang with their laughter. Ibrahim set the scene with educated ease, his language flowing and elegant, his tone full of love and humour.

'It isn't just an account of children playing in the garden.' Xurxo turned the letter over again, his eyes darting along the lines of script. 'He goes on to say that Sara is turning into a beautiful young woman. She's nearly thirteen, and he's worried about her. What will her future be? Will she ever find happiness as an adult, he asks?

'It's a pity we can't see the letters Jabir wrote back,' I said. 'They would have revealed a lot. Where did you find all these, Joan?'

'They were in his holy book. He knows I never open it. It is sacred to him, and I never touch it.'

'Then what made you do so?'

'I searched everywhere, Rory. I knew I had to find something. I knew nothing of this correspondence before today, and I'm shocked by it.'

I was also shocked. It was these secret letters, the product of the strong bond Jabir had forged with Husain and Elmira, that had culminated in Rashid's and Sara's escape from Christian-held Murcia. Their subsequent latching on to my own journey north had been lucky for them, but bad news for the rest of us.

'Aren't you worried about Rosa?' Joan asked, watching my face.

I grimaced. I suppose I was concerned. Perhaps not as much as I should have been.

A thought occurred to me. Beckoning to Xurxo, I hurried back to the laboratory. Where was Yehudah's crate? What had Jabir done with the astrolabe, the Alfonsine Tables and the various books with their vast array of knowledge and literature, so hastily swept away while I crouched, blinded, on the floor? I flung open the laboratory door. Inside, everything looked as it should. Wooden benches, glass tubing, flasks, bottles of specimens, Sappo munching on a slug in her wooden box. I'm used to all this now, and I know it's Jabir's stock-in-trade. I looked all over the room, but found nothing suspicious. It was Xurxo who pushed open the door to what had been Rosa's convalescence chamber and looked under the bed. Yehudah had guarded his crate against all possible damage or vandalism, even down in the hold of a sinking ship, but in death he could not guard it, and now here it was.

'I'm pretty sure,' I said quietly to Xurxo, 'that all the things Yehudah had in that crate were the property of Don Alfonso. I don't believe any of it was Yehudah's at all.'

The crate was locked and there was no key. Jabir would have that on him.

Xurxo raised his eyebrows. 'Crowbar it open?'

'No. Not yet. But we'll move it to the house.'

That was an interesting move in itself. The crate was heavy. Xurxo and I struggled to carry the bulky, awkward thing between us, cursing it for having no handles.

We managed to get it into the house and shoved it under the high table. In spite of my assertion that I was not concerned for Rosa, she was somehow in the back of my mind, along with a melody line that just would not go away.

Rosa das rosas e fror das frores...

45

I ADVISE YOU TO GO TO HER

Kit returned from his trip into Hambrig Town.

'I found Richard and Cristina's house eventually,' he said, dusty from his walk. 'I had a letter for Cristina. From her mother, Enes. Remember?'

I did remember. Kit had told us long ago on an Iberian hillside that Enes was ill, and Joy was caring for her on the top of the mountain. Enes had written to her daughter, Cristina, who is married to my former steward. I glanced across at Xurxo, who had joined us at the gate.

'That is good,' Xurxo said, nodding to Kit. 'I am grateful to you and to your mother.'

'Do you know what the letter was about?' I asked Kit.

He shook his head, but Xurxo said, 'It is her Will. I have a copy, and now my sister also has one.'

There was nothing more to be said, since none of us knows if Enes is even still alive. I was deciding what to do next when, to my astonishment, Rosa and Jabir came round the corner of the laboratory, walking slowly, Rosa leaning on Jabir's arm. She had put on a different gown, and around her shoulders was the fringed scarlet shawl.

'I asked to go for a walk, Lord Rory,' Rosa said. 'I've had enough of being indoors and of being ill. I wanted some fresh air and to feel well again. I washed, I brushed my hair, and I changed into this gown. It made me feel good.'

But she neither looked nor sounded good. Her complexion was pale and her voice lacklustre, her speech slow, belying her words.

'You found the crate?' Jabir asked abruptly. 'You must have found it. But did you open it?'

'Yes, I found it, and no, I didn't open it.'

'I fear you still don't understand. You probably think—'

'Don't you dare tell me what I think,' I snarled, my temper suddenly snapping. 'I'll bet you directed the whole "Mudéjar" business. Guido was your plaything all along, wasn't he? Rashid and Husain were your friends, and you're involved in this somehow. You set me up, and it's because of you that Joseph, Isaac, Yehudah and Aldara are all dead.'

'No! It is not like that at all. Let us return to my home and I will explain.'

'We've read your letters, Jabir. The ones Husain, Elmira and Rashid sent you. The ones you kept hidden in your Qur'an.'

His face went suddenly furious, the eyes hard, the mouth set. Then he relaxed, though there was no smile in his eyes. 'My Qur'an? Oh yes. But it is of no consequence. I am hiding nothing, as you will see.'

In the great hall, Jabir glanced at the large wooden crate under the table. Ellen had cooked dinner. Soup, bread, cheese and pears were brought to the table, and Xurxo slid the box out of the way. Joan was still upset. She put a wooden board down on the table, turning to go without a word.

I followed her into the kitchen. 'Why are you not joining us?'

'I have no wish to. I was deceived by Jabir. I should have been told about Husain and Rashid, about Elmira and the girls. Why didn't he tell me? It was such a big part of his life. He was writing secret letters to them for thirty years!'

'But you and Jabir have not been together for very long. Have you told him everything about your own past?'

'He knows most of it. He knows about William. He knows my father was in textiles and that I helped him with his work.'

'But he doesn't know everything, does he. There must be a great deal he doesn't know about you.'

I returned to the hall, but Joan remained in the kitchen, where she was collecting utensils for washing at the well.

'We should open this,' Kit said after the last mouthfuls had been eaten. He pointed to Yehudah's crate.

I agreed. 'Jabir, why did you take it into your laboratory?'

'For protection. You know how much rain we have had. I did not know if the crate were waterproof, or if it contained valuable equipment.'

'Why did you open it by yourself?'

'I was curious. Inside, I found a beautiful and sensitive astrolabe, and a number of books, pamphlets and writings. I have not yet examined those, but I did look closely at the astrolabe. You will remember that Sir Bernard of Hambrig had such an instrument, which was destroyed in the fire two years ago. Since then, I have not had access to an instrument that charts the heavenly bodies and their passage through the skies. You may know I have been working on the design of an instrument of my own, one that will give an accurate measurement of time passing...'

'Ah yes. The Castle Clock.'

Kit looked up, interested. 'What's the Castle Clock?'

'The Castle Clock, Kit, is the invention of a Persian mathematician, after whom Jabir's donkey seems to be named. Ismail al-Jazari.'

Jabir's eyes gleamed, but his voice was steely. 'You know nothing about this. Ismail al-Jazari was a wonderful mathematician and inventor, but he did not build the Castle Clock.'

'He invented it. Joseph told me.'

'Al-Jazari *began* the design. It is I, Jabir of Tusa, who will bring the design to perfection and construct the Clock itself, so we can see it in action. This is the way all science works, if you but realised it. Someone has an idea and they take it so far, but others have to carry the torch a little further, and still others, maybe centuries on, bring it to fruition.' He turned to Kit. 'You will understand this, Kit, son of Anthony Merry, Duke of Casuel and seer of the future. You will know that all inventions and discoveries work like this.'

We all looked at Kit.

'That is so,' he said dreamily.

Jabir sat back, vindicated.

'How is Kit a "seer of the future"?' Xurxo asked with interest.

'I'll tell you later,' Kit said, which astonished me, since he's never agreed to tell me anything at all about his strange knowledge of what is to come. But then, mischievously, he added, 'In the future!'

Joan stood in the doorway, her hands on her hips, her mouth set in a straight line. 'Jabir. Are you going to explain the letters to me? Those letters you received from your Andalusian friends, calling me your wife, saying you have created life, that you can work miracles! You told me none of this and you hid the letters away so I could never read them, never know of your past life and your lies. How do you think I feel about that? You lied to me, deceived me and concealed things from me. I am no longer willing to live with you or have any connection to you. I will be returning to Castle Rory as soon as I can, if Lord Rory will have me.'

There was a stunned silence. If a dark-skinned man could go white as a sheet, that's what would have happened to Jabir. He looked shaken.

'You had to make a public announcement of this?' His tone was soft, but under the table his fists were clenched.

'I don't care who knows about it,' Joan said. 'You are not the man I thought you were. This is your house, even though I paid for it. I wish you joy of it, for I am leaving.'

'I can explain the letters—'

'You should have explained them months ago. It's too late now.'

Kit, Xurxo, Ellen and I were helpless witnesses to this breaking of the relationship between Joan and Jabir. If, I wondered suddenly, that was even his name. Had he taken a dead man's name as his own, as, without compunction, he'd taken al-Jazari's invention, Yehudah's astrolabe and Alfonso's celestial tables?

I came to a decision. 'I will examine the contents of the crate. And I will do it alone.'

'There is a letter in it.' Jabir's voice sounded suddenly desperate. 'It's addressed to me, so I have read it. It is an offer. For both of us, Joan, an offer from Don Alfonso of Castile himself!' Jabir had turned to talk directly to his lover, and his hands were clasped under his chin. 'He asks me to go and join his court, to work with his scholars and conduct my experiments in a brand-new laboratory. You are also to come, my love. Alfonso wants you to design his garden! Yes, a most beautiful garden! Working in that place, it's my dream come true, my – my paradise…'

But Joan was stony-faced. Jabir went to her and took her hand in his. 'It will be everything we want,' he said softly.

'Everything *you* want, perhaps,' Joan answered. 'You have always wanted to meet Alfonso. You've told me that. Now he wants to meet you, it seems. This garden idea is just to lure us there, knowing I might not otherwise let you go. This is your dream, not mine. And since you have never once asked me what *my* paradise looks like, I assume you're not interested. Go, then, Jabir. Go to Castile. Be a hero in Spain.' She gave a sob, turned, and walked away.

Jabir, devastated, trailed back to the table. He sat down heavily, his eyes closed. I knelt by the crate. It was locked.

'How did you open it?' I asked.

'It is easy if you know how.'

'Open it now.'

The Persian knew how, all right. He had a small knife blade, which he inserted into the lock. The blade flickered back and forth, and the lock clicked open.

'My God,' Kit breathed. 'How did you learn the trick of that, Jabir?'

Jabir didn't answer, but returned to the bench by the table. We all knew he'd been close to Joan, but I had not realised until now how very much he loved her.

I peered into the crate. The astrolabe sat on top of everything. I suppose we shall have to send it back to Alfonso, and if Jabir is going to join Alfonso's court, he might as well take it with him. Underneath, there was the bundle of books and documents I remembered from before; I'd already looked at the tables of the planets. I laid them carefully on the floor beside the astrolabe, and saw Jabir's letter, his name plain to see on the folded parchment.

'Here it is,' I announced. 'Your formal invitation, Jabir. How amazing that it is the very paradise you spoke of to Guido!'

I read the letter carefully.

Honoured Jabir ibn Hayyan of Tusa,

Because I know you are well versed in the arts of astronomy, astrology, mathematics, science and medicine, I wish to offer you the most superior and creative place in which to study, work and progress your knowledge and understanding. To this end, I am having constructed a building, which I believe is to be called a 'laboratory', in which you will be free to carry out experiments and to pursue your own ideas and either prove or disprove your theories and philosophies. Whatever equipment you desire will be supplied, and you will have all the time you require to work. In addition, if you need to test your ideas on people, there will be no shortage of men and women willing to advance the sum of human knowledge by putting themselves entirely in your hands.

I am particularly interested in your invention of a clock, which I understand is called the Castle Clock, and which relies on the movement of water for its functioning. I have heard there are mechanical musicians who play instruments at certain times of the day! I will be fascinated to hear these, as I am something of a musician myself. Your Castle Clock is intriguing, and my court is agog to see it in action.

You are well known, also, as the inventor of the Elixir of Life, and further knowledge of this is eagerly anticipated by my physicians and apothecaries. Please bring samples with you, together with the precious recipe for its creation.

Naturally, you will share your ideas with the other men of intellect who surround me, and they are eager to meet you and to discuss moving the boundaries of knowledge forward. The inventions and discoveries that will take place in Seville will be the talk of the civilised world, and I know you will want to be part of this.

As well as the laboratory, you can be assured of a spacious new house which will be built for you and your wife here in Seville. You will have servants to attend you and cook your meals, and I am sure you will enjoy the wonderful climate, food and drink that Spain has to offer.

It is also my wish that the Lady Joan design for me a garden, which I am intending to call the Spanish Garden. It will be similar to one I have observed, with symmetrical pathways, beautiful trees and gentle fountains. The Spanish Garden will bring solace and peace to all who walk and sit there, and I will entrust its design only to your gracious lady.

Don Alfonso X of Castile, León, etc etc

'That is a very flowery invitation,' Xurxo observed. 'You are highly thought of, Jabir.'

'Yes, indeed,' Kit said drily. 'And you look very well for your age, too. Ibn Hayyan died four hundred years ago!'

'I am a descendant,' Jabir cried hotly. 'I have always stated this fact. Always. There is no dissimulation. Do not take Don Alfonso for a fool!'

'Jabir,' I said. 'Joan will forgive you in time. But that time will pass more quickly if you talk to her now and explain yourself properly. I advise you to go to her.'

46

ADIO QUERIDA

'What is he like? Alfonso of Castile?' Joan asked.

'He appreciates fine things. He is a musician, but...'

'But what?'

'He loves power. Castile is taking over the whole Iberian Peninsula. The Christians are getting rid of the Moors. Rashid's family are in danger; that's if they're even still alive.'

'That's not Alfonso's doing, though. We know now it was Jaume of Aragon who conquered Murcia.'

'That's naïve, Joan. Jaume was supporting Alfonso; they're related by marriage. Aragon or Castile, it makes no difference.'

'What will happen to Sara?'

'I don't know what to believe about that. I can't think that a son of the mighty Jaume of Aragon would be interested in a pathetic little misfit like Sara.' I held up my hand to forestall Joan's protests. 'He would see her like that, Joan. Surely even you will concede she's a misfit? And she's too young and unimportant to make a difference to anything. They're clutching at straws if they genuinely think a Prince of Aragon is calmly and patiently waiting for Sara to return to him, her body transformed by Jabir's mystical powers, and thereupon the *taifa* of Murcia is returned, intact, to the Mudéjars.'

'What's a *taifa?* I haven't heard that word before.'

'It's an independent Muslim state in al-Andalus. There used to be a lot of them; now there are none left. All have been subsumed by the Crown of Castile.'

'But Rashid and Sara believe—'

'No. Sara's father is a powerful man in Murcia, but even so, it's not going to happen.'

'What will you do?'

'I? Nothing.'

'But they'll be riding to their deaths! And Rashid's family, hiding away, waiting...'

'They'll likely have been killed long since, Joan. It's the way things are there. The Muslims are killed or evicted; their mosques converted into churches and cathedrals. Only Granada is still under Muslim rule, but even *that* is a tributary state. It's not independent.'

'Ibrahim is still alive.' Kit came into the house and sat down next to Joan. He looked her in the eyes. 'You can be sure, Joan, that he is alive. As for Rashid's family, they worked for Ibrahim in the paper mill. He and his wife and children, they were all employees. Alfonso wants to work the mill. He wants his paper to be a key commodity when he trades with the Hanseatic League. He *needs* the mill to work, and he'll build more mills, so he'll need Ibrahim to take on apprentices and train them. He'll not kill the goose that lays the golden egg, you can be sure of that.'

Joan sighed in relief, and I was glad Kit had come in just then; his words made sense. But I wondered what would happen if Rashid and Sara did not get back to Murcia within their year's grace. What would happen to the golden egg then?

I changed the subject. 'Have you decided what you're going to do, Joan?'

'I will go to Seville with Jabir. I have to give him this chance.'

'You're going to Seville *because* of Jabir? Or because of this so-called Spanish Garden?'

'I can design things, you know that. I'm a creative person; I see pictures in my head all the time. I can create this Paradise Garden, and it will be beautiful. Be glad that I will finally make something of myself.'

This last sentence of hers so astounded me I became speechless. Hadn't Joan already made something of herself? She was liked and respected throughout Hambrig Town, and my father had loved her. *I* love her. She must know that.

But it turns out she has never felt proud of anything she's done. Her father was an honest tradesman, but *my* father made Joan into a pseudo-lady, *the Lady Joan*, a title she hates and despises.

I didn't know this until she told me that afternoon as we sat together on the courtyard wall, watching Ismail al-Jazari munch turnips. He was wearing one of Joan's shawls, I noticed. A bright green one with blue stripes.

'I thought he looked cold,' Joan said apologetically, and I smiled. Only Joan would think of it.

I mulled over the things she'd just told me. 'You know, all my life I thought you were a high-born lady.'

'You haven't known me all your life, Rory. I came to live in the castle while you were away. You didn't know me before that.'

'I meant all my life that I've known you.'

'But even that's not true! You knew my father was a

textile merchant. You knew I lived in the Merchants' Quarter in Hambrig Town, in the house next to Anthony's, and you knew I was sleeping with Anthony long before his wife died. You knew all about me! Don't try to tell me you didn't. High-born lady, indeed!' She turned away, and I saw she was genuinely upset.

'I'm sorry, Joan. I wasn't thinking. You're right, of course. I knew all that, but you've always been "The Lady Joan" to me. And it was you who helped Kathryn. That was the most important thing to me. I suppose I never really thought about the rest of it.'

'Well, it's time you did. You're the Lord of Hambrig. I'm a very ordinary woman, a merchant's daughter, and this is my opportunity. My chance to do something big. I don't want power or wealth, and I don't want to be famous. But I would like the chance to do something special, and designing a garden for the King of Castile would be very special indeed.'

'Then I won't stand in your way,' I said lightly. Ismail al-Jazari looked quizzically at us, and Joan jumped down to give him his nosebag.

Then she turned, her hand to her face in horror. 'I've just thought! Who will look after Ismail al-Jazari when Jabir and I go to Seville? Will you have him, Rory?'

'Of course,' I said at once. 'He can work with Samson. Branca will be happy to look after him.'

Joan looked relieved. The donkey's feelings being more important than mine, I watched her fill the bag with oats and twitch Ismail's shawl more comfortably around his ears.

Well, what do you expect? my father asks, sauntering across to lean against the wall. I move over for him and he tips his head back to look up at the cold blue sky. *Of course she loves the animal. He doesn't give her any trouble.*

I don't give her any trouble, I mutter morosely.

Father laughs. *She would say differently. But, seriously, you need to let her go. This is her opportunity. Don't make it difficult for her to grasp it, boy.*

Joan's head is filled with images of immaculate grassy walkways; cool, sparkling fountains; shady bowers surrounded by fragrant citrus trees; and geometric patterns of channels filled with clear water on a bed of pink and grey pebbles. A perfect paradise. She's borrowed my charcoal and has made a number of sketches. Jabir has been involved, the designs thrust under his nose for approval or comment.

'In Persia, you would have circles,' he intones. 'Always circles, my love. The waterways should radiate from the centre, like the spokes of a wheel—'

'But they do!' cries Joan, resting her hand on the parchment in front of them. 'Look, Jabir! And in each segment of the circle there's a different tree, representing different stages of life, together with other plants and fragrances—'

'That is not a Persian concept,' Jabir reproves, and Joan looks distressed. She says something about Alfonso being a Christian not a Muslim, but Jabir takes no notice, sweeping on with some suggestion about including a bridge in the design. It's to be called the Chinvat Bridge, apparently.

'I don't understand what you're talking about,' Joan says, irritated. 'The Chinvat Bridge? I have never heard of it. But a bridge over the channels, yes, I like that idea…'

Neither of them has noticed that Rosa is also in the hall, listening. She is standing by the door. Jabir and Joan are at the end of the table, still arguing in low voices, and Jabir has not yet explained his 'Chinvat Bridge' to Joan's satisfaction. I'm at the other end, sitting near the fire, which, if I'm honest, is making me drowsy and rather too hot, even on this bitterly cold day.

I catch Rosa's eye and jerk my head. She comes to sit with me next to the fire. Joan and Jabir, deeply engrossed in their conversation, still haven't noticed her. I can't hear everything they're saying, but odd words reach me.

'…a bridge of choice,' says Jabir.

Joan's voice. 'Oh, I don't think so. That sounds horrible.'

'The House of Lies…' hisses Jabir, stabbing at the parchment.

I've missed the sentences in between, and I have no idea what they're talking about.

Rosa raises her eyebrows. 'What's the House of Lies?' she whispers.

But I'm as ignorant as she is.

'…and on the arch, a big sign!' Jabir's voice is suddenly stronger, clearly reaching Rosa and me. 'A big sign, Joan! It will say 'Good Thoughts, Good Words, Good Deeds'. Something for that lying, deceiving Christian to aspire to!'

'Good thoughts, good words, good deeds,' Joan repeats, doodling on the parchment. 'Yes, I rather like that, Jabir. But not your 'Bridge of Choice'. You still haven't told me what the choices are.'

'Haven't I?' Jabir says absently. 'I thought I had. The Chinvat Bridge offers those who cross it the choice between good and evil. This is a choice that all must face, and even if you enter the House of Lies, it will not be for all eternity…' His voice trails away.

Rosa's expression is serene and she has closed her eyes, but I am simply confused. This doesn't sound much like Islam to me, and it's definitely nothing to do with Christianity. So where is Jabir getting his ideas from?

Joan rolls up the parchment. The discussion is finished. No, wait. She has one more question for her lover. 'What is the alternative to the House of Lies, Jabir? If there's a choice between good and evil, surely there must be two houses, one good and one bad?'

He looks at her with adoration in his eyes, and his arms reach out to draw her to him. 'But of course, my lovebird of paradise! There is also the House of Song. The white roses that scramble over the bridge will direct you there. You must fill the House of Song with songbirds who sing exquisitely of longing for their love – which is the rose. Surround the House of Song with white roses, and let the thrushes, nightingales and bluethroats sing their hearts out.'

And then Jabir makes a 'shall-we?' gesture with his hand, and he and Joan walk out, arm-in-arm. I roll up my parchment, unsure if they even knew I was there.

I heaved the cart out from where I'd parked it behind the outhouse, and I bundled them all into it, Jabir and Joan included. Jabir, whom I've tolerated out of respect for his learning, turns out to have very little learning after all, while Joan, it seems, has to 'prove' herself. Her father's honest trade wasn't enough, nor was my father's love for her, nor, apparently, are my own feelings. And yes, I *do* love the Lady Joan, who abhors her title because she doesn't, so she says, deserve it. As for moving to Castile – that idea is dead in the water, and became so as soon as Jabir's tower of lies had been exposed. The Paradise Garden will be built in Hambrig after all. The laboratory I paid good money for is a fake. Jabir is a sham, no more a mystical alchemist than I am. I intend to pull down the ridiculous 'laboratory', stone by stone, and I shall do it with my own hands. Standing, it is a monument to my gullibility, mocking my attempt at atonement.

Castle Rory, on the other hand, is a building to be proud of. It stands high on a windy hill, and it's where I belong. Not down in the reeking valley of the River Hurogol where everyone is trying to deceive everyone else. Naturally, Kit has had 'a quiet word' with me, pointing out that not everyone's a liar, and that *not* being on a high windswept hill has its good side. Did I listen to all that? Yes, I did, but it changed nothing. I was in a foul mood and everyone knew it.

We arrived in the bailey of my home an hour or so before supper. We'd been seen, of course. The Watch on the wall-walk had spotted us easily, so everyone was ready for us, and there was food on two trestle tables in the great hall. Scowling, I looked around. It was so familiar, and yet so different. Where was Jonny, my garrison commander? Long gone to be an English baron. And where was Sir Patrick of Myrtile, who was my father's steward before he was mine? Back in his remote estate, taking Deborah, his Jewish bride, with him. And what of Richard, who succeeded Patrick as my steward? Married to Xurxo's sister, Cristina, and living in a grand house in Hambrig Town. So many changes over the years. No Sammy, who was once the Lady Joan's apprentice, now a sailor. No Kerry, who used to be a captain in my Special Guard. Now she's Lady of Nightmolben, presiding over a haunted forest and an indestructible castle of black granite.

I greeted my household as they emerged, some shyly, others with enthusiasm. A fanfare sounded, and Archer Ben paraded the troops in the courtyard. I inspected them, feeling disappointment. In the six months between Ben becoming garrison commander and my departure on pilgrimage, he had only managed to recruit three people to Training Company. That in itself is disappointing, but I also noted that every one of his recruits was male, and though they were well turned out, none showed much spark. Mallrovia is alone in Europe in encouraging women to become soldiers, doctors and lawyers. It's true that the numbers taking this opportunity are small, but I would have expected at least one female recruit in my new garrison, and I would certainly have expected Training Company to be full by now. Ben marched his men back to their quarters in the gatehouse. The garrison is not in a good state, however smart the men's uniforms, however impeccable their drill.

After a hasty bite to eat, I scribbled a list, handed it to Ben, then made my way to the south-west tower. At the very top of this tower is a room I constructed many years ago. I call it my library. It has shelves full of books, which qualifies it for the name, but mostly it's a sanctuary for me, with its comfortable green leather chair by the fireplace and my father's old desk against the wall. There's a chest full of documents and all the historical files I keep on the estate, the castle, and everyone who lives and works here. In the old days, I'd meet my steward here every Thursday morning, and we'd go through the accounts and the records together. Now I have no steward, but my intention today was to interview each person on the list, one at a time. This would take several hours. I arranged parchment and quill on the desk, thinking fleetingly of Kit's prediction that the new material, paper, will take over from parchment. I wonder what it's like, this paper? Parchment is expensive, but I invest in vast quantities of it for my estate records – and to write this journal. After all, why else am I here?

The interviews took place, but no one had anything special to report. The day-to-day life of a thirteenth-century castle is fairly mundane in peacetime. The garrison have been exercising daily, drilling and parading as usual. Ben has done nothing new, merely continuing Jonny's routines. I'd been hoping for more individuality from him, more initiative. Still, Jonny was a good commander, and perhaps Ben could think of no way to improve on his former general's work. A loyal soldier is Ben, but not really a leader, and definitely not an innovator.

Eliza's interview was interesting. She wanted to know if I had news of my brother, Nicholas. Perhaps I'd even seen him? Mallrovians don't always understand the distances involved in travelling in Europe, or even in England, our closest neighbour. I explained we'd gone nowhere near Somerset. She nodded, which I thought was the end of it, but she then told me she's been receiving letters from Nick.

Increasingly anguished letters, and in the last one he was threatening to come home.

'Home? Treborough's his home now. He has his own estate!'

'I know, lord. And he's married. Perhaps I should just show you the letters.'

'Another time, Eliza. And I'll write to him myself.' Though what I'd say, I had no idea.

My last interview, well after supper, was with Rachel, our cook.

She came straight to the point. 'There's been a messenger. He brought a letter for you and one for a person called Sara. I told him there was no one of that name here, but he insisted that you and she would arrive together. I have the letters with me.'

'Tell me about the messenger.'

'He was a foreigner, and he had come a very long way. With Archer Ben's permission, I gave him food and lodged him overnight in the new granary.'

'That's odd. Ben didn't mention this visitor at all.'

'No, lord. We arranged that only I would tell you about it, since I had most to do with the man, and it is I who took custody of the letters.'

The reasoning didn't ring true to me, but I didn't pursue it.

'Did he leave the next day? Do you know where he went?'

'He stayed two days, for his mule needed to rest, he said. He wouldn't let Branca look after it, though. He didn't make many demands on us; he ate a little but not much, and he kept to himself. On the third day, he left early, although I did see him before he went.'

'Did he say anything before he left, Rachel?'

'He flung some words at me, although I didn't understand what he meant. He said, "Tell your lord, the men of justice will never get me." And then he was up on his mule and riding fast out of the gate. Was he a wanted man, lord?'

'Not in the sense you mean, Rachel; but I know who he is. Let me have the letters now, please.'

She felt inside her apron pocket and pulled out the letters. I had never seen anything like them before. The surface of each was shiny, and Rachel showed me that if you held one up to the light you could see strange patterns. They disappeared when you lowered it onto the table again. I realised that, for the first time, I was looking at a sheet of paper. The new material. The stuff that Ibrahim makes. The letters were folded, my name in ink on one of them and Sara's on the other. I thanked Rachel, and let her go back to her kitchen.

I opened up and read the letter addressed to me. It was, as I'd thought, from Isaac ben Sid. He apologised for fleeing from Saintes. He knew he wouldn't survive if he stayed; the *Justiciers* would have found him, as surely as they'd found Joseph. Isaac asked my forgiveness, and then he told me something I hadn't realised. Alfonso had ordered the three Jews to accompany my party, not as warriors, as I'd first thought, nor as bait, as I'd decided later, nor yet as guarantors of the delivery of his letter to Jabir. In fact, Alfonso had sent them to determine Jabir's authenticity. Those three scholars would know at once if the Persian were faking it. If Jabir seemed false, they were to destroy the invitation to Seville. In his letter to me, Isaac hoped Yehudah had been able to carry out this mission.

Perhaps it was just as well Joan had made the decision she did. Alfonso was no fool. He wasn't taking Jabir's boastful proclamations on trust. He'd wanted his advisors to check him out first. That they hadn't been able to do so was the work of the Mudéjar, of course. Isaac also mentioned an offer from Alfonso for me. It would need careful thinking about.

I sent for Xurxo.

Xurxo watched me open Sara's letter, and I handed it to him. He read it aloud.

> *Adio, querida. Esta terminado. Va busacate otro amor, aharva otras puertas, aspera otro ardor que para mi sos muerta. Debes volver á túa casa para axudar a teu pai. Debes volver ser rapaz para que poidas traballar. Iago de Aragón*

From James of Aragon. I understood a few words, but not enough.

'He says goodbye,' Xurxo said sadly. 'He says he does not love her. He says she must return home to help her father. And he says she must become a boy again.'

So it had all been for nothing. I ground my fist into my hand. All the suffering and the pain, the missed deadline, the terrible, long, hard journey, undertaken for Husain's cure and Sara's treatment; but Jabir had been unable to cure Husain, and now Sara's lover had rejected her. There had been no point in any of it.

Kit joined Xurxo and me in my library.

'You've had supper?' I asked.

'We weren't all that hungry,' Xurxo said.

'Perhaps because Ellen's got rabbit stew bubbling away

at the Cottage,' Kit said with a grin. I smiled too. Rachel always serves leftovers for supper, so rabbit stew probably seemed much more welcome on this cold night. I gave Kit the letter to read.

'*Adio, querida,*' Kit quoted at the end. 'That's interesting.'

'Why?'

'Because it means 'Goodbye, beloved.' But then he goes on to tell her he's going to look for someone else. He even says she is dead to him. So why call her his beloved?'

'Perhaps he loved her, but his father won't let him marry her?' I hazarded.

Xurxo looked doubtful. 'Jaume of Aragon is a powerful king. But he wouldn't interfere in that. Can Sara have babies?'

Kit looked at him in surprise. 'No, of course not, Xurxo.'

'Then perhaps Jaume *has* forbidden it. A king must have descendants.'

'James is the second son, though,' I pointed out.

'But he must still have an heir. Just in case.'

An argument I've heard many a time on my own account.

'Well then,' I concluded, stretching in my chair, 'Sara, when she arrives home, will be put to work for her father. As James says in his letter.'

'As Darakhshan bin Ibrahim?' asked Xurxo.

'Yes. Probably.'

'Poor Sara,' said Kit.

The rabbit stew was calling, and Xurxo and Kit hurried away to enjoy their supper with Ellen out by the eastern wall. Two young men and a girl without a care in the world, I thought sourly, before reminding myself that Xurxo's sister, Carlotta, had committed suicide, and his mother was seriously ill. Still. They are all good company for one another, and I'm good company for no one. I glanced with distaste at the notes I made during the many interviews I'd conducted this evening. I'd written much but learnt little. No matter. Things, as Xurxo is always telling me, have a habit of revealing themselves when they're ready. And right now, I decided, I was ready for bed. I damped down the fire and snuffed out the candles and the oil lamp, then tramped back down to ground level.

I pushed open the door to my chamber and started in surprise, for Rosa sat on the bed, her hair loose around her shoulders. She wore a thin, lacy gown and her legs and feet were bare. A fire burned in the grate; the room, normally so chilly and draughty, was warm. I've never contemplated having a curtain at my window, but one had been found and the window was now covered in a bright, striped fabric. Two candles stood on the chest, their flames flickering and dancing. In the firelight, Rosa's hair looked like burnished metal, and her shoulders, like bronze. Involuntarily, I gasped.

During the long night, I thought once or twice about Sara and the letter from her lover. Rosa slept in my arms, her breathing steady, her skin soft and warm, but I could not sleep at all. The room was too hot; the air was too close; Rosa was too tempting. I shifted slightly but didn't want to wake my wife. In the end, I managed to disentangle her limbs from mine, got up and dragged the striped fabric away from the window. I leant on the sill and found relief breathing in the cold, fresh air, then hoisted myself up and sat on the ledge for a long time, aware that the rest of the castle was fast asleep. I thought about Alfonso's offer: a vast sum of money for the use of our new *kontor*, an ideally situated trading post for his new writing material.

Suddenly I wanted to write some notes, and I thought of pattering out down the passage and making my way back to my library, but I was naked, and my clothes were mixed up with Rosa's in an undignified frenzy of undressing. I was sure I would disturb her if I rummaged through the pile of garments, so I stayed where I was, contemplating the futility of it all. Poor Sara, Kit had said, and I caught a sudden sob in my throat. *Put things right,* Father had instructed me. *It is this new child you must not fail. A disturbed and miserable child. Solve the problem. Put things right.*

I heard a noise, and when I turned I saw Rosa, wide awake, staring at me.

'Sorry,' I said, sliding back into bed, aware I was shivering with cold.

'That was a foolish thing to do,' she upbraided me, but for once her tone was not harsh. 'You will make yourself ill.'

I turned away from her, lying on my side, facing the now exposed window.

Adio, querida.

EPILOGUE

Maybe it'll feel like paradise once it's completed, but right now it's nothing but a nightmare. The bailey down by the refurbished House of Colours has been dug up. No one can walk down there, and earlier in the autumn it became completely waterlogged because it's on a slope and we've had torrential rain. All the water ran down, but instead of draining into the River Eray and being carried away down Baudry Hill to fall harmlessly into the Hurogol, the water stayed on the ground. It couldn't get past the banked-up walls of earth, and then it couldn't soak away because the soil was already full of water, so it just stayed there in unsightly ponds and puddles, preventing anyone from getting round with dry feet.

If you want to get to the mill, the dairy or the laundry house, you can't just slip out of the kitchen and run round the south wall anymore. You can either go into the keep, by climbing up the steps to the second level, then *down* a different set of steps into the bailey, which, if you're carrying bulky bags of laundry or heavy churns of milk is not easy, or, arguably worse, you come out of the courtyard, run to your right, going halfway around the entire bailey until you finally get to the dairy, or wherever you're headed. At least that way there are no steps, but it's a bloody long haul.

Kit and Ellen are all right; they can get to their cottage quite easily. And Branca's not bothered either, since the stables are easy to reach from the courtyard gate. But a great many of my household curse the day the Lady Joan decided to create our very own Paradise Garden in the grounds of Castle Rory. Or perhaps they curse me for allowing it. But they don't swear at the person they ought to be swearing at, because King Alfonso of Castile is not a well-known figure around here. King Alfonso never got his Spanish Garden in Seville – or at least he never got one designed by the Lady Joan. We are getting it instead, and it's taking forever to make.

'Don't blame me,' Joan says crossly. 'It was you who said it would be a good idea.'

'That was when you were living at The College,' I point out.

I've seen the drawing. Joan got rid of the one she'd roughed out for Alfonso and started again, this time on *paper.* Kit procured some for her, God knows how; I didn't think you could get paper in Hambrig. Joan makes her own ink, and the complicated diagram is pinned to the wall of the House of Colours. Joan and Jabir study it intently every day.

Jabir has changed. It's hard to put my finger on it, because he's still an infuriating, sarcastic fraud. I've warned him I'm going to dismantle the College, but still he goes off on a too-small pony every morning to 'work' in his laboratory, staying a night or two in his house. The next evening, he clatters back over the drawbridge just before supper and joins Joan in the great hall before they retire to the House of Colours. Joan has spruced it up, of course, and it's almost the same as it used to be, although she no longer uses it to create textiles and garments. Instead, she's thrown herself into this new project. The water channels will be filled by the Eray of course, but, she tells me earnestly, the fountain will need to be fed from a rush of water downhill, so the course of the Eray will need to be diverted to inside the curtain wall somewhere near Kit's Cottage. Does she realise how difficult, expensive and time-consuming that would be? I make a face and tell her I'll think about it; it takes me less than a moment to think about it and reject the idea. Joan's Paradise Garden will have to be fountainless. I haven't yet told her that, though.

In the year that's passed since my return from pilgrimage, little has happened here. We are on a reasonably even keel, and seedtime and harvest were the highlights of the last twelve months. Once the harvest was in, the weather changed, and now, in November 1268, it's constantly cold, frequently wet, and invariably windy. Work on the Garden has ceased. Joan gazes in horror at the state of the land outside her House of Colours, squelching through the mud and, occasionally, poking at it with a small shovel. But no one can dig in this weather.

'The original Persian Gardens weren't built in this climate,' I remind her. 'You're trying to do the impossible.'

'I'll make it possible. See if I don't!'

'Hmm. Cypress and pomegranate trees? Sun-drenched patios? Are you quite sure about this?'

She turns away, frustrated and hurt. I should be supporting and encouraging her; instead, I'm endlessly critical. I can't forget that Joan ached to show the great Don Alfonso that she could do his design. His garden would have been world-famous, and the Lady Joan, its designer, would have finally felt worthy of her title.

'Why did Father give you the title?' I ask, although Joan still has her back to me.

'Ask him yourself,' she replies tartly. 'You're always saying he appears in some sort of vision.'

I send for Jonathan, who is now my squire. He's been learning how to polish a sword, and now he must show me his work. Our blacksmith, Andrew, has let Jonathan practise on an old, chipped blade. He brings me the blade, and we go and stand on the high wall-walk, where the wind tears our words to shreds, and the steady rain soon soaks through our clothing. Jonathan shivers a little, but I don't know if it's from cold or nervousness. This is the first piece of work he's shown me.

I take the blade from him and hold it at arm's length. Raindrops fall on the steel surface. If it is well polished, they'll run off easily. If not, they will form mini puddles which will soon mark the metal and corrode it. I watch them fall, make rounded blobs and run off. It's good. The blade has been polished to a high shine, and it shakes off the wet like a water spaniel.

'This is good work, Jonathan,' I say to the boy, and he blushes with pleasure.

I give him back the sword and dismiss him. I am pleased with my new squire. Hanging on the wall in my great hall is a Templar shield. It once belonged to Jonathan's father, a man I met just once, when we discovered we had fought in the same Crusade, although we didn't know each other then. I'm pleased Jonathan is shaping up so well. For his father's sake.

The wind has penetrated my knitted jersey and chills my whole body, but I love it. I love this hill and my castle on the top of it. I look north, where I can just see the winding ribbon of the Wartsbaye Road. I can't see the River Hurogol, partly because I'm at the wrong part of the ramparts, but also because the day is so drear, the river has merged in with the sky and the whole thing is a mass of grey watery nothingness.

But surely there is something there, something moving on the road? There's been no shout from the Watch, no alert given. So perhaps I'm mistaken. I blink the rain from my eyes and put my hand up to shield them. At first I can see nothing, and I decide my eyes must have deceived me. They are no longer a young man's eyes, after all. But I continue looking and blinking, looking and blinking, and yes, I'm *sure* something is out there. It is coming towards us. I make my way down the tower, across the courtyard and down to the gatehouse. I'm yelling for Ben. Where the hell is the Watch? Why has no one alerted the garrison?

I pound up the steps. Ben and his troops are inside, and it's clear there is no Watch. I demand an explanation.

'Lord Rory, the weather's too bad—'

'The weather's never too bad! For God's sake, Ben! You have to set the Watch, day and night, no matter the weather.

Relieve them more often, that's the only difference. There is someone on the Wartsbaye Road and he's approaching at speed. I want armed warriors at the gate, and I want a report from you every five minutes.'

I'm rattled. This would *never* have happened under Sir Jonny. Has Ben been this lax throughout my absence? If so, it's a wonder the castle is still standing. I'm pleased with my reference to 'five minutes', although I know Ben won't understand it. I've studied Jabir's Castle Clock, and I know now how the hours divide themselves. Five minutes, though, is not long. I struggle up the next flight of steps to the top of the north gatehouse tower. This gives me the best view of the road, and now I can clearly see the river, its surface whipped up by the wind into swirling, treacherous waves. There are no boats out today. The road looks almost as dangerous; it's awash with water, and the surface is crumbling badly.

It's clear now that the movement on the road is someone on horseback. Ben does not let me down, but I can see what's going on for myself. The troops muster in the bailey. It should have been done an hour ago. The rider digs in his spurs and turns onto the track that leads up Baudry Hill.

I'm down at the gate; the rider is here, requesting permission to cross the drawbridge, though he can see it's been left down for him. Ben, at a nod from me, bids him cross. The mare's breath is thick in the cold air, and she's tossing her head, her flanks heaving. The rider dismounts. He's enveloped in a long, woollen cloak, sodden now, but still wrapped closely around his body. Head down against the rain, he hurries forward, then looks up at me. The visitor has a Mediterranean complexion. I am instantly transported back to Castile and the shimmering palace in Santo Domingo de Calzada.

'I have a letter for Lord Rory of Hambrig,' announces the stranger, and his accent is Alfonso's. Involuntarily, I shiver. It's too recent, and yet too long ago. I'm done with the pilgrimage, the Mudéjar, the bright colours and hot, hot sunshine of Iberia.

I hold out my hand, and the man burrows into his bag and extracts a parchment. He passes it to me, and Ben takes charge of the messenger from then on. He and his horse will be fed and watered, then offered rest. I know all this, but I don't give it a moment's thought. I hurry to the south-west tower, to my library, where I open the letter. But it is not from Alfonso. It's from Rashid, and I learn that he and Sara arrived safely in Mula. They did not make the deadline, and arrived to find James gone from the town. Sara was unsurprised. She knows she will never see him again. Sara's father, Ibrahim, and Rashid's boys, Malik and Hanif, are safe and well. But Jamila, Rashid's wife, is dead. The letter does not explain how or why.

Large-scale production of paper is underway in Mula, and new paper mills are to be built as quickly as possible in other towns. Rashid concludes his letter by asking if Jabir will recite the Du'a for Husain every month, saying: *Oh Allāh! Forgive those of us that are alive and those of us that are dead; those of us that are present...* There is more, but I skim over that. The final paragraph of the letter is a confession: yet again, Rashid has stolen the collarbone of Joseph of Arimathea; he hopes I will forgive him.

Jabir is not in the House of Colours, so I fetch my horse, Blue, and I ride over to The College. I find him in the laboratory, which seems different. Something is missing, but I can't put my finger on what it is.

'Good,' says Jabir, dancing down the room. 'I knew you would come. You have read Rashid's message, and you had to talk to me.'

'How do you know about Rashid's letter?'

'It is not hard, O Lord of Missed Connections. Rashid is the son of a great friend of mine. I do not mean his father, Husain; I mean his mother. Elmira looked after me as if I were her own son. I lived with that family for one year. I was fifteen years old when I arrived, a very impressionable age. When I heard what had happened to Elmira and the girls I was devastated. Ever since, I have been trying to avenge their violations and their deaths. The Elixir of Life? For Elmira. The *takwin?* For Shakira and Amira. Not for you, not for Richard, not even for Rupert. Sir Bernard knew all about my friends in Murcia; he knew all my work was for them. Now I am here, and I am still working for those women, whom I loved.'

'But they're dead, Jabir! How could the Elixir or the *takwin* help them?' For some reason I feel like crying. I am certain Joan knows nothing of this.

'Death happens to us all,' says Jabir quietly. 'But what happens afterwards? Have you ever thought about that, O Lord of Morbid Mortality?'

Of course I have. And Laurence reminds us of it at Mass every day. Jabir is making me angry, with his questions and his assumptions, but he continues with his philosophy. 'For some people, death is also birth. It is the birth of the soul. But the soul has to go on a journey, and that journey involves crossing the Chinvat Bridge, the Bridge of Judgement. Some souls will go to Heaven, others to Hell. I know, beyond any doubt whatsoever, that Elmira, Shakira and Amira are in Paradise.' He raises his voice. 'My inventions are not to bring them back to life; they don't need that. My inventions are to honour them. And *they* are the inspiration for everything I do.'

Having spent several years in Egypt and Palestine, I know something about Islam. And I know this isn't it.

'Jabir, you're not a descendant of Jabir ibn Hayyan. Everything about you is false and you are an imposter.'

He turns flashing eyes on me. 'I am an opportunist. Jabir ibn Hayyan was a famous alchemist, and he wrote many important books. I have done nothing to discredit his name.'

Well, that's open to debate. I ignore it though, and ask about the Chinvat Bridge. He tells me it is part of the belief held by Zoroastrians. I have heard of this faith, but know little about it. I remember Jabir telling me how the Muslims drove the Zoroastrians out of Persia some six hundred years ago, and how many Zoroastrians subsequently converted to Islam, while others were badly abused by the invading Muslims and, if they survived, fled from Persia. Jabir reminded me of the name of their sacred text, the *Avesta*.

'So that's why you ran from your native land?' I ask, intrigued. 'Because of the Muslim invasion?'

'Do not be ridiculous. I am not six hundred years old.'

'What are you working on now? Have you abandoned the quest for the Elixir of Life?'

'Not at all. Rashid's wife, Jamila, needs treatment. If I can help her, then—' But he reads the expression on my face. 'What has happened?'

I tell him.

Jabir's response is curious. He hides his face in his hands, his long fingers working, bending and straightening as if they don't belong to him but to some multi-legged creature that has climbed onto his face. He rocks back and forth in distress. 'Why must they die?' His voice is indistinct and full of tears. 'Elmira. Shakira and Amira. Rupert. Aysha. Jamila. All dead, long before I could save them.

'The Elixir of Life. It is within my grasp! I have so nearly created it. I *will* do it.' He looks up, his face streaked with tears, but his voice stronger. 'I *must* do it. That is why Alfonso wants me in his court. He wants me to make the Elixir in the laboratory he is building for me. And his Persian Garden will provide inspiration for his scholars, of whom I will be one.'

'Joan is building her garden here, Jabir,' I begin, but he doesn't hear me.

'In the Muslim *Qu'ran*, Heaven is a garden, but there are eight grades of Heaven, the highest of which is called Paradise. The Jews, in their *Talmud*, describe the Garden of Righteousness, which was created at the beginning of the world and will appear in glory at the end of time. Then of course, you Christians stole the Jewish sacred books, so you have the Garden of Eden. But did you know that Archangel Michael buried Adam, the first man, in Paradise, even though God had expelled him from it after he succumbed to the serpent's temptation? Even the great Saint Paul describes his vision of Heaven. Oh yes, we are all seekers after paradise.' He breaks into crazy laughter.

In a corner of the laboratory smoke is coming out of the furnace. I know this furnace, and it's a dangerous thing. It's called an *athanor*, and strange things happen in the athanor. I move over to it, intending to lift the lid, but Jabir comes running after me and his bare brown arms wrap themselves around my waist. With surprising strength, he pulls me backwards, and the two of us tumble to the floor.

'What are you doing?' I have knocked my elbow painfully on a corner of the bench.

'I would ask *you* that, O Lord of Meddle and Muddle.'

And now he's standing over me, and in his hand is a glass bottle of something. I'm nursing my elbow and don't pay a lot of attention, until he raises the bottle.

'I am about to drink this,' Jabir says calmly.

'What is it?'

'It is the proto-type.'

I have no idea what he's talking about. I stand up and peer at the bottle; it's full of something dark, and I see patterns swirling inside it. They're moving. They're alive!

'This is the starter for the Elixir,' Jabir says, holding the bottle at arm's length. 'You know what a starter is? Your cook will use one to bake bread. It has living things in it. You must feed it; it must never be allowed to die. This is the same, but it is not for making dough, it is for making life. Do you see the connection yet, O Lord of Dunderheaded Stupidity?'

'I see it,' I say grimly, ignoring the meaningless and unnecessary insult. 'You claim to be holding the starter for making life, as in the Garden of Eden. That's what you mean, isn't it? That's why you've been babbling on about gardens in the world's religions. They're all the same really, no matter what your faith. Only the details differ. And all of them mark the beginning and end of life. Is that it, Jabir?'

He looks at me in astonishment. 'Remarkably perspicacious,' he murmurs. Even his compliments are insulting. He draws himself up to his full height, which is barely average. 'All right. But you have disturbed my work, so I would like you to go now.' He swings the bottle by its neck. The brown swirly stuff pops slightly, and bubbles appear on the glass.

And then I remember. 'You said you're going to *drink* it? Drink your – your proto-type? Why?'

'That is not your business. I am doing vital research. Sometimes that involves personal risk. Now please go.'

'Does Joan know what you're doing?'

He looks furious. However enraged he is, he must know that in a fight I would easily beat him. If I choose to stay here, he can't stop me. I sit on the bench, my feet swinging just above the floor. 'I'll watch,' I tell him. 'If you're in trouble, I'll fetch help. If it works, I'll be a witness. You can't object to either of those things, surely.'

His face clears. 'You are right, O Lord of Unexpected Inspiration. Yes, a witness is exactly what I need. Take your manuscript from your jersey, and write down everything that happens. Do it now.' He snaps his fingers, and the bottle gives a sudden shudder.

I take out my journal and smooth the parchment on the bench. The charcoal I already have in my hand, but Jabir darts to a chest and fetches a quill pen and a jar of black ink. 'Use this,' he commands. 'Write down everything, and it must be indelible. Even if I become ill, or scream in agony, *even if I die,* you must not help me. You must record every single detail of what happens. Promise me this.'

I promise, which is easy, since I don't intend to keep my promise if things turn out badly. But Jabir dashes again to the chest, and this time he brings out a book. He thrusts it at me. 'Hold this in both hands, and then swear you will not move until it is over.'

I see that I must now swear on the Bible. I swallow hard.

Jabir's eyes are boring into mine. In his hand, the bottle of proto-type Elixir is jumping, swinging, turning. My heart is in my throat. 'Joan,' I start to say, my knuckles white on the cover of the Bible.

'Do not bring my lady into this,' Jabir hisses. 'This is you and me only, O Lord of Intimate Knowledge of the Unthinkable. We have this bond now. It is unbreakable. It is for life, and it is for death. Now swear!'

I swear on the Bible. I swear to record everything, down to Jabir's final breath. I swear not to move until he has drunk the entire contents of his bottle, and I swear to miss nothing, neither with my eyes nor with my pen.

Finally, he steps away from me, and with shaking hands I put the Bible down on the bench. I hope I can write. I hope there is enough ink. I hope my bowels do not betray me. I hope Jabir survives this ultimate of experiments. And then, pen in hand, I wait, I watch and I write.

Jabir is uncorking the bottle. He does it slowly. The bottle is jumping in his hand, and I think he may drop it. He does not drop it, but the cork will not come out. He holds the bottle between his knees, and applies a metal tool to the cork. Now the cork is slowly coming out, and I see more and more of it appearing. But suddenly it explodes out of the bottle, as an arrow from a bow. The cork flies high into the air and travels some distance, landing on the floor beside the athanor. The athanor is still emitting smoke.

The cork rolls towards it, but stops before it touches the furnace. The smoke is thick and has a purple tinge. I must not watch the athanor, I must return my gaze to Jabir. He has the open bottle in his hand and he looks terrified. I have never seen a man look so frightened, not even when I pointed my lance at a disarmed Mamluk warrior in Egypt, all those years ago. Jabir is petrified. His whole body shakes, and there is perspiration on his face, neck and hands. He loosens his tunic and undoes all the buttons. I wonder if he's going to undress, but he leaves it at that.

He fetches a goblet from a shelf. I thought he was going to drink from the bottle, and now I wonder if he's playing for time, putting off the dreadful moment when the stuff touches his lips. I watch, fascinated, as he tilts the bottle over the goblet. I am expecting a brown liquid to pour out, but that isn't what happens. Instead, the neck of the bottle seems to swell. I think Jabir knew that would happen and was ready for it, for he is grasping the bottle with both hands. He snatches up a towel, which he wraps around the neck of the bottle. He tilts it further, but the whole bottle is changing shape, stretching and shrinking alternately. I'm reminded of the *takwin* and the 'Sludge-Thing'. But this is a bottle! I can't understand what's happening, but then I see the stuff begin to emerge; it's brown, but it's not liquid. A gloopy lump of something falls into the goblet, and then another lump. Now the lumps are coming thick and fast, all plopping into the goblet. Surely it should be full by now? But more and more globules fall into the container.

Jabir lowers the bottle onto the table. It looks like a normal bottle again, though it's only half full now. Jabir's hands are clammy, and he wipes them on his breeches. So what's left in the bottle? I lower myself from the bench and walk over to scrutinise it. I can see the level of the swirly brown stuff, below halfway down. In the bottle, there are no globules, only a viscous liquid. The swirls are clearer than they were. They are thick white streaks that move around, twisting to the top, then down to the bottom, then hiding inside the liquid before coyly peeping through and swimming to the surface. They look for all the world like white worms swimming in a thick, dark, muddy puddle. I begin to feel sick, and retire hastily to my bench. I know I must keep scribbling. I've sworn to record the tiniest detail, to miss nothing.

Jabir picks up the goblet. He raises it to his nose and sniffs cautiously. He recoils, rocking back on his heels, his hand to his mouth. I swallow hard. What must it smell like to cause such a response? Jabir is shaking again, and something dribbles from the side of his mouth. His eyes look glazed. And he hasn't even tasted it yet! The goblet is back on the table. Unlike the bottle, it doesn't move or change its shape. It's just a simple pewter goblet, resting on a sturdy oak table.

Jabir approaches it again. He picks it up. I wonder suddenly if he'd be doing this if I weren't here. Yes, he wants a witness, but perhaps I'm also spurring him on. Without me watching and recording, he might withdraw. After all, no one would know. But here I am, and now I understand why he has let me stay; he was frightened he wouldn't have the courage to go through with it. Now he has to. And so the goblet is lifted again, this time to the alchemist's mouth. Jabir's lips touch the metal, but only on the outside. There is a long wait, and it's almost palpable how much fortitude Jabir has to summon up to do this.

And now he tilts the cup and his lips are over the rim. He tilts it more. I look to see if he's swallowing. At first the answer is no, but as his head tips back, the rim of the goblet rattling against his teeth, I see his Adam's apple move. This is the moment I have to watch, record and report on. Jabir is swallowing the Elixir of Life.

He swallows several times. I see his knees buckle, and he reaches out to grasp the table, setting down the goblet. I want to ask how he feels, but he probably won't hear me. He pours the rest of the bottle into the cup. The bottle, empty, is put down again. On an impulse, I slide down from the bench and go across to the table. I peer into the cup. I see the swirls on the surface, the white 'worms' appearing and disappearing. The rest of the stuff is dark, almost black. It's liquid, even though it didn't look like it as the globules came out of the bottle. How this works, I can't imagine.

Eventually, Jabir drinks again, though there's a long wait as he screws up his courage. He drains the cup, tipping the last dregs of it down his throat. But now the cup is falling. It clatters to the floor. Jabir's legs give way. He's down on the ground, both hands to his throat, and his eyes are popping. I don't think he can see. I call his name, but there is no response. I hurry over to him. He's lying on his back and his eyes are staring. His lips and fingers look blue. I try to hear and feel if he's breathing. He isn't breathing. I panic, running around the laboratory, looking for something, anything, but I've no idea what I need. After wasting several precious moments, I scurry back to Jabir, kneeling down beside him, feeling him all over. His body feels cold. He's still not breathing, and his skin looks waxy. He is quite, quite dead.

Elixir of Life? No! This was a Potion of Death! I pick up the fallen cup and sniff inside it, recoiling at the ghastly smell of rotting putrefaction. Something has died some time ago, and its body has been used to make this potion.

Immediately, I know I'm going to vomit and my bowels are about to void. I manage to get outside and finish up leaning against the wall, tears running down my face. I know I can't go back into that place of death, but my parchment is there. It's not just the record of everything that's just happened, it's my whole journal, and I have to have it. I wait, leaning against the wall, unable to move; I haven't even pulled up my breeches. The sky is darkening, and my horse, Blue, is whinnying a little. She can sense I'm in trouble. I can't leave without my journal, but I do not want to go back into the laboratory.

I make myself go back. I wonder if I can possibly resuscitate the alchemist, but Jabir's body is already starting to stiffen. His skin is tight, his limbs rigid, wide eyes staring at nothing. Treading softly, I reclaim my journal and leave this place of horror.

I won't go home. Not yet. Instead, I keep a vigil for my dead friend. Was Jabir ever a friend? I can't say that he was. He arrived out of nowhere, with nothing, made a great reputation for himself out of gossamer promises, outright lies and unsubstantiated claims, but Joan loved him, and for her sake I will stay with his body until daylight.

I spend the night in the cold outside the laboratory. I've dressed myself, but that's all I've managed to do. I don't sleep, but crouch against the wall. I don't know whether the night passes quickly or slowly, I just know that eventually the sky lightens a little, although it's not yet dawn. And someone has arrived. It's my squire. I've been missed at home, and someone guessed I might be here. I tell Jonathan that terrible things have happened. I don't mention Jabir, but Jonathan wants to know where he is.

'He's in there, Jonathan. Don't go in. Things are not good.'

'He's dead, isn't he?'

My silence tells him he's right.

'Where's Sappo?' Jonathan asks, squatting down beside

me. It's a good question, and I don't know why I haven't asked it myself.

'I don't know,' I say, and the sickness overwhelms me again as I realise I *do* know where Sappo is. And I now know the origin of the putrefaction in the drink. I know why Jabir drank it. I know how it was made. And I identify the 'something missing' that I felt when I first entered the laboratory last night: there was no comforting chuntering of the toad in the corner.

I stare at Jonathan, and as the sun begins to show itself, he sees the truth in my eyes. He stands up, a tall boy of fourteen, with a look of his father about him. Or as his father must have been when he was a brave Crusader. The boy squares his shoulders and walks towards the laboratory door.

'Don't go in there,' I cry hoarsely. Jonathan looks round. As my squire, he's bound to obey me. But he takes another step forwards, facing the laboratory door.

I'm sitting on the cobblestones, my hands on my queasy stomach. Jonathan is still several yards from the laboratory. In disbelief, I see the door opening from within, and there in the doorway stands the alchemist. Jonathan hurriedly retreats to my side. His hand is to his mouth and he looks terrified. Both of us stare at the vision in front of us.

Jabir is immobile, framed in the doorway as the sun rises. The sun's rays are golden fingers, reaching out to touch him. Slowly, he raises his head. Holding his arms out wide as if he were the Messiah, he walks confidently out into the sunlight.

Thank you for reading *The Paradise Garden*, Book Five in *Tales of Castle Rory*!

Lord Rory's adventures will continue in *The Foucois Legacy*, to be published in January 2025.

Did you enjoy *The Paradise Garden*? Leave a review, and let everybody know!

Have you read *The Box of Death*, which is Book One, *The Soldier of Fortune*, Book Two, *The Man in the Moon,* Book Three and *The King's Ransom*, Book Four in the series?

Want to know what happened to Rory before he became Lord of Hambrig?

Rory and Jonny, barely out of their teens, join King Louis IX of France on Crusade.
This Crusade is a disaster for the Christians, but it forges a tremendous and lasting friendship between Jonny and Rory, who go to war as boys and return as men.
Read about their adventures in Egypt, the women they fell in love with and their miraculous escapes from the Saracens!

This story is told in Mansurah: Jonny's Tale, a free ebook only available to members of **The Household**!

Joining is free and also gives you access to fortnightly

newsletters with behind the scenes action, giveaways, fun competitions and much more!

Go to www.talesofcastlerory.co.uk to find out more about **The Household** and get your free copy of *Mansurah: Jonny's Tale*

Go to www.talesofcastlerory.co.uk to find out more about *Tales of Castle Rory.*

You can also follow me on Facebook.

ACKNOWLEDGMENTS

Thanks to my mum (as always), to Patrick, to Kit and to Kerry for their support and encouragement.

Thanks to Pat from church, and Simon from down-the-road-from-Kit. You were my first readers!

Thanks to Peter for the cover design, and to Sharon for editing the manuscript.

Thanks to Rebekah for her invaluable help in getting my books in front of readers.

Thanks to Debbie and the Awesome Self-Pub WhatsApp group for keeping us all going and for oodles of encouragement.

And thanks to all my readers. You are the backbone of it all.

AUTHOR'S NOTE

***The Paradise Garden* is a Medieval Fantasy Adventure. But how much is medieval? And how much is fantasy?**

During the Middle Ages, the Iberian Peninsula was known as al-Andalus. The *Reconquista* was the attempt by the Christians to re-take (re-conquer) al-Andalus from the Muslims, who had themselves seized it from the Christians in the eighth century. Although the term "reconquista" was not used at the time, I have used it to emphasise the struggle of different religions to take, and re-take, control of nations and their people. Of course, the Muslims were guilty of crimes against displaced people when they invaded al-Andalus in the first place, and this point is also made when Jabir describes the persecution and subjugation of Zoroastrians from Persia, who were forced either to flee or to convert to Islam. The Christian "reconquest" of Spain was equally barbaric to the Moors (the Iberian Muslims). This was not a time of religious tolerance by those seeking power and territory.

Santiago de Compostela is the capital of Galicia, a community in the north-western tip of the Iberian Peninsula. Pilgrims flock to the famous shrine to Saint James the Apostle, travelling along the Way of Saint James, the *Camino*. The *Camino* has been the pilgrim's route for centuries. On arrival at the shrine, provided you have walked at least part of the *Camino*, you are presented with a symbolic cockleshell. In *Tales of Castle Rory*, Galicia is renamed Smander, and Santiago de Compostela becomes Santiago das Cunchas (Saint James of the Shells). Why are some place names real and others made up? You will have to wait until *The End of Time* to find out!

Kit's Red Mountains are the Aquilanos Mountains, the main site of which is the historically fascinating Las Médulas. I've moved the mountains westwards into Galicia/Smander, although they are actually situated on the Castilian side of the border with Galicia. The Romans really did mine gold from these mountains, causing the *ruina montium,* which Xurxo is so incensed about.

My returning pilgrims stay in many abbeys, monasteries and convents. Most of these exist, or used to exist. The *Abbaye aux Dames* in Saintes, the *Abbaye Grestain*, close to Honfleur in Normandy, and The Newarke, which is the oldest quarter in Leicester, and certainly had a hospital during medieval times, were all real places with real facilities for the sick in 1267.

Alfonso X of Castile was a power-mad tyrant. Or he was an intelligent scholar and musician. Or he was a scientist, who wanted to know more about everything, and compiled the world's first set of useable astronomical tables. In reality, he was all those things. Medieval music students know him as the composer of a set of more than three hundred *Cantigas*, all hymns to the Virgin Mary. *Rosa das Rosas* is Number Ten in this collection. Yehudah ben Moshe, Isaac ben Sid and Joseph Alfaquin were all genuine members of Alfonso's elite circle of intellectuals, the "Toledo School of Translators". There is no record, however, of the three Jews ever travelling to Mallrovia, nor of their falling foul of vigilantes and murderers.

Rosa herself is my own creation. Alfonso had many children, and not all were legitimate. He did indeed have an affair with Mayor Guillén de Guzmán, and their daughter's name was Beatrice. I have endowed this couple with a second daughter, Rosa. It would be nice to think that Alfonso was fond enough of this daughter to write a *Cantiga* in her honour!

I have modelled the *Justiciers*, who are my own invention, on the *Vendicatori*, a group of twelfth century Sicilian vigilantes. Unlike the real-life *Vendicatori*, however, my French *Justiciers* specifically target the Jews. I wanted to show the rampant anti-Semitism of this time (and of this area), and the constant clash of religious doctrines by those hungry for power and dominion, while, at the same time, ordinary people were almost always tolerant and inclusive of all.

The Mudéjar Muslims were like slaves in southern Spain, forced into lowly and humiliating status by their Christian conquerors. Yet they themselves had done exactly the same thing to the Zoroastrians in Persia five hundred years before. This is the first time Zoroastrianism has appeared in *Tales of Castle Rory*, and I believe it to be a much overlooked faith. Jabir has always been portrayed as a Muslim, but in *The Paradise Garden* he gives a flavour of Zoroastrianism to Joan's garden design. So what exactly is his holy book? Is it the Quran? Or is it the Avesta?

I did a great deal of research into Husain's "wasting disease". Of course, Rashid is the unnamed boy in the Prologue, and Husain is his father, forced to endure months of being besieged within the town of Mula in Murcia. Starvation would force people to eat unclean animals (unclean according to their Muslim faith, but also clinically diseased). Chronic wasting disease (CWD) is classified as a transmissible spongiform encephalopathy, or prion disease. It is mostly found in animals, and is caused by eating contaminated deer or elk. There has not been much zoonotic transmission, although I found one or two cases of humans being infected. I could find no cases reported from Spain (they're all from the USA), but I have given poor Husain this condition, together with variant Creuzfeld-Jakob Disease. Variant CJD can take years to show symptoms, and this would explain why Husain becomes so ill twenty years after the siege of Mula.

Lord Rory first encountered crossdressing when he was on Crusade, although he's quick to point out that the *mukhannath* he met didn't consider himself female. And in many ways, medieval attitudes to transgenderism were much more broad-minded than you would expect from such an intolerant age. Often, transgender individuals were seen as special, expressing, rather than opposing, God's plan for them. That plan might be different from His plan for other people, but it was just as important and valued. However, transgenderism in the thirteenth century did not involve surgery (and no one knew of hormones then either). So a transwoman might dress as female, and transmen were even known to enter monasteries, but they relied on their acceptance by others, within the limitations of their biological bodies and secondary sexual characteristics. Clearly a medieval transwoman could shave her face, but she could not grow breasts. It's unclear if Sara is truly transgender, or if her problems actually stem from multiple personality disorder, now known as dissociative identity disorder (DID). She certainly has several distinct identities, and some of these are probably due to the trauma of knowing her best friend was stoned to death in mistake for Sara herself.

Of course, very little of this was understood in the Middle Ages, and Lord Rory, Xurxo and the others try to make sense of Sara's behaviour. While Rosa and Aldara accept her unconditionally, the men find it harder to adjust. I think this would indeed be the case. Given Sara's condition, it's unlikely she would ever find happiness as a woman without the underlying causes of her DID being addressed.

And finally – paper! Paper was first made in China, around 200 BC. In Europe, paper making started in the Iberian Peninsula and spread slowly to the rest of Europe. Although paper was first made by hand (using rags and linen cloth for fibre), it was not made at scale until the thirteenth century. Water-powered paper mills began to appear in the 1260s, again in Iberia, the first being run by the Mudéjar Muslim community. I have Sara's father, Ibrahim, as the entrepreneur who made the first of these mills. More mills were built, all in southern Europe, and the price of paper soon undercut the price of parchment and all other writing materials.

As Kit said, 'Paper will replace every writing material currently in use. It doesn't just have a future, it *is* the future. Of writing, at least.' And he was right.

R. Marsden, September 2024.

Printed in Great Britain
by Amazon

48488483R00283